This book contains the following:

- Emotional child abuse
- Allusion to physical child abuse
- Sexual assault (not FMC nor by MMC)
- Depictions of drugs
- Profanities
- Very graphic scenes of a sexual nature

Painted TRUTHS

PAMELA O'ROURKE

This book is a work of fiction. All names, characters, locations, and incidents are products of the author's imagination or used in a fictitious manner. Any resemblance to actual persons, living or dead, or actual events is purely coincidental.

Cover Design: Y'all. That Graphic.

Editing: NiceGirlNaughtyEdits

Formatting: CPR Editing

"ABSENCE IS TO LOVE WHAT WIND IS TO FIRE; IT EXTINGUISHES THE SMALL, IT INFLAMES THE GREAT."

—Roger De Bussy-Rabutin

For James.

MY HUSBAND. MY BEST FRIEND. MY LOVER. MY ROCK.
MY WORLD.

THANK YOU FOR ALWAYS LOVING ME—EVEN WHEN I'M LIKELY TO EAT YOU WITHOUT SALT FOR INTERRUPTING ME WHILE I'M EDITING, I ADORE YOU.

For Katie.

IF I'D NEVER MET YOU, THIS BOOK WOULD STILL BE LIVING SOMEWHERE IN THE DEPTHS OF MY IMAGINATION. YOUR FRIENDSHIP, LOVE AND UNCONDITIONAL SUPPORT AND POSITIVITY MEAN EVERYTHING TO ME, AND IF I NEVER SELL ONE COPY OF THIS BOOK, I'LL REMAIN FOREVER GRATEFUL THAT THIS JOURNEY BROUGHT ME TO YOU.

MY SOUL SISTER.

- "Brother" – Kodaline (*The Brotherhood* theme)
- "Walls (Naked Edition)" – Ruben
- "These Arms of Mine" – Otis Redding
- "One (Your Name) Radio Edit" – Swedish House Mafia feat. Pharrell
- "Ignite" – Alan Walker, Julie Bergan & K-391
- "Drown" – Martin Garrix feat. Clinton Kane
- "Hard To Love (Mahogany Sessions)" – Hamzaa
- "Hurt" – Johnny Cash
- "Don't Take Your Love Away" – Vast
- "Beneath Your Beautiful" – Labrinth feat. Emeli Sandé
- "Don't Call Me Up" – Mabel
- "Save Tonight" – Eagle Eye Cherry
- "Wait For You" – Tom Walker feat. Zoe Wees
- "Yellow" – Coldplay
- "OUT OUT" – Joel Corry, Jax Jones, Charli XCX & Saweetie
- "Yours" – Ella Henderson
- "Roses (Imanbek Remix)" – SAINt JHN & Imanbek

Prologue

HENRY
AGED SIX

"Stay here and do not leave this room. You hear me, you little shit?"

Opening my eyes wide at Nanny Lauren's words, I nod rapidly, crossing my feet at the ankles to stop the sudden need to use the bathroom.

"I mean it. There will be hell to pay if you so much as *attempt* to touch the door handle. You don't want to test me, Enrico."

"It's *Henry*."

As though of their own accord, those two words fly from my mouth as her lips turn up in distaste. "Not anymore, it's not. She's not here to save you now."

And with that as her parting shot, she slams the door as she marches down the hallway, leaving me to my thoughts.

My chest burns as I remember these last couple of weeks

leading up to this horrible day when Dad and I buried my Mum, and he drank all the funny-smelling special juice in his office, refusing to leave even though I'd cried and begged for hours through the locked oak door.

A single tear escapes and tracks along my already tear-stained, puffy cheek, dropping down and landing on the black shoes Nanny Lauren had made me wear this morning before we went to the funeral service.

I've lost count of the number of days since Mum left us.

Since she left *me*.

But I miss her like it was only yesterday, and I can still hear her magical voice telling me crazy stories about pixies and elves, knights and dragons, princes and princesses.

My favourite one was always the one about the Prince meeting his true love.

Dropping my head forward and closing my eyes, I let the memory of her voice wash over me, cleansing my heart of everything that has happened since she's gone away.

"Once upon a time, there was a Princess, whose father, the King, ruled his empire with an iron fist. The Princess had everything she could ever have even dreamed of wanting. Until one day, a Prince from a faraway land arrived at the palace. They immediately fell wholly and irrevocably in love with one another, but the King didn't believe in their love, proclaiming that they were too young and foolish to know their own hearts and minds, so he sent the Princess away for many years.

The Prince and Princess wrote letters of love to one another in their time apart, falling deeper in love with each passing day. Their passion had started as a spark, and although the winds of time tried to extinguish that tiny ember, their forced separation fed the fledgling flame, allowing their devotion to grow to unreachable heights.

After a time, the Prince, a good and noble man with the courage of conviction and the strength of his love driving his actions, returned to the King to tell him he wouldn't rest until he had taken the Princess for his own and the King, pleased that both of them had passed his test, happily gave his daughter to her Prince. So they lived in a never-ending cycle of happiness until one day; the Princess discovered she was having a little Prince of her own, and it was from that day forward, the Princess discovered the meaning of undying love."

I wasn't so little that I didn't realise she was telling me the story of how she had met my father, even though I didn't understand the details. The part I loved hearing was how she meant her undying love was for me, and though it didn't ease the pain of her death, it did dull it ever so slightly, knowing that she would love me from wherever she had gone to after she'd closed her beautiful brown eyes.

Raising my head, I take in my bedroom, checking to see if there's anywhere I can relieve myself after Nanny Lauren's threats have left me too scared to leave the confines of my room, but unfortunately, there's nothing. She's meticulous about enforcing a tidy bedroom.

Knowing that if I wet these clothes, the punishment will indeed surpass all previous infractions, I choose what I think is the lesser of two evils. So, slipping off the pinchy black shoes, I tiptoe on stockinged feet to the door before pressing down on the handle, praying to a God I'm not sure is listening, especially after all the unanswered prayers I'd sent up to him to save Mum, that she doesn't catch me.

The door opens easily into a thankfully empty hallway, the

only visible light coming from much further down the long, dark corridor. Slipping into the bathroom several doors down and opposite my parents' bedroom, I quickly do my business before washing up and checking the hall once again.

This time the light is brighter, and I can hear music floating up the stairs from somewhere below. A small smile creases my face as I wonder if, perhaps, my dad has finally emerged from his office, and, helpless to stop myself, my feet move closer and closer to the top of the enormous staircase.

Crouching low, I try to figure out where the soft laughter is coming from as I hear two voices speaking quietly, laughing together at times, and I could *swear* I catch a hint of my mother's perfume along the balustrade.

I'm desperately hoping these last few days have been a bad dream. That my parents are both alive and happy together downstairs.

That *she* never entered our home.

Just as I'm about to throw caution to the wind and go down there, I hear Nanny Lauren shout the F-word loudly and clearly. My dad's answering low tone is one I've never heard from him before.

Knowing she's down there, I can't risk her punishment. They get worse each time, so shutting off the yearning in my heart, I quickly and quietly return to the safety of my bedroom and force my mind to push this night to its furthest recesses, never to be thought of again.

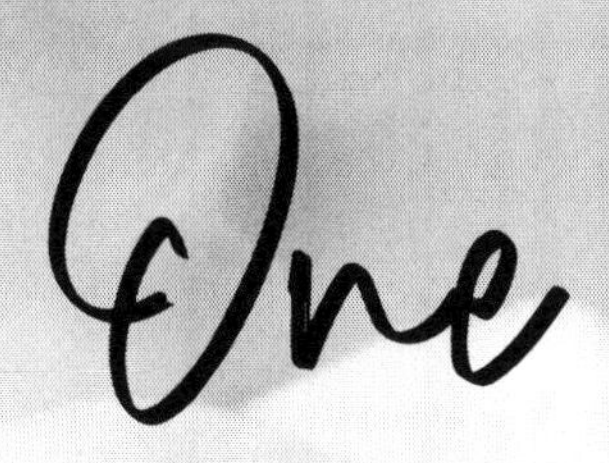

HENRY

As our chauffeured car pulls up at the entrance to Velvet, London's hottest new nightlife, my phone rings with an ear-splitting shriek.

"Christ, DeMarco. Ever heard of muting that shit?!"

My companions for the evening, one newly signed rock star in the making and one washed-up award-winning author, have clamped their hands over their ears as my heart sinks. That's the tone assigned to my asshat of a father, undoubtedly ringing to give me shit over some misconstrued fault or other, ruining the night before it's even begun.

Knowing better than to ignore the old wanker, I give Nate and Caden, the writer and the rocker respectively, my middle finger before using said finger to swipe the answer button.

"Dad. What's up?"

"Rico." My jaw ticks instantly at his unwillingness to call

me Henry, the name I prefer. Yet another reminder of our lack of familiarity. "You never answered my email. Lunch tomorrow, yes? I need to talk with you about something important, and it cannot wait any longer."

Internally heaving an exhausted sigh while gritting my teeth, I reply the only way you can to my father. With an unwilling affirmative. "Fine. Have your assistant text me the details."

I'm about to hang up. After all, my previous conversations with my neglectful, workaholic father over the past twenty-one years since my mother died have been short and lacklustre. Then I hear his voice again. His hard-won British accent all but gone as he speaks in his mother tongue.

"Grazie… Figlio Mio."

My brow furrows in confusion, but he's already dropped the call. I don't remember the last time he called me anything other than my given name, despite the fact I go by Henry. I prefer the English version of Enrico, which is my father's name, having been named for his father, and his father's father and, I'm sure you get the gist. The joy of traditional Italian forebears.

But Mum was British, born and bred. She'd wanted to honour her own heritage, and so she'd always called me Henry. My father had too.

Before.

After her passing, everyone referred to me as Enrico, and as time passed, it was easier to just let them. My friends have continued to call me Henry and still do, and they're the only people who truly matter anyway.

The business world and everyone else knows me as my father's heir, Enrico, but Christ, it burns. I want as little to do with that man as possible.

Rapidly compartmentalising the conversation with my sperm

donor slash boss, I shake my head to purge it of him. Of the ridiculous life choices he'd made that led me to become the cold bastard I am today.

My mother would be turning in her grave.

Just then, the driver comes around to open our door, forcing me from my reverie, allowing Nate to exit, followed by Caden, with yours truly drawing up the rear in our band of brothers.

As quickly as I've exited the vehicle, I want to return to the safety and anonymity of its confines. But instead, the swarm of paparazzi surrounding us is at least three bodies deep—a disgusting, heaving mass with no security in place whatsoever.

He'd sworn to me there'd be little to no media.

I'll kill the prick!

"I'm never going anywhere with you again, North, you fucking asshole!"

Careful I don't hurt one of these paparazzi wankers hungry for a glimpse of the latest golden boy on the music scene, I inch interminably closer to the door. At the same time, the object of my frustration throws his blonde head back, laughing long and loud.

More flashes and jostling continue as the vultures attempt to snag their money shot of a laughing Cade. Velvet's security team gets the crowd under control, allowing us to enter the building as civilised as possible, considering the circumstances.

At long last. North has always loved creating drama, and this evening's shitshow was him and his antics to a goddamn T.

"I told Noah to make sure the security was in place, but he said the free publicity was worth its weight in gold, man. Don't get your knickers in a knot!"

Unable to stop the grin that appears on my face, as if by magic, in answer to his bright, fun-loving smile, I throw my hands up in mock exasperation, earning chortles from both of my friends.

"Good evening, gentlemen. I'm Brielle, your liaison for the night. If you could just follow me this way, please."

A petite brunette, with a generous helping of curves on display, wears a low-cut red dress that clings to her ass like it has been spray-painted on, leads us through a maze of dimly lit corridors before ascending a staircase with two doors at the top.

The first door is set back from the stairs with a large black and gold sign pronouncing it: *The Powder Room.*

As our host reaches the second door, with a matching black and gold sign marked simply as *VIP Only*, Brielle turns the handle so I can hear the music, which up until now has been a semi-muted bass thumping through the walls.

Dance music roars to life, the beat dropping as though on cue as we enter the area reserved just for Caden's and our pleasure by proxy.

The space is a suspended box with floor-to-ceiling glass walls. This allows us to observe the club below without the masses losing their shit over the presence of one Caden North, lead singer of Misdirection and bad boy extraordinaire, like the paps had done already upon our arrival. The area comprises plush black velvet booths and matching high-backed chairs with gold cushions strewn artfully across them, all set around low black tables with gold accents. There is a long black bar underneath spotlights in the far corner, along with another set of stairs which, I assume, leads to the main club but is currently being blocked off by a rope alongside a huge ass security guard wearing a scowl to rival my own.

"The management here at Velvet has provided a range of drinks, and a server shall be with you shortly. The dance floor and main club area can be reached via those stairs, and Burt will be on duty all night, so you won't be bothered by anyone unless you, the hosts, wish to bring guests up here."

Brielle glances in Caden's direction, blatantly having done her due diligence, a knowing smirk on her pretty face before she continues. "If you go back out the way we entered, you'll find a door to your right. Those are your private facilities, The Powder Room, for the evening."

The door opens once more, and in walks who I presume is our bartender for the night.

"Ah, here's Toby now."

He nods in our direction before taking his place behind the bar.

"There is also a private roof terrace reserved solely for your pleasure if you go back through here." She indicates behind us with one delicately manicured hand. "You can't miss it."

Placing her hands on her ample hips while arching her back to push her tits out front and centre, our host's lips turn up in a provocative smile.

"I shall check back in with you every twenty minutes or so, gentlemen. If there's *anything* you need. Anything. At. All. *Please,* don't hesitate."

She exits the same way we had come in, with a saucy wink and a matching smirk that encompasses our trio.

"Did you *see* the tits on that one?"

Caden is most certainly the tit man of our motley crew, not that you'd know it to look at his long-term main squeeze, who looks like she's stepped off a runway but has no curves to speak of.

Nate and I, though, are most definitely ass men.

"Was too busy looking at her ass." Nate confirms my thoughts as he continues. "Didn't hear a word she said, to be honest. Too busy thinking about how hot my cock would look between her perfect cheeks."

"Which cheeks, friend?" Cade shoots a devilish look his way

as Nate just shrugs.

"Either would do. That mouth was entirely as fuckable as that ass."

"And with that thought in mind, let's get this party fucking started." Caden makes quick work of getting the drinks in, not bothering to avail of the ready and waiting bartender, instead opting to grab some bottles and a handful of shot glasses before settling down between Nate and me to observe the already heaving dance floor.

The music has changed to some familiar song; the guy is singing about just wanting to know someone's name, and the dancefloor goes apeshit when the bass drops; I even see Nate manage a foot tap or two, bringing a smile to my lips.

"Christ almighty. This place is un-fucking-real! Check out the view." The dance floor is teeming with swarms of barely dressed women of all shapes and sizes. In varying states of deshabille, just how we like it.

Someone must have researched the shit out of Caden and his proclivities to have this place set up like it has been made for us. And us alone.

"Is that Alex? That is *not* Alex!" Caden's brow is furrowed as he looks my way.

"What? Where?"

It doesn't take long to locate my estranged younger brother in the multitude of gyrating bodies. We both got our father's significant height, so it's relatively easy to spot him head and shoulders above most others.

Alex.

Fuck.

I've lost track of how long it's been. My stomach sinks as unwanted images play across my field of vision, but blissfully,

I lose my train of thought as my half-brother moves to the side, letting me glimpse the absolute goddess he's dancing with.

Her head tosses back, allowing her long blonde hair to graze the curve at the base of her spine, highlighting an ass that makes my palms itch with the desire to squeeze those perfectly proportioned peachy cheeks. Her high-waisted black leather pants are moulded to her body like a second skin, and as she turns to face me, my breath falters.

With her eyes closed and her face turned upwards, an array of colours from the club's strobe lights dance across her body, while she sways seductively to the sultry beat. Then, raising her hands above her head keeping her eyes closed, her lips lift ever so slightly in a barely-there smile.

A half-smile that makes me think she's privy to secrets I'd like nothing more than to uncover.

Her eyes slowly open, and as if she has a sixth sense that she is being watched so blatantly, our gazes clash. Her smirk turns into a full-blown smile showcasing perfectly straight white teeth and deep dimples that, on anyone else, would be overkill.

She glances down coyly before lifting her face to mine again, chin tilted almost in a defiant act before sending me a cheeky-as-fuck wink as she catches her bottom lip between her teeth.

She looks like the perfect mix of sass and, dare I say, innocence. Jesus Christ, the two combined are a potent mix, particularly when you consider the wrapping it comes in, and suddenly, the words of this high energy dance song are ringing so true. I want to know her name. I want to know *her*—more than I've wanted anything in my entire life.

I take my time making a leisurely perusal of her glorious body. Those pants make her legs look unbelievably long, and even though her torso is encased in a full sleeve, high-necked black crop top, her breasts are thrust forward and slightly more than a handful. I do not doubt that her tiny waist, flashing an inch of skin with each movement, is the breadth of one of my hands.

From this angle in the half-light of the club, her face seems to have petite features.

Except for those eyes. They are impossibly wide and fringed with lashes so dark and long I can clearly see them, even from this distance.

To say this woman is the thing of dreams, and in particular, *my* dreams, feels lacklustre. It falls short. She is perfection embodied.

And I *want* her.

My stomach clenches and sinks as the realisation hits.

Alex has moved around behind her now. He's placed his hands on either of her hips as they sway together in perfect synchronicity.

Of all people to see my dream girl with, I wasn't expecting it to be Alex, the half-brother I haven't seen in person in ten long-ass years. And though he was only ten when I'd left home, our parting had not been on the best of terms, so there is no way I am making any approach, even if they are just friends.

I am not opening that can of worms. Not a goddamn chance.

As our eyes meet again, her brows pull together, making the most adorable frown as she tilts her head to one side questioningly. I'm guessing my horror is reflected on my face because all signs of flirtation have ceased.

At that precise moment, I feel a hand descend over my eyes.

Fucking North.

Grabbing the offending appendage, I throw it away as though it has burnt me and frantically look back to where the girl had been gyrating, only to find she has disappeared in the crowd.

An emotion somewhere between disappointment and loss

ravages my body with anger hot on its heels as I pivot to face a laughing Caden, his blonde locks pushed back over his face.

Nate stands beside him, arms folded over his chest stoically, watching the gyrations beneath us, almost ignorant of my outrage.

Almost ignorant but not quite, as evidenced by the expression on his stupid face. His sneering face that's almost wholly hidden by all that face fluff he calls a beard.

"What the fuck, man? Get off!"

"Jesus, DeMarco. What's with the eye-fucking? The night is young, the booze is plenty, and the pussy is endless, my friend. This is *my* big night, so you tossers have to do what I say, and I say, get fucked up now, get fucked later."

Ducking down, he plucks two shot glasses brimming with clear liquid off the table before straightening up and holding one out for me. I take the proffered olive branch as some of the contents splash out onto the back of my hand before I smirk, putting the glass to my lips.

"Bottoms up, wankers!"

Two

OLIVIA

My first night out *ever,* and it's looking like disobeying Mum and Dad is paying off.

And in spades.

I tried, and mostly failed, to ignore the guilt that churned in my gut. It had been swirling on and off all night. The joy of growing up in a devout Catholic household, I guess. Feeling guilty over simply living my life the way I had always wanted.

Freely and independently. As my own person, not just as an extension of them and their over-the-top beliefs.

My only sibling, an older sister Holly, had died in a hit and run when we were eleven and seven, respectively, and since then, my place in the family had become even more immovable. Unfortunately for me and to the delight of my pious parents, I am being groomed to marry a member of our devout little community in the suburbs of London and will be expected to live a faithful and downright staid life filled with devotion to both our Lord and Saviour. To whomever my parents deemed a proper husband.

I am still utterly devastated over the fact they hadn't allowed me to attend university, citing that I would primarily be a wife, homemaker, and mother and, as such, it would be "foolhardy to waste" another level of education on me.

Being graciously afforded the privilege of volunteering at a local homeless centre, St. Fintan's, operated by Father Thomas, is the only bright spot in my life. He's less judgemental and less old-fashioned than my parents. I love the work we do and have plenty of friends because of my time at the shelter, even though I hate how stifled I am by the life I haven't chosen.

The life I would *never* willingly choose.

Through St. Fintan's, I had come to meet Nola and her partner Josie. However, if my parents knew that I had befriended an openly gay couple, I would be doing penance for months, and I could kiss goodbye to my volunteer work, which would absolutely break my heart.

Nola is one of the kindest souls I've ever met, with a wicked sense of humour. She reminds me of my big sister, and I suppose that's part of why I felt so drawn to her in the first place.

Our paths had initially crossed about six months ago when I was assigned to run a playgroup with some of the homeless kids that stayed at the centre. Nola had been paired with me, and as it was her first day volunteering, I spent most of it explaining how we did things, who was who and where everything was.

By the end of the day, we had become fast friends, and the following day, she invited me to have lunch with her and her partner, whom she neglected to tell me was another woman. My jaw nearly hit the floor when she introduced Josie, or Jo, as she had insisted I call her, and greeted her with a great big resounding kiss on the lips when we met her at a nearby cafe.

It was all due to these two beautiful souls that my eyes had been opened to a whole realm of possibilities, and tonight's foray into this crazy world was the first of what the girls informed me would be many mini rebellions.

I had never lied to my parents; never once had reason to, though I didn't tell them that my friends were a cohabiting couple. To my defence, that's a lie by omission, not an outright lie.

Yeah, Liv, keep telling yourself that.

When I told them I had been invited to Nola's house overnight for pizza and a movie, they had no reason to say no. After all, I've always been a good and respectful daughter, never giving them an ounce of trouble.

Plus, Mum had met Nola many times in the past six months. We'd even had her over to dinner several times, so she had no reason to believe I would ever lie to her.

The night was going so, so well. Of course, we had started the evening with pizza, so that part at least wasn't a lie.

Keep trying to validate your excuses to yourself, you great big lying liar.

Then we got ready, which involved a lot of stuff I had never done before. There were so many different types of makeup and hair potions and body lotions; I just let the girls have free rein and was honestly blown away with the final result.

They had given me a smoky grey eye with several coats of mascara over my naturally long thick lashes that made my blue eyes stand out. I had a light, natural pink shade on my lips and some rose blush on my cheeks. They had blow-dried my hair and used a whole array of products to define the different shades of blonde.

Jo said it was the "just been fucked" look, and both my friends had giggled contagiously when they saw my already pink cheeks deepen with my natural blush.

After all, profanities are still new to me.

My friends had wanted me to dress in more revealing clothes, but years of being a good girl warred with their wishes, so we'd eventually settled on black leather pants and a black crop top that covered all but a sliver of my flat stomach.

Once we got to the club, the girls told me we were meeting some of their friends, so I was pleasantly surprised to find my dear friend Alex there too. The girls pull both of us out onto the heaving dance floor, and I can't help the self-satisfied mini smile that I allow to play across my lips at the thought that this is it.

I'm doing it. I'm living my life.

And on *my* terms.

The thought fills me with joy. A rush of sheer delight, as I've never felt, fills me from the tips of my toes to the top of my head. I am simply happy and present in this moment.

When I open my eyes, I lock gazes with the most magnetic human being I have ever seen. Alluring eyes draw me in, holding me in place with their outright fixation on me.

Dark, almost black hair falls across his brow, though he is quick to brush it away in a practised, slightly impatient move. It looks as though it's a little too long, and I find myself wishing it were *my* hand running through the length that's once again fallen forward across his forehead, giving him an almost boyish look.

My smile broadens, and when his lips lift into a smile to match mine, I swear I can feel the earth move.

It's as though our souls recognise each other even if our bodies and minds don't, and in that couple of seconds, my entire life shifts. Which is completely insane, right?

Josie has spent the night referring to the male population of the club as "McHotties," which I've found beyond hilarious. And so, I have claimed it for the beautiful man looking down upon me.

My McHottie is momentarily distracted by his friends, so when Alex grabs my hand to ask if I'd like a drink, I use that as my opportunity to leave the dancefloor and, by proxy, my admirer's attention.

I don't want to hide away from that beautiful man upstairs; it's not that I don't want to see him again. It's more that I just need a breather. His gaze was… ardent.

Intense, to put it mildly.

I just need a moment to gather my senses as it seems they've been scattered to the four winds.

Also, I'm parched, so Alex's offer comes at the perfect moment.

After trying several different cocktails, we dance and chat for several hours as the club gets more packed. My eyes keep straying to the VIP area upstairs, which is now at capacity, but I've yet to glimpse the McHottie again, and I can't help the discouragement that flows through me.

Alex offers to grab another round, leaving our table to go to the bar as Nola announces she needs to use the little girls' room.

"I see you, you know." Jo looks at me, a knowing smirk playing on her purple painted lips.

I'm not even attempting to pretend otherwise, because, with Jo, I've learned that there's no point. The girl is unrelenting, so my lips lift into a big grin, highlighting my dimples.

"Am I that transparent?"

"Yup!" We both dissolve into a fit of giggles. "But you're so freaking cute, girl! Why don't you just go and see if you can blag your way up there?"

Shutting my giggling off as suddenly as it started, I shake my head vehemently.

"No. Way. Not happening. I'd never get in there. Those women look like they stepped straight out of a fashion magazine."

Jo looks at me askance, slowly shaking her head of shoulder-length black curls, her deep brown eyes flicking skyward.

"What?"

"Oh, baby girl, you have no idea how much of a knockout you are, do you? You are an eleven, and those bitches can't be more than four, or five at a push, on a really good day."

My cheeks flare with embarrassment as I laugh nervously. "You're so kind to say that, Jo. I don't think so, though."

I send a rueful glance her way, noticing when my eyes meet hers that they are narrowed as though in deep thought before she grabs two shots of something Nola bought, but no one wanted to drink.

It's syrupy looking, dark brown, and smells of liquorice, which I always liked as a child. It had been Holly's absolute favourite, though Mum didn't really buy it after the accident.

"Liquid courage, hmm?" Handing me one, Jo nods, encouraging me to knock it back, which, after taking one final longing look at the VIP area upstairs as an incentive, I quickly do.

The shot burns my throat as it makes its way down my oesophagus and into my abdomen. It settles with a flickering warmth in my stomach, and I find the sensation entirely too pleasant, so when Jo passes me the second one, I don't hesitate to send it to join the first.

"I'd say you're as ready as you'll ever be, baby girl. Come on. I'll walk with you. Moral support and all that."

Tossing a wink at me, Jo catches me under the elbow, linking our two arms. Together we walk out from the seating area near the bar, around the side of the heaving dancefloor, eventually coming to a stop at the base of a roped-off spiral staircase.

The syrupy shots are still fervently burning in my stomach, dimming my doubt, and keeping much of my anxiety at bay.

I can do this.

Turning to face each other, Jo places both her hands on my biceps, rubbing them up and down briskly.

"You got this, girl. Go and live a little. We'll be right here for you."

Then she swats me on my rear before sauntering back toward our table to wait for our friends. Giving myself a bit of pep talk under my breath, I slip beyond the rope and slowly ascend the stairs before reaching an absolute hulk of a man guarding the entrance.

The sight of his sheer bulk has me slamming to a standstill, pivoting on my heel with a grimace. There's *no way* he's letting me in there.

"Are you alright, Miss?" The Cockney accented voice behind me is soft, in complete contrast to the Hagrid-esque man I just turned my back to.

I look over my shoulder, catching his earnest eyes with mine and deciding that honesty is the best policy, as Father T. always says. It may be the wrong way to go, but lies don't come easy to me. It's as simple as that.

"Hi." I peer at the white, bright name badge on the side of his dark suit. "Umm… Burt. I'm Olivia, and I've not been invited up here. As a matter of fact, I don't know a single person in that room."

I plough on, cringing internally at the word vomit while pleading with myself to quit it. But, once it starts, it's hard to stop the spew.

"I've never been to a club before, not even a pub if you can believe that. I've been very sheltered by my parents, and I'm breaking a bazillion rules by being here tonight. But, I *need* to meet a guy who is a guest up here because he saw me earlier, and I've been too nervous about coming and finding him, and now I've drunk some strange alcohol that tastes like liquorice for some 'liquid courage' as my friend called it, and I'm blabbering on like an idiot to meet a McHottie, though my head says I should know better… and I should just go now."

Inhaling a deep breath because my tirade had been one long, breathless sentence that had picked up speed the longer I'd gone on, my face flushes in a deep pink blush from the lack of oxygen and complete embarrassment at my idiocy. Still, as luck would have it, just as I'm about to cut and run, Burt, the gentle giant, catches my wrist, pulling me closer with a facial expression as close to a grin as I reckon his stoic face can get.

"After a spiel like that, I'd have to be a right bollocks not to let you in, wouldn't I?"

My face breaks into a wide smile that reaches my eyes as I look up into his slightly less angry looking face, but just as I'm about to utter my thanks, a sudden movement through the crowded room draws my attention.

The sight of the McHottie bearing down on us at light speed, with such intensity on his handsome features, turns the still burning ball of warmth from those syrupy shots to molten lava in the depths of my stomach.

What would Jo do? I can almost hear her voice whispering in my ear, like a miniature devil on my shoulder.

"Game face on, girl." And so, channelling my inner Jo, I meet his eyes with mine, ready for whatever the night may bring.

Three

HENRY

Three hours later, the VIP area is overflowing.

Caden has always been prone to excess, a product of being the only son of the world's best-known rocker.

From the age of fifteen, when he lost his virginity to our thirty-year-old English teacher on her desk at the stupidly posh school for rich assholes where we met, his favourite vice has always been a pretty face—and an even prettier pussy.

If the man were told he could either have food or pussy for the rest of his life, he'd happily die gorging on exquisite pink tacos.

The star of the show is currently holding court with twin redheads adorning each knee and his long term, more-off-than-on girlfriend, Layla, at his feet with her hand palming his blatantly hard cock through his ripped denims while her other hand disappears under one of the redheads' short skirts.

Catching my eye, he gives me his signature self-satisfied

Cheshire Cat grin, before turning to one of the redheads and running his tongue up and down her exposed neck, playfully nipping at it to the delight of the groupie.

He and Layla are into sharing, always have been. Nate and I don't get how he can share his bird but have just given it up as a lost cause, having asked too many times to count.

Considering Cade and his band have just signed a multi-million-pound contract with Spellman Sounds, one of the world's biggest record labels, I think the man deserves to let loose. They are starting an extensive world tour in a couple of weeks, so who knows when the three of us will be together next time.

Shaking my head at his not-so-surprising antics, I turn back to Nathaniel, who has been unusually quiet this evening, even for him. Nate often comes across as aloof or just plain rude as the most reserved of our trio, but that isn't the case.

He is an observer, forever taking in everything around him and committing it all to memory.

For such a quiet guy, the man gets almost as much pussy as North, and that's saying something; the perks of being an award-winning, internationally best-selling author and all by the tender age of twenty-three. Four years and three revelatory books later, he's more than a little aimless. In his own words, he "peaked at twenty-fucking-three and it's all been one big shitshow since."

"You fucking any of these wannabes tonight?"

"If I hadn't been ruined by that luscious blonde earlier, I would be." He snorts into his Jack and Coke as I grin, continuing. "Seriously, man, did you fucking see her? On a scale of one to ten, she was a stone-cold one-hundred. Did. You. *See.* That. Ass?"

An ass like perfect peaches.

I make an O shape with my lips as I suck air through them. Nate nods fervently. "Fuck yeah, I did. De-fucking-lish. A thing of beauty!" He stops, then questions, "What the hell was she doing with Alex?"

Rubbing a hand down my scruff, I shrug my shoulders as I nod.

"Maybe he's got a massive cock." My words feel like sandpaper on my tongue. The thought of my kid brother getting to put his hands on the hottest woman I have ever seen is a severe buzzkill.

"Jesus, DeMarco, I'd rather not think about your baby brother's cock; thank you very much."

Raising a sardonic eyebrow to match my half-smirk, I chuckle at the grimace on his face.

"Well, I never want to think about you or Cade's cocks, but that's all I seem to hear about lately. Mostly, where you're sticking them. You're a fucking manwhore if I ever met one."

He laughs good-naturedly at my ribbing, knowing full well I'm right. He rode the success of his bestsellers all the way to the bank, and then rode the banker's wives for shits and giggles.

"Ah, but, DeMarco, I'm one sexy ass manwhore." Chuckling harder at his exaggerated wink, I'm about to reply, when I catch sight of a head of blonde hair on the stairs near our security who has had the evening from hell keeping all but those Caden deemed the "tastiest pussy" in the club out.

Ever the gentleman, our Cade.

Without so much as acknowledging Nate, I stand and begin to make my way toward the staircase in an attempt to ensure my eyes aren't playing tricks on me. Spotting that same blonde head, now engaged in conversation with Burt, whose lips are tipped into something suspiciously smile-like and whose perma-scowl seems to have disappeared for the first time since we arrived, I lengthen my strides to close the distance in mere seconds, despite the crowd.

Just before I reach my destination, or perhaps that should be quarry, because the way I'm stalking toward her makes me feel like a hunter closing in on its prey, she spots me, her eyes widening like a deer in the headlights.

"I've got it from here, Burt." I nod at the chain keeping my beauty from entering the room, and Burt quickly unlocks it, holding it open so that she can enter.

I'm taken aback by the sound of her laughter. It's like a wind chime, and Tinkerbell made a baby, and it's, undoubtedly, the most beautiful sound I've ever heard.

Until the next words leave her mouth. "Who says I want to come in?" Her eyes sparkle with mischievous delight at my apparent confusion.

The first thing that registers is the fact that the sound of her voice instantly has my cock stiffening uncomfortably in my pants. The second, she doesn't seem set to fall at my feet like the rest of the female species.

Women tend to throw themselves at all three of us at all times of the day and night. We're accustomed to not having to graft.

And the thought that I may have to work for this one makes my semi throb painfully against the fabric of my jeans.

The thrill of the chase.

I knew I'd always been a sadistic bastard.

Inclining my head, with my hand on my heart and a cheeky grin plastered to my face, in an exaggerated toff accent my father would be proud of, I tell her, "My most heartfelt apologies to the most beautiful woman I have ever laid eyes upon. I had but hoped to make your acquaintance."

Laying it on with a trowel, I extend my hand in the hopes she will take it, lift my head to display my teasing, now fully loaded smile, and seal it with what I've been told is a cheeky-as-fuck wink.

Once again, I'm greeted by her tinkling laugh before she accepts my outstretched palm, placing her petite fingers on it.

A bolt of electricity runs from her fingers into mine and all the way up my arm, hitting me square in the chest. Her eyes, which up until that point had been laser-focused on my hand, shoot up to meet mine, meaning one thing.

She felt it too.

Her smile widens impossibly, displaying her enticingly deep dimples to perfection, and I find my lips mirroring hers.

Jesus, who the hell am I, and when did I turn into a complete fucking idiot?

Still holding her hand in mine, I draw her closer and weave our way towards the back of the room near the door we entered through earlier. I turn from the table I've nabbed for us to alert our server of my desire for two drinks, which he delivers within seconds of having seated my little Miss Peaches and even before I have taken a seat for myself.

"Dom okay for you?" I nod at her drink, which she moves to pick up from the low table in front of her. She smiles almost shyly before taking a sip from her champagne flute. "It's delicious. Thank you."

Having barely spoken more than a handful of words, it's crazy to feel this level of attraction between us.

The desire is palpable. Tangible. The ultimate aphrodisiac.

Up close, she's even more mouth-wateringly delicious than I had earlier thought.

Younger too.

Caden's pulling motto races through my brain: before you tap it, make sure you wrap it.

No, you twat, not that one.

I shake my head before asking, "You're old enough to drink that, right?"

It's entirely out of left field, but it doesn't throw her in the slightest.

Daintily swallowing the sip of Dom she's just taken, she utters words that make my stomach drop. "Would it matter to you if I wasn't?" One side of her mouth lifts into a half-smirk as she pops a brow in what I hope is sarcasm.

Seeing the confusion mixed with mild horror on my face, she reaches out and pats the hand resting on my thigh, putting me at ease.

"Relax. I'm turning twenty-one in a couple of weeks." I immediately feel my shoulders descend from my ears, where they had migrated.

There's that sweet laughter once again. I glance around to see that most of the men in our secluded area are staring straight at my girl. Her head is tipped back, her slim neck on display, and her breasts thrust forward in her delight.

I am *not* like Cade; I don't like sharing. I don't even like these asshats looking. But, as I remember the host telling us earlier about a roof terrace, a lightbulb goes off in my head. "Would you like to go somewhere a little quieter?"

Her eyes shoot to mine, and I see temptation and hesitance play across her features in equal measure.

"To talk. Just talk." I don't want to spook her now that I have her within reach.

"We… I… That's to say, you haven't even told me your name yet."

Her bumbling is cute and a little bit out of sync with the bold sassiness she's displayed up to this point. Hmm, interesting. My girl has two very different sides, and I'm honestly not sure which one turns me on the most.

"Let's start with your name so that I can stop referring to you as Peaches in my head."

There's that damn trowel laying it on thick once again. Her eyes sparkle with laughter as she reverts to that saucy minx from before.

"Well, isn't that a coincidence!" Her cheeky grin is contagious as hell. "That's my name." The amplified innocence on her face sends a shot of unfiltered lust straight to my cock, making my balls tingle in anticipation.

"Nice to meet you, *Peaches.*" The fact that I placed extra emphasis on the word doesn't go amiss, and mischievousness flashes in her eyes.

I think it's fair to say we're both enjoying this game.

"I'm Henry. But you can call me Get-your-coat-love-you've-pulled if you'd like."

Cocking an eyebrow at her, we both dissolve into floods of laughter, my deeper tone rumbling just under the lilting resonance of hers, before she unfolds herself gracefully from the large seat.

"I just need to use the little girls' room, and then we can discuss what you can do to earn the knowledge of my name, Henry."

Bending to press a small peck on my scruff-covered cheek, she straightens up, sends me an exaggerated wink, and sashays in the direction of the Powder Room.

That fucking peachy, perfect *ass.* Yup, definitely reinforcing the fact that I am an ass man through and fucking through.

There's a scuffle to my left as Nate and Caden collide when they both try to crash into the seat she's just vacated before I can even take a breath. You'd swear we were teenagers all over again with how these two were acting.

"What the fuck, dipshits? Act your goddamn age!"

They don't even acknowledge my annoyance before launching into a round of twenty questions.

Who is she? How does she know Alex? Is she legal?

That last one is all North. Obviously.

Both pricks grin manically at me, and I can't help the cheesy ass smile that slashes across my face at the thought of possibly having found the woman that all wet dreams are made of.

"We've barely exchanged a handful of words, and none of them included my brother. She's gone to freshen up, and then I'm going to bring her upstairs to the roof."

Caden elbows Nate frantically, as if I can't see what the idiot is doing right in front of me.

"And no, it's genuinely only to talk, dickhead. She's worlds beyond being a quick fuck and dump, yeah?"

Nate snorts out a disbelieving laugh. "That does *not* sound like you, DeMarco. I've known you forever, and your only rules are no kissing…"

"Always said that was the weirdest fucking thing I've ever heard, Henry. You're one strange tosser!"

I kick Cade's shin under the table at his interjection, earning me a howl.

Prick.

Kissing is an intimacy I don't do, and the boys know it. I've kissed one person in my life, one goddamn time, and she ruined the closeness of the act for me. But this girl. There's something about her that makes me almost… *feel*. Something I gave up doing a long damn time ago.

Ignoring our side banter, Nate goes on. "So, zero kissing and only ever fuck and dump. What gives?"

Nate and I grew up in similar environments. Absentee father, dead mother, no siblings to speak of—my long-lasting estrangement with Alex doesn't even come into the equation.

The one difference between Nathaniel Hawthorne and me is that while my mum had died when I was young, younger even than Nate had been when his had passed, I could still remember my mum's passion for true love.

I could still remember the love she and my father had shared with one another. And with me. Theirs was an epic love, an unforgettable love, a once-in-a-lifetime love.

I still relive her words regularly, as though she had spoken them only yesterday, her voice soft and melodic. Her eyes dreamily remembering her own great love as she stroked my messy, dark hair from my forehead while we lay wrapped up in each other on her bed during one of her final days.

"Henry, my darling boy. If there's one lesson I can teach you before I leave this world, let it be this: when your heart finds its other half, you will just know. You mark my words; when you meet your true love, you'll fall hard, and you'll fall fast. And when you know, you know."

And fuck me if I hadn't already fallen halfway down that rabbit hole.

Four

OLIVIA

I can feel Henry McHottie's eyes following me, or more accurately, my swaying bottom, as I stride towards the Powder Room. And of course, that devilish little Jo on my shoulder tells me to keep up with that little bit of sass, so I add a little extra undulation to my hips, just for him.

Entering the luxurious space for the first time, having heard about it from my friends, I knew I would be blown away as I had been with the rest of the club's interior, but seriously... Wow!

There are several groups of drop-dead gorgeous women chatting and giggling while fixing their makeup or fluffing their hair at the numerous golden, individually spot lit mirrors, each with their own high-backed velvet armchairs. The colour scheme is black and gold with accents of a beautiful deep purple splashed here and there for contrast, and there's a giant purple velvet pouffe dead centre of the space where some girls appear to be sharing some lines of white powder off the back of a hand mirror.

All eyes land on me as I enter, yet they return to what they had been doing previously, just as rapidly. Being able to melt into the background has always been easy with the lifestyle I've been raised in, but tonight, I'm craving to be seen in this whole new world. And I think that is what pulls me toward Henry. The way he makes me feel seen, genuinely *seen* for the first time in my whole entire life.

Moving to an empty cubicle, I close the lid and take a moment just to sit and think. I don't have to pee or anything. I just need to take a minute to make a choice. Go upstairs with the handsome virtual stranger or go back to my old life of being the perpetual good girl and hating it inside.

Don't pretend you don't know what he wants. You're not that naïve.

Furrowing my brow in contemplation, suddenly, the silence in the Powder Room permeates my thoughts. I rise to stand inside the cubicle, then strain my ears to hear if there's anyone left out there.

Suddenly there's a *bang*. It sounds like the door to the Room has been opened and someone's coming inside.

"Leave."

One word. That's all it takes for me to instantly recognise the owner of that deep, goosebump-inducing voice.

"Oops, sorry," is followed by giggles and another *bang* as the door slams behind the newcomer, leaving me alone with the owner of the deepest, huskiest voice I've ever heard.

A voice that makes me clench my thighs together in a desperate attempt to create friction to alleviate the desire pumping through my veins.

I may be devout by force, but I'm blatantly not by nature.

"Come on out here, my sweet Peaches. You've been gone *far*

too long."

I can't hold back the giggle that erupts out of me at his nickname as I unlock the cubicle door and find Henry standing in the centre of the room just by the pouffe with his legs braced apart and his arms crossed, the very epitome of power and strength.

His boyishly messy hair belies his age, which I would place around mid-twenties or so, and once again, it's falling into his eyes.

"You really should invest in a haircut."

He chuckles as he unfolds his arms to use his right hand to swipe it out of his eyes once again. His head is bent forward as he looks up at me from under his long lashes.

For the first time, I can see his eyes are stunningly green with the tiniest flecks of gold that seem to sparkle with playfulness as he asks, "Want to volunteer?"

"I'm no barber," I say, shrugging, "but I could give it a shot. I tend to excel at everything I put my heart and soul into, FYI."

He pops a brow at me as I continue. "What's in it for me?"

My heart is beating out of my chest at my sheer audacity. Who am I, and what happened to Olivia Parker? Safe to say that the Josie on my shoulder is still whispering devilish ideas into my ear.

Before I can even blink, he's crossed the distance between us. I inhale sharply, and its echo rebounds through the empty space.

Taking in what I'm sure is the look of pure shock on my face, Henry raises his hands and places his warm palms on each of my cheekbones. For a moment, we stand just breathing each other's air. He smells out of this world. Like a mixture of Sunday walks in the forest, my favourite Earl Grey tea, and a scent that is all male and wholly intoxicating.

Running his tongue across his bottom lip, he sucks it into his mouth as though in contemplation before allowing it to pop free.

"I want to try something."

My heart stalls in my chest at the intimate tone of his words.

I'm not entirely innocent. I've sneakily shared several experimental kisses with boys in our circle when opportunities have arisen. Still, I've never felt as drawn to another living person as much as the man standing before me.

It's as though he is the Sun, and, like the planets of our solar system, I am utterly powerless to fight the gravitational pull that surrounds him.

He waits for a beat, and almost as if the words are ripped from deep down inside his throat, he rasps, "I'm going to kiss you now."

Then, without hesitation, his warm, large palm slides around my neck, nestling in the hair at the nape, making the base of my spine light up in delicious tingles before his lips softly press against mine, almost tentatively.

A moan is torn from my chest as he teases my lips with his tongue, and when I part them to allow the sound to escape, he thrusts his tongue inside, running it along my own.

What began as a gentle teasing of each other's mouths rapidly turns into consuming each other with a voracity I didn't know was possible. His tongue and lips are soft, in direct contradiction with the kiss itself, which is hard, demanding, and I never want it to stop.

In response to my own unchecked whimpers and moans, Henry's deep groan sends a lightning bolt of pleasure straight to my innocent sex as he continues his assault on my mouth—and my senses. One hand moves from where it cups my cheek to run along the side of my breast, skimming past my rib cage and finally down to my ass, where he splays his palm underneath.

At his urging, in a perfectly organic move, I lift my legs to wrap them around his waist, locking my heels tightly behind his hips. I can feel his rock-hard erection pulsing right at my core, and instead of following years of ingrained repression, I let my inner desires take flight.

It's so absolutely unlike me, yet nothing has ever felt more authentic, more *right* in my whole life.

Without taking his lips from mine or changing the arduous tempo of our kiss, I can feel him moving me across the room until my back is pressed against the cool wall as he grinds his hardness into me, sending red hot flames through my centre. I'm slightly embarrassed to feel a sudden flood of moisture in my panties.

But not nearly enough to stop the torrent of downright carnal madness from seeping into my body and drowning my soul.

Still fully clothed and in an act of utter lunacy, we move together, my body untried but intrinsically knowing what I want, what we both *need.*

We grind our fully clothed pelvises together in a way that makes my body sing as he plays it so expertly.

Henry rips his mouth from mine, wrenching a gasp of horrified disappointment from my lips at the loss of contact before he reattaches his own to the curve of my neck, his pelvis pressing against me harder than before as my whimpers get louder and more uncontrollable.

Realising his intention, I tilt my head to the side, allowing him to lave hot, wet, open-mouthed kisses from my earlobe to the sensitive flesh where my neck meets my shoulder, nipping and nibbling as he goes until I'm a panting, writhing mess.

Sensation after sensation builds where our sexes meet as I throw my head back against the wall, mouth opening wide in a silent scream.

My mind is whirring at a thousand miles per hour, all manner of thoughts swirling desperately, screaming for acknowledgement, yet I can't seem to focus on a single one because my entire being has come to life under Henry's fiery touch.

My body is alight, reaching for something. Something in the distance that feels unobtainable, and I desperately try to chase it, needing more, when Henry licks a path to my ear, resting his lips on my lobe as his breath ghosts across the shell when he whispers, "Let go, Peaches."

Abruptly, the building sensations in my core reach a peak, and I squeeze my eyes shut tight as I see stars, my body shattering into a million tiny little pieces. As consciousness slowly returns to my body, my eyes flutter open to find his intense green orbs, pupils blown wide, fixed firmly on mine.

For several long moments, we focus solely on one another, an array of thoughts and emotions passing wordlessly between us as though our very souls are speaking to one another without either of us ever uttering a word.

Both of us are breathing hard, inhaling each other's breaths like two people starved of oxygen, and I can't quite distinguish whether it's Henry or me who's shaking slightly.

Perhaps it's both.

Once his breathing is more controlled, a beautiful smile graces his handsome features. He blinks those unusual green eyes once.

Twice.

"You even taste like a peach."

I can't stop a small answering smile from dancing across my lips.

His hands rake along every newly awakened, vibrating nerve ending. I hesitantly move my hands from where they are clasped behind his neck to inch the hem of his deceivingly plain black, no doubt designer t-shirt upwards to place my slightly trembling hands on his torso.

His abdomen is silky smooth with a smattering of coarse hair, his abs rock hard and well defined.

His body quakes under my tentative palms as he bends forward, dropping a smattering of butterfly kisses along my neck and jawline until he comes to my lips, where he stops, whispering so softly I strain to hear him even in the room's silence.

"Kissing is entirely underrated."

He returns his hand to the back of my neck. It feels right; his hand is now where it's meant to be.

Home.

With his palm right at the top of my spine, he exerts a little pressure to pull my head forward so that our brows are resting on one another.

Then he leans in to brush his lips to mine before setting me down on the floor between himself and the wall. I feel so small in his presence. There's got to be at least a foot between our heights.

Bending at the knees, he wraps my hand in his much bigger one and looks me straight in the eye, the intensity of his gaze bringing butterflies to life underneath my breastbone.

"Come with me, okay?"

Smiling almost shyly, which is ridiculous after what has just passed between us, I nod, and he smiles broadly in reply.

Lacing our fingers together, we exit the Powder Room and go downstairs, where we enter through another door with a sign pointing up that reads, *Roof Terrace.*

Upon stepping through the door, I pause momentarily, the enormity of what we've just done hitting me like a freight train, until Henry turns questioning eyes to find mine. His exquisite gaze allays my doubts as rapidly as they surfaced so I smile softly before nodding my consent to move forward once more.

We climb several flights of wrought-iron stairs before emerging into the coolness of an early spring night, the lights of London blinking around us and the sounds of the hustle and bustle below us a muted din.

Henry leads me to a seat covered with cushions and blankets surrounded by loops of tiny twinkling lights with a firepit crackling away in the centre. The entire thing looks as though it's been placed here for secret interludes.

"This is beautiful."

Without missing a beat, Henry's husky voice washes over me.

"You're beautiful."

Turning to face him, I'm taken aback by the sincerity blazing in his eyes. It's like nothing I've ever seen before. I'm utterly unable to stop myself from blushing profusely at his ardency. I'm unused to such blatant flattery, or such intense eye contact. A blazing intensity that both floors me and bolsters me in equal measure, and I find myself desperate to bask in the depths of his gaze for as long as I can.

I whisper a thank you as I tear my eyes from his to look down at my hands resting on my lap.

"Have I earned your name yet, Peach?"

Switching on my newfound sass, courtesy of devil Jo, I meet his eyes with my chin lifted. "Not yet, Henry."

"Ooh, you really are intent on making me work for it. I don't know whether to be proud or pissed."

We laugh a little—our eyes never leaving the other's as the conversation flows between us, alleviating the previous tension.

We talk about everything from the mundane, like the unseasonably cold weather of this past weekend and favourite foods, to deeper topics like religion and family.

At some point, Henry's arm winds itself around the back of the seat behind me, his fingertips resting lightly on my sleeved shoulder. Despite being fully covered, I can't help the eruption of goosebumps from head to toe when he begins drawing light circles along my arm so softly that I'm not even sure he's aware he's doing it.

And so, I'm utterly unable to help the dimpled smile from breaking across my face, Henry jumping on it with a smile of his own.

"What's so funny, little Miss Peaches?"

I can't stop a hugely unladylike snort from escaping between my upturned lips.

The thought that Mum would surely be horrified if she heard me tries its utmost to enter my conscious mind, but this me—the new me—shuts it out as quickly as it rears its repressed ugly head.

"I'm sorry. It was your hand—"

"Oh, are you ticklish? I didn't even realise I was doing it."

Henry moves his hand back to rest on the seat behind me and instantly my body misses his touch. Sliding closer to him along the bench, in a move I know Jo would be proud of, I reach back to pull his arm closer around me, my eyes once again finding and holding his.

My voice is low and doesn't sound like my own when I speak. "I didn't say you had to stop."

His eyes glitter in the semi-darkness as they rove along every contour of my face before he tugs me closer to drop a lingering kiss atop my brow. When he pulls back, he waits for a beat, then shakes his head as though he's confused before slipping back into our conversation—all the while skimming his fingers along my arm and collarbone.

He's empathetic to my strict upbringing, though I don't go into it in any great detail, and once we realise that we've both suffered a significant loss at a young age, we bond over the deaths of my sister and his mother.

Before I know it, almost two hours have passed in the blink of an eye.

During that time, I come to discover that Henry works for his family, his favourite pastime is painting still lifes, which he claims he's "not half bad at"—and his all-time favourite TV show is *12 Monkeys.* Although I've never heard of it, he makes me promise I will source it and give it a shot.

"A science-fiction love story tragedy, right?"

He looks at me, scepticism blazing from his eyes as I try to contain my giggles. "I'm telling you, Peach. You'll love it. Trust me, okay?"

My face promptly loses all hints of tomfoolery and sarcasm. "Okay, Henry. I trust you."

His nostrils flare as his jaw tightens at my simple, genuine words; however, as the fire has begun to die, I unwittingly choose that moment to shiver. It's gotten a lot cooler since we first walked up here.

Henry pulls me into a standing position until I'm flush against his body.

"I've got to go let the guys know I'm leaving, and then I'll get my guy to bring the car around."

Brushing his knuckles across my cheekbone, he continues. "Got to make sure my Peaches gets home safe and sound! Maybe then I'll have earned your real name."

He raises his brow as I laugh softly. "I'll be right back, okay?"

Warmth fills my belly as I realise that he could have taken things further here if he wanted to. After all, I lost my mind and morals to the passion swirling between us earlier.

Instead, he wants to ensure my safe journey home after spending time getting to know me.

I nod my head solemnly once. Then, leaning up onto my tiptoes, I wrap my arms around his waist and nuzzle into his hard chest. He folds me into his body like we were made to fit each other, and for long minutes, we stand motionless. Henry's head is resting on mine, which is pressed against his chest, listening to the steady beat of his heart as we drink in each other's bodies. Each other's souls.

If ever there was a moment in time I wished I could bottle up and keep for always, this would be it.

The trance is broken by the sound of feet thumping on the stairs.

"What the fuck are you doing up here, Henry? Cade is on a murderous rampage you've fucked with 'boys' night'—his words, not mine."

Henry's body stiffens ever so slightly as I move my head away from the safety of his broad chest and peer around his body to see another darkly handsome man.

His face appears to have been chiselled from marble; it's all smooth lines and perfect shadows. With a jaw covered by an almost full dark beard, I can't help but think it looks a little out of character with his features. Almost like he's trying to hide his true self behind his facial hair, though that could be the romance reader in me talking.

He's dressed in a shirt and slacks; much more sophisticated than Henry's youthful t-shirt and jeans, and it makes him appear older, but if I were to hazard a guess, I'd place him to be the same age as Henry.

His almost black eyes widen as he spots me, hidden mainly by Henry's width. Then, grimacing in apology before opening his mouth to speak, revealing shockingly perfect teeth, Henry spins to cut him off, still hiding me from the view of the newcomer. Well, mostly.

"I'll find you in a minute, idiot."

His friend's lips roll upward on one side in a self-deprecating sneer before he turns and returns the way he'd come.

We follow behind him, my hand wrapped inside Henry's much large one, our feet dragging, knowing the night is coming to an end.

Urging me into the virtually deserted Powder Room, Henry presses a chaste kiss to the top of my head before drawing back to find my eyes once more.

"I'll be right back, then we'll leave via this entrance. My Peaches better not go anywhere."

I giggle at the name he is so insistent on calling me and nod.

"I'll be right here."

Raising our joined hands to his lips, he presses one final kiss onto the back of my hand before slowly unlacing our fingers until just our fingertips are touching.

He peers deeply into my eyes, all signs of playfulness gone.

"Promise me, Peaches."

Throwing caution to the wind, for the—I've lost count of how many times tonight—I raise his fingertips to my lips to drop a kiss on each tip, ending with his pinkie finger, which I intertwine with my own.

"Pinkie promise."

Dropping one final kiss on my upturned mouth, he makes to leave, stopping once to glance back with a mixture of longing, desire, and something else I can't place in his eyes, yet I know instinctively is mirrored in my own.

"Go! I promise I'll wait right here."

Then, remembering the brand-new cheeky side that Henry brings out in me, I blow him a dramatically noisy kiss just as he walks out the door, his loud laughter the final sound I hear before the door whooshes closed.

Deciding to take this time to make myself more presentable, I settle into one of the luxurious armchairs and take in the damage. My eyes are glassy, and my hair is tousled even more than Jo had teased it into artfully earlier. It's definitely got that look she was going for after Henry got his hands on it. And in it.

My lipstick is a thing of the past.

I wonder if he's got it all over his face.

A thrill ripples through me at the idea of having marked him as mine.

It's just then that I notice the marks on my own skin. There are several not-so-subtle bruises along my neck and collarbone from his attentions. I smirk at the thought of marking each other.

Claiming each other.

Blatant wanton. That's what I'm most assuredly becoming!

In the first five minutes after his departure, the Powder Room sees a conveyor belt of an array of model-esque women as I wait. Eventually, the crowd, alongside my hope of Henry's return, tapers off to a slow trickle. When he's been gone twenty minutes, and I haven't seen another patron in more than five minutes, I shoot Nola a text to ensure they haven't left yet.

No response, yet I'm adamantly clinging to that final look Henry and I exchanged. The look that promised so much *more.* Another fifteen minutes pass before I hear my phone ring.

And with it, my heart sinks.

"Hey, girl. Where are you?"

"Jo, I met him! I'm in the Powder Room waiting for my McHottie to return, but he's been gone for so long, and this place has long since cleared out. I'm feeling a bit. Ummm...." I trail off, not knowing how to finish without sounding as naïve, as I so clearly am. Not wanting to admit to myself that he's just not coming back, and I've been taken for a fool.

"Liv, sweetie. Head downstairs now, okay? We're waiting for you at the foot of the VIP stairs."

Confusion knits my brow, but I make an affirmative sound before making my way to the VIP area.

Which is now fully cleared out.

I'm unable to stop my steps from faltering as I inhale deeply, still pushing the reality to the back of my mind—still wanting to bask in glorious ignorance just another moment longer.

Four staff members are piling glasses onto trays, and Burt, the somewhat friendly security man from before, is no longer anywhere to be seen.

"Excuse me, Miss. This area is now closed if you wouldn't mind making your way to the main floor."

My stomach churns with nauseous anxiety, not unlike the feeling I had when I'd first come up here only a couple of hours ago.

I manage to walk down the stairs in a daze to find the girls waiting for me just like they said they would, an oblivious Alex in tow; God love him.

Jo is the one to bite the bullet, telling me what I already know.

"I thought maybe you'd gone with them. Just about everyone except a handful of stragglers left the VIP area more than half an hour ago."

Doing the maths in my head, I realise that would mean that Henry had left the club without me within minutes of telling me to stay put.

I can't wrap my head around it. In my utter naivety, I had

thought we had a connection.

My heart plummets, and my stomach bottoms out at the thought of how I had been with him.

How honest and open we'd been with each other.

How easily discardable I am to a man like Henry.

How easily I'd believed the lies he'd fed to me.

Nausea, guilt, and something else I can't quite put my finger on swirl, like a sickening cocktail of regret in my stomach.

Jo is the picture of contrition as she rubs her hand soothingly along the back of my hand.

"I should never have sent you up to that stupid McHottie."

I catch her hand with my other one, holding tightly. "Don't do that, Jo. My life, my choice, right? The entire purpose of our night."

Alex looks ready to kill whoever has hurt me, and I feel my heart expand in my chest at the thought of what good friends I have.

Putting my arms around his waist, he drapes his over my shoulder and pulls me in close for a side hug, allowing me to feel sheltered from the hurts of this evening.

As I leave Velvet, wrapped up in Alex, with Nola and Jo leading the way, I swear right then and there to never allow my good nature to be taken advantage of by anyone ever again. And I know, hand on heart, that I won't let it happen either.

After all, recalling the words I had spoken earlier, I excel at all things I put my heart and soul into.

Five

OLIVIA
TWO YEARS LATER
PRESENT DAY

Coming to a halt outside the door of the apartment I share with two of my best friends, I take a moment to listen to the ongoing maelstrom still going full tilt.

I'd hoped they would be finished after I got back from my morning run, but I'd been overly optimistic, or so it seemed. I could make out some words here and there, but their tone said it all.

Nola and Jo have been having issues for years now. For probably longer than I've been living with them, their blow-ups are legendary throughout our building. It has made being the third wheel a lot harder at times, and that's without mentioning their at least bi-nightly marathon fuck-fests.

Yes, Olivia Marie Parker curses these days. Upon occasion.

These ladies have blown my once innocent eyes wide open, and I've never been so grateful to be the proud owner of noise-cancelling headphones. So, let's just leave it at that.

The voices stop suddenly before I hear a thud, then silence. Hoping the thud was a door closing instead of a dead body hitting the apartment floor, because yes, their arguments could get *that* volatile, I slowly slot my key into the lock. I twist it quietly before entering on almost silent feet, relieved at having had the foresight to remove my trainers before entering.

My mum had never allowed shoes to be worn indoors. Mum hadn't allowed a lot, to be fair. Years of repression can be hard to change, but I'm proud of this person I'm becoming now that I've been given the chance to spread my wings—as awful as that sounds.

Even so, some habits are hard to kick.

Rounding the corner at the end of the hall, which opens into our open-plan living area, I spy Josie with her back to me at the island in the centre of our kitchen. Her head is down, and I can hear her whimpering softly.

My heart goes out to her. The thought of how bad the fight must have gotten for her to show such emotion when she never cries makes me feel all twisted up inside.

"Are you okay, Jo…?" Trailing off as I walk closer, I freeze, realising Nola is at Josie's feet, on her knees with Jo's short skirt roughly gathered and held up in a fist. She has Jo's leg haphazardly thrown over her shoulder, as she loudly feasts on her lover.

Both women are oblivious to my intrusion, as focused as they are on each other.

Josie grasps at Nola's long red hair as she throws her head back, eyes clenched shut and panting desperately. "Yes. Yes, baby, that's it. I'm coming. I'm…"

A shock goes through me as I slowly and silently back away toward the safety of my room just off the entry hallway. Closing the door with a quiet *click,* I let out the breath I didn't realise I was holding, and instantly, I'm flooded with the absolute certainty that I am so utterly jealous of what my friends have. I want it too.

Not *them*. I want that spark. That *connection* that these women have.

That passion.

That all-consuming fire where you'd prefer to let the world burn than go without having them in your life. Even for just one night.

Dropping my old, used-to-be-white-once-upon-a-time trainers to the floor, I fall onto my single bed and let myself soften enough to remember Henry, that beautiful liar. The one who made me feel like he promised me the sun, the moon, and the stars, only to toss me into dark despair in one callous act.

Unfortunately, to remember Henry is to remember everything that had come so rapidly after the loss of my naivety. Despite the passing of time since losing my parents, the grief mixed so potently with guilt never faded.

After Henry's no-show, I spent the night at the apartment Nola and Josie shared. It was smaller than the one we currently rent, so I had wrapped myself up in a blanket on their sofa bed, wearing a white t-shirt Josie had given me that ended up smelling like the elusive Henry just from being draped over my body. Hours passed as I ran the gamut of emotions from sorrow for myself to desperate hatred for both of us.

The next day, I'd surreptitiously shoved the t-shirt in my overnight bag, hating myself while doing so and still unable to force myself to stop. Then, after having a quick breakfast with the girls in their local greasy spoon, I'd made my way home.

If only I had known what awaited me.

As I walked closer to our neighbourhood, a feeling of such horrible foreboding washed over me. A wretched smell lingering in the air seemed stronger with each step homeward I took.

Rounding the curve onto our street, I saw two ambulances, a massive fire truck, several police cars and, what appeared to be, the *entire* neighbourhood.

Before any of it could really register with me and the implication of *why* these people were all here, I was swamped by the entire hoard, and snippets of sentences from different voices penetrated my hazy mind.

The words "fire," "parents," and "dead" stood out above all else, and I began to feel lightheaded in the face of the onslaught. Thankfully, two plainclothes detectives had chosen that moment to take it upon themselves to clear the crowd, each gently grasping an elbow to steer me closer to what had been, up until that day, my childhood home.

Now it was just some burnt, blackened, crumbling walls and a whole lot of ash and smoke.

Taking in the devastation, I felt something switch inside of me. It was almost as though I went into autopilot and stayed there for several weeks. Pulling myself out of the haze of guilt that gnawed at me daily took a strength I didn't know I possessed. But I did it.

The fire turned out to have been caused by a candle one of my parents had left burning in the kitchen, so the house and life insurance pay-outs were minimal, to say the very least, but just enough to put towards going to university.

I opted to get a qualification in office management, something the girls and I agreed definitely played to the strengths I'd developed during my time at St. Fintan's. And even if it's not something I'm overly passionate about, it will pay the bills.

I'm grateful to be where I am now, having graduated only a couple of weeks ago, so I'm finally at a place in my life where I can begin to apply for positions, to stand on my own two feet.

To live the life I so desperately wanted before my parents had died, even while knowing that this life wouldn't be possible if circumstances were different. If my parents had remembered to extinguish the candle before going to bed. But that's a guilt I've had to learn to live with, just as I've learned that their expectations of me were borderline abusive, according to the girls and Alex.

They'd been astounded to learn the manner of my upbringing, but it was in disclosing some long-held truths to my best friends that I was able to grow and embrace this new me with all I am.

I've even started to get out on the dating scene—not that it's all it's cracked up to be.

I'll give it time; after all, not every possible relationship feels like an instant connection, and going on past experience, that can only be a good thing. I've had a handful of almost-boyfriends since finding my feet. Several random kisses and cuddles.

Still, I'd never felt that instantaneous affinity for another soul like I'd had with Henry. Even though I've tried my utmost, everyone else comes up lacking when I subconsciously make comparisons.

But I will continue to be happy to *try* at least.

Or at least that's what I try to tell myself at a moment like this when emptiness is bearing down on me, and I feel a visceral *need* for that intimacy, that sense of belonging that I felt so long ago, even if it was all just one-sided naivety on my part.

My mobile rings, breaking through the silence that had been enveloping me in its embrace like an old friend. Glancing at it where it's been charging on my bedside locker, I can see it's Alex calling. Panic flutters through my stomach as I quickly pick it up and slide the green icon across to answer the call.

Before letting him get a word in, I cry, "I'm *so* sorry I'm late! I'll be there in twenty if you have time to hold on for my stupid ass!"

He chuckles knowingly on the other end of the line. I can almost see the curve of his lopsided grin as he says, "I'm outside your door because, sweet girl, if I don't know you and your habits at this stage, it's all been for nothing." He snorts at his own joke, putting a large smile on my face with his easy-going nature. "Come on and let me in before your coffee gets cold."

I'm sliding along the wooden hall floor in my stockinged feet before he has even finished speaking, almost crashing to my ass in my haste. I throw open the door, bursting with delight just as he's slipping his phone back into the laptop bag hanging over his shoulder, resting lightly on his hip.

He's leaning against the doorway with that grin I love so much and have missed even more. Two coffees are stacked on top of each other and held in front of him in offering. I can't help the answering grin that breaks across my face in genuine delight.

I stand to the side and theatrically flourish my hands before putting on my poshest voice.

"I bid you good morrow. Please, kind sir, enter my humble abode."

It's an ongoing joke between us. Despite looking and sounding as normal as my other friends, Alex comes from money. A *lot* of money. Not that you'd know it. He's as down to earth as they come.

When I first met a teenage Alex and his Mum, Lauren, who looked more like a slightly older sister than a mother figure, at St. Fintan's, I'd been somewhat taken aback by his Mum's overly exaggerated accent. But, over the years, he's confided in me that it's entirely forced. After that, hoity-toity accents became a running joke between us, always guaranteed to make him chuckle.

"You're a classic idiot, Liv. Here! Take this before it gets cold. I've already added the sweeteners that you like. All five of them." He grimaces a little green at the gills.

Linking my fingers together, I rest my chin on them while batting my eyes rapidly. "You know, you can never be too sweet!"

Reaching forward and taking the reusable cup out of his outstretched hand, as he laughs at my silliness, I peer down the hallway cautiously before making my way into the living area with no sign of the girls. I don't want to imagine how our conversation would go if I'd brought him into that hot mess.

My best friend takes a seat on the sofa while I perch on the arm on the far end.

"It's so, so good to see you! Are you working today?"

He's dressed in a dark grey three-piece suit over a light blue shirt with a dark blue skinny tie. His naturally highlighted brown hair is styled back off his face, and it's longer than the last time I saw him on video chat, but it suits his handsome face.

His physique seems to have filled out too while he's been away, and in general, he looks so much more confident than the Alex who flew to New York a scant six months ago to work his way up the corporate ladder at his late father's company, DeMarco Holdings.

"Yes, unfortunately. I wouldn't be dressed like this otherwise, but the office dress code fucking sucks. So, needs must and all that shit." Rolling his eyes, he sets his coffee on the table in front of us before turning to me with wide, amber eyes and a quick smile that comes to him as naturally as breathing.

"Speaking of work, how's the job hunting going, sweet girl? Surely, you've been snapped up already."

Of course, this is one of the first questions out of my friend's mouth. He's always taking care of me, another of the many things I appreciate so very much about him.

"Nope. Not a single call. Yet! I'm remaining optimistic. Father T. always says—"

Finishing the much-used phrase, he cuts me off, "'What's meant for you won't pass you.' Yeah, he loves that one, doesn't he!"

We both burst out laughing at the many memories we have of an un-ageing Father T. reciting his favourite positive thinking phrases until Alex suddenly sobers beside me and levels me with his whiskey eyes.

"Well, I think I have something meant for you."

My stomach immediately ties itself up in knots before I cautiously nod for him to continue, my apparent interest bringing that lopsided smile to his lips and instantly quelling some underlying unease.

"Well. You know that before going to the New York branch, I'd been given quite a bit more responsibility at DeMarco, right? And now that I'm back here full time, with that responsibility comes the added bonus of… a personal assistant."

He stops, leaving me to digest his words for a second before verifying, "A PA. You know?" Frantically taking in my disbelieving face, he ploughs on. "Hear me out, sweet girl. I know it's not what you want to do in the long run, *but* it would be a huge stepping stone to help you gain experience to get where you need to go. And obviously, when you want to move on, I'd give you the best recommendation letter *ever* –"

He stops when I put my hand up, palm facing him. Then, taking a deep breath, I rise from my perch on the arm of the sofa and gesture for him to stand too. Once he does, I throw my arms around him, fitting my shoulder underneath the nook of his arm the same as always.

"Thank you so much."

The words, while heartfelt, just aren't enough. I'm so overwhelmed by this unwavering belief my best friend has in me. I don't remember ever having anyone believe I was capable of anything other than Holly, and those memories are so old and faded they don't feel real half the time.

He stands frozen for about half a minute before slowly and lightly draping his own arms around my shoulders. I'm so grateful for this little group of friends who have helped me more than I could have ever hoped for. I feel a little choked up, so I continue to hug my friend for another minute or so until I have managed to pull myself together.

Drawing back and looking up at him, I smile as his face mirrors mine.

"So, when do I start, Gaffer?"

Smiling indulgently at me, he shakes his head. "Less of that, you insubordinate wench." Both of us descend into fits of laughter.

We chat for the next thirty minutes about my duties and salary, which isn't entry level, but he insists that it is before he has to leave for work.

"How does dinner tonight sound? We can catch up properly then, yeah?"

"Yes! Definitely. I've missed you so much. The girls don't like Italian; it's positively blasphemous!"

He laughs. "Well, with a surname like DeMarco, it'd be *excessively* blasphemous to dislike the food of my people." He hugs me one more time, then makes his way to the door. "I'll send a driver around 5 pm and meet you there."

"I can walk, you know. Or Uber!" Pinning me with a stare, I hold my hands up in defeat. "Okay, okay. You win. I'll take your driver and see you then if you insist. I have a hot date all afternoon anyway."

His eyebrows raise in question until I wink at him pointedly, and he tuts in mock exasperation, knowing precisely what hot date I'm talking about. Then, as he pulls the door closed after him, his final words find my ears as the door clicks softly shut.

"When will you give up with this James Cole slash McHottie obsession?"

Tossing a cushion at the closing door, I shout, "My Cole obsession has nothing to do with him!" But all I can hear are my best friend's soft chuckles before the door clicks shut behind him.

Idiot! This *12 Monkeys* obsession has nothing to do with Henry what's-his-face, I swear.

Liar, liar, pants on fire.

Six

OLIVIA

I spend the rest of my week preparing myself for starting work on Monday at the global entertainment and communications giant, DeMarco Holdings. Josie informs me I need a whole new wardrobe, and being our resident self-confessed fashion guru, she takes great pleasure in bringing me shopping and spending way, way, *way* above and beyond my means.

But fuck—and although I *generally* keep curse words to a minimum, this calls for a profanity or two—the outfits she helps me choose are so flattering to my body that they make me feel like pure sex. Not that I'd know what sex feels like considering I still haven't gone any further than kissing with anyone since the night-that-cannot-be-named with you-know-who when *he* made me you-know-what. Still, when I put those form-fitting dresses and jumpsuits on that Josie is so insistent on buying, I can't help but feel desirable.

Not just regular, run-of-the-mill desirable. Desirable, like I was to *him*. Damn him for still occupying space in my brain even after two long years and a whole stomach full of tragedy.

Josie's clothes shopping extravaganza also consists of the non-negotiable must-have new killer heels, no less than five pairs, and the fear that I'll probably break my neck wearing them is real and very present. There are also all-new silky, lacy, and very itty-bitty lingerie pieces that she insists I need in my life because she claims, "you never know."

The obligatory trip to the beauty salon she owns is also non-negotiable, so I get my hair trimmed and nails shaped and painted a simple white colour.

Josie, and Nola, via video call, as she's been travelling for work this week, insist I get the full-service hair removal treatment. At their behest, I can feel my face turn purple with embarrassment.

"Jo, I can sort myself out. Seriously, there is *no* need for this."

My words are landing on deaf ears while Josie continues to speak to her lover over FaceTime, as though I'm not even in the room.

"And who knows! Maybe she'll even let me vajazzle it. Heaven knows it's the most action—"

"No! You can do the waxing, but I draw the line at jewels on my vag, okay?"

The two girls smile knowingly at each other, and I can't help the hint of a smile that graces my own lips, knowing full well this was their intention all along.

"So what if I'm boring and set in my ways. I happen to like being a wallflower, thank you very much."

Nola's voice crackles over the video chat. "Liv, your name might sound like it, but you most certainly haven't figured out how to *live*. We're just giving you a little push to get you closer to your best self, okay?"

I huff out a laugh, knowing they're not too far off from the truth.

"Okay, okay. You win. Wax me up, Scotty."

Several hours later, I'm primed and ready to take on the world—even if I am walking like a cowboy.

In fairness, I have always tended to my own maintenance. Although, in my defence, I wasn't a Yeti down *there*, but hello? An upbringing of repression ring any bells?

Let's just say it definitely wasn't as bald before as it so surely is now.

Ouch!

But despite my reservations and empty purse, the whole process makes me feel like a new woman, so when Monday morning rolls around and the time comes to leave for my first day as Alex's PA, I feel amazing. I've decided on a long-sleeved black silk blouse that's unbuttoned to show a hint of cleavage, paired with a black leather pencil skirt that comes to just below the knee. I've chosen black patent heels with a bright red sole, and to tie the whole thing together, I've added a matching bright red lip.

I've automatically opted for muted colours or neutrals, but this job is for the new me, and the new me loves her red lip, thanks to Jo's encouragement.

Throwing a black tailored winter coat over my arm, I make my way out of the building, buzzing with nervous excitement.

It doesn't take long to realise that Alex had sent a driver for me, even though I told him I had no problem catching the tube. I've met the driver, Samuel, on several previous occasions, most recently last week when I had dinner with Alex, so I greeted him with a small "Hi!" and a big smile, knowing Alex's feelings would be hurt at my slight if I declined his gift.

Traffic is light, so we make great time from my apartment right to the doors of the DeMarco Holdings building in the city proper.

"Goodbye, Miss Parker. I shall be available at your discretion throughout your day, courtesy of the DeMarco family, so please call if there's anything you need."

Handing me a card that presumably has his number on it, Samuel nods sharply and gets back into his seat, smoothly pulling out into traffic before I can utter a single word.

Shaking my head, I turn from the sidewalk and make my way inside the building, where I see Alex waiting for me with that signature grin on his face.

I can't help stopping dead in my tracks to take in the absolute elegance that is the foyer. High ceilings and an oversized matte black reception desk take over the majority of the floor. There are art deco light fittings interspersed along all the varying shades of grey walls, and to the rear of the space, there is a long row of elevators with throngs of people milling about.

As I'm taking this in, Alex has grasped hold of my elbow and has begun steering me to a set of elevators set slightly away from the rest.

"These elevators are for management only, Liv. You'll need this code to ride." He stops to key in 8-4-9-1 before continuing. "You will get a weekly email from building security advising you of the newest code. And you'll be introduced to Tim Nash and the guys in the security department later today. They'll need to get you set up with a work ID and all that stuff, okay?"

I nod slowly, taking it all in as the elevator smoothly whisks us past umpteen floors.

"What floor are we going to?"

"Good question. This elevator and the one beside are

reserved strictly for employees needing access to floors 25 and 26, which are the top two of the building. That's where you'll find all management have their offices. In addition, DeMarco Holdings owns the entire building and operates all divisions of our international branches from these offices. But in reality, you won't need to venture much further than the twenty-fifth floor, Liv. That's where my office is."

The elevator stops, and we disembark into an ample open space with a reception desk directly in front of the elevator doors. An obscenely gorgeous and utterly fed-up-looking redhead is filing her nails at the desk. Dressed in a skin-tight pencil dress that dips so low at the front, I swear if I looked closely, I'd see her belly button; she's so beautiful she could have been recruited off Victoria's Secret.

Blowing out a breath without even glancing up, we are greeted with, "Good morning. Welcome to DeMarco Holdings Management Division." Her voice is monosyllabic and sounds like she's two seconds from launching herself off the top of the building.

"Good morning, Andrea. I'd like you to meet my new Personal Assistant, Olivia."

Andrea just about manages to tear her eyes away from her blatantly fascinating nail filing to give me the once over. But, whatever she sees, she obviously finds it as dull as the rest of her surroundings as she returns to her task with a barely mumbled, "Hey."

Alex glances at me, rolling his eyes, to which I just grin.

To each their own. Another one of Father T's favourites.

We make our way across the open area with several doors lining it. Outside each door is a small desk space with a chair and all the tech stuff needed by a PA. It is still early enough that the rest of the staff hasn't arrived, so I have plenty of time to settle in and get my bearings.

Alex stops as he reaches the fifth office on the right. I smile like a proud big sister when I see his name and title on the door.

ALEXANDER DEMARCO
ACQUISITIONS

"Here we are." He steps to the side of what will be my desk going forward. I can see a little rainbow-coloured banner with *Congrats* on it running along the computer screen and a red foil balloon tied to the desk. To one side, there's an enormous bunch of sunflowers, which we always call the "happy flower," since both of us agree that the sight of the big yellow blossom always brightens our days, and an envelope with my name on it.

I'm floored by all of it.

"Alex. I don't know what to say. You… you are just too good to me." Stepping forward, I hug my friend before recalling where we are.

"Umm… what's the deal with office fraternisation? Oops, you know, umm. That's to say, is it still okay to hug you even though you're my boss now?"

His eyes light up with barely suppressed laughter, knowing my tendency to blurt things out without thinking when I'm flustered. He reaches for me and pulls me in for a side hug. "Boss best friend, Liv. First and foremost, I'm your best friend, though. Don't forget it!"

Stepping away, Alex tucks his hands into his suit pants pockets and rocks back on his heels as I walk around him and get settled at my desk.

"Martha Goode from Human Resources will be swinging by

within the next thirty minutes, so she will go through all the ins and outs of your position, holiday entitlements, company perks, et cetera. She'll also give you a tour of the building and bring you to the places you most need to know about. If you need to use the Ladies', there's one back the way we came, just to the left of the elevator. I've got a 9 am meeting that I cannot be late for; otherwise, I'd wait with you…."

I cut him off with a quick, "Nope. No. No. No. You will not be giving me *any* preferential treatment at all. During working hours, you have to treat me like everyone else."

Looking up at him and that wide ass grin on his smug face, I know my words are landing on deaf ears. Alex has always been a fan of listening to your demands and doing his own thing anyway.

"I mean it, Alex."

He raises his hands in defeat, but not actually acquiescing, slowly moving backwards away from his office and my desk. "I'll see you later, Liv. Have a great first day."

Watching him leave, I can see a steady stream of employees begin to appear as if by multiplication, and it is only when I realise HR will be popping by soon that I make any kind of move from where Alex had left me.

I bend down to grab my handbag from where I'd abandoned it on the floor, spotting the envelope with my name on it that had somehow been forgotten until now. Picking it up, I rip it open without pause. Upon further inspection, I see it contains four tickets for Misdirection, my absolute favourite band, who are playing a London gig at the O2 Arena in a couple of weeks, and a card from Alex that simply says:

Happy first day, sweet girl.
Love, Gaffer!

I can feel my mouth drop most unbecomingly. Alex has always tried to spoil me whenever he can, not that I often allow him to do it in fairness. After my parents' deaths, he was such a constant, despite needing to go away for work and other commitments regularly once he started at DeMarco.

This was a different kind of spoiling, though. While extravagant, Alex knew I had been desperately wanting to go and couldn't get tickets for love or money. They'd sold out months ago.

No way was I looking this gift horse in the mouth.

Misdirection, I'll be seeing you *real* soon.

Martha Goode from HR is an absolute godsend. After introducing herself later in the morning, we get the boring stuff out of the way before she brings me to meet Tim Nash, a tall, thin man with sharp eyes hidden behind the most enormous pair of horn-rimmed glasses I've ever seen.

"His bark is worse than his bite, sweetie."

Martha winks exaggeratedly as she explains that Tim has been the Head of Security for the London branch of DeMarco for almost as long as I've been alive.

He has everything set up and ready to go—my ID badge, all my company logins for email, intranet and, of course, all the logins for Alex's accounts, too, which I will need to access from time to time. After we visit with Tim on the second floor, Martha takes me to several different floors, showing me the ropes and the perks of being a DeMarco employee.

Finance and Human Resources share the fourteenth floor, which I file away for future reference. Unlike any regular canteens I've seen, the ninth floor houses the most extravagant workplace restaurant imaginable. It serves food all day, and not just any food—gourmet, Michelin star quality stuff.

I can see myself needing to do a whole lot of running in my future to offset the excellent food if the smell alone is anything to go by.

It's a good thing that there is an office gym with every kind of exercise equipment known to man, with floor-to-ceiling windows wrapping the entire floor, allowing gym goers to experience the most spectacular view of the Thames and the city beyond the eighteenth floor. Each employee is welcome to use the floor as they choose, but must enter their details on the office intranet before using it to avoid overcrowding.

Martha shows me how to do it for both myself and Alex, as booking his gym time also falls under my jurisdiction.

I am astounded to find a creche and childcare facility on the third floor. Martha snorts a laugh as she sees my jaw drop in her peripheral vision.

"The company recruits only the best, and we want to hold on to our staff at almost any cost. Providing this service for mums and dads also happens to be a great recruitment strategy. Mums are more likely to return to employment following their maternity leave, not to mention that they have access to their little ones as they wish throughout their workday."

I can definitely see the appeal and believe it is a very successful addition to an already impressive company.

I spend the rest of my first day learning the ropes but don't see Alex again as he's booked in back-to-back meetings off the premises. I'm kept busy, and before I've even realised it, the day is done, and everyone makes their way from their desks, filing out of the building like worker bees leaving a hive.

Deciding to take my time, I pack up slowly and am one of the last to leave the office. Punching the elevator call button, I'm surprised to find Martha standing inside.

"Going down?"

"Not yet, sweetie. I have some papers I need to grab from Henry."

Two things happen at once that make nausea swirl in the depths of my stomach. Martha's casual mention of a name that I can't escape, at the exact moment the elevator begins to move.

"I forgot to mention earlier that there is a pool, sauna, steam room, and jacuzzi in the basement of the building. They are only for the top brass, but you may need to schedule some time for Alex if he so requires." She leans closer, almost conspiratorially, despite no one else being present. "It's a relatively new part of the building, installed by Alex's older brother."

Enrico, or Rico, as Alex refers to him, was estranged from his brother for years. Alex has never gone into the reason for their hostility, though I've often gotten the impression that the fault lies with his older brother.

When their father died around the same time my parents did, the business was left to Rico. Still, he reached out to Alex, who'd just applied to study business at Cambridge and offered him an entry-level management position—entirely unheard of for someone with zero experience.

It took several weeks of talking him around, though eventually, Alex agreed to his brother's proposition. From all accounts, they seem to be getting along decently, considering their years of separation.

The elevator doors ping before opening on the uppermost floor as Martha bids me farewell, then strides determinedly from the lift towards a tall man, whose broad back fills out his black suit indecently well. A jolt of familiarity shoots through me as the door closes just when Martha reaches him, a bright smile on her matronly face.

Hitting the button to take me to the ground floor, I put all thoughts of tall, well-built strange men from my head. Instead, I begin looking toward the evening with my tall, not so well buffed best friend, and I can't help feeling sorry he's never had a relationship with his brother.

I'm just grateful now that Alex seems to be past whatever set the wheels in motion to make them cut each other off so many years before. Everyone deserves a second chance, and the Alex I've been seeing since he'd granted one to his brother is a happier, more well-rounded version of himself.

And so, the time has come for me to become a more well-rounded version of *myself*. This new life of mine calls for a new apartment. Or a studio at the very least because there's no way I can afford somewhere on my own on entry-level wages, even if those wages are totally *not* entry-level, regardless of what my new boss maintains.

It's not until a couple of nights later, after talking to my housemates, that they understand my desire to live alone for a while and are happy to support me in entering a new phase of my life.

The first four weeks at DeMarco pass in the blink of an eye, my days flat out, organising Alex's schedule along with general duties in the office, which all the PAs on the floor chip in with.

Since Alex is generally out of the office much more than the other management staff, it seems as though I have become everyone's go-to girl to do the odd jobs that really should fall upon our fair-weather office manager, Andrea. She has a serious fixation with her nails, playing with her hair, and reapplying her varying lipstick shades on a continuous loop throughout the day.

Basically, she's shit at her job.

Besides her, I've made some great friends on the twenty-fifth floor. The whole office, not just the handful of other PAs, has taken me under their collective wing, and I am never without someone floating by my desk to chat or ask a question or for a favour.

I finally manage to tie Alex down for lunch in the massive canteen on Wednesday of my fourth week before he flies back to the States for some big merger Rico is entrusting him with.

We're seated side by side, just about to tuck into a veritable feast of Italian cuisine as both of us reach for the arancini at the same time.

"Alex." Side-eyeing him, I can see his smirk clear as day.

"Olivia." Damn it, I knew we shouldn't have said we'd share.

"Ladies first." His hand inches closer, despite my words. He's got no self-restraint for these little morsels of culinary pleasure, and true to form, with the speed of a rattlesnake, his hand flies forward, grabbing two and jamming one in his mouth before I've even registered his actions.

Narrowing my eyes, I turn to him to find his mouth full and stretched wide with that stupid smile of his. "You shouldn't piss me off, Gaffer. I still haven't forgiven you for those Misdirection tickets."

His sudden laughter rings out across the canteen, before rapidly turning to cough when he nearly chokes on the arancini in his mouth. I help him with some water before he swallows while pounding his chest with his fist and clearing his throat.

Raising one eyebrow in challenge, he deadpans. "Why? You want to have them returned?"

Wanker.

We both spend the entire hour filling our faces and laughing ourselves silly. We're wholly unbothered when more than a handful of tables nearby watch us like we're crazy.

I take the opportunity to tell him face to face about my new apartment.

With the receipt of my first payslip, I just took the plunge. Ringing several leasing agents, finding somewhere within walking distance of work, *and* within my budget, didn't seem possible.

Until the other night, I'd arrived home to find Jo's laptop open on the coffee table with the advertisement for the most perfect place within my price range, which was miraculous, seeing as city rental prices are astronomical.

"I must have a guardian angel or something!"

"Liv, that's amazing! I'm so fucking proud of you."

His delight at my newfound independence makes my heart happy.

Reaching for him, I take his hand in mine, which he squeezes gently. "It's all thanks to you, my friend."

You and your unwavering faith in me.

"Speaking of the concert, did you want to do a double date again?"

Throwing my head back, my loud guffaw draws even more eyes to our table as I try to pull myself together. Eventually, I wind it down to hiccupping snorts while Alex continues to deadpan me across the table.

"I rather enjoyed the last double date night we had—"

I cut him off, raising my hand between us.

"No way. No. Way. The last time that guy, Rhys, got way too handsy, and you had far too much fun laughing at me while shoving your tongue down Gwen's throat."

Not missing a damn beat, his response is nothing less than I'd expect from my best friend, the adorable lady-killer he's become.

"That wasn't the only part of my anatomy that met her tonsils that night—"

Clapping my hands over my mouth, I can't stifle the bark of laughter that erupts from my lips as his lopsided grin takes pride of place on his delighted face.

"Nola and Jo, it is then, yeah?

Seven

HENRY

The events of the night my life changed so drastically will be forever ingrained in my memory. So many things happened in such a small space of time, some good, but mostly shit.

After forming a thought-provoking connection with Peaches, I'd left her in the Powder Room at Velvet, but my phone had rung before I'd ever even entered the VIP area to find the boys, and all previous plans flew out the window. The caller was a woman called Charlotte, or Lottie, who, I'd later find out, my father had been living with for years.

She was calling from his phone to let me know he'd just been brought to the Royal London hospital by ambulance after going into cardiac arrest while at dinner. He was currently in theatre, and it wasn't looking good.

Knowing that now was the time to make amends despite our

less than stellar relationship, I lit out of Velvet like the hounds of hell were at my heels. Somehow, in the backseat of the cab I'd flagged down, I remembered I'd left Peaches with no explanation.

I quickly shot off a text in our group chat.

ME

Can one of you find the girl I was with tonight and give her my number?

CADE

I've just left. No sign of her.

NATE

She left with your brother.

Shit.

The next couple of days were nightmarish. My dad was in and out of lucidity, so Lottie and I set up camp at his bedside, and it was then I discovered I had a younger half-sister, Mila—the one bright light to come from the whole sorry mess. She turned fourteen the day before our dad gave up his fight and passed away, surrounded by the three of us.

In his lucid moments, Dad told me what had happened when I was just a kid, the whole sorry mess with my stepmother, more like step-monster, Lauren, and he begged my forgiveness for his abandonment all those years ago. Not wanting to burden an obviously dying man, I forgave him, keeping my secrets locked up good and tight while also taking on the burden of righting his wrongs as my own.

He'd known he had made mistakes with Alex, freely admitting that he'd spent years blaming him for things that were not his fault and refusing to allow his younger son into his life, firmly alienating him from his heart.

I'd agreed to his request to make things right for Alex wholeheartedly, aware that in doing so, I would need to build bridges between my brother and me, despite the reasons why that seemed an impossibility.

And in doing so, I knew I couldn't come between my half-brother and someone he was seeing, or at least had an interest in seeing, despite the connection I'd had with her.

Forcing our interlude to the back of my mind, I had resolved to leave Peaches firmly in the past, even though here I am, two goddamn years later, still fighting myself to stop thoughts of her drifting through my mind.

"You're in a right pissy mood!"

Mila's voice brings me to the present as I notice her Converse resting lightly on the not inexpensive dashboard of my Ferrari.

"Feet!"

Crossing them at the ankles while settling herself deeper into the seat, she folds her arms and looks at me in challenge. I may worship my kid sister, but Jesus Christ, she does my head in when she wants to.

Changing tack, I lower my voice, keeping my eyes fixed on the road while softly requesting. "Please?"

I can feel her eyes rolling from here, but she does as I've asked, and within moments she's forgotten her animosity at my inattention, launching into a story about one of her friends preferring iced tea to hot tea. The inner workings of a teenage girl's mind will forever baffle me.

"And then, Eliza was like, 'oh, you can't do that,' and I was like, 'well, Simon told me I could,' and she was like—"

"Who's Simon?"

"Hmm?"

Turning to me with wide green eyes that mirror my own, she's the very picture of feigning innocence, so I automatically know she's about to try to fill me with shit.

"Simon? I've never heard you mention that name before. Who is he?"

We pull up at valet parking outside our favourite non-Italian restaurant just as I finish speaking. Since she has all the recipe cards from our Nonna's kitchen that Dad had given to her, we don't ever eat out for Italian. My sister is an outstanding cook.

Jumping out and rounding the car, I grab Mila's door before straightening up and tossing the keys to the valet. Tucking her arm underneath mine, we walk in and are seated within moments.

Sitting opposite each other, I gesture for her to continue, but her full-on motor mouth seems to have suddenly and rather abruptly run out of fuel.

"So, you were saying?"

Her face flushes a deep red that I notice quickly, even under her olive tones, and I can't help the self-satisfied smirk that grows on my face as I take in her discomfort. It's not often my baby sister gets flustered, and even on those rare occasions, she's capable of extricating herself from them with ease, though it's looking like I've got her now.

"Isn't that Nathaniel?"

She stands, waving him over with a bright, easy smile on her pretty face. The man in question is unable to keep his answering smile from his heavily bearded face once he spies us.

Well played, sis.

It's almost three hours later and well past teatime when I'm finally dropping Mila home, promising to be back next week for a repeat of today. Our weekly dinners are one of my few highlights.

Knowing I've got an absolute barrage of work ahead of me, I'm unable to find the will to give a flying shit, having allowed my thoughts to roam free today after so long of self-disciplining myself to keep all memory of her firmly where it should be.

In the fucking past.

But she's not in the fucking past, is she?

I'd tried to put her out of my mind, especially after inviting Alex to come and work with me. But, unfortunately, mending fences with my brother has been a slow one, and it's not been helped by my inability to put her out of my head, only made worse once I'd seen that *stupid* fucking photo on Alex's desk in his office.

Both wearing huge smiles and little else, her dimples popping for all to see, and their arms wrapped tightly around each other on some beach, the wind blowing the long curtain of her hair around them. There's an intimacy between them that hit me right in the gut. Their love for one another is clear as day on their faces.

It made me feel sick. Physically fucking sick.

I'd scheduled my first appointment at Valentine's, which is basically Tinder for rich wankers like me who want a no-strings-attached fuck and zero small talk, that same day in an attempt to fuck the image out of my head, not that it had worked.

And like a junkie, I can't stay away. So I continue to find a reason to visit his office every couple of weeks. And all just so I can torture myself with that fucking photo where her gorgeous blue eyes look past the man I show the world and instead see me as the one I *should* have become if circumstances had been different.

So, I sit here in my stupidly expensive sports car, tormenting myself with the promise to not ruin Alex's life any further than my absentee father did and instead continue to destroy my own.

I don't even need to see that photo tonight to know a visit to Valentine's is an absolute must. So, after parking in the underground car park at my building, I shoot off a quick text to Nate, even though I'd shot down his earlier invite when he'd asked at dinner while Mila was gone for a pee.

ME

What time will you be at Valentine's?

NATE

Already there.

ME

Why am I not surprised!

NATE

You coming then or what?

Cade's here.

ME

Well, I'll have to now, won't I? Can't let you two wankers have all the fun.

Calling my driver, I let him know I'll need him in the next fifteen minutes before I quickly rush to get showered and changed into fresh clothes.

The journey to the highly sought after, members-only sex club Valentine's, takes another thirty minutes, being that it's on the outskirts of the city, set on an old estate that gives everyone the privacy they crave for the debauchery engaged in while on property.

When my car pulls up, Cade is waiting out front, cigarette smoke swirling around his half-lit features. I exit the back seat as he reaches for me to pull me into one of his legendary bear hugs.

Caden's just a touchy-feely guy, always has been. He is most definitely a product of his picture-perfect upbringing.

"How the fuck are you, man? It's been way too long!"

"You're the one who's too busy for us mere mortals."

Handing me the spare black masquerade mask in his hand, I quickly slip it over my face. This is an extra layer of privacy for Valentine's club members, and the mystery adds to the excitement for most.

Pulling back, one of his signature, huge ass smiles firmly in place; it's good to see my friend looks happy. And I'm pretty confident he's neither high nor drunk.

His girlfriend, Layla, is the one who has issues with using. It's more than apparent, and she's doing her damnedest to drag my best friend down with her. But, thankfully, he's stronger than that.

Although he still refuses to see the bad in her. Like with everything, Caden always wants to see the best in others, even when they've repeatedly shown their worst.

"The other tosser is in here. Or, well, he was a few minutes ago unless he's getting his cock sucked!"

Approaching Nate from behind, I whisper-shout, "Even so, a few minutes is plenty for him to have blown his wad at least half a dozen times."

His scowl is at odds with the twitching lip he's desperately trying to fight as he spins in his seat. "Better too fast than not being able to get it up, eh, DeMarco?"

"Tou-fucking-ché, brother."

The room we are sitting in resembles a drawing-room like something from Downton Abbey but with darker red, black, and gold accents.

Our trio happily spends over an hour shooting the shit before Caden's phone beeps.

"That's Lay, guys. Her flight just got in. I'll catch up with you in a couple of weeks when we're back for the concert, yeah?"

Another round of hugs, and he's out the door without so much as a backward glance.

"Strange seeing North so uninterested in the pussy here." I can't help uttering my musing aloud while Nate nods, not really paying attention as his eyes land on something, or someone, behind me, and his lips quirk in a questioning smile.

His mouth widens in a downright devilish manner before he stands, buttoning his jacket and, without so much as taking his eyes from whatever has held them captive, takes his leave.

"Catch you in the next cartoon, Henry."

Shaking my head, I quickly get down to the business end of why I'm here.

"Soraya?" I recognise one of my favourites as she walks into the room. She's also masked with curly black hair and dark eyes, which she heavily accents with thick black liner. She's a knockout and as far from my light-filled Peaches as possible.

I never opt for blondes here.

Her face breaks into a smile as she grabs my hand, wordlessly leading me through a maze of rooms until we come to an unused one, and before I've even slammed the door, she's already sinking to her knees, expertly popping my buttons to get to my swelling cock.

Standing against the door, I let her take control, aware that she knows exactly what I need. Throwing my head back and closing my eyes, she takes the head of my dick deep down into her throat before hollowing her cheeks and sucking with abandon.

And while this is precisely why I came here—no outside noise, no bullshit, just a pair of full lips wrapped around my hard cock, moving up and down with enthusiasm, despite her evident prowess in the refined art of cock sucking, it's not enough.

It's never e-fucking-nough.

It isn't until I allow a single flash of wide blue eyes to cross my vision that I'm able to hold my shaft deep inside her mouth as she gulps down my hot, sticky cum.

And the torment continues.

Eight

OLIVIA

It's Friday, the end of my fifth work week and my first proper work friend, Freya Thornton, PA to Ryan Solomon, Senior VP of Marketing, asks me out for drinks after work with the whole floor.

"Come on, Liv. You've survived over a month of the madness at DeMarco. So it's only right that we celebrate!"

Freya went out of her way to befriend me. I've learned that's just her nature. Her boss is a dinosaur who stomps his way through the office every morning, snarling left and right. His favourite past-time is issuing unnecessary grunts and growls at Freya for things like not getting his coffee order right, even when she does every single time, and for being late, even though he always arrives after her. *Plus,* she is never, ever late.

Added to that, the fact that his marketing strategies belong somewhere in the seventies, he is just a fossil too far past his prime. Like our oh-so-friendly Andrea, it's yet again a question of how on earth do these people keep their jobs when they're so bad at them? Freya said she stayed on with him because underneath it all, he'd be lost without her, and I knew then that I'd found a kindred spirit.

Call me sheltered or not, but my idea of a good friend is someone who is essentially kind. Kindness is everything to me, hence how I knew she was meant to be my friend.

Shooting a big smile her way, I tell her, "Give me five minutes."

I quickly jot down a text to Samuel to let him know that I won't need him for the evening and would be okay to get an Uber at a later stage. I hate the idea of him waiting around for me. It's bad enough that he remains outside for me every evening; I couldn't make him wait for me to finish drinks with the work gang on top of that.

Plus, it was the weekend, after all. So Samuel deserves his time off too.

Or at least that's what I'll tell Alex when he surely admonishes me for not letting him make sure I get home safely.

Having touched up my makeup, which I'm now a semi-pro at, courtesy of Jo, I hightail it out of the Ladies' and to the elevators where most of the other PAs from the management floor are waiting.

Sans Andrea, obviously, because we peasants are clearly beneath her.

Today's outfit is another pencil skirt, except this one is red linen and, again, it's tight to my curves. I've paired it with a plain white shirt with long sleeves and an oversized collar and my skyscraper heels that I've come to love. They imbue me with boundless confidence every day, kind of like the red lip.

Our destination is a live music Irish bar called Mulligans

that serves pub grub and is just a stone's throw from the office. According to Martha, who I was delighted to see joining our ragtag bunch, Mulligans serves the best margaritas in the city. We quickly grab several tables and get down to the business of office gossip, which they all seem to be pros at.

I'm not much of a drinker, which I've been informed by Jo is a scandalous state of affairs in this day and age. But I have been drunk occasionally, so I know I can have one or two drinks now without saying or doing something embarrassing.

Martha was spot on. The margaritas are cosmic, as in, out of this world yummy, and I end up having the best chat with Freya and another PA, Anna, about the best shade of red lippy for our complexions.

"I don't know how you got that shade so perfect for your complexion and hair. I have tried *so* many shades, and I just can't pull off a red lip."

"Give me one second, Anna. I have my friend's salon's phone number here. She's a *miracle* worker."

I grab my bag to get my mobile phone as the girls continue their chatter. Another round of drinks is delivered, courtesy of a table of hot, significantly older businessmen across the room. The men smirk when the three of us raise our glasses in thanks.

"Right, ladies." Freya raises a carefully groomed brow. "Time to move on because those guys think they're in there like swimwear."

I snort into my margarita while still rooting for my phone with my other hand. "Where the hell is it?"

Frustrated, I tip the entire contents of my bag out onto our table as Anna and Freya quickly grab all the odds and ends that go flying everywhere.

Maybe I'm an easier drunk than I thought.

Shrugging off the thought, I look through the mess. Wallet, keys, a compact mirror, lipstick, mascara, EarPods, a sachet of ketchup from Maccy D's, and some old receipts, but no phone.

I could scream.

"Ladies, that's my cue. I've left my phone at the office."

My announcement is met with groans and pleas to just forget about it, but I think I might have reached my shut-off valve anyway. Those margaritas were more potent than I thought.

"Sorry, girls. Raincheck?"

"Of course, sweetie. Here's my phone. Put your number in it, and I'll give you a ring in, say, twenty minutes to make sure you're okay and in your Uber."

After doing as Freya instructed, I spy my almost full margarita looking so lonely on the table. Grabbing it, I pop a brow at the girls.

"Waste not, want not." I put the glass on my head and drain every single delicious drop to raucous cheers from all and sundry.

Depositing my glass onto the table with a flourish and slightly flushed cheeks, I hug both girls goodbye. Then, turning, I bid farewell to the rest of the office, who are still drinking and bantering at the table next to ours and make my way to the bar's front door.

Great! It's coming down in buckets.

I rapidly debated the pros and cons of just leaving my phone until tomorrow as the building only closes on Sunday and just using Freya's phone to order an Uber, but in the end, I decided to just get it over with. A little rain never hurt anyone.

Steeling myself against the torrent, I pull my coat over my shoulders and tie it tight around my waist. Then, realising the lesser of two evils is to use my handbag as an umbrella, I hold it over my head and dash out into the deluge without second-guessing myself any further.

The DeMarco building is a mere two-minute frantic dash down the street. Well, it *would* have been two minutes had I not been wearing ridiculously high shoes. The price women pay for fashion!

By the time I reach the foyer, I look no better than a drowned rat, though my handbag has kept my hair and face from getting overly wet from what I can see in the silver of the elevator door while I wait for it to descend.

I begin to feel a little bit wobbly, which I suspect is from both the adrenaline-filled sprint through torrential rain and the margaritas. I somehow managed to lose count of how many I'd had, but I think it was only four.

Oh no, make that five. I'd almost forgotten that last one I'd downed, courtesy of those silver foxes.

Oops.

Giggling to myself, I hop into the elevator and stab the button for my floor while eyeing myself and the damage in the mirror. Not as bad as I'd initially reckoned. My hair is dampened, but not drenched. My face is clean and rain-streaked. My clothes are plastered to my curves, though my coat keeps most of the moisture off my body. I'm not feeling the cold, at least not yet.

Upon further inspection, I see that my eyes are slightly glassy, but, in my defence, I never really let loose. This new me, she damn well deserves to let her hair down for once.

The elevator *ding*s as it reaches my floor. Before I get my phone, I decide to nip to the loo to dry off using the hand dryers. Bee-lining to the Ladies', I duck inside the familiar door, though I would put money on there having been more cubicles in here earlier.

Once I finish my business, I wash up and stand by the hand

dryer for several minutes, just trying to warm my cold hands. My hair is all askew now from standing so close to the hand dryer, so I quickly unclip the hair grips holding up what had been a sleek chignon when I left my apartment this morning.

My hair cascades down my back like a familiar safety blanket when I release the final clip. I run my fingers haphazardly through it in an attempt to tame the tangles before grabbing my slightly less wet coat, thanks to the hand dryer, and making my way out of the restroom.

Furrowing my brow upon my re-entry to the office, I'm slightly turned around.

"What the-?" My murmur sounds louder than it should in the low lighting of the empty office space. Office space that looks like mine… but doesn't?

Did they give the office an overhaul?

They couldn't possibly have. It's only been a couple of hours.

Edging my way past the elevator, I pop my head around the reception area. My eyes are blown wide as I spot several large glass offices, unlike anything I'd seen previously.

Tiptoeing past these huge glass boxes, I can see they are laid out like meeting rooms with oversized dark wooden tables surrounded by a handful of black chairs on all sides. The view beyond the meeting rooms is spectacular. I can see so much of the city lit up with the moon full and high in the sky above.

I cringe, realising that I must have hit the button for 26 instead of my own 25 and slowly begin to walk back the way I'd come.

Until I hear a large *crash* followed by a woman's scream.

My heart skips a beat and my mouth goes drier than the Sahara as my alcohol addled brain struggles to catch up with my body's natural reaction.

Why, oh why, did I ever come back here tonight? I'm going to die a virgin.

My stupid do-gooder side makes leaving without checking the floor for signs of distress impossible.

Damn you, the virgin martyr Olivia.

So instead of running like I know I should, I quietly dash into the nearest meeting room, grab the phone in the centre of the desk, and dial 0 for security, only to be met with an automated message to hold the line.

What the actual fuck?

Hanging up, I scream internally as I look down at my trembling hands. I can hear my blood pounding through my veins, the sound drowning out everything else and almost deafening me in its vigour.

Even so, I opt to take my chances, which I would later realise was the margaritas talking.

Glancing around to survey my surroundings in the hopes of finding a weapon, there's nothing free-standing in the area small enough to carry with me. Until I look down, squinting my eyes as my shoes come into view.

Gives a whole new meaning to killer heels.

Slipping them from my feet, I pick them up, slide one into my discarded handbag, and then grip the sole of the other one with the heel facing forward. I feel minutely less scared until my delusion is shattered when I catch sight of myself in the windows, and the absurdity of the situation alongside how asinine I look is almost enough to set me off.

Smothering a giggle, I make my way into the main office area and, on bare, silent feet, walk in the general direction the noises had come from. I peer anxiously into each meeting room I come upon, and having passed the sixth and final one, which is as empty as the first five, I'm beginning to doubt whether I heard anything in the first place.

A closed door lies at the furthest end of the space, which also has glass walls, but as I edge closer, I discern the internal shades must be drawn. There's a tiny sliver of light coming from under the door, and, as though magnetised, my feet are drawn ever closer.

I palm the door handle with the killer stiletto raised higher over my shoulder, ready to attack whatever lurks within. I don't know whether to be pleased or discomfited by the discovery that it isn't fully closed.

The thought that someone may be hurt just beyond this door spurs me on, so I gently push the door inward.

An oversized desk similar to the boardroom tables and a substantial throne-like desk chair take up the centre of the room. Beyond, the London skyline lights up the night sky as far as the eye can see, and I notice a lamp in the far-left corner, which must have been the light I'd seen from under the doorway.

I'm just about to turn and leave, when movement from the opposite side of the room catches my eye. Cautiously, I peer around the door's edge to be met with the object of the noise.

An oversized black couch is right there against the wall that runs parallel to the now open door behind which I stand. Lying stretched out and buck naked along this couch is none other than Andrea.

Her pale skin is shockingly bright against the dark furniture, as is her flame-red hair. She has her head draped over the arm of the sofa as a very tall man in a black suit holds it in place with his palms on either side of her face while he drives his hardness ruthlessly into her open, dripping wet mouth.

His thrusts get more forceful, and he holds his length in place for several seconds at a time, his mussed dark hair hanging over his face as he watches while she gags around him.

My eyes widen, and my core clenches when, to my utmost shame, I feel a rush of warmth between my legs as he leans forward and pinches her red, pointed nipple. Her body arches, thrusting her breasts forward, almost searching for more, before he grabs her hand in his much larger one and brings their joined fingers down to her glistening sex.

"Make this pussy weep for me, Andi."

I feel my nostrils flare at the rasp in his voice, and I can't make myself look away as he pulls back his hand. Andrea begins to touch herself, gently at first, but picking up speed as she rocks her own pelvis to match the tempo of the hips pumping into her mouth.

She trembles and shake, her movements faltering as he pounds with even more ferocity until she arches her hips into her own hand in desperation. I can hear the muted screams of her muffled orgasm wash over her in waves.

Just as her body comes back down, he groans loudly, throwing his head back and revealing his face for the first time.

Even in the dimly lit room and after all this time, I'd still know him anywhere. My mind whirls in unparalleled shock as he opens his bright green eyes, pupils blown wide, landing on me, the voyeur in the doorway, before I spin on my heel and run as fast as I can.

Nine

HENRY

I'd had the day from hell. My monthly visit to the step monster went swimmingly. Warning her, yet again, she's overspending on her more-than-generous stipend always goes down like a lead balloon.

At least it's over and done with until next month, although I'd be pleased as punch if she could do me a huge favour and die in the meantime.

My ex-nanny turned stepmother is possibly the bane of my existence, with good fucking reason. Her faults are many, not least of all that she'd conned my grieving father into getting her pregnant and marrying her when my mother was barely cold in her grave.

A blind man could see he had loved my mum with his whole heart, so my father's revelation had made a hell of a lot of sense. My parents were each other's soulmates, and the little bits

I remember of our life together as a family are the only bright places in my darkened, heavily fortified heart.

A heart that Lauren had been the one to blacken with her poison. I'd avoided seeing the bitch since I'd left before Uni, but since my father had bestowed me the gracious gift of holding her financial purse strings, I now had the unwelcome task of facing my demons monthly.

Lauren had everything she could possibly want; a mansion in the countryside that no one visited other than the entire staff she insisted upon keeping. As many jaunts abroad as she could manage, excessive clothes, cars. Anything. But in true Lauren style, everything is never enough, and the DeMarco name means she can find creditors everywhere willing to feed her need for *more*.

Doubtless, she's milking my half-brother's inheritance, too, though, with our precarious relationship, it's not as though I've been able to ask him.

There's also the fact she insists on referring to me as Enrico. A fact that wouldn't bother me, seeing as she's always preferred the Italian variation of my name. The difference now is that the crazy bitch is adamant that I am my deceased father.

I'll admit, the resemblance is most assuredly there, and while I've long known her to defy reality in favour of her own gains, at this point, her delusion is nothing more than an enormous pain in the ass.

When she sees me, she sees him and, depending on the day's humour, I'm subjected to the gamut of interactions.

Last month's meeting resulted in an antique vase flying past my head and smashing to pieces on the driveway. Today consisted of her stripping down to her underwear and barring the door closed. You never know what she'll pull, and after two fucking years of it and a quarter of a goddamned century of that bitch in my life, I was done.

I am beyond done. And have been for a long time now.

On top of the shitshow that is visiting that cunt, Alex had fucked an acquisition stateside earlier today, so now, I *must* be in New York first thing tomorrow morning to fix his cock-up.

After two years now, I feel that we are in a good place. And by that, I mean my brother can just about stand to be in the same room as me without openly scowling anymore. So, I think we are on the right track.

Barely.

And I'll just have to continue to bury all thoughts of his girl down deep, knowing full well she's out of my reach.

I've heard him talk about his nights with Peaches, or Liv as he calls her, often, and though the urge to reach out has always been undeniable, I've restrained myself, knowing that she firmly belongs to my brother.

No one needs to know how I came so close to letting her in that night two years ago. Hell, she was the first and only woman I've kissed since… *her*.

But the desire to reconcile with my sibling is so strong that even if that means backing off from the first woman to make my long-deceased heart beat since my mother died… well, then, yeah, I'd just have to continue through life as I always have.

So, I was stressed. And needed to blow off some steam.

Badly.

My usual Macallan 64 wasn't cutting it. And I didn't have the time, nor the inclination, if I'm honest, to organise a last-minute blowie at Valentine's. And so, I'd rang down to Andi, the lacklustre Office Manager on the twenty-fifth floor who is always more than willing to make time for me.

Her mouth is like a fucking hoover, and it isn't long before I'm really going at it as I fuck her face harder and harder, her throat gagging around my length repeatedly.

Making her play with her pussy as her mouth takes the punishing pace I'm giving to her sends a ripple of pleasure down my spine, and I'm close. So close.

I groan deep in my chest. Almost there, I see movement in my peripheral vision, which is somewhat distorted with being balls deep in Andi's mouth. My eyes locking with navy blues, I hold her head steady and ram my hips flush with her distended face, coming in thick, hot jets, which she swallows only too eagerly.

Peaches!

It takes a moment for my vision to clear, and as it does, I *swear* I see a flash of blonde hair swish in the open doorway before I blink heavily, and it's gone.

Pulling out of Andi's drenched mouth, I tuck my still hard dick back into my boxers and zip my suit pants up before walking to my office door in quick strides. The floor space is dark and seemingly empty.

I venture further into the office and call out, but there's no sound.

Not wasting any time dwelling on my wishful thinking, I turn back, knowing I need to kick Andi out before she wants to have the favour reciprocated, which is something, like kissing, I just don't do.

Finding myself on my office threshold, I see Andi has made no move to cover herself or re-dress, an issue I remedy quickly and efficiently.

"Get dressed." My voice is loud, harsh, and brooks no argument.

Her face falls, her mouth pulling itself into the most unbecoming pout as she jerks herself to a sitting position.

"Quickly, *Andrea*. I have places to be."

She winces visibly upon hearing the inflexion I purposely place on her name, confirming her suspicions that playtime is over. But to her credit, she dresses swiftly and quietly before walking to the doorway and turning to face me.

"Call me *anytime,* Rico."

"It's Mr DeMarco, Andrea. Goodnight."

Without so much as glancing in her general direction, I march toward my restroom and close the door behind me, clicking the lock loudly on the off chance my ex-fuck buddy didn't get the message before now.

I won't be dipping my wick in that office ink anymore. Judging by the hopeful look in Andrea's eyes, it seems she's gotten attached, when I've been forthright from the first that I am not interested in anything more than a quick release.

Divesting my three-piece, slightly rumpled suit, I turn my rainwater shower to a cool temperature and duck underneath, allowing the water to sluice along my body, washing away both the day from hell and the orgasm that has forced me into *feeling*.

Or at least that blaze of blonde hair I am 99% certain I saw as I came has me melancholy.

Two years. Two damn years, and I'm still mooning over a piece of tail. It's a fucking joke, but it's on me because the thought of Peaches still gets my dick harder than granite. Despite having just come, my cock stirs to life at her memory. But, unfortunately, it's not just her ass I'm hard thinking about. It's the entire cock teasing package.

Her big blue innocent eyes. Her hair that had looked and felt like spun gold. Her perfect smile. Her tinkling laughter. Her hesitant hands as they felt my body vibrating with barely restrained need.

My cock is fully hard again as precum drips from the slit freely. Grabbing the offending appendage in my right hand, I run my thumb through the slickness and grip it hard before jerking off viciously to the thought of Peaches. Not that she's mine to dream about, but my cock has yet to get the memo.

Picturing how it would feel to sink into her tightness from behind while grabbing her hair with one hand and slapping her peachy cheeks with the other is my go-to wank-bank material and never fails to get me off.

Slapping my left hand against the shower door, I come with a bellow and more intensity than I ever have with a woman since I laid eyes on her. Just the mere thought of her does this to me.

Fucking hell.

As I rinse off, I'm more than a little pissed at my lack of discipline. Once I'm done and dry, I set to the task of getting ready for my flight. The jet is booked to fly in a little over an hour, so I ring down to my driver and tell him to pull the car around.

My flight to the States is quiet, having opted for one male flight attendant, mainly because I've fucked the female ones, and I couldn't be bothered dealing with them tonight.

Instead of sleeping, as I should be, I shoot off an email to Tim Nash, my head of security at the London office, telling him that I need the surveillance footage on 26 from earlier tonight.

I can't stop the nagging feeling that someone was outside my office earlier, though I don't expect an answer as it's still the middle of the night back home. So, I'm guessing it will be tomorrow afternoon New York time before I hear a word.

There's a car ready and waiting when I land, and within minutes, we are on the way to my penthouse in Manhattan. Of course, it's still the middle of the night, but here in New York, it's a bustling concrete jungle at all times of the day and night.

My Upper East Side penthouse is a 12,500-foot space with monolithic windows taking up floors 46 and 47 in the building. It's currently painted in lights from the bustling city, so I grab a bottle of water from the well-stocked refrigerator, chugging it down in two gulps, before abandoning my luggage at the foot of the stairs and taking the steps two at a time.

Stripping out of my travel clothes, I fall face-first onto my super king bed in just my jocks and am asleep almost before my head meets the mattress.

It's still dark outside when I awake to someone beating my door down. I feel like I've just been asleep for ten minutes, if not less.

The door attendant of the building knows better than to let just anyone in, especially at this time of the day, so my sleep-addled brain can at least acknowledge it can only be one of three people.

It can't be Nate. He's stuck back in London, wading through his late father's estate.

It can't be Alex. He's undoubtedly worked himself into a frenzy over shitting all over this fucking deal.

So, there's only one remaining culprit, and I'm damn sure it's him. Who fucking else, though how he's tracked me down is anyone's guess.

After locating last night's pants on the floor where they've been abandoned, I pull them up over my jocks as I make my way down the stairs and, without bothering to button them closed, I pull open the door to my apartment.

Sure enough, right there, in all his glory, is none other than Caden fucking North.

Of course, it'd be him. Who else?

"It's still dark, man. What the fuck gives?"

Unperturbed by my less than welcoming manner, Cade crosses the distance between us and envelops me in one of his tight hugs. I stand there, hands hanging uselessly by my sides for a moment.

Eventually, I awkwardly pat him on the back before withdrawing to find the big blonde rock star flushed a dark pink with tears glistening in his big blue eyes.

"Jesus, what's wrong?"

"Nothing's wrong, Henry, my man. Everything is *right* with the world!" He steps back to puff out his chest, almost comically, if his following words weren't the ultimate tragedy.

"Lay's pregnant!"

Oh shit.

"And we're getting married."

Bigger shit.

An intensely amped up Caden spends the next hour waxing poetic about how being a good dad is his top priority now. About how he can't wait for their family to settle down and "live the dream," which I've long known is the endgame for him. But Layla?

Really?!

An unusual feeling of nervous anxiety, one I'm wholly unused to feeling, takes over my body. I can't help myself from going there.

"What about Layla's little *habit*?"

I don't want to rain on anyone's parade, but I can't help the words from spewing out of my mouth.

I'm happy for him. And even as I tell myself that lie, I can feel my stomach churn as I try to swallow it, knowing it's utter shit.

I can envision an intense conversation down the line where Nate and I will need to address some hard truths for our best friend. Unfortunately, Cade has always been blind to Layla's many, *many* faults and, for some reason, both Nate and I know he's holding the truth back. I just can't for the life of me work out what it could be.

He and Layla have known each other pretty much forever. They'd spent time away from each other in their teen years, eventually coming together in the on-again, off-again scenario we are so used to witnessing. Their bond initially came through their mutual love of music, but for Layla, that encompassed the dark underbelly that came with excessive fame.

"She's clean, DeMarco. We've both been seeing drug counsellors. Obviously, I'm just there to support her, and it's going really well." He snorts. "Privately, of course. The label would have a shit fit if any of it went public." We both laugh, though it's without any genuine mirth. Misdirection's manager, Noah Spellman, would rather sell his own kid than have any negative press touch his cash cow.

"She's finding it hard right now, man. This morning sickness is no joke. We're going to throw a huge ass party once she's feeling better, and I need my boys by my side for the big day!"

Clapping him on the shoulder, I smile in response to his contagious delight. "Wouldn't be anywhere else, North!"

A while later, once I've sent him on his merry way, I get myself together quickly, not bothering with catching another lousy hour of kip. Due to my early morning wake up call, I'm ready earlier than anticipated. My driver is waiting curbside and quickly ferries me downtown to the hotel my half-brother has opted to stay in.

Rather than use one of the homes in every major city where DeMarco Holdings has a branch, Alex still refuses to stay anywhere associated with our father. With time, maybe he'll get past it as I did.

Knowing from his increasingly frenzied emails throughout the last twenty-four hours when the deal began to tank that he is in room 1607, I bypass reception and ride the elevator to his floor.

It's still early, but as the business district never sleeps, it takes several stops before I finally reach his floor. I walk briskly down the corridor to his room, and after pounding on his door three or four times, he answers, wearing nothing but his jocks.

His face falls. "Rico!"

"Alex, seriously." Rolling my eyes for effect, I hold his eyes. "How often do I have to tell you it's *Henry*." Then, marching past him into his suite, I take in the room and the pigsty it currently resembles. The glass coffee table has two empty wine glasses on it, and the open door beyond displays a bed filled with rumpled white sheets and blonde hair splayed across them.

Is she here?

My stomach sinks at the thought, but I quickly mask my feelings with sarcasm and anger, my go-to weapons of choice.

"Sorry to interrupt your sleepover, little brother, but if you don't kick your companion the fuck out and get yourself downstairs right fucking now, I don't care if you're family or not. I will sack your ass faster than you can say would-you-like-fries-with-that, you got me?"

Jesus, I don't mean to be so harsh, especially considering the frail threads of trust I've painstakingly built between us, but Christ, the thought of her being so close and undeniably freshly fucked by someone who *isn't me* gnaws away at my guts like a rat. My stomach swirls sickeningly as I suck in oxygen through my nose. The unmistakable smell of sex lingering throughout the suite makes me feel worse, and there's a genuine possibility that I might throw up.

Without giving him the chance to reply, I yank open the door and get the fuck out of dodge, heading toward the lobby to await his arrival. He's caught up with me within five minutes, looking none the worse for wear and with his business game face firmly in place.

The reps from Van Deutsch Applications arrive earlier than we'd planned, but Alex and I have had plenty of time to form a plan of attack, and within ten minutes, they're rolling over, practically begging us to take the company off their hands.

After we sign the relevant documentation, we all shake hands and bid them farewell before Alex spins to me. "You are like the Jedi fucking Master of this shit. That was awesome."

Heat spreads across my chest, settling in the place my heart should be. It's been such a long time since Alex has willingly spoken to me—and words of praise at that. I'm at a loss, forgetting how to react to his positive words.

"Umm. Thanks."

"Thanks for flying out to salvage the deal. I'm sorry I made such a cock-up in the first place."

Shaking my head at his words, I pat his shoulder encouragingly. "Alex, you're doing *great*." Unable to help myself, I look at him intently, willing him to understand what I'm trying to convey. "We all make mistakes."

"Safe flight, Rico."

And without another word, he turns and walks briskly across the lobby to the waiting elevators, not glancing back once.

Returning to the penthouse, I find Tim Nash has come through for me with the footage I mailed him for. It's waiting in my emails; a copy of the entire twenty-sixth floor from 8 pm to midnight the night before last.

Pouring myself a glass of Macallan 64, despite the hour, before settling at the desk in my office. I turn on the reel, starting at 10 pm, as I reckon I was with Andrea around then.

When I start thinking that I must have gotten the times wrong, I see the elevator doors open and out walks a light-haired woman, who immediately takes a left to the ladies' room. Then, after a couple of minutes, she re-emerges, long blonde hair cascading down her back.

My heart picks up a beat.

She steps further into the offices before making her way back to the elevator, but something in the background stops her in her tracks.

She spins her head around, looking almost directly at the camera. All breath leaves my body, and I pause the track.

I was fucking right.

It's her!

Peaches.

So, if she's not with Alex, then who the fuck was in his room this morning?

Does that mean she's fair game after all?

And what the hell is she doing in my building?

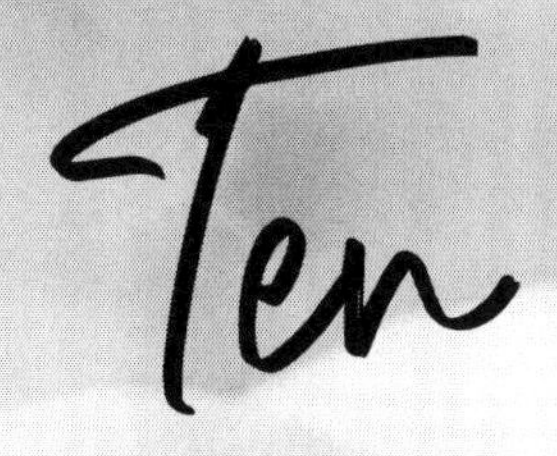

OLIVIA

When I fly through the foyer doors from the DeMarco building into the rainy night, I've never been as relieved to see Samuel's car by the curb.

My bare feet splash through puddles as I race across the path. As though by magic, the door opens to allow me to jump inside out of the downpour. Samuel is still stretched toward my door, obviously having reached for the handle to open it from the inside.

Shooting him a watery smile, he nods, silent and stoic as always, before smoothing his hand across his fair brow and turning in his seat to start the car. I've never been more grateful for his lack of aimless chatter as I am at this moment, and I curl up into a ball in the backseat as he whisks me home through waterlogged empty streets.

I arrive home to an empty apartment, soaked through, and

head straight to the DeMarco Holdings website to confirm the fact that Henry, *my* Henry, is indeed Alex's brother, Enrico DeMarco, CEO of DeMarco Holdings. Seemingly the same Henry that Martha had visited earlier this week, but judging from several more Google articles, he goes by Enrico, at least in the business world.

A little more digging unearths the information that his father had died three days after our meeting at Velvet two years ago. I'd obviously known that Alex's father had passed away around the same time as my parents, but he'd not attended the funeral, citing that as his father hadn't wanted to know him in life, he didn't want to know him in death either.

It all just seems too crazy to be factual. Having been friends with Alex for years now, it's beyond frustrating to discover that his rarely mentioned older brother is the man who has kept me up so many nights, lost in memories.

The McHottie we joke about on the regular!

Alex and I have an easy friendship. We've always had an unspoken understanding between us that our families are most definitely the Mariana Trench of deeply complicated drama. So, over the years, we have never delved too deep into the nuances of why we are the way we are.

I'd met Alex's mum, Lauren, many times. She'd initially volunteered at St. Fintan's, which was how I'd met Alex, who she'd forced to accompany her, but had taken to volunteering like a duck to water. It always felt like her actions were disingenuous. Which was later confirmed by my best friend. So, in a move orchestrated by Father T, he'd encouraged her to help out by sponsoring several homeless who resided at the shelter. She'd accepted by giving a handful a place to stay and a job on her staff.

It was kind but wholly selfish as she'd used it as an excuse to never darken the shelter doors again, having felt she'd done her bit in the sponsorship.

She'd shocked the hell out of me by showing up at my parents' funeral, perfectly made-up like she'd stepped off a catwalk in Milan, albeit cold and aloof as usual. Now that I know she had been the older Enrico DeMarco's second wife, call it a hunch, but I could see how a woman like her wouldn't take kindly to being second at anything.

Thinking of Lauren as Henry's stepmother was strange; she barely seemed old enough to be Alex's mum.

I still can't let my newly acquired knowledge impact my work. I need the job, end of story. And having signed a lease last weekend for my new apartment closer to the office, my desire to get my own place trumps all else.

Arriving at work the following Monday, I'm on edge, but after some subtle questioning, Freya lets it slip that Mr DeMarco, Enrico, not Alex, flew to New York over the weekend and won't be back for a while. According to the absolute queen of office gossip, our CEO spends rather a lot of time stateside, which allows me to relax ever so slightly.

I still spend the week with my ear to the ground and glancing over my shoulder.

Finding it strange to hear Henry referred to as Enrico, my nosiness gets the better of me, and I ask Freya what the story is.

"His father was Enrico. Named after him obviously, though from what I've heard, he goes by the English version, Henry, with his inner circle. I don't think even Alex calls him Henry, though…" She tilts her head to the side as though this realisation has only become apparent to her before lifting one shoulder. "Strange that!"

Seeing my eyebrows knit together, she goes on. "You seem

very interested, Miss Parker! Have you happened to catch sight of him around the office? He's unmistakable. Just watch for the most gorgeous man you'll ever see."

She bursts out laughing, and I join in, but only half-heartedly. Yeah, I've seen him, alright. Balls deep in the most enormous pain in my ass.

Andrea basically runs the show on 25, and, while I have no idea why she's the only one who so openly doesn't like me here, having witnessed her performance upstairs, I hate to admit it, but the feelings are reciprocated or at least in part. Though I don't like the idea that I'm capable of *actually* hating someone, so maybe I just dislike her.

Intensely.

It's the middle of the week when I get a call from Alex informing me that he wants to catch up over lunch at our favourite Italian place, so I gather my stuff and head out to meet him, Samuel at the ready obviously because, well, Alex, duh.

Lunch is a quiet affair, both opting for our own food today, smiling slightly at each other at how predictable. Alex gets a call after ordering a Tiramisu to share, and when I say share, I mean he'll take a bite, and I'll finish the rest.

"Hold on one second, sweet girl. I absolutely *must* take this." Then, sliding the button across before the third ring, he puts the phone to his ear.

"Hey, Rico, is everything okay?"

Lo-and-behold, it's none other than the CEO of the moment. There's indistinct chatter before Alex flushes slightly, then nods. "Yes, yes, of course, Henry. I apologise."

Hmm, that's interesting.

There is more chatter from the other end before Alex raises his eyes, meeting mine across the table. "Well, I'm at lunch with Liv.

Can't it..."

More chatter, and Alex's flush deepens. "No, no, no. It's not a date *date*."

Silence follows for several long beats as my stomach bottoms out at Alex's words. Does he know who I am? That his brother's best friend is the same girl he'd ghosted in Velvet two years ago?

Get a grip, idiot.

"Is it okay if I get to it tomorrow, Henry?" The stilted hesitance in Alex's voice is so sweet. And it makes me a little angry that his own brother would strike such apparent fear in my kind, dear friend.

Alex nods along before grabbing a pen and scribbling something on a napkin.

"Okay, great. Thanks, bye."

Letting out a huge sigh, he stuffs the napkin in his pants pocket before looking at me, still a little pink.

"Since starting this new position, I see things differently. Well, the business side of things. My brother is still a prick in general, but he's a fucking *virtuoso* in the business world. Ten steps ahead of the competition at all times..." He drifts off for a moment, a glazed look in his eyes. "It's... it's kind of awesome."

My heart tightens in my chest at hearing the reticent praise in Alex's voice.

"Not that I'd ever tell him." He quickly recovers. "As I said, *prick*."

The end of our lunch passes rapidly, and soon, he rings Samuel to pick us up. We sit in the backseat quietly for several minutes before I realise we're going the wrong way.

"I thought we were headed back to the office."

Alex chuckles before shrugging nonchalantly.

"The annual DeMarco Holdings Gala is this weekend."

I already know this but have opted not to go, having pumped all my cash into securing my new place.

"Yeah, I know. But I'm not going."

"Do you honestly think I'll allow you to miss it now that you work with me? Hmm? And over what? A few hundred pounds to kit yourself out or whatever?"

I raise my hands to stop him from speaking, but he gently clasps both of my wrists in his, effectively stopping me.

"Liv." His tone is pleading, and I can already feel the fight leave me. "Let me do this, please? It's as much for me as it is for you. I've had to go stag since starting at the company because I don't want any ladder-climbing socialites, or worse, staff getting the wrong idea, but this year"—his lips begin to twitch, and I'm already fighting the urge to match him—"this year, I have *you*."

He grins broadly. It's lopsided.

Crap, I'm screwed.

"You know everyone. If I must disappear for business crap, you'll have plenty of people to shoot the shit with!"

I snort out a laugh. In total Alex mode, he's quickly and efficiently undone all my resolve. Extricating my hands from his, I throw them up in fake exasperated surrender.

"Ugh, fine!" I wag a finger directly under his nose, striving to keep the mirth from my features for another moment. "But you owe me, Gaffer."

Both of us dissolve into floods of laughter, knowing full well that I'm the one who owes him everything.

Eleven

OLIVIA

I was shocked as all hell when a makeup artist and hairstylist rocked up to my apartment on Saturday afternoon alongside a bouquet of sunflowers. Our happy flower. The accompanying note reads:

Enjoy the pampering.
Be seeing you soon,
A

Popping the flowers into a tall glass vase, I plant my ass in a seat and let the pampering commence.

Jo is working, but Nola sits and watches everything, like free entertainment or something. She snaps some pics and sends them to her lover as I am done up to the nines.

"I feel like Julia Roberts in Pretty Woman, girls."

Nola snorts as Jo shouts down the line, "Except the whole

hooker part, girl, unless you got a side hustle—"

My sudden burst of laughter cuts her off as we all break down, giggling uncontrollably.

There's another loud rap on the apartment door as we're recovering, with Nola and I shaking our heads at Alex and his over-the-top treatment. She rushes to answer it, returning with the most exquisite bouquet of dark blue roses I have ever seen.

"I didn't even know blue roses were real!"

Nola, who has an issue remembering to replace coffee pods or buy loo roll but has the uncanniest ability to retain utterly useless information, shakes her head, all hints of mirth gone as she launches into what Jo playfully calls her "clever clogs" mode.

"Well, they're engineered, not grown, Liv, but they're mega expensive. They are known to signify an unfulfilled wish or, to some, love at first sight."

Jo's voice comes down the line, making me jump. I'd forgotten she was still there.

"Ooh, watch out, girl. Alex is making mooooooves."

Both Nola and I burst into a fit of belly laughter, with Jo joining in a nanosecond later.

All three of us know, as surely as he's one of the best people I've ever met, that Alex is far too much of a fuckboy to be making moves on anyone. In his own words, he's a "one and done" kinda man.

Being the first to compose myself, I look to Nola. "Who sent it, then?"

Unease prickles forebodingly down my spine at her words when Nola speaks again.

"There's another note. Want me to read it?"

"Um, thank you, but I think I'll read it myself." Handing it over reluctantly, she picks up the phone, removing Jo from the speakerphone and allowing me some privacy to see what the note reads:

A rare rose for a rare beauty.

They reminded me of your eyes.

Furrowing my brow, I hold the note out to Nola, who all but takes my hand off in her eagerness, and once she's read the words aloud to Jo, she faces me, looking perplexed.

"Well, do you have a secret admirer we don't know about, hmm?"

Green eyes, tanned skin, and a perfect broad smile flash across the front of my eyes before I shove the image to the extreme back of my mind, locking it in a little box and throwing away the key before I can dwell on it another second.

"No, not that I'm aware of! I don't know—" I break off as the hairstylist puts her hands on either side of my head, stopping me from shaking my head vehemently, almost ruining her work. Instead, I mumble a quiet *sorry* and spend the remaining time as she finishes my hair, chewing my lip, deep in thought.

I am slipping on my gold heels to match my high-neck gold satin full-length dress with a completely open back and indecently high slit up to my thigh, when the doorbell rings. Adjusting the girls, I straighten up as I hear Nola let Alex in.

"You scrub up well, my friend. A tux really suits you!"

I can hear some loud cheek kisses and deep chuckles as they walk further into the apartment, past my door.

I step into the hallway as they reach the living area, catching sight of them just as Alex spots the two bunches of flowers side by side on the low coffee table.

"Wow. Who owns the roses?"

His words cause me to stop dead in my tracks. Nola spots me over Alex's shoulder, her eyes widening as confirming realisation strikes.

If Alex truly didn't send them, then who did?

I'm torn from my musing as Alex turns to face me and takes me in from top to toe.

My blonde hair has been pulled back in a simplistic updo with loose wisps softly sitting on the nape of my neck. My makeup is minimal, and instead of the office red lip that I usually opt for, I've gone with a soft blush pink and smoky brown eye Nola had insisted would be perfect on me.

"You look stunning, Liv."

"You don't look so bad yourself, Gaffer!"

My ongoing nickname causes the three of us to laugh, breaking the tense undercurrent of the moment before Alex leads me to the waiting car.

He produces a bottle of champagne and two flutes as I send Samuel a small smile, settling myself into the back seat. Quickly popping the cork with efficiency and handing me a glass, I sit back and gratefully sip. We make some small talk on the way, shortly reaching the Landmark London, the hotel where the Gala is being hosted.

"Oh my God. Paparazzi? I didn't realise there would be celebrities in attendance!"

Alex chokes out a laugh. "They're here for Enri… I mean, Henry. The life of an extremely reclusive CEO, eh? They're well aware he's no option but to be here and as one of Britain's most eligible singletons under thirty…" He raises a shoulder, knowing he's made his point.

I'd forgotten he would even be here in my stupid preoccupation, and I'm so utterly unprepared to come face to face with him after all this time.

Cop on, Olivia!

This is two years ago we're talking about here. Henry definitely does *not* remember me. I don't want him to remember me.

I don't *need* him to either!

So why does that thought make my heart sink and my stomach sick?

Once we enter the Grand Ballroom, Alex grabs us another flute each, but it's not even been a full minute before he's being called off to some little chinwag or other that the bigwigs from DeMarco simply *must* have him be a part of.

As he's being pulled away through the crowd, he scrunches his face up in distaste as he mouths, "I'll be back."

I smile at him, allowing my dimples to pop, letting him know it's okay. That I'm fine and within minutes I've found my people. Freya gathers me close, like a clucky mother hen, telling me all the who's who of the party, and it's not long before Henry makes his debut.

Walking into the ballroom as though he owns the place, his black tux and crisp white shirt fit his body like they've been made for him.

His strides are long, even, and so cock fucking sure of himself; I don't know if it makes me even sicker or turns me on.

Sadist!

The butterflies that only seem to appear for him flutter in my stomach.

And other places.

The rest of my gang take turns dancing with each other and continue to drink like fishes, along with the rest of the party, but I limit myself to sipping, very, *very* slowly. I don't dance so as not to draw attention to myself, but I have a blast all the same.

Alex returns twice and is pulled away again within minutes of his reappearance, so we've not spent any proper time together, but I'm still having a brilliant evening.

I'm just exiting the little girls' room, when I round a corner and run straight into a wall of rock-hard muscle, my clutch flying from my hand, scattering the contents all over the hallway.

"Oh, I am so sorry."

Crouching down to retrieve my belongings, I look up to come face to face with spectacular, unique green eyes.

Unforgettable green eyes that have haunted my dreams for the past two years. My breathing becomes laboured, and I feel my cheeks flush under his focused attention.

My eyes meet his and entirely unconsciously, I find mine begging him, pleading with him, to remember me. To remember our moment.

His eyes flicker across my face, and there's zero sign of recognition to be found as hopelessness settles in the pit of my stomach like a lead weight.

Gathering my purse, I force myself to stand tall under his indifference, so squaring my shoulders, I slip past him.

"Excuse me."

I can't help the disappointment that runs through my body at the confirmation that he doesn't remember me.

Get over yourself, Liv. He forgot about you the moment he left that stupid terrace.

I get through the next torturous twenty minutes, hoping Alex will return soon so that I can let him know that I need to go home. Still, I can see he's wrapped up in a group that includes Henry, alongside Martha and Ryan Solomon, so it'll be a while.

Turning to Freya, I'm about to tell her that I want to call it a night when the band stops playing to announce the traditional management dance.

"Oh, here we go. My annual dance with Ryan."

I snort behind my champagne. But, of course, no one else would have the ability to put up with the old codger for the entirety of a song.

Each member of management will pick someone at random to dance with, kind of like a show of unity so that all employees know that everyone is equal within the company.

"Enrico always dances with Martha. She's like, old enough to be his grandmother, and obviously, if he were to pick someone more age-appropriate, the office gossip aka yours fucking truly would go into overdrive."

The two of us chortle at that, knowing full well that she's the ringmaster of said office gossip. If there's gossip to be had, Freya will source it like a sniffer dog in Amsterdam. She's in her element.

She side-eyes me when I smile as Ryan reaches us and holds his hand out for Freya, which she dutifully takes. I glance across the room, wondering where Alex is and who he'll ask to dance, when my eyes land on him and Henry. They are speaking quietly together with Martha close by, but even from this distance, I can see the anger bristling between them, wholly at odds with the stilted but polite conversation I was privy to earlier this week.

Suddenly Henry turns his back and strides away, leaving Alex clenching his fists repeatedly at either side of his body, his face like thunder, before he turns sharply to hold his hand out to Martha.

He looks across the room, his eyes finding mine as my head tilts to the side questioningly, brows in a deep V, the very picture of confusion as Henry comes to a stop in front of our table, causing the entire room to gasp audibly.

"Miss Parker."

His voice is as deep and downright sexy as I remember, and I feel more than a little lightheaded when he affects a slight, stiff bow before continuing. "Would you kindly do me the honour of this dance?"

If my eyes widen any more, they'll undoubtedly fall right out of my head, yet I stand, as though magnetised by his mere presence, making my way around to take his proffered hand, allowing him to lead me to the dance floor.

Turning to face me, our eyes meet as he keeps hold of the hand I gave him while I place my other one on his broad shoulder, and he slips his warm palm around my waist, gently tugging me closer so that our bodies are flush together.

The band begins to play *These Arms of Mine* by Otis Redding, sending a shiver of longing down my spine as we slowly start to sway to the music. My mind instantly flashes back to when he'd told me his favourite show of all time was *12 Monkeys*.

This song is the love song between the two main characters who weren't supposed to meet, but as fate would have it, they did, and their love would go on to change the world. My mind is whirring at top speed as I think about it.

Did he have them play it on purpose?

Does he remember me?

Am I a complete and utter paranoid wreck, making something out of nothing?

Yes, Olivia. Get a fucking grip!

Not a single word is exchanged between us as his green eyes never leave my blue ones, and I can feel the attention of the entire Ballroom upon us. Though my worries slowly begin to ebb away, I can't find it in me to care.

Not one bit.

My knees feel weak, like I might stumble and fall at any moment, but his strong arms and even stronger gaze fixed firmly on mine keep me upright.

As the song's final bars begin to play, his eyes move from mine down to linger on my lips for several beats. His nostrils visibly flare as I can't help but tug my bottom lip between my teeth nervously before he leans in close. So close I'm enveloped by him and that bergamot that makes it impossible for me to enjoy a cup of Earl Grey without remembering his indelible scent. His lips brush my ear so softly it sends a shot of pure, unfettered yearning straight to my core.

My breathing hitches when the hand upon my waist drifts to the bare skin of my lower back, his thumb drawing lazy circles once again, except this time it's on my naked flesh. When his lips by my ear begin to move as he speaks oh-so-softly, it sends sweet shivers of desire all the way along my bare spine.

All the way to my wet, needy centre. The part of me that only seems to come alive for this man.

"I'm pleased I got the exact shade right, Peaches."

He pulls away at my sharp inhalation, bowing low over my hand to dust his lips across my knuckles as though we're in a scene from *Bridgerton* before straightening up, turning on his heel, and leaving the ballroom. I'm forcibly tossed back into the here-and-now as our audience gapes open-mouthed at the show performed so heedlessly in front of them.

Thankfully, Alex has the presence of mind to stride forward, grasping me firmly at the elbow before directing me out of the Grand Ballroom, just as the gossip starts up with a cacophony at our departing backs.

Twelve

OLIVIA

Holding my elbow in one hand while resting his other one at the base of my exposed spine in his reassuring way, Alex quickly steers me out of the Grand Ballroom, out of the Landmark, and onto the street. Almost miraculously, Samuel is waiting like a white knight but with a black town car instead of a horse. The thought sends me into hysterical laughter while both men look at me like I've lost my mind.

In a way, I have.

Henry has blown it away with his eyes and the promises held within them. And when he'd leaned in and spoken those words, it was as though I had left my body and was watching the scene unfold from afar. Those words confirmed my deepest, darkest, most secret hope; that he'd been the sender of those divine blue roses, the ones Nola claimed signified things I'd only ever dared to dream of.

Alex brings me back to the moment, ushering me into the car just as Freya runs out onto the street, brandishing my clutch.

"Liv, honey, I've got your bag. Are you okay?"

Bending my head as he places his palm gently but firmly on the top to urge me inside the vehicle, Alex answers in my stead.

"Thank you so much, but she's fine, Ms Thornton. I'll make sure she gets home."

He gently plucks the bag from her grasp before sliding into the car beside me as I send wide eyes to Freya. Alex continues as he buckles me in and settles himself.

"See you on Monday. Goodnight."

I don't think I've ever heard Alex as… succinct. As in charge. And it makes me wonder what happened between the brothers.

"Alex, is everything…."

Cutting me off swiftly with a finger to my lips, he takes me in with his unusual amber eyes before speaking.

"Liv. I know what you're going to say. Because I know you better than almost anyone."

His forehead crinkles into a deep frown. "And it's because I know you so well that I need to be honest with you, okay?"

He waits for my slight nod, telling him to go on, before dropping his finger from my lips and holding my hands lightly between his.

"My brother is a fucking god in the business world. And maybe, long ago—"

His voice breaks before he clears his throat, continuing. "As a child, I adored him with something akin to hero-worship." His emotions are bubbling to the surface, these words telling me more about their obviously fraught relationship than he's ever let slip before, and my heart breaks for my best friend. "But, sweet girl, he's *not* a good person."

He swallows heavily, as though a tonne weight rests on his shoulders.

"Something happened tonight. I *wish* I knew what, but it was like a switch flipped, and he decided that you were his for the taking."

My stomach swirls and nauseates at those words, not knowing what to make of them. Only knowing that they are sending little thrills of hope through every crevice of my being.

"It's my fault you've been caught in his crosshairs, sweet girl, and for that, I'm sorry."

The car pulls up outside my building, stopping with a jolt that jerks us both forward suddenly as Samuel solemnly catches my eye in the rear-view mirror. Alex leans over to unbuckle my seatbelt, then reaches for his own then exits, coming around the back of the car to open my door before walking me to the building.

The words are on the tip of my tongue.

Henry is McHottie. Those three words and Alex will know it has nothing to do with him. That this is no coincidence. But my throat has seized shut. My whole body is numb as I try to swallow down the lump keeping me from voicing my truth.

We stand on the pavement facing each other as he holds my chin between his forefinger and thumb, his brow furrowed, so at odds with the happy-go-lucky person I usually see.

"You're my best friend in the whole wide world. I want nothing more than to see you happy… but my brother is incapable of making anyone happy. I know that, more than most."

Wrapping his arms around me, his mouth rests by my ear as parting words send my heart plummeting. "He will just break your heart, Olivia. This I can promise you. This I *know*."

He breaks our embrace, giving me one last firm squeeze before turning and walking back to the car, leaving me in the chilly night, allowing the events of the past hour to sink in.

Sleep doesn't find me for a long time that night.

I spend all of Sunday holed up in my room, avoiding everyone. Going over and over Alex's words. My head tells me he is exactly right; any interaction with the enigmatic Enrico DeMarco will undoubtedly result in breaking my silly heart. And so, my head has ruled that we stay as far from him and our inevitable downfall as humanly possible.

But my foolish heart, that traitorous bitch, tells me that deep down, underneath the bluster, and far behind walls too high to breach lies a man who could want me, need me, love me the way I've wished for so many times.

Having my head and heart at odds is exhausting, and the thought of adding other voices to the two doing battle in my mind is too much for me to even entertain.

Nola, being the heart of our little trio, drops three square meals at my door and doesn't push any conversation, confirming in my mind that Alex has indeed spoken to the girls about what had happened the night before.

Once I'd worn my brain out thinking through all possible scenarios and outcomes going forward, I shut down the only way I knew how, with yet another *12 Monkeys* binge-fest. Re-watching my favourite episodes always calms me, and tonight is no different. I devour the final three episodes of the series, ending with tears, once again, like every time I do this, streaming down my cheeks, finding pieces of my own life within each of these characters' stories.

Settling into a fitful sleep, I dream of walking through an endless black void with no hope in sight until I relax as the feel of solid arms lock tight around my body, soothing my restless slumber. I dream of my head resting on this unknown person's chest, listening to the rough cadence of their heart under my ear, the smell of soap and citrus surrounding me, and my sleep becomes slightly less uneasy as I take the comfort offered to me.

Waking the following day, I feel okay until I remember the Gala and the gossip that is no doubt circulating before the day has even begun.

The unavoidable rumour mill will be in overdrive at the knowledge that I had danced more intimately than appropriate with the company CEO and proceeded to leave the event with his younger brother, my direct boss.

Queue.

The.

Vomit.

As I finish the last of my makeup for the first workday of a new week, I give myself a fleeting glance in the full-length mirror, turning this way and that to make sure I look okay. Having opted for all black once again in a sleek, fitted pencil dress with a flirty little kick at the hem, landing on my knees, with my signature heels and a red lip, I know I look good.

Small mercy.

I grab my bag and my coat and add a black scarf to the ensemble as the seasons seem to have bypassed autumn and jumped straight to winter, judging by the icy breeze that has descended upon the city over the weekend.

It's only August!

Placing my palm on my stomach to quell the rising nausea, the events of Saturday replay as though in fast forward, though each time I remember his eyes, the flashbacks move in slow motion. The memory of those golden-green orbs looking at me with such intensity felt like they could see right down to who I am, at my very core. It's an unsettling yet utterly addictive feeling that I've only ever experienced at the hands of one man.

Rushing from the building to the waiting black town car, I jump straight in, only to recoil in shock when I spot another person in the back seat.

"Jesus fucking Christ!"

My stomach plummets as I hear the unmistakably deep, sexy voice following my exclamation.

"Your vocabulary seems to have taken a swan dive since we last exchanged words, Peach."

Butterflies flutter and come to life in my stomach when I turn to face him, just as the driver, blatantly *not* Samuel, pulls out into traffic.

My voice is breathy and entirely not my own. "Henry."

"The one and only. Although you may call me Mr DeMarco going forward. If you last at my company, that is. Voyeurism in the office, Peaches. Tut tut. Naughty girl."

The smirk on his face is nauseatingly sneer-like.

My cheeks bloom a deep red with both embarrassment and shame and while I should question him about what the hell kind of a stunt he pulled on Saturday, thus making me the unwilling victim of petty office gossip, my rarely seen temper flares.

I'm angry. *Really* fucking angry.

Angry that he would bring that up.

Angry that he obviously knew who I was on Saturday, which had led me to believe he didn't remember me at all.

Angry that I'd let my guard down as a result.

Angry that he so blatantly has the upper hand here.

Angry that my stupid heart won't let go of the idea that he's not what he portrays to the world, despite my head *knowing* it to be true.

Angry that he filled my innocent head with such complete

and utter bullshit that I still can't get past that singular night two long-ass years later.

But most of all, I'm angry, I'm *so* fucking angry that he still makes me *feel*. That he retains that power over me.

Yeah, that last one tips me right over the edge, so I can't stop myself from lashing out.

"You can go and *fuck* yourself, you giant asshole." My eyes are narrowed as the words come out in a hiss from between my clenched jaws. "Threatening an employee, Henry, or is it, *Enrico*? Who the hell knows! Tut fucking tut yourself, Mr DeMarco!"

Before I can even take a breath, he's unbuckled his seatbelt and is on me.

My heart rate stutters in my chest before galloping at top speed, threatening to jump out of my palpitating chest.

One big hand comes up, catching my chin to force me to look him in the eyes. Those unforgettable, evocative eyes, more black than green at this moment, threaten to devour me.

I swallow roughly under his searing gaze while my disloyal body purrs from the power he exudes.

The other hand catches my hip, pinning me in place so that all I can do is look up at him, hating myself for coming alive under his obvious disdain. "Peaches, baby," he growls, the words sounding as though they're being torn from deep within his broad chest. "I hate to disappoint you, but I don't make threats. I make promises, and I keep them. Unlike some."

At the last two words, his eyes flicker with something.

Pain?

I've seen it often enough in my own eyes to recognise it instantly, and regardless of the words he's just spewed at me, despite it *all*, I can see the Henry my heart believes hides away from the world behind fortified walls too high to be scaled.

My idiotic heart softens at the glimpse into his humanity for a nanosecond before giving myself a mental shake. I need to listen to my head where this man is concerned and stop letting the emotions he forcibly pulls from me take flight.

I stiffen my spine and push the empathy I feel for him deep, deep down inside. I force myself to remember his beautiful lies, his treatment of my best friend, and his unnecessary exhibition at the Gala. I steel myself to his proximity, scent, voice, and beautiful fucking face. Ugh, it's so fucking beautiful, but I plough on.

I plough on, regardless of my wayward thoughts. "You clearly love to disappoint me, seeing as you do it at any given opportunity."

"What the hell is that supposed to mean?"

"It *means*," I seethe, ruffled and entirely out of character, "maybe people in glass houses shouldn't throw stones."

His eyes narrow into angry slits, his jaw tightening even more than before as we stare, at each other at an impasse.

Having realised moments ago that we were just about to pull up outside the office, I'm ready to duck out from under his grasp.

"And I'm so far beyond done with this conversation."

I grab the handle, push the door open wide before the car has even reached a stop, then run as fast as my heels will carry me.

As I reach the foyer, I glance back over my shoulder, just once, but it's once too many. Henry has gotten out and is now leaning against the car, looking disgustingly gorgeous, his hands in his pant pockets and his green eyes bright as they follow me on my dash into the building.

Picking up the pace, I can only hope he leaves me alone going forward. I'm not a confrontational person by any means, but there's something about him that makes me become someone else, and I'm not altogether sure if I like it.

Or maybe you like it a little too much.

The day goes from bad to worse. Much, much worse.

It's barely 10 am when I get a call from Martha asking me to come down to the fourteenth floor, where she reigns supreme, though I've never had a reason to visit for a "chat." The whole way down in the elevator, my stomach is churning with where this conversation will inevitably go.

I've already endured pitying looks from the whole of the twenty-fifth floor, except from Andrea, who has spent the morning so far up my ass she undoubtedly knows what I've had for breakfast.

She's in flying form. Barking orders at me and basically making life miserable.

Obviously, Henry has spoken to Martha, and despite Alex's newly found clout, even he won't be able to save me if Henry has decided I'm out on my ass.

"Good morning, sweetie. Come on in and close that door."

Doing as she says, I take the seat she gestures to, crossing my ankles and tucking my hands between my thighs to stop nervous fidgeting.

"Now, this is just a regular review to see how you've gotten along in your first six weeks here, okey-dokey?"

My shoulders relax ever so slightly before she continues.

"And having reviewed your work first hand, I can see it is exemplary. So much so, in fact, we might be considering re-assigning you elsewhere."

My mouth drops open unbecomingly before I gather my wits.

"May I ask why, Martha? Alex would have definitely told me if he was unhappy with my work thus far."

I'm not averse to having a new boss, and though I think Alex might not be thrilled, maybe this is my chance to get off the management floor and away from the incessant rumour mill.

"Well, Liv, to be honest, your work is excellent. Impeccable, in fact. Your presence has boosted office morale on the entire twenty-fifth floor. All management adores you and would happily take you on as their own, as they can clearly see what a diligent worker you are. On a side note, *do you know* the last time we all went for Friday drinks after work to celebrate a new employee's first month on the job?"

Her eyes twinkle with delight as she goes on. "I'll give you a hint."

Leaning forward furtively, she winks. "*Never*. And that was because of you. Everyone gravitates toward you. Even Ryan, and he's as set in his ways as they damn well come!"

I can't stop the small giggle that escapes me as she hoots at her own joke. This meeting is looking *way* better than I'd initially thought.

"Liv, sweetie, I really feel your talent is wasted where you are, not to mention that you are entirely overqualified for the position you're filling."

I'm seriously considering talking to Alex about it until the next words leave her mouth.

"So, what do you say? Will you move upstairs and work under Henry?"

Thirteen

OLIVIA

I nearly lose my breakfast, and my eyes almost fall out of my head from how wide I've opened them, but she goes on, lowering her voice confidentially, which is complete overkill considering the office door is fully closed.

"Olivia, I know you're bound to be hesitant after… well, to be honest, after the events of Saturday's Gala. However, I can assure you, Henry is the very picture of a gentleman. Your presence would be invaluable to him. He's found it hard to retain a PA, though I think you'd be the ideal person for the position."

I snort internally as my mind flashes to his penis rammed down Andi's throat.

Yeah, he's found it hard because he can't quit fucking them.

"So… what do you say, honey?"

It's clear that she thinks I'll just jump at the chance like anyone else in their right mind would. But I just can't. My head is telling me I need to stay as far away from him as humanly possible for the well-being of my irrational, incompetent heart.

"Umm, I… I… Martha, I don't think that's a great idea." My stupid mouth won't work right.

I could scream from the frustration this ass causes me.

"I… I'm flattered, b-b-b-but I am friends with Alex, um, the other Mr DeMarco, and I would hate to leave him in the lurch right now."

My face is puce with a concoction of anger, distress, and self-frustration at my inane word vomit. I need to get out of here before I lose my fucking rag.

Returning to full-on business mode as I've effectively shut her down, Martha is the very picture of sincerity. "Well, Liv, I'll relay your concerns to Mr DeMarco. He hand-picked you for the position, you know. After reviewing your performance last week, and between us girls, I believe he asked you to dance on Saturday to get a feel for how you two would get along on a professional level."

Bless her. She really has no idea of this man and his manipulations.

"Okay, Martha. That's great. Thank you. I'll see you at lunch, yeah?" And with that, without waiting for a reply, I fly from her office on winged feet, knowing exactly where I'm going.

Punching 26 on the elevator with a little more force than necessary, I'm entering Henry's office space before seeing anything other than the red haze behind my eyelids.

To say that I'm fuming would be to put it delicately.

Very, very delicately.

I don't remember the last time I've ever felt such unfettered rage coursing through my veins. What is it about this man that makes me so erratic—that makes me want to dance with the devil himself? How does he manage to bring such potent emotions to life in me?

He's in one of the glass board rooms with a whole room full of dull-looking business types, alongside Andrea, who looks spitting mad at the sight of me descending upon them. But I don't hesitate for one split second before I walk right in the open glass door, pointing a white glossed finger directly at Henry as I grit out, "Your office. *Right now.*" Spinning on my towering heels, I march straight into his office, the entire floor staff staring at me.

The rumour mill will be running solidly on me and my actions for the foreseeable. And I couldn't care any less.

Henry arrives less than thirty seconds later, shutting the door and closing the electric blinds after him before sauntering around me to lean nonchalantly against his desk.

"No need to afford either of us any privacy, *Mr DeMarco.* I got your offer from HR," I snarl, "and I just wanted to let you know face to face that you can ram your 'promotion' right up your *fucking* ass. I'd rather clean public toilets with my tongue than work under you."

Having said my piece, I turn quickly, but not quickly enough.

He captures my wrist in his much larger hand, but rather than jerk me around to face him, he presses forward so that he is right at my back, my hand locked between us, and my front pushed up against his office door.

I can feel his rock-solid cock pressing forcefully against the top of my ass as we both breathe heavily, as though having run a marathon.

His breath is hot on my neck, forcing my heart rate to kick up yet another notch. His free hand lifts, running his forefinger along my cheekbone before he gently splays his palm across my neck. I gasp at the sensation, and he pauses his movements. For reasons that I can't comprehend, I find myself relaxing into his hold, wanting more. And as though he's heard my body's silent assent, his hand continues down to palm my breastbone. He slowly inches further, stopping as he reaches the top of my breast to pass over my pointed nipple, lightly pinching it through the fabric of my clothes.

Goosebumps light up my whole being as I hum under his touch, and I can't help but curse my traitorous body's willingness to forget everything in his mere presence.

Get it together, you idiot.

He continues lower, his breath hot and heavy against my nape, sending another shock of goosebumps tingling along my spine. His chest is rising and falling at my back, almost as rapidly as my own.

"You know, Peach, you really are quite edible when you're angry."

Blowing out an unsteady breath, I whisper, "Stop."

At least pretend you mean it, Liv!

I don't think he's heard me anyway as he continues along my abdomen, lower and lower, before brushing lightly above my pubic bone, making me inhale sharply through my nostrils.

"And surely, you've realised by now…" His voice is a hypnotic drawl at my ear, holding me in place more firmly than his hands.

My hips jerk of their own accord as my face flushes red with the shame of desiring him this strongly, the utter bastard.

"I like to play with my food before I eat it."

Oh God quit pretending and just go with it, you hussy.

His pinkie finger moves lower, barely grazing over the top of my clit. His breaths become shallow, and I whimper helplessly when he rolls his hips forward into my ass cheeks as I press back against him.

Craving more.

Needing more.

I feel his hardness grinding against my rear as I'm transported to the time before there was any animosity between us.

A low moan slips unbidden from my lips as I lay my head back against his broad shoulder and close my eyes in delicious anticipation, allowing my heart to take the lead—to hell with the cost.

Until he obliterates everything.

"But don't get excited, Peaches. I'm not into my brother's sloppy seconds." Then, shoving away from me as though I've stung him, he crosses the room in quick strides. I don't wait to see what he does next, instead choosing to run from him.

For the second time today.

I take the elevator to the foyer, emailing Alex on the way to let him know I'll be continuing my work from home for the remainder of the day.

I really am beginning to think this job is more hassle than it's worth.

"Come *on*, girl! Alex is downstairs."

"Just a sec, Jo. I've got to grab my heels."

Moving past my best friends, who are both looking fine as hell tonight in matching rainbow sequin co-ords, I almost trip over my own two feet as I race into my room to locate my new silver sandals that lace up to my knee. I've matched them with a white bandage dress that almost shows my underwear, but I'm trusting that Josie's innate fashion sense hasn't steered me wrong yet.

I don't think I've ever been as grateful to see the end of a work week. I felt like I was walking on eggshells until I got word midweek from Freya, who has somehow managed to mostly keep a lid on the rumour mill, that Henry had been forced to go away for the rest of the week on an unscheduled trip stateside. And so, Thursday and Friday were much more relaxed, knowing he wouldn't pop up anytime soon like an unwanted pimple.

Plus, I had tonight's concert to think about, which definitely brightened my week.

I shimmy out of the room, excited for the night ahead, with my hands in the air to meet the waiting high fives of my girls.

"Okay, let's get this show on the road, ladies."

Grabbing our bags and coats from the hall table, we make our way out of the building and jump into the stretch Hummer that Alex had Samuel driving just for the special occasion.

The man himself is inside, sprawled out on the neon-lit seats with his lopsided grin front and centre, the very picture of chill.

After the angst of last weekend, Alex rocked up to work on Monday, before the showdown with wanker extraordinaire, like a fucking god, light brown hair slicked back, brushing the collar of his shirt. His eyes had flashed amber fire, ready to defend me to the nth degree, not that I'd needed it. Other than Andrea's remarks, no one else had said a single word about the spectacle at the Gala.

I had to hand it to him; he was really coming out of his shell since the semi showdown with Henry, and I was proud as all hell of him. Even though I am still gagging to know what words had been exchanged between the brothers before Henry had claimed me for that dance.

The trip to the O2 is a relatively short distance, but during that time, we fit in three bottles of Dom Perignon between the four of us and being the cheap drunk I have realised myself to be, I'm properly buzzed as we go inside.

The place is absolutely packed and about ninety-five percent female, but Alex has spoiled us by booking a private suite so that we can take in the atmosphere without being crushed in the throng.

He chooses this moment to produce VIP backstage passes for our group after the show, resulting in lots of screaming and a few tears, all of which are from me as Jo and Nola aren't half as in love with Misdirection as I so obviously am.

The warm-up act is really good, but they only play a handful of songs before making way for the main event.

We spend the time chatting amongst our little foursome, downing several more glasses of champers and generally soaking up the electricity within the stadium. The night is charged with excitement and possibility.

Each member of Misdirection arrives separately, as they always do, garnering individual cheers, which seem to ramp up their own excitement.

Of course, the loudest screams are for Misdirection's frontman and lead singer, Caden North, whose blonde locks, panty-dropping smile, and devil-may-care attitude have enamoured women and men the world over.

"Good evening, London!"

The screams reach a fever pitch, and it feels like the ground is shaking beneath us, despite being in a box well above the earth.

"How're all you wankers doing tonight?"

As Caden continues his spiel that we, the fans, know and love so well, Alex turns to me while Nola and Jo are busy shouting alongside the rest of the O2.

"I heard you had a meeting with Martha this week. You never said. Everything okay?"

His brow is furrowed, and his eyes are full of concern as he looks me straight in the eye. I look right back and lie blatantly.

"Yup. Everything's just peachy."

Hmm, memo to self. No more peach references.

"Well, as long as you're happy with me. Martha told me about that promotion..." He eyes me intently, and I realise he knows exactly what was said. "I know I'm just a stepping stone, and working under Rico—I mean, Henry, would open doors that I don't have access to yet. If you want to work…"

"Alex." I place my hand on his arm to stop him with a massive smile on my face. Despite his reservations, he still wants me to do well in my career, even if it means placing me right in the path of temptation—or potential heartbreak—but now isn't the time or place for melodramatics. Mis-freaking-direction is about to perform. "We'll talk later, okay? Let's have the time of our lives now!"

Putting my arm around his waist, I give it a reassuring squeeze, then turn and face the ongoing concert, just as the band breaks into their breakout hit *Layla*, which North had supposedly written for his teenage sweetheart. It's an upbeat tune with lots of bass and Caden's deep and husky vocals that never fail to get the crowd pumped.

Several more songs, some tequila shots, and a whole lot of screaming later, my heart stalls in my chest as Caden North strums the opening bars to my absolute favourite song ever, *Brothers.*

It's one of their only heart-rending, sad songs, and the lyrics speak to me every time I hear it.

The whole arena sings along, loud and unrepentant, with the words Caden penned himself, detailing the loss of his twin brother and how, although he hasn't replaced him, he has found other brothers to keep his memory alive.

"You don't fade away; you still burn the same.

And we can't let you go. We revere your name.
Not left behind."

By the time he's finished the last haunting note, I have tears streaming down my cheeks to mirror the ones Caden has glistening on his tanned face on stage, and I can't help reliving the loss of my sister. I miss her every single day.

And, in my slightly, or maybe very, inebriated state, while remembering her tragic passing, I'm shaken to my core to realise I haven't faced my parents' deaths. Not yet. I've been too busy just trying to survive.

I can see now, clear as day, though the world around me has become blurry from a mixture of tears and alcohol, that I've been moving through life on autopilot. Going through the motions, but not really taking part in the journey.

The worst part of losing a loved one suddenly is being unable to say goodbye. I hunger for that. To be able to say farewell to my sister. To my parents. To find closure. To face my losses. To ease my guilt.

It would mean everything to me.

Indicating to the others with hand signals that I need to use the loo, I quickly rush out of the suite and don't stop until I reach the bar.

Standing there with one hand on the bar, the other on my stomach to quell the nausea rising with my head down, my long hair shielding my face, I take several deep breaths.

In through the nose, out through the mouth, over and over for several long minutes until I can feel the nausea begin to ebb, and the overwhelming grief becomes more bearable.

I'm about to look up and make my way back to our suite, when I feel a hand on my shoulder.

"Olivia?"

My newly recovered stomach sinks as I realise I know the owner of that inimitable voice, and I keep my face down, hair sheltering my surely red eyes and tear-streaked face.

"Not now, Henry. Jesus, just… not now, okay?"

My voice is a croaky whisper that I'm not even sure he can hear.

I close my eyes, willing myself to disappear. To fade into the background. I'm too weak, too fragile for this man and his mind games right now.

My head won't win this war because my heart is ablaze tonight.

Fiery with long-veiled emotions and fuelled with way too much alcohol.

I can't allow him to be kind Henry with me in this state. The hidden version that allowed me to experience life for the very first time before it was all snatched away in some cruel cosmic joke.

Inhaling oxygen like a dying woman, my shoulders rise and fall more quickly than usual, and I *know* he can feel it.

"*Please*. Henry." My voice breaks on his name, the words part plea, part prayer, and wholly meant. I can't handle this crazy thing between us, whatever it is, on top of the emotions barrelling through me like a freight train.

He's ambushed me, embarrassed me, and made me question my promise to myself repeatedly. The promise I'd made after his callous actions that I'd never again let my guard down for anyone. That same promise has kept me from making viable, romantic connections with another man for fear of being discarded and forgotten about.

For fear of *feeling*.

He continues to stand there for long minutes, his hand remaining on my trembling shoulder, my face still turned to the floor until I decide, enough is enough.

I lift my face and pivot my head until I look right at him. Green eyes on blue. An intense mixture of confusion, frustration, and resignation meets my teary gaze as his hand closes the distance between us so his thumb can reach up to brush a falling tear from my cheek.

"Come here, Peaches."

My teeth grit as his nickname sends a shock of unwanted hope through me. "I'm *not* Peaches, Henry. My name is…."

"Olivia," he breathes softly. "Yes, I'm aware."

"So, stop with the nickname."

"Just… please. I… I need to make sure you're okay."

He holds out his right hand, palm facing upward, as his lips hold an unsure half-smile.

"Why?"

I look at him, uncertain, and try—oh my God, do I try—to remember all of the reasons I *shouldn't* take his hand and run a million miles at light speed away from this man.

His brow furrows, as though confused by my question. "I just *need* to."

And I can't find it in me to care about the rationale of why I should stay away. Not one single iota.

I've given chase, and Henry has caught me, albeit in a moment of weakness. Maybe it's just time to succumb.

Fourteen

HENRY

When Olivia had steamrolled into my meeting on Monday, I don't think I'd ever been as turned on in my fucking life. She had no idea how fucking sexy she looked with her long blonde locks sporting a delicious just-been-fucked look, eyes flashing blue flames, and her demand to see me with no care for the onlookers. Fuck me. She was glorious.

The fact that I had no clue what promotion she was talking about didn't even enter my mind.

It had been a natural reaction of my default dick mode to insult her and push her away.

I had stayed away from her for two damn years in a wholly misguided attempt to honour a dead man's wishes, regarding the lifetime of mistakes he'd made with his youngest son. But when I finally grew the gall to ask Alex if they were an item, he had claimed they were just friends. Those words had sent my hopes soaring and pushed me to finally make a move.

I'll never know exactly why I sent those blue roses that night. I had seen on some spam email that I usually just bin without ever reading that blue roses signify attaining the impossible, or to hopeless romantics, which I most assuredly *am not*, love at first sight.

Whatever the reason, I had just been compelled to send them, like I hadn't been given a choice.

I'd known from Alex that she was his date, and while it had eaten me up inside, I couldn't help myself from a small show of remembrance of having the band play *Otis Redding*, her pupils widening in recognition, fanning the flames of longing she stoked within me.

She'd watched *12 Monkeys* since that night.

I hadn't been able to restrain myself from claiming such a significant moment with her. Even though my brother's actions and the angry, territorial words exchanged when I had made my intentions known had belied his claims from earlier in the week of them being "just friends."

The way I could feel him staring daggers into the back of my head as I'd moved across the floor with her had definitely felt like there was something between them. The possibility of them together, laughing, kissing, touching—fucking... it made me lose my fucking head.

I wanted to rage against my promise to the man who'd all but ignored me in life, forcing me to clean up his fucking mess.

I wanted to crumble in the face of possibly losing what little relationship I had recovered with my brother forever.

I wanted her more than I needed my next breath.

But, instead of making her *mine* and owning her as my body demanded, I'd called her my brother's sloppy seconds before slinking off to my shower to wank my cock so hard it chaffed.

It was that emptiness in my chest's way of punishing me.

A subconscious way of hurting me for hurting her.

For taking a little sliver of light from her radiance, and once more reminding me that my reason for staying away was not just limited to my father or even my brother.

I need to stay away because my words and actions once more reminded me that I only know how to hurt and destroy. How to raze lives to the ground. I'm living proof of that fact, and I can't do that to her.

I won't.

That night we met, I was able to forget—if only for a fleeting moment—that I don't have to be the man this world has made me. I *could* be so much more.

I'd wanted to be. For her.

But she deserves so much more than I am capable of giving. She deserves nothing less than the sun, the moon, and all of the stars in the night sky.

Everything that had followed that night had firmly reinforced the fact that I can't even offer her tomorrow—let alone today. I'm broken.

Defective.

Needing the escape, I call the boys later in the afternoon. Following the last of my meetings on Tuesday, Nate and I fly to New York to spend some time with Caden before the first leg of their UK tour begins on Friday.

Knowing me as well as they do, it doesn't take long for my friends to realise something is wrong.

North opens the can of worms, delicately as ever.

"What the fuck crawled up your ass?"

Levelling him with a stare that would have lesser men shitting their pants, I deadpan, "Your mother."

Nate's deep chuckle beside me vibrates through the sofa, soon drowned out by North's guffaw. Having an ex-model as a mum invited a lot of MILF jokes back at school, but Cade's too laidback to give a rat's ass about any of them. However, he'll freely admit his mum is still hot as fuck.

And he'd be right. His father is one lucky prick and treats his woman like the queen she is. I can see a lot of him in Caden and his desire to do anything and everything to make Layla happy, though I can't see why when she's such a fucking cunt.

The vibrations from Nate's chuckle have ceased as he turns to look at me, his brow wrinkled in concern.

"Seriously, man, what gives? You never bunk off work, and you've definitely never turned down a quick transatlantic fuck with an air hostess or two, but both have happened this week."

Blowing out a breath I didn't even know I was holding, I raise my eyes to meet Nate's.

"Do you remember I met that blonde in Velvet the day Misdirection signed with Spellman Sounds two years ago?"

Both men nod. "Yeah, the one with that epic peachy ass." Of course, Nate would remember an ass like hers.

"Well, she works for me. At DeMarco Holdings. In London."

Both men's jaws fall open, and Caden's eyes pop so much they nearly fall out of his face.

"I've kept track of her, in a way, but from a safe distance after the promise I made to dad, you know? But she's Alex's PA now, though I reckon there's more to it than he's saying, judging by his actions."

Cade is the first to react, throwing a bunched-up napkin at my head.

"Come on, man. You can't still be hung up on her. At least

shoot your shot, man. You'll never know if you don't try. Right, Nate?"

Nate nods along before adding, "North's right. At least *ask* Alex what's going on there."

"I did a couple of weeks back. He said they're just friends."

Caden slaps his thigh in an ah-ha moment. "See? Told ya, idiot."

I level him with dead eyes. "Well, that *was* his story before the Gala on Saturday, but then he blew that to shit when he all but said they were friends... with benefits."

The two boys grimace as I go on.

"Not to mention the way he looks at her. It's like he'll kill me if I so much as glance in her goddamn direction." Then, inhaling deeply while I shake my head, I blow it out before murmuring quietly, "And it fucking *kills* me because I really felt like we were making inroads, he and I, but it's like... Peaches comes into the equation, and all bets are firmly off the table."

Two sets of eyes watch intently as I scrub my hands down my face, blowing out a heavy breath. "And after the last conversation that we had, well... I can safely say, she now sees me for the prick I am."

I screw my eyes up at the memory of hurting her yet again, even as I tell myself it's for the best.

"Look, man"—Cade leans forward, resting his elbows on his knees, concern dripping from every feature, all hints of his usual joker self gone—"maybe now is the time for you to ask her what *she* wants because from where we're sitting, you've never moved on from whatever the fuck happened two years ago. You've been stuck in a cycle of fuck, rinse, repeat your whole sodding life, Henry, and she's the closest we've seen you ever get to letting anyone in."

Throwing his hands up in the air, he adds, "Least if you ask, you'll get some answers. Hell, maybe she'll tell you to sling your hook, but at least you'll know!"

Nate and I are as still as statues by the time he has finished, unable to look away.

"What? What did I say?" He looks sincerely baffled as both of us begin to piss ourselves laughing.

"Caden North, the lady-killer to end all lady-killers, has been well and truly fucking henpecked."

Reclining in his seat, arms unfurled across the back of the sofa, legs braced apart, he can't help but nod slowly in self-satisfaction as the biggest shit-eating grin spreads across his smug face.

We spend the remainder of the week shooting the shit and catching up on all the current baby mama drama from an over-eager North, who has become a walking encyclopaedia for all things pregnancy and baby-related almost overnight. Still, the image of navy-blue eyes doesn't leave my mind once in all those days.

As my jet touches down in London on the evening of the Misdirection concert, I am heavily contemplating throwing caution to the wind by doing as Cade said and just turning up at her apartment and laying it all on the line.

I try and fail to think of the Alex I'd known as a child. The one who had loved me unfailingly right through my worst years to when my whole world had spun on its axis.

Physically shaking my head to stop my wandering thoughts, I climb into the waiting town car with an even more sombre than usual Nate in tow.

However, trapped in my own melancholy, I just stare out the window, not a word passing between us as the traffic whizzes by on this rainy, dull London evening.

It's not long before we've reached the O2 arena, where the band have already started their performance.

The suite for family and friends of Misdirection is jam-packed, and Layla, who is now "glowing" in her second trimester, according to one pussy-whipped, ex-bad-boy of rock, is holding court, front and centre.

Oh, goodie. I can hardly contain my delight.

Exchanging a grimace with a less than enthused Nate, we stand at the back of the crowded space, taking it all in.

Looking out on the packed O2 arena as Caden sings the song he'd penned for me, Nate, and his twin brother, Archer, who'd died when we were fifteen, I become lost in remembrance of simpler times. So lost that I almost miss that unforgettable flash of blonde hair passing by the wide-open door to our overcrowded suite.

It feels like fate. It's like a divine intervention of some kind. And so, I jog from the suite, on her heels, finding her with her head down, long tresses shielding her face from view, but I can tell that she is distraught from the frenetic movements of her body, trying to gulp in air as though she can't fill her lungs quickly enough.

My initial thought is that maybe now we can put this thing to rest between us. But I need to get a hold of myself, and she needs to stop being so fucking divine it blows my mind.

Hmm. Sounds doable. Ish.

Holding my hand out tentatively, I wait for her to spurn me again. After all, I've been a right cunt to her, and the hot and cold act I've got going on is even giving me whiplash.

However, I'm beyond surprised when she reaches out her petite hand and places it in my vastly larger one. My mind flashes back to two years ago when she first trusted me enough to hold my hand.

I'm almost floored by the surge of possessiveness that flows through my veins. The level of protectiveness that assaults me fills up my empty chest and makes me want to turn the world to ash for whatever has made her sad.

Turning her tear-streaked face up to mine, I can almost see her walls lower, and the similar long-standing fortress I've erected around my blackened heart shifts in its foundations.

She takes a hesitant step toward me before I close my fingers around her hand and draw her closer. Closer still until we are standing toe to toe.

Like we had at the Gala, but this feels entirely more intimate. Infinitely more organic.

And now that I've seen her in the flesh after all this time, I can't help being pulled into the gravitational force that makes up her very essence. She moves me.

Doing something that comes more naturally than breathing, but is inherently unlike me, I let her hand go now that she is within touching distance and close my arms around her small, fragile body. Then, sensing that I have done this, as though we are *that* inextricably intertwined so that she has a place to let it all out without the world watching her fall apart, her forehead falls against my chest as she sobs quietly, locked in the safety of my arms.

Standing still and tall, I feel a dormant part of my soul awaken in recognition of its other half as I inhale her very essence.

The realisation shoots through me like a lightning bolt.

I don't want to be like my dad as a rule, but more importantly, I don't want to make the same choices he did. I don't want to regret choosing the wrong woman like him, or in this case, not choosing the *right* one, especially when she keeps being set in my path, like serendipity.

Leaning down and placing a gentle kiss on the top of her golden head, I can feel her body jolt, as though she had been in a trance and was just now coming back to awareness.

Speaking with her face still turned in against my chest, I have to strain to hear her hoarse words above the noise of Misdirection and their legions of fans.

"I'm so alone. I'm..." Her voice hitches alongside my heart. "They're gone. Hearing 'Brothers' and the emotion poured into it, everything just hit me. How much I've lost—my sister, my parents, my home and...." She trails off, sighing deeply, and I think she won't finish her sentence for one long minute.

Instead, she takes a deep breath and swallows audibly.

"You, Henry. I feel like I lost you, which is ridiculous when I never *had* you to begin with, and that feels like the hardest loss to take because you're here, and I still can't have you. I'm an idiot to even think anything could ever be between us."

The innocuous way she voices all the thoughts that have been bouncing around in my fucking mind all week drives home just how broken she is underneath her fiery, feisty exterior and the idea that she resides in her own lonely world, just like me, takes root in my mind.

Could we be more alike than I had thought? Both of us have lost so much and yet here we are—despite it *all*.

Could we be the light to chase away the other's fears, the other's misgivings, the other's... brokenness? And suddenly, the vow I made to my father doesn't seem overly significant. Fixing things with Alex seems an impossibility. The only thing of value is this woman in my arms, giving me honesty and, dare I hope, zero judgement.

"Olivia, look at me."

Her face remains steadfastly facing my chest as her hand comes around my body to be placed palm down against my faltering heart.

I gently pinch her still quivering chin between my thumb and forefinger, forcing her to meet my gaze. Blue on green, each colour warring for dominance, both wanting so badly to forget everything outside of this moment.

"Peaches. Please."

She closes her eyes as though unable to face the longing in my eyes, her nostrils flaring the only indication she has heard me before she places both her hands on either side of my face, all fight relinquishing from her body.

And in that moment of her glorious surrender, I know as surely as I know I need air to breathe that if I don't kiss her now, right this fucking second, I'll regret it for the rest of my miserable fucking existence.

Releasing her chin, I wrap my hand around the nape of her neck.

Jesus, it feels like home.

Her eyes open and meet mine again, way too innocent to be real, before I close the distance between us. Our lips meet gently, hesitantly at first, before she inhales a ragged breath, deeply through her nostrils, then opens her mouth to allow our tongues to dance together in an age-old rhythm. Her low moan into my mouth shoots desire the length and breadth of my body.

Her kiss is as lethal as a shot of venom straight to my cold, dead heart, but instead of finishing me off, it brings the fucker back to life.

First, a slow throb.

Then a steady thump.

Followed by a galloping beat.

We kiss as though we'd never stopped. Her body moulds to

mine like we are meant to be. Her firm breasts are pushed hard against my chest as she presses against me, seeking more, wanting what only I can give her.

What only we can be when we come together.

Surely, she can feel my cock pressed hard and wanting against her abdomen. He knows her and recognises her as I lay claim to *my* Peaches, uncaring of the hustle and bustle of the ongoing concert around us.

Mine.

The single word echoes inside my brain repeatedly as I take every single ounce of what she has to give me.

I move to deepen the kiss and cup her heavenly ass, only to hear and feel her low moan of approval in my mouth. Her reaction makes my cock weep in my jocks as I feel her move her hand to the front of my pants that hold my straining dick.

Grasping it through the material of my jeans, she moves her palm against my erection, giving me the friction I so desperately need. At that moment, despite the debauchery I've been part of in my life, despite how I have needed so much more to get off with someone other than my own fucking hand, I'm barely able to stop my cock from coming under her touch.

As I desperately try to focus on holding myself together, I hear a familiar voice behind me, pulling us both back to reality in a flash.

"Rico?"

Slowly and unwillingly, I relinquish my hold on the fractured creature held within my embrace, turning to face my seething half-brother.

Fifteen

OLIVIA

As Henry breaks our kiss, all my senses come rushing back as though they had been on hiatus while a heady mix of desperate longing and unchecked desire run riot throughout my being. The feeling of being back in this man's arms, when it's been my heart's wish for more than two damn years now, it just feels so *right*. It feels like coming home.

The first thing I'm aware of is the distance he's put between us, which makes me scowl indignantly at the loss of his warmth and the safety of his embrace.

The second thing, and what knocks the grimace clear off my face, bringing me back to reality with a bang, is Alex's face, not entirely unlike a thundercloud, as he glares at both of us. I can see the disappointment in his usually soft gaze, sending my previously soaring heart hurtling into conflict.

"Liv? What did he do to you?"

His gentle but firm tone belies his frown as I struggle to set things right, knowing that some invisible boundary was crossed tonight. I don't want to be the cause of further dissension between these brothers. I won't be.

"Alex, I… I'm sorry. I lost track of time, and I—"

Alex reaches for me, putting his arm over my shoulder in a gesture that would look like he's claiming his territory to anyone who didn't know better.

Dropping a kiss to the top of my head in almost the exact same spot Henry had, he squeezes my shoulder. "It's okay, sweet girl. I've got you now."

My brow puckers in confusion. "Alex, what—"

I'm cut off by my best friend dropping his hand from my shoulder to rest lightly on the curve of my hip, just above my ass.

"What—" But before I can ask Alex what on earth he's playing at, Henry cuts me off, his eyes narrowing as his coolness hits me like an Arctic blast.

"It's been entirely too emotional, brother. Have a nice evening, Miss Parker."

He turns curtly, marching directly out of the arena, our eyes on his wildly broad back the whole way, but he doesn't look back. Not once.

Spinning to face my friend as I dislodge his arm from its perch on my lower back, I'm triggered and ready to do battle. He said he'd never tell me what to do, but his actions are a lot more heavy fucking handed, and that shit isn't going to fly, but he steps backwards, giving me space before holding his hand up pleadingly, an agonised look on his face.

"Liv, I'm just doing what's best for you. I told you, he's not good enough for you. Can't you see? He'll *ruin* you."

"Can't *you* see? That's my choice to make, Alex. *Mine*."

Turning and walking away before I say or do anything that may damage us irreparably, I stop after a couple of steps, my back still turned. "I have been a puppet my entire life, Alex, you know that. I can't—no, I *won't* go back to being powerless ever again. I choose how I live my life, and no one, not even you, who I love beyond measure, will tell me what to do."

I continue to walk toward the exit until Alex closes the distance between us, placing himself between me and the door with a hangdog expression on his face.

"Liv." Alex heaves a sigh, like he has the weight of the world on his shoulders. "I won't ever tell you what to do. That's not my place."

He takes another step closer.

"I'll always have your back. I'll always be in your corner. *Always*. You're my favourite person in this whole world, and your happiness means everything to me."

Scrubbing his hands down his face before shaking his head as though to shed his mind of unwanted thoughts, my best friend looks at me with such deep intent I am fixed to the spot, and my stomach physically churns as he finishes what he has to say without inflection.

"But, Liv, my brother can't keep it in his pants and has the penchant to turn everything he touches to shit."

In the deepest reaches of my soul, I feel that Henry DeMarco is not who he pretends to be, and I want now, more than ever, to disclose the fact that I've met Henry before starting at DeMarco. But now isn't that time. Emotions are overwrought, and I can feel the tension emanating off of Alex from a mile away, so I take the only avenue left.

"I'm genuinely not feeling up to going back inside, Alex. Mind if I just call it a night?"

I can sense he wants to push things, but being the kind of person he is, he just smiles indulgently and calls Samuel to ensure he's ready to drop me home; despite my assurances, I can just Uber.

"Come on. I'll walk you out."

Minutes later, we exit the arena together, and Alex gives me a gentle side hug before I slip into the backseat of Samuel's waiting car.

Pulling out into the busy Friday evening traffic, I look back to see him standing there staring after me with his hands stuffed in his pockets and the saddest expression I've ever seen on his face.

What is really going on between these brothers?

The journey back to the apartment is quick, and as I let myself in, I see the flat-packed boxes I'd bought for packing for my move. I pop on some *12 Monkeys* as background noise and begin the arduous task of packing up my entire life into a handful of brown boxes.

My mind is an unnatural disaster as I try to focus on the task at hand, but it's impossible to keep my thoughts from wandering back to that kiss.

Shivers of sheer delight race up my spine, settling at the nape of my neck as I recall each brush of our lips, each touch of our tongues, each mingled breath. My heart kicks up a notch as my cheeks flame bright pink at the thought of openly feeling his hardness through his pants—where anyone could have seen us. And they probably did.

My eyebrows gather as I remember Alex's arrival and his ill-advised attempt at putting his brother off. That's the very last thing I want, if I'm being totally honest.

Knowing that I need to sort this out with him, I grab my phone and shoot him a text.

ME

Can we do lunch on Monday? 1 pm in the DeMarco canteen?

The reply is almost instantaneous.

ALEX

Of course, Liv. See you then.

Well, here's hoping we can clear the air then. One thing is for sure, I'll be saying those three important words.

Henry is McHottie.

I've just put the last of my packable belongings into the final box, as I hear the girls twist a key in our front door. I'll add the last couple of bits over the week before moving day arrives.

There's a loud rap at my bedroom door, followed by Jo sing-songing my name.

"O-liv-eeeeeeeeee-aaaaaaaaaa!"

Without waiting for my reply, both girls shove open my door, with poor Josie falling inside, obviously three sheets to the wind.

"Where did you go tonight, baby girl? You missed all the backstage action, and let me just tell you, those Misdirection boys know how to par-tay!"

Nola snorts as Josie continues.

"You should have seen the shit that went down, though, seriously. Everyone was forced to sign DNAs leaving the arena. It was a shitshow."

Nola's giggles reach fever pitch at Jo's obvious error.

"Baby, you mean NDAs, and FYI, that means we can't tell our girl here either, so zippity zip that loose lip of yours before it gets you in trouble."

My curiosity is piqued, but despite Jo's obvious inebriation and her desire to share the events of the night with me, I know there'll be a fallout if she opens her mouth, so I rapidly change the subject.

"Ta-dah! I'm basically already dust, girls. This time next week, and it'll be like I was never even here."

Nola pouts her coral painted lips as her lover stumbles across the room to sweep me up in the biggest hug.

"Girl, you have always got a place here with us. Forever and ever and ever. We are going to miss the hell out of you. Who will listen to me moan when Nola forgets to replace the coffee, hmm?"

The lady in question chuckles loudly at this, knowing full well it drives both Jo and me insane when she forgets, which is all the time.

"Come on, drunky."

Jo shrugs her off. "And *don't* get me started on how she never replaces the toilet roll. Ugh!"

I can't help my loud chortle as Nola tries again. "Let's leave our girl to finish up, baby. It's late, and you've got work tomorrow."

Bestowing me with a sloppy kiss intended to land on my cheek but somehow ends up on my shoulder, Jo crab walks from the room, holding her arm up in farewell.

Nola goes to follow but stops at the door to turn and look at me.

"Are you okay, Liv? You were so excited about the show tonight, and then you just up and disappeared. It was so unlike you. You had me worried; we both were."

I love this girl. Meeting her changed my life in many ways, and I'll be forever grateful for her and Josie's friendship.

I'd fallen on my feet when I met these two; that's a fact.

But tonight is not the time, and that's soon confirmed when we hear drunky down the hall shouting, "Noooooooo-laaaaaaaaa! I'm going to start without youuuuuu!"

The woman in question shrugs sheepishly, eliciting a laugh from my smiling lips at their obvious lust for each other while simultaneously reaching for my earphones. Then, leaving me feeling lighter than I have all night, Nola swiftly closes the door leaving me to stew amongst my packing and my unwanted thoughts.

Arriving at my desk bright and early on Monday morning, I'm confounded by a single blue rose with a small note attached.

Approaching it like it possibly has rabies, I eventually pluck it from its resting place, unable to keep from brushing my fingertips across the soft petals, and read the note, written in an obviously masculine hand.

Please forgive me for leaving so abruptly and callously.

Yours,

Henry

What.

The.

Fuck?

This man is like Jekyll and Hyde. Yet, even so, I can't help the tiny bubbles of delight that keep popping within my stomach for the rest of the day. Things like this don't happen in real life. This is like something from one of my romance novels.

Could he be a Prince Charming in disguise?

Freya's mouth drops open when she spots the flower tucked away, almost out of sight, on the corner of my desk.

"Is it from him?" she mouths, pointing her forefinger skyward, indicating the floor above us, to which I nod before I can catch myself, unable to stop a dimpled grin from breaking out on my face. And in true Freya style, she can't let it go, so even though she doesn't make one of her signature announcements, the entire staff of 25 have been by my desk for one reason or another by the time lunch has rolled around.

They're about as subtle as a car crash, but they don't mention the rose, even though they all nearly strain their eyesight in an attempt to read the note tucked in beside it.

I'm sorting through Alex's work week when I spot an email from the man himself, which I find strange, as we're due to meet for lunch in a little over an hour.

> **Sender:** Alexander DeMarco
> (alexanderdemarco@demarcoholdings.com)
>
> **Recipient:** Olivia Parker
> (oliviaparker@demarcoholdings.com)
>
> **Subject:** Banished to the Desert
>
> Hey sweet girl,
> I've been unexpectedly and unceremoniously (thank you, CEO dearest!) sent to the Dubai office for the next month. I got the call late last night and am only just now getting around to checking in.
>
> I'm sorry we'll have to raincheck our lunch. I promise I'll get you extra arancini next time.
>
> Please run through my calendar and I'll call soon to go over the immediate changes with you.
>
> Love you!

Had Alex not aired his suspicions in his email, I'd have known a mile off that this last-minute transfer—that I'm the last to find out about, mind you—has Henry DeMarco written *all* over it.

And even so, I don't know whether to be relieved that I've avoided a hard conversation or disappointed to still have that conversation hanging over my head.

Either way, I decide to join Martha for an earlier than anticipated lunch. She doesn't make unnecessary conversation, and that's just what I'm in the mood for right this moment.

Disembarking from the elevator, I spot an extremely pissed looking Andrea as I try to return to my desk. Heaving out the breath I didn't realise I was holding, I brace myself for impact. She fucking hates me, and now I won't even have Alex here as a buffer from her machinations.

"Olive! You broke the copier earlier and never reported it to fucking I.T."

I can't help the fleeting wish that she'd choked on Henry's cock all those weeks ago, the thought causing one side of my mouth to turn up in a subconscious smirk.

"Do you think it's funny? I had to spend almost my entire lunch hour fixing your cock-up!"

Her unfortunate choice of words makes me choke on the snort of laughter I almost manage to contain. Her face is nearly the same colour as her hair at this stage.

"Okay, *Andi*. First of all, my name is Olivia, which you *damn well know*. And second, you were the last person to use the copier on Friday evening, and, if memory serves, you said, and I quote, 'tough shit for the unlucky fucker left to deal with this on Monday. I'm out of here, folks!' So, back the hell off, or I'll have no choice but to lodge a complaint upstairs."

And with that, I shoulder past her and march to my desk, feeling like a million pounds. This Liv doesn't let anyone walk all over her, least of all cum buckets like that wench.

Settling at my desk, I begin to sort through emails before one, in particular, catches my eye.

Sender: Enrico DeMarco, CEO
(enricodemarco@demarcoholdings.com)

Recipient: Olivia Parker
(oliviaparker@demarcoholdings.com)

Subject: Colour

It has come to my attention that I don't know your favourite colour. Please reply at your earliest convenience.

Sincerely,
H

My earlier merriment bubbles to the surface, with fireworks beginning to explode in my stomach, extending to my trembling limbs as I type my response, nibbling nervously on my bottom lip as I go.

Sender: Olivia Parker
(oliviaparker@demarcoholdings.com)

Recipient: Enrico DeMarco, CEO
(enricodemarco@demarcoholdings.com)

Subject: RE: Colour

I'm not entirely sure I should be engaging you, Mr DeMarco.

But if you must know, my favourite colour is the one found just as the sun is setting after a long, hot summer's day. It's a mixture of fire and light, and each hue has the ability to remind me that I'm lucky that I get to witness such beauty at the end of another glorious day.

I've told you mine. Now it's your turn.

Regards,
Olivia

Despite waiting on a reply to ping in, one never arrives, and I leave the office feeling a little—more like a lot—bereft, though the blue rose between my fingers as I climb into the waiting town car helps to soothe the burn.

Sixteen

OLIVIA

The next day, another single blue rose appears on my desk as if by magic, with another note which reads:

Please forgive me for sending Alex to Dubai.

Yours,

Henry

Well. I can't help the huff of laughter that escapes me.

At least he's owning up to that manipulation, regardless of the fact it would be apparent to a blind man he'd gotten him out of the way intentionally.

"Another one today, Liv! Someone really wants to impress you." Freya, who's perched her rear on the corner of my desk, sends a knowing wink my way, causing me to roll my eyes skyward in a good-natured fashion. She's incorrigible.

As I'm settling in to get everything started, my mobile rings.

Glancing at the screen, I can see that it's Alex calling. My stomach bottoms out at how we left things, but I rapidly hit the *Answer* button before I can talk myself out of it.

"Alex." I'm sure he can hear the relief in my voice. "I'm so glad you called. You're in Dubai?"

"Liv, this is the life!"

Hearing the smile in his voice makes me smile in answer. My shoulders relax from the subconsciously held tense position they've been in since Saturday and my whole heart feels lighter at our normal easy exchange as he continues happily.

"The only thing missing is you, sweet girl!"

We both collapse into gales of laughter, our disagreement of the past weekend no longer hanging between us, just as I spy Andrea making a beeline for my desk.

"Hold on one sec." Then, placing my hand over the mouthpiece, I look up to meet her glare with one of my own.

"Olive, you are at work, and the time for personal phone calls is at lunch or after five. So you can leave your mobile at my desk in the mornings from now on if you are going to insist on being so unprofessional."

Where does this bitch get off? Taking my hand off the mouthpiece, I return to my call.

"I'm here, Mr DeMarco. Sorry about that. *Some staff* are using your absence as an excuse to try to intimidate me."

Her eyes open wide, and she retreats at top speed back to her own end of the office, making my lips inch upwards in a hint of a smile.

Olivia 1.

Cum bucket 0.

"Is everything okay there?" The smile has gone out of his voice, and I'm quick to attempt to return it. "Everything is perfect, I promise. Just Andrea being her usual cunt-ish self."

He chuckles down the line. "Cunt-ish? Christ almighty, Liv, what would Father Thomas say!"

We spend another half an hour on the line, during which time he gives me the details of the hotel he's staying at, along with emailing over his itinerary for the upcoming two weeks. Of course, I'll still be dealing with his UK-based itinerary, rescheduling meetings and sorting his personal commitments too.

"Alex, you've got a dinner booked off in your schedule for Thursday evening, but it doesn't have any details other than the time. Do I need to move that?"

He heaves a world-weary sigh. "Ugh. I'd forgotten about it. I'm booked for dinner with Mum. Just back from another *retreat*, and looking for more money, no doubt."

My heart fills with sorrow for my best friend. His mum has several annual "retreats." He's never exactly gone into why she needs them, just that she has a delicate mind from when his dad left. She'd never gotten over him or his abandonment of them, and although both of us know things shouldn't be as bad as they are with the kind of help she's forking out for, it's not my place to force him to address the issues with his mum, no matter how much I want to.

"Do you need me to reschedule?"

"You're good to offer, sweet girl. I'll sort it out. Thank you, though."

The unspoken words lie heavily between us as silence fills the line for the first time on this call, until I can't take it any longer.

"Alex, you need to know… Henry is Mc—"

But before I can finish, Alex speaks up, drowning out my words. "Gotta go, sweet girl."

And with that, without even a farewell, he's gone, and my

heart is heavy all over again.

Sorting through the emails and requests that have inundated my inbox since last night, I immediately spot what I was waiting for all day yesterday.

Sender: Enrico DeMarco, CEO (enricodemarco@demarcoholdings.com)

Recipient: Olivia Parker (oliviaparker@demarcoholdings.com)

Subject: RE: RE: Colour

A sunset doesn't touch on your beauty, Peach.
As for my favourite colour, only one comes to mind. Have you ever seen a stormy sea with the waves swelling and cresting? The sheer beauty is awe-inspiring.

You need only look in the mirror if you haven't, because your eyes are that exact shade and twice as breathtaking.

H

When I've finished reading, my chest rises and falls rapidly as my heart threatens to jump right out of my chest. I can't help nibbling on my bottom lip as I re-read the email another two times. A lump forms in my throat at these words, and I swallow roughly in an attempt to dislodge it.

It takes several long minutes before the goosebumps have receded, the lump has dissipated, and I feel myself return to a semi-normal state, settling into the right mindset to get into my workday.

The day passes without incident, with no more communication

between us; however, I can't deny that his gestures have cracked through my already lowered walls.

Despite the well-meaning warnings from Alex, the only thing that dominates my thoughts for the rest of the workweek is Henry.

It's hard to forget about him, considering he's either placed himself or had someone else place in his stead a blue rose each day on my desk, and each day the sight of it sets my soul aflame.

Each exquisite rose chips away at my wavering resolve.

Each divine bloom questions my ability to stay away.

On Friday morning, after I've tucked my daily rose away into my top drawer, the previous days having drawn unwanted crowds to my desk, I am kept excruciatingly busy right up until lunchtime. So I decide I'll just grab a quick salad and eat it at my desk, but before I can leave the floor, I get a call from HR.

"Liv, honey." She beams. "I'm so glad I caught you."

"Is everything okay, Martha?"

"Oh, everything is *great,* sweetie. I wanted to let you know you have been given the rest of the day off, courtesy of Mr DeMarco. Well, courtesy of Alex. He emailed me earlier, telling me you have your big move today, so you can take the rest of the day off to get it done quicker. Isn't that wonderful?"

The smile that brightens up my face is big and genuine. Even from Dubai, he's still looking out for me.

I bid Martha a farewell and return to my desk, where I grab my things to leave, happy but already exhausted at the thought of what's ahead of me. As I'm looping my bag over my shoulder, my desk phone rings.

"Good afternoon, Alex DeMarco's office. How may I help you?"

"Have you had lunch yet? I've ordered far too much."

Promptly recognising that singularly electrifying voice, my heart speeds up, and my palms get sweaty before I shakily agree to meet him upstairs. Then, hanging up, I grab my coat and take the elevator up, arriving at his door within five minutes of his call.

Tapping gently, remembering what I'd witnessed the last time I'd entered the same door uninvited, I hear his voice call from within.

"Come on in, Olivia. Make yourself comfortable."

I cross the threshold, and my smile widens as I sit down in the seat across the desk from Henry's own. "Thank you for inviting me."

He makes quick work of divvying up several different types of Thai food and, after handing me a plate that holds way more than I would ever manage, he sits back in his seat and tucks in.

He handles his chopsticks the same way he does everything else in his life; like he was born to do it.

We eat in silence for several minutes, avoiding eye contact until the words I've been anxious to say tumble from my lips.

"Thank you. For… for the roses." I blush at my stuttering. "They're beautiful."

He raises his eyes to mine, pinning me with an intensity so blinding I have to force myself to hold his gaze. "They can't compare to how exquisite you are."

Unable to last under the ferocity of his gaze, I drop my eyes to my food and push it around my plate, suddenly not in the least bit hungry.

Lifting my head to meet his steady stare again, something inside me shifts as I remember the newly empowered Olivia, and she refuses to be intimidated by him or anyone.

"So, Thai food. Is it your favourite?" I'm drawing inspiration from his emails earlier, and he well knows it.

His lips twitch imperceptibly as he answers. "Well, it's the safest choice when you plan on having company."

"Is that right?" My eyes narrow as my chin tilts upwards in rebellion, and I ask, "So you ordered enough for two, and I'm invited at the last minute. I'm your second choice, then?"

Sitting forward in his chair, he places his food on the desk before steepling his fingers and resting them under his chin as he observes me in silence for several long beats. At the same time, I hold his gaze unblinkingly, wearing my insolence proudly, until his words send my head spinning, along with my undeniably obsessed heart.

"Peaches…" He waits a moment. "You could never be anyone's second choice. You're spectacular inside and out. Anyone who doesn't know that immediately is a fucking idiot."

His tone is matter of fact, his greens shining with authenticity, yet I can't stop the fleeting thought that I obviously wasn't spectacular enough to make him stay on the night we met.

We sit with our eyes firmly on each other, not eating, not speaking, barely even breathing, until he asks, "So. Any plans this weekend?"

And just like that, the moment has passed, and I can breathe again as I feel the tension slowly ebb from the room.

"Um, yeah, actually. I do." His jaw ticks, something I've seen him do when he's fighting speaking his mind, but I surge forth, undeterred. "I'm moving today… into my own apartment. I'll be living alone for the first time in my life. I've been with my friends since my parents died."

"I meant to tell you how sorry I am. For your loss." He pauses, as though unsure for the first time since I walked into the room.

"Do you mind me asking what happened? I... I know a little about losing parents."

"Umm, no, it's okay. They died in a house fire two years ago."

His face crumples in sorrow.

"I'm so very sorry. A sudden passing can be hard to accept."

"I felt relief more than anything." My hand flies to cover my mouth, having not meant to voice the words that had lain dormant deep inside my soul, never to be spoken aloud.

Henry's intense gaze holds mine for a beat before he speaks again. "I can relate."

My eyes widen as, almost by its own volition, my hand drops from my mouth. "I've never said that out loud before—but it's true. My immediate response was relief. Relief at not abiding by their prehistoric way of living; their holier than thou bullshit that I never bought into, especially after Holly's death. My parents loved me—in their own way, but they loved their religion and their standing in the community more than they ever loved their kids."

Henry hasn't moved a muscle as he takes in my word vomit. Old habits die hard, I guess.

"My own father died three days after I met you. Our relationship was... fraught, to say the least, so I can empathize with what you've had to overcome." He stops in contemplation. Indecision plays swiftly across his handsome face as he debates whether or not to share the next words that come out of his mouth.

"I'm sorry too."

At his confused look, I continue. "For *your* loss. I'm sorry."

He nods his thanks, his eyes holding mine for a long beat before he looks away, deciding to continue with whatever he was at odds over saying a moment ago.

"Actually, I got a call from his..." He shrugs, before continuing.

"His paramour, for lack of a better description. Unfortunately, he'd gone into cardiac arrest and been admitted to the Royal London Hospital."

His eyes find mine once more as he clearly assesses my reaction to his next words. "I took the call just moments after I left you that night."

I can't help my sharp inhalation. There *was* a reason he hadn't come back, and it wasn't because he was a fuckboy who'd had his fun with the token virgin blonde. His dad was dying, and I'd spent the last two years resenting all memory of him for something beyond his control.

"Charlotte—or Lottie—that's her name, called from my father's phone to let me know he'd just been brought to the Royal London by ambulance. He never fully recovered. Just enough to share some long overdue truths… among…" His lips twist before he finishes, "...other *requests*."

I can't help myself from opening up more to this version of Henry, Alex's caution a long-forgotten memory.

"I'm so sorry, Henry. I had no idea."

"How could you have."

We sit quietly until he leans back in his chair and speaks in a tone that isn't quite accusatory, yet I can't help but feel the veiled intention behind his words.

"Anyway, my friends had seen you leave with Alex. So—"

His eyes roam over the cityscape, never once meeting mine after the words have fallen from his lips.

And while he sits in silence, I can clearly see so many more pieces of the puzzle that make up this man fall into place. And the more that fall, the more I can see that my intuition is correct. Henry *is* more than he appears, more than he shows, under that facade.

Underneath that suit he wears in place of armour lies a soul that calls to mine. A kind soul with a good heart that has never been given the chance to flourish.

I know it. I can *feel* it.

Yet, right now, his provocative words have incited me, and I can't hold my tongue despite myself.

"So, you *assumed* Alex and me were more than friends, is that it?"

I can't withhold the ire from my tone. I'm pissed off with men making *assumptions*. And in particular, the DeMarco men! So, I don't stop there.

"You *assumed* that what you and I had shared that night meant nothing to me?"

He's utterly impassive, looking out over London like a king surveying his birth right. And Jesus, does it piss me off.

"I have no idea why *you* get to be the one who's so pissed off. After all, *I'm* the fucking idiot who waited for you that night."

His eyes swing to meet my narrowed ones as his jaw tightens almost imperceptibly, yet he doesn't say whatever is so obviously on the tip of his tongue. I hadn't planned on disclosing that fact. How I'd kept my promise and stayed in the damn Powder Room.

So, before I can word vomit any more long-buried feelings about that night, I clamp my lips shut and silently will him to open up even further, begging him with my eyes, but it appears it's too late.

Henry's invisible but impenetrable walls had lowered enough to allow me a glimpse into the man beyond the mask; however, they are firmly on the way back up as I see his eyes harden. Finally, he straightens himself to stand, walking to the floor-to-ceiling windows to stare across the cityscape.

Knowing we've reached an impasse, I sigh internally and I rise to stand too.

"Well, I was just on my way out when you rang down. Alex gave me the rest of the day off to get a head start."

His shoulders rise visibly at my mention of Alex's kindness. "Ah yes, Alex rides in on his white horse and saves the day. The hero to my villain in your eyes."

Kind and polite Henry brings out my inner bumbling idiot, and while she's not the coolest person ever, she's alright.

Offensive and mean Henry brings out my inner bitch, and that's where I'm headed at light fucking speed.

Bristling with barely restrained anger at his rude presumption, I try to keep a lid on her for another minute or two until I can escape the floor.

"Alex and I are best *friends*."

Spinning to face me, he pins me with a look as he grates out, "Yeah, right. Try telling *him* that. What do you think we were getting into it about at the Gala, hmm?"

I will myself to stop my face from falling. Blinking several times owlishly, my mind is brimming with questions I still need to ask Alex.

Squaring my shoulders, I tilt my chin upward ever so slightly and thrust my chest forward as I pull myself up to my still fairly short full stature. This *lunch date* is souring more quickly than a carton of milk left out of the fridge on a hot summer's day, and I can't help feeling as though his actions are to blame, which only incites me further.

"If you thought I was seeing your brother or even suspected it, why would you be dropping expensive roses on my desk every day with intimate handwritten notes or popping flirty emails into my inbox?"

He strides across the office until he's right in my face, glaring down upon me like a vengeful god in all his glory. Every inch of my body vibrates into awareness at his proximity—to the extent that I can almost feel the visceral pull his body has.

His beautiful green and gold eyes take me in for a moment before the fire within him slowly diminishes at whatever he sees on my face. My breathing stalls in my throat when he visibly softens, his eyes filling with a longing I see daily in my own reflection. He reaches a hand around the nape of my neck, and I can't help but exhale heavily in total and utter completion before he pulls me forward to place a gentle kiss on my brow.

Still, with his lips against my skin, he speaks straight to my foolhardy heart. "Because *I'm* the fucking idiot. Because I stupidly forced myself to stay away, Peaches. And now that you're *here*, in my world, in my periphery, so close to me, I can't fight the urge to see you, to know you, to *want* you. If you were to be mine, to be really and truly *mine*, I'd never let you go."

I'm stunned into silence, my mind racing as it tries to catch up to what this man has just said. For so long now, I've dreamt of this being a reality. Of this being *my* reality.

Prince Charming doesn't have anything on Henry DeMarco.

We stand in each other's space as time passes irrelevantly. It may have been a minute; it may have been an hour before there's a rap on the door, breaking the spell.

Stumbling backwards, life returning to my frozen body, I reach for the door. He's attacked my senses with his artfully chosen words, and now bumbling Liv is back in full effect.

"Thank…thank you for lunch. It was wonderful. Uh, really… excellent." Awkwardly pointing back and forth between the two of us, like some sideshow freak, as Henry looks on with a smirk playing around the edges of his mouth, I manage to squeak out, "See you Monday, yeah?"

Opening the door to find none other than Andrea on the other side, my heart and my hopes make a quick swan dive. Her plump lips rise upwards into a full-blown sneer as she shoulders past me.

Hard enough that I almost stumble.

"You wanted to see me, Rico." His name is a purr from her throaty, seductive voice, sending a shot of unquestionable envy to my depraved, jealous heart.

Was she his first choice?

Feeling physically sick at the knowledge that she can only be up here for one thing, and I was just filling time as he waited, I race from the floor, hurt and more confused than ever.

Seventeen

OLIVIA

Hitting the button for the ground floor and praying that no one calls the elevator to see my barely bridled tears, I can't help one of them sliding down my cheek as I recall the safety of his arms, the sincerity of his words, the sense of belonging. Only for it all to be blown away by the appearance of his fuck buddy.

Heaving out a deep breath, I mumble to myself, "When are you going to get a clue, idiot!"

Alex has warned me several times now, and despite *knowing* he has my best interests at heart, I've still let Henry wriggle his way in.

I begin to relax as the elevator has almost reached the ground floor, when it grinds to a gentle halt on the second floor, and Martha steps on.

"Olivia, my dear. What are you still doing here, honey?"

The sight of a friendly face is too much, and I can't stop the barrage of tears as they fall unbidden, causing Martha's face to drop.

Hitting the *Emergency Stop* button, she gathers me in her motherly embrace and just holds me, waiting for the onslaught to recede, and once it does, we stand there for several long minutes while her arms chase away the worst of the sting.

Once I've pulled myself together, mostly, she hits the button again, and we descend to the foyer, where she grasps my hand to lead me out onto the bustling footpath and across the street to a small, hole-in-the-wall pub I've never noticed before.

"Mike, can I get two shots of tequila, please?" A greying gnarled old bartender, in a blue flannel shirt, nods as we sit on the bar stools in front of him, the only two patrons in the place.

Turning so that the tops of our knees are touching, Martha takes my hand in hers again. She reaches for the shots Mike has just deposited in front of us, holding one out for me to accept with my free hand.

Gripping it like it's a lifeline, I put it on my head without pause, only to smack it on the counter with a wince and find she's holding the other shot out for me, too, to which I pop a brow in question.

"Sometimes, honey"—a wry grin appears on her face, encouraging my own lips to twitch in response—"one just isn't going to cut it. And crying at work warrants two, at the very least."

Gesticulating for a repeat order to Mike, she rubs my hand between hers in a comforting way. Her warm actions make my heart lighter already. "So, come on, then. Out with it. What happened?"

Nibbling my lower lip between my teeth as I draw my brows

together in confusion, I wonder if perhaps I should open up to her, but she astounds me when she leans forward, almost conspiratorially, to ask, "It's Henry, right?"

I have zero clue how she knows, but before I have time to debate the pros and cons of inviting a third party into the hot mess residing in my brain, my mouth moves almost of my own volition.

"I met Henry over two years ago before his father passed. Before my parents died. We had this… I don't know what to even call it. This… connection, like an invisible tether that we couldn't see or touch, but was there as surely as I'm sitting in front of you right now. I didn't know he was Alex's brother or future CEO of a multi-national company. Jesus, I was so sheltered I had no idea what a CEO even was."

"So, you were friends with Alex first?" I nod. "And you met Henry but didn't know they were brothers?"

Another nod.

"And then?"

"Well," I murmur, "then he left after telling me his name was Henry, but without exchanging anything more than a broken promise."

And saliva.

"Over lunch today, I found out why he broke that promise. He told me he'd received a call that his dad was gravely ill, and he had rushed to his side. I'd waited for him that night but left with Alex and some girlfriends and have spent the last two years caught in a cycle of regret, reminiscence, and resentment…" I trail off as she continues to look at me very intensely.

I go on, under her fervent stare.

"I knew Alex had an older brother, but he's always called him Enrico, so… so it never even entered my head to ask more about something he was so undeniably closed off about, you know? It wasn't until just before the Gala that I realised they were brothers and, well, we all saw what happened there, didn't we?"

Shrugging helplessly, as I lay it all bare for my friend, who is more a mother figure than my own had been to me, I look at her with wide eyes, taking in her demure figure that belies the strength underneath.

She gazes into the distance and speaks so quietly I have to strain to hear, even though there's nothing but the background noise of Mike loading the dishwasher.

"I remember when Henry took up the mantle after his father had passed. He was adamant about doing right by the man, despite his father's treatment of him. And his brother."

"You knew Henry's father?" She nods her head. "Yes, very well. We started at the company around the same time. His own father was a moody shit, but he was fair, and even though women in business would have been very unpopular then, he gave me the chance to move on from your basic secretary role, which is where I'd started. Now, consider that the whole industry back then was nothing like today's world. Of course, it's a lot more complicated these days, but Henry runs a tight ship, and he's good at his job, no thanks to his father."

"Were they not close, then?"

"Goodness, no, honey. I remember when Enrico married his first wife, Katherine, or Kat, as she went by. It was like she was the sun and his whole world revolved around her. When he took the reins, he brought her in as an advisor, a role she excelled at, and it was her input that truly helped propel the company into the global giant it is today. They'd often leave Henry running riot around the building—not where we're based now, you know? It was a lot smaller back then. Anyway, he had the entire staff wrapped around his pudgy little finger, none more so than Kat. Their bond was a thing of beauty." Her face changes, her eyes becoming veiled as her lips turn down.

"When she got sick, Henry was only four years old. Just a baby! She fought it for two years. Cancer. Ravaged her until she was a shadow of her former self, and even so, she pushed on for *them*. Enrico and Henry, they were her reason for living." She stops for a moment, shaking her head as though she can hardly believe it despite living through it.

"Eventually, she passed, leaving a gaping hole in the lives of her husband and young son."

Regardless of how I'm feeling towards adult Henry right now, I can't help my heart's overflowing sympathy for the child he was when he lost the most significant female influence of his life. And judging from our conversation the first night we met—a conversation I can still remember word for word—it's something he has never entirely accepted.

Knocking a shot of tequila back, Martha hands the other one to me, holding two fingers up for Mike to replenish. "When Kat was diagnosed, they travelled worldwide to find a solution. They tried everything. And so, they hired a nanny for Henry to accompany them on their endeavour. I don't know if you've met Alex's mum, Lauren…"

Grimacing, I nod. "Yeah. Eh, she's not my biggest fan."

Martha snorts out a laugh. "I wouldn't feel bad about that, honey. She's a fucking bitch if ever I met one. I'll never know how Alex turned out half as well-rounded as he is."

My eyes are wide, my mouth dropped open, catching flies at the shock of hearing Martha speak about anyone in such a manner, but she continues as if she's not just blown my mind.

"Lauren was their nanny."

My ears can scarcely believe what they are hearing, and true to form, my eyes almost fall from their sockets as Martha nods slowly. "An innocent-looking, beautiful nineteen-year-old when she was hired. By all accounts, she gave a fantastic interview, coming highly recommended. But, unfortunately, at least from what I witnessed, she never really interacted with Henry, called him Enrico despite both parents preferring the English version, at least initially. His baptismal name had been purely to satisfy his Nonno.

"She had a blatant obsession with Enrico, although she kept Kat sweet enough that dismissing her was never even on the table."

Her eyes narrow at the memory of whatever is coming next, almost as though she's forgotten I'm here.

"When Kat passed, it was two months before Enrico came back to the office and the day he did, looking tired, rumpled, and no longer the man he'd been, he announced he was getting married to Lauren. Then, less than eight months later, Alex was born, which shocked everyone to say the very least and, though his arrival didn't mean much of anything to either parent, as sad as it is to say that, he was doted on by Henry from the very start."

And the hits keep on coming…

"That boy had barely turned seven years old, and he was feeding, winding, and changing nappies like a seasoned pro. Lauren refused to hire help; obviously, it would reflect poorly on her to need help, considering her previous occupation. Regardless, Henry adored his little brother, and as Alex grew, he adored his big brother in return."

We sip on two margaritas Mike drops on the bar without being asked, confirming my suspicion that Martha is undoubtedly a regular here as she sits back quietly to let me take the time to absorb what she's just blown me away with.

I'm mostly floored at the thought of Henry and Alex being true brothers—none of this estranged animosity they've got going on. And I can't help but wonder if perhaps there's a way to fix things.

Maybe whatever happened isn't as deep-seated as they make out. Maybe their relationship *can* be mended.

"After Alex turned three, Enrico bought a place here in the city proper, and that was the end of office visits for both boys. I didn't see Henry again for another eight years when he started work at the bottom of the food chain, slowly working his way up the ladder with an inherent knack for knowing what moves to make, *just* like his mum. It wasn't until after Enrico's passing that Henry brought Alex on board and fast-tracked him to his current position. But the first time I saw both boys together, well, now men, they were barely tolerant of each other, so whatever happened to their relationship happened in the interim."

Draining her drink and signalling for two more, meaning I'll probably spend the night fighting a waking hangover instead of moving, her eyes meet and hold mine. Both hands firmly clasping my own as she speaks again.

"Olivia, what I'm about to say now should have no bearing on your relationship with the DeMarco brothers, but I'd feel remiss if I kept the knowledge to myself when you are so desperate for answers."

She waits for half a beat.

"At the Gala..." My sharp inhalation cuts her off. I hadn't expected this. Nodding for her to continue as I remove one hand from her grip to grasp my margarita, draining it in one gulp, she squeezes the hand she holds.

"At the Gala, when the management dance was announced... Henry asked Alex if he could dance with you."

He asked to dance with me?

She pauses to take in my reaction, presumably to ensure I'm not dead from a coronary before she floors me.

"Alex told him that your friendship had blossomed into something more since you'd started at DeMarco. When I took in Henry's reaction, he seemed caught off guard by this, like he was under a different impression. Then he asked Henry, nicely at first, mind you, to just continue the tradition his father had started by asking me to partner with him."

I'm sorry, what?

I knew he'd insinuated it at the concert, but knowing he was purposely trying to force Henry to believe there was something between Alex and me—to make Henry back off from his pursuit, taking my choice away from me, albeit in a much less straightforward manner, pissed me the hell off.

While my mind is going fifty million miles per hour, Martha keeps the blows coming.

"Henry told him he'd waited long enough, but after seeing you there that night and in person, he couldn't stay away from you any longer. Which, after what you've just told me, makes perfect sense. He's been thinking of you for years, that much is clear. Alex looked as though he were going to hit him and, even more oddly, Henry looked as though he'd have let him. Until Henry removed himself from the situation and, well, you know the rest, sweetie."

Taking another sip of her drink before placing the glass back on the counter, she looks me squarely in the eyes, her no-nonsense practicality front and centre.

"What I'm saying, Liv, is that the relationship between those men is fraught, to say the very least. I don't know why and, honestly, it's not my place to ask, but… maybe now that you know more, you may find the right time to mend what's broken, hmm?"

Eighteen

HENRY
AGED SEVEN

"Can he sleep in my room, please, Nanny Lauren?" My new stepmum's hand lashes out to slap the side of my head as I realise, too late, my mistake.

"Mummy, I mean Mummy. I'm sorry, Mummy."

"Good boy, Enrico."

She pats my head as she would our kitten, Millefeuille, while smiling broadly.

"Your brother shall sleep in your room, of course, dear. Your father will be pleased to see you caring for his newest son in his absence. He's your responsibility now."

I look down upon the sleeping baby in the crib beside Mummy's chair. He's pale and small. Almost too small to be real until he opens his eyes, and they focus unerringly on mine.

Reaching forward, I hold my pinkie finger out, which he

latches onto it quickly, making me giggle.

Glancing up to gauge Mummy's reaction, I realise she's gone, and I heave a sigh of relief.

"Hi, Alexander."

My words are barely a whisper, though they sound too loud in the silence of the drawing-room.

"Alexander is much too big of a name for such a small baby. So I think I shall call you Al until you grow into your full name, okay?"

He coos up at me as a small laugh escapes from my mouth.

"I'm Henry, but *she* makes everyone call me Enrico, like our dad."

As soon as the words have left my mouth, an idea hits me out of the blue.

"But you can call me Ri, so that way I can keep my real name, and she'll never know!"

I dance on the spot as joy fills my chest at this secret act of defiance until my little brother kicks in his swaddling before his face scrunches up, and he begins to cry.

Softly at first, but his mewls escalate quickly.

His dislodged blankets draw my attention to his vest underneath, noticing his nappy is obviously dirty and needs changing.

"Oh, I see, Al. You've done a poo. I'll just run and get Mummy."

Extricating my finger from his firm grasp, I fly from the room in search of Mummy.

I do hate calling her that, but the punishment is worse than the taste of the word in my mouth, so I go along with what she wants.

She doesn't force it while Dad is here, though he's not been home in weeks now.

I can't wait for him to meet Al. I bet he'll be around more now that there's another DeMarco man in the house.

Dad always told Mum he wanted a house filled with kids. So perhaps Al is a gift from Mum; maybe he's her way of telling us she's okay and watching over us, just like she promised.

"Mummy!"

Eventually, I find her on the phone in the kitchen. She puts her hand over the receiver upon my entry.

"Enrico. You rude boy, I'm on the phone."

She steps forward threateningly, but I don't flinch. Not this time. My brother needs help.

Instead, I step toward her.

"Mummy, Alexander needs a clean nappy."

Rolling her eyes, she makes a shoo-ing motion with her hands.

"Well, the changing table in your room is stocked with everything you need. Now, go and get your brother cleaned up."

She arches a perfectly shaped brow. "I told you, he's your responsibility."

Then she turns her back, returning to her call.

My shoulders slump, and my forehead creases as I slowly plod from the kitchen back toward the drawing-room until Al's high-pitched cries reach my ears once again.

I got you, brother. I won't let you down.

AGED ELEVEN

"I told you, Lauren, you get your stipend, which isn't a small sum, mind you, and not a goddamn penny more. So what could you possibly need more money for?"

My dad's words carry across the open foyer where I've just entered, Al riding high on my shoulders, having spent the last hour chasing butterflies in the garden.

He's overtired, having woken this morning to his mother's screaming down the phone, demanding our father come home for a visit. I hate it when he hears her like that, so I've worked hard to distract him in the hours since.

"Down, Ri. I want down!"

Alex's impatient hands swat absentmindedly at the top of my head, and I chuckle before lifting him from his perch to drop him gently to his feet.

He takes off across the foyer, and I instantly know I've made a colossal mistake, but before I can reach him, he's already thrown open the door to Dad's mostly unused study at the far end of the vast open hall.

Lauren strides past us without a glance, but Alex ploughs forward, throwing his arms around our father's leg.

"I missed you, Dada!"

My stomach bottoms out when I raise my eyes to my namesakes. His face is ashen, his eyes cold, and his mouth hard.

Hope swells within my chest for a split second as I look at my little brother's light amber eyes. Eyes so like his mother's, yet filled with light and love and, as such, entirely opposite to hers. How could anyone look at him and not love him with their whole heart and soul?

Then I glance back at my father and remember his heart and soul died the day my mother did. He grasps Al's shoulders to forcibly push his youngest son away from his leg, Alex's shoulders slumping forward in defeat. His eyes fill with barely restrained tears.

"Come along, Al. Let's get some toast with honey from Iris in the kitchen."

Catching his small hand in my much bigger one, I lead him from the room until the sound of our father's voice stops me.

"Enrico. A moment, please."

Squatting down so that I'm at eye level with my baby brother, I hold both his hands in mine.

"You run on and tell Iris that Ri wants extra honey on his, okay?"

He nods once, solemnly, before doing as instructed, allowing me to stand and face our father.

He doesn't mince his words as he thrusts his hand into his pocket before holding it out to me.

"I found this in your mum's safe deposit box in an envelope marked with your name."

Brow furrowing, I gingerly pluck the item from his raised palm.

Then, without another word, he marches past me, shouting once again for my stepmother.

"Lauren, I'm leaving. You'll have the additional funds in your account by this evening."

And with that, he departs without so much as a backward glance.

As I slowly meander toward the safety of Iris' kitchen, I hold up the necklace he gave me. It's an oval silver locket devoid of decoration, and it looks to be quite old.

Upon opening the clasp, my breath stills in my throat.

Held within the confines is a photo of my mum holding a newborn me. Her face is the picture of happiness, her eyes shining with radiance, just as I'll forever remember her.

My dad may be a neglectful parent, but he's just bestowed the most beautiful gift I've received since Alex was born.

"Enrico, what are you doing?"

Guiltily jumping, I drop the locket into the back of my pants, away from her suspicious eyes. If she found it, there'd be hell to pay.

"Has your father left? Did he say anything about sending the money?"

Without waiting for a reply, she walks to the foyer window, obviously checking for the presence of his car.

"Yes, Mummy. He said it would be there this evening."

Clapping her hands together with unhampered glee, I can't stop the words from leaving my mouth even as I know I'll surely earn another punishment.

"What do you need the money for anyway?"

Instead of the backhanded slap I fully expected from this woman, she smiles. But, as always with her, it's not a genuine smile; it scares me.

"Investments and such, my dear Enrico. Nothing to concern yourself with."

AGED FIFTEEN

"Thank you for a great afternoon, Mrs North."

My best friends Caden and Archer snort in the back seat of the Range Rover, driven by their mum, Clarisse.

"I've told you, Henry, call me Clary." Her pretty face breaks into a bright smile similar to her sons' when they're not being tossers.

"Are you sure there's someone home?"

I glance back at the sparsely lit house, knowing without a doubt she is inside. After yesterday's argument, when I'd outright refused to refer to her as "Mummy" any longer, I know with certainty she'll be home.

Waiting.

Planning.

Very little goes unpunished in the DeMarco household; not that I'd ever share that with a living soul.

Pride cometh before a fall.

Words I'd heard spoken around my dad's offices upon the rare occasion I'd visited in the last couple of years ring through my ears, but I swallow them down into the depths of my stomach, where they churn like bile.

"Thanks… Clary." I nod, a blush suffusing my cheeks, which my friends will no doubt plague me for tomorrow at school.

Waving my farewell, the Range Rover ambles down the extensive driveway with Cade and Arch stuck to the back window, flipping me the bird.

A wave of unwanted jealousy threatens, but I push it down, knowing those two are well aware of just how lucky they are to have such a beautiful family.

And besides, I have Al.

Entering the mostly unlit house, I immediately notice something unusual: a light coming from the wide-open door of my father's study.

Making my way across the foyer, thrilled at the thought of him visiting, having not seen him since before Christmas, I'm sorely disappointed to find Lauren sitting in his chair.

Her legs are elevated, her feet resting on the desk, and my cat, Millefeuille, is stretched lazily across her lap.

"And where have you been?"

Swallowing deeply, I raise my chin in silent refusal to be cowed.

"I told you, the Norths had a sleepover for the twins' birthday."

Nodding slowly, she raises her eyes to mine.

"And what of Alexander?"

"He went to Iris' for the night. He'll be back tomorrow."

Giving her my back, I walk as quickly and as evenly as I can toward the sanctuary of my room, but she's faster. Upon reaching the foot of the stairs, she's caught up to me.

"Don't you have something you wish to say to me, Enrico?"

Narrowing my eyes, I shake my head once.

"No."

She pops a brow, tilting her head questioningly.

"Last chance…"

Shaking my head sharply, I shrug her off to move past her, and that's when I see it. I realise I've walked straight into her carefully laid trap as her face transforms into a sinister grin, making my stomach roil with nausea.

"I thought you might say that. Here!"

Instead of the slap or punch I expected, she thrusts her closed fist forward, only opening it to display her palm once my full attention is focused on it.

"Take your punishment, then."

Her words are plain, but her tone is full to bursting with sick, twisted delight. Something I've come to learn she relishes.

Another's pain.

Their suffering.

And that's exactly what shoots through me in this moment—years of repressed pain and suffering.

My heart stutters in my chest cavity as I take in the annihilated silver locket I'd been left by Mum. There are deep gouges along the outside, and the hinges have been snapped off. The picture inside has been burnt to black, the image underneath wholly unrecognisable.

And fuck her if she thinks I'll give her what she wants.

The satisfaction of knowing she's hurt me.

Shrugging nonchalantly, I force my feet to propel my

body up the stairs, vowing that *someday* that bitch will get her comeuppance.

I should have known that wouldn't be the end of it.

After a fitful night's sleep, I'd come downstairs the next day to find Iris in the kitchen, but no Alex in sight.

"Where's my brother?"

"Mrs DeMarco came and picked him up late last night, Enrico." Her brow furrows in clear confusion.

"She said you were aware of her intentions."

My stomach plummets. Nodding blindly, I walk back the way I'd come, only for Iris' voice to stop me in my tracks.

"She said to tell you she left a message for you in your father's study."

Without turning to face her, lest she see the horror on my face, I find myself in my dad's office before realising I've even moved.

Dead centre of the mostly empty desk lies a white sheet, my hated name highlighted and underlined at the top.

Enrico,

I believe you need a couple of days to think about your transgressions.

I've taken your brother to visit the city until Monday, and when I get back, I expect a full and genuine apology.

In the meantime, I've left you a reminder. You'll find it in your father's study.

Let's call it a small indication of what happens when you don't give me what I want.

Be good,

Mummy

My nerves are on fire, my insides rioting at what could be awaiting me upstairs, and even so, I drop the note and rush towards my "reminder," knowing undoubtedly it can't be anything good.

Slowly crossing the threshold into my father's private sanctuary, my first thought is how dusty it is. There's but a slit of light entering the space through the barely separated heavy drapes, so I grab them, throwing them back to reveal my punishment—because that's all my step-monster ever gives me.

In the centre of the dusty desk, there lies Millefeuille's red collar and another note.

My poor Millefeuille; my last gift from Mum. I can only pray whatever the note says that she's okay and not another casualty in this war with *her*.

My gut heaves, threatening to expel a breakfast I've yet to consume as I unfurl the script.

You're damn lucky that I've just re-homed the cat.
Next time. I'll take away the one person you truly care about.

Throwing my head back to stop the tears that threaten to fall from my eyes at the complete and utter hopeless situation my brother and I are living in, I can't help the words as they cross my mind.

Message received loud and clear, Mummy.

Nineteen

OLIVIA

Monday rolls around with a bang. A banging fucking headache, that is.

I drank *way* too much wine with Nola and Jo on Sunday evening while having an *Outlander* marathon. I ended up entirely too fucking horny from those Jamie and Claire scenes, going home to my empty apartment to scan the internet for the minimal pap shots of one overly smug bastard CEO, who shan't be named.

Only to find the sight of his sickeningly handsome face turned me on even more. So much more, I couldn't sleep until having wrung three orgasms from my traitorous body at the memory of his rock hardness beneath my palm.

At the thought of his tongue tangling with mine, stoking the fire of need within me to an almost boiling point.

But it was the memory of that fervour, that *longing* barely contained within his gaze, that tipped me right over the edge under my own fingertips, all the while thinking they were his.

Turning on my desktop, I'm surprised to find the first of many exchanges over the coming days, considering how we'd left things on Friday.

Sender: Enrico DeMarco, CEO
(enricodemarco@demarcoholdings.com)

Recipient: Olivia Parker
(oliviaparker@demarcoholdings.com)

Subject: The Big Move

I hope you had a lovely weekend, Miss Parker, and everything went smoothly with your move on Friday.

Thinking of you,
H

Sender: Olivia Parker
(oliviaparker@demarcoholdings.com)

Recipient: Enrico DeMarco, CEO
(enricodemarco@demarcoholdings.com)

Subject: RE: The Big Move

Sending movers to shift my crap to my new place doesn't earn you any brownie points with me, Mr DeMarco.

Regards,
Miss Parker

Sender: Enrico DeMarco, CEO (enricodemarco@demarcoholdings.com)

Recipient: Olivia Parker (oliviaparker@demarcoholdings.com)

Subject: RE: RE: The Big Move

Good to know. Is there anything that might dissolve the tension?

Another lunch date, perhaps?

Yours,
H

Sender: Olivia Parker (oliviaparker@demarcoholdings.com)

Recipient: Enrico DeMarco, CEO (enricodemarco@demarcoholdings.com)

Subject: RE: RE: RE: The Big Move

Nope. Hope you enjoyed your little tryst with Andrea on Friday.

Was glad to help you fill the time while you waited for your first choice.

Please stop emailing me.

I'd had the entire weekend to ruminate on everything that had been said and done on Friday, particularly that conversation with Martha, who was away this week at the L.A. office, unfortunately. My head had concluded that my heart had been swayed even more than before by hearing about childhood Henry, and so going forward, my head would deal with all matters Henry-related.

Get lost, ostrich.

I'd tried calling Alex to verify what Henry claimed, what Martha had confirmed, but we couldn't catch each other between the time difference and his schedule.

Instead, we'd texted, which can always be hit or miss when you can't hear the inflection in the other's tone.

ALEX

So sorry I haven't been able to catch you, Liv. Everything okay? How did the move go?

ME

Yeah. Everything is fine. The move was good. Settled in well. I kinda wanted to talk to you about Henry.

And then radio silence for thirty-six hours, his reply coming in late last night or very early this morning. If I want to face facts, I've barely slept all weekend.

ALEX

Sorry, Liv. Time just moves at a different pace here. You'd love it. We have to have a holiday here.

ME

Can we discuss your brother? Please?

ALEX

How are things with big bro now that he's taken me out of the picture?

ME

Well, he told me you exaggerated our relationship at the Gala. Is that true?

I'd rather not insinuate Martha in this, so I leave her out.

The dots blink and disappear and then blink again for a long time before…

ALEX

I did.

I won't lie to you, Liv. I told you that before.

I was trying to keep you safe from him. If he thought you were mine, he'd have backed off. He SHOULD have backed off!

Liv?

You know I'd never hurt you, right?

Alex lying is hurtful, but it is his keeping it from me that I've found so strange. So unlike him, it makes me wonder what he isn't telling me and if, maybe, it would change how I feel towards either brother.

Whatever his reasons, I can't wait to see him face to face to do this. He needs to know what he's interfering with.

ME

Your brother is my McHottie. From two years ago.

And I need time to figure this all out on my own. I understand your concern, Alex, whatever your issues with Henry are, and I won't press you for that, but I need to be able to make my own mistakes. To follow my own heart, even when it goes against what you want for me.

So please, unless it's work-related, I need a breather, okay?

I love you.

And just as I'd asked, there are no replies, even though I know I've hurt him deeply with my words. And no doubt with my disclosure that *should* have come before now, but if I don't figure out my feelings and Henry's true intentions by myself, I just know, in my heart, I'll regret it forever.

Despite my words with Alex, I am aloof and purposely obtuse in the exchanged emails with Henry, and thankfully, he is away on business for the first part of the week, so the emails are the only contact we have.

Well, those and a small delivery of one little gift box that I make Freya open, her mouth falling open in awe when she reveals a beautiful rose gold necklace inside. Held within is a single large rectangular cut gem that seems to glow and sparkle with a range of pinkish hues reminiscent of a setting sun in the middle of tiny dark blue gems that I know if compared side-by-side will be the exact colour of my eyes.

It is, hands down, the most beautiful gift I've ever received, and it brings a lump to my throat at his thoughtfulness while simultaneously chipping away at my wavering resolve.

Sender: Enrico DeMarco, CEO (enricodemarco@demarcoholdings.com)

Recipient: Olivia Parker (oliviaparker@demarcoholdings.com)

Subject: Favourite Song

I don't know what you think happened with Andrea,

but I can guarantee you, you're the only woman on my mind.

Indulge me, please, Peach. I'm surrounded by boring wankers, and all I can think of are your stormy eyes. Sat in a meeting with EarPods in, listening to my favourite song.

I'll tell you mine if you'll tell me yours.

H

Sender: Olivia Parker
(oliviaparker@demarcoholdings.com)

Recipient: Enrico DeMarco, CEO
(enricodemarco@demarcoholdings.com)

Subject: RE: Favourite Song

If you could hear me right now, I'm sighing. Loudly.

Only the fact I'm being forced to sit in a meeting with the dinosaur, aka Ryan, I wouldn't even entertain your absurd email.

My favourite song is Mabel's "Don't Call Me Up."

Get. A. Clue…

Sender: Enrico DeMarco, CEO
(enricodemarco@demarcoholdings.com)

Recipient: Olivia Parker
(oliviaparker@demarcoholdings.com)

Subject: RE: RE: Favourite Song

That's a decent tune. I think her uncle's "Save Tonight" is more our pace, though, Peach. No?

My favourite is "Hurt" by the inimitable Johnny Cash.

H

When I find the song on my Spotify, being unfamiliar with it before now, tears fill my eyes as the raw emotion in the music hits me squarely in the feels, once again endearing this man to me without meaning to let him burrow further under my skin.

And as if that wasn't enough of a killer, those damned blue roses that send my foolhardy heart racing continue to appear every morning.

That same heart is lying to my head, but my head has decided to play ostrich and stay buried in the damn sand, allowing my heart to run riot.

Every evening when I return to my quiet apartment, I must press that day's blue rose in a scrapbook that I bought custom-made from Etsy because I can't bear to part with them.

You fucking loser, Olivia!

And each day has its own page, with his handwritten notes taped alongside.

Each of them makes my heart beat gloriously faster.

All of them force my feelings to the surface with each magnificently blue petal.

But my head doesn't know about any of that. Obvs.

Remember? Ostrich.

Then, on Thursday, everything comes to a head. Reaching my desk, I see that today's rose has been crushed. Like, stomped underfoot and scattered across the desk, floor, and beyond. The note has been torn into teeny pieces and is thrown haphazardly on the floor.

I can see a red haze descending over my eyes as I run them around the office to find the perpetrator, only to land upon Andrea. She's staring straight at me with a smug smile and raised eyebrows on her overly made-up, utterly cunt-ish face.

My heart pounds in my ears as I feel my adrenaline kick in. I have never been a physically violent person, but before I can consciously determine what I'm about to do, I'm tossing my shit to the floor and marching across the distance between us.

I see fear flash across her eyes as I reach her, and a rush of twisted delight like never before flows through me. She takes several steps backwards before her perfectly rounded ass meets the reception desk, effectively stopping her, and I close the gap, moving right up into her face, careful not to touch her. She's a total fucking Karen and would have me sued in a heartbeat.

Instead, I slam my hand on the desk beside her and just stare her down until she can't hold my incensed glare any longer, glancing to the side, obviously seeking help from someone she won't find here.

"Don't," I grit out through clenched teeth, "you *dare* touch my things ever again, or I will *fuck* you up. You got me?"

Withdrawing from my intimidating pose, despite the fact she towers at least five inches over me, I see none other than Henry in my peripheral vision.

Arms crossed, feet braced apart, and steaming fucking mad.

Nothing in this world is as downright *hot* as an impassioned Henry. My head has gone all ostrich on it, just when I need her to keep up this angry tension between us. The delicious push and pull that we've been feeding via email all week, but my soft heart, that stupid bitch, is soaring at his presence.

"Andrea." Her name is a bark across the dead silence of the entire floor. "My office." Spinning on his heel and marching to the waiting elevator, she tosses me a knowing wink that sets the fire in my belly to fever pitch as he steps on, snarling.

"NOW!"

Once both he and Andrea have left, Freya, Anna, and several others gather me up as I'm rapidly deflating from my earlier anger. Then, bringing me to the Ladies', they all fuss over me, checking my hair, my makeup, and getting me a cup of tea to calm the nerves, as Freya declares it's the only thing for it.

It must be about half an hour or more after the whole thing has transpired when I get back to my desk to find another beautiful blue rose, the evidence of the previous one disappearing as though it had never existed.

She's gone. For good.

Meet me in my office when you feel able.

Your Henry

Shrugging my shoulders as I decide there's no time like the present to rip this man a new one, so I head to the elevator, catching Freya's eye and sending a reassuring smirk as I leave.

This man, who has the audacity to refer to himself as *my* fucking Henry. I'm steaming.

I move on autopilot, and within no time at all, I'm standing outside Henry's door. Lifting my hand up to knock, I'm surprised to see the door jerk open before touching it as though he knew I was right outside at this moment.

"Peaches, I'm so sorry for what happened earlier. But, Andrea… well"—he groans deeply, his face the very image of regret—"let's just say, she was having issues getting the message

I've been sending."

He closes the door as I step further into his space, when I spin to face him with my brow drawn into a deep V.

"Getting the message? Umm… surely, she got the message when you were balls deep in her throat, no?"

I shrug, both for effect and because I've overtly had enough. I can't believe a damaged blue rose turned me into someone I don't recognise.

"Or maybe it was balls deep in another orifice!"

He looks at me with sad, *hurt* eyes, reminding me of that stupid song. Another manipulation, no doubt, or at least my head tells my heart that must be the case because I am not prepared for the opposite to be true.

"It's okay, Mr DeMarco. I have my own ways and means of sorting myself out. If you catch my drift."

Popping a brow while folding my arms underneath my tits, I push my chest out in defiance alongside my chin.

"No need for comparison, Peach. Andrea was just another easy lay I've no interest in repeating. Unlike you and my brother, obviously."

His jaw ticks, only to make him even more impossibly gorgeous.

Prick.

The sudden, overwhelming need to wipe that smug sneer off his face is not about to let a little thing like the truth get in the way of knocking him down a peg or ten.

And his sudden flip of personality drives me flying over the edge of reason. Jekyll and Hyde have nothing on this guy.

"Is that jealousy I hear in your voice, Mr DeMarco? That's rich coming from you!"

He has slowly moved closer to me, his eyes fixed firmly on my face.

"Things are not always as they seem, Peaches." His words are a warning I choose to ignore, despite all the flashing red lights screaming at me to hit the brakes before things spiral out of control.

But maybe I want to lose control. Just for once in my stupid life! So, feigning a nonchalance that I don't feel, I shrug. "Doesn't matter to me. I have Alex anyway."

I take small steps to the left, towards his office door, as he continues to close the gap between us, my words like a red cloak to a raging bull.

"What is it then, Olivia?" The question is spat at me through gritted teeth, and I can't help the thrill of sadistic delight that runs through me at being able to tear emotion from him unceremoniously.

He steps closer, stalking me slowly.

"Fuck buddies?"

I huff out a laugh as he takes another step closer. He's almost within arm's reach as his intoxicating scent reaches me, drowning me in all things Henry.

"A good old friends-with-benefits arrangement?"

I narrow my eyes as he shuffles slightly closer, his eyes never once having left mine nor decreasing in intensity.

"I can get behind one of those, though I don't indulge myself."

He raises a brow, almost questioningly, but too heavy on the sarcasm. "Oh no, don't tell me." He grasps his chest as though pained. "There are *feelings* involved, right?"

Prick!

The need to one-up this almighty asshole washes over me like a tsunami as the following words leave my stupid fucking mouth.

"Let's just say, when I have an itch, he'll give it a good scratch.

If you know what I mean."

I drive the point home entirely too well when I follow my blatantly provocative statement with a wink. A fucking *wink*. I'd be shocked if I wasn't so damn angry.

Sensing his demeanour change rather than seeing, I realise I've pushed him too far. I spin on my heel, finding that I'm closer to the exit than I had thought.

As I close my hand around the handle, he roughly grabs my shoulder, yanking me around to stare down at me through eyes spitting green and gold flames.

He slams both of his palms against the door on either side of my head hard and loud, effectively caging me in.

I swallow roughly when my heart stutters and stalls for a beat, my senses kicking into overdrive under the sheer power this man exudes.

"I was *trying* so very hard to be nice, but you had to go and poke the beast."

He bends his knees until his eyes are level with mine, the tips of our noses barely touching as his hot breath skates across my panting mouth.

"You have no idea what you've just done, Peach."

My heart is racing behind my breastbone when his eyes drop to my parted lips, my mouth suddenly drier than the Sahara as I run my tongue over each one.

Without shifting his attention from my actions, he hisses, "I don't give a fuck who's been inside your sweet cunt before me. My brother or any other small-dicked wanker you've allowed to scratch those fucking itches, but I can guarantee you, Peaches, no one else will be enough after I've spent myself in every hole of your body."

My nostrils flare at his crude words while my pussy weeps

unbidden into my satin and lace panties and damn it all to hell because I want this man more than I've wanted anything in my whole entire life.

And so, putting my head in the sand like the good little ostrich I so clearly am, I let my body take control.

Leaning in, Henry moves closer and closer until our lips are brushing and the butterflies in my stomach turn to fireworks exploding, shooting undulating waves of desire right to my throbbing clit.

Praying to a god I stopped believing in years ago, I *need* him to touch me before I spontaneously combust.

Running a thumb across my quivering bottom lip before dipping it inside, I don't think before drawing it further into my mouth, sucking hard as Henry growls deep in his chest.

"In fact, I think I'll fuck this perfectly pouty hole right now."

Twenty

HENRY

The way her blue eyes fill up with a heady mixture of innocence, anticipation, and outright desire makes my rock-hard dick grow impossibly larger, throbbing in my suddenly too tight pants.

My voice is guttural, and I can barely choke the words out, desperate to see how far she'll let me take this.

"On your fucking knees, Peaches."

Dropping my arms from where they've been braced against the door on either side of her guileless face, I take the smallest step back to allow her room to do as I've demanded.

My eyes make a slow descent down her delectable body, highlighted today to perfection by a tight jumpsuit I've seen on her before. As my gaze reaches her pussy, a knowing smirk stretches across my lips when I catch her rubbing her thighs together, desperately seeking friction.

Our eyes meet as she realises, I've seen her movements, and her chin lifts in the most delightful show of defiance.

My hand shoots out as she speaks, grasping her throat. Not tightly, but firmly enough that she doesn't say a word, popping a haughty brow instead.

And *fuck* me, if her additional small act of dissent doesn't make my balls draw up almost painfully.

Narrowing my eyes while slightly increasing the pressure around her throat, I growl, "Don't make me say it again."

I release her neck as she holds my eyes for several long moments before she slowly lowers herself to her knees, never breaking eye contact, arching a perfect brow as though calling my bluff.

Fuck me. There's no way she's going to suck it.

Once her face is right in front of my barely restrained cock, she leans forward to rub her cheek against the obvious bulge in my suit pants, eyes closed as though in worship, before sitting back on her heels and reaching her hands up to undo my belt. The button and zip soon follow, and she grabs hold of my pants and jocks to pull them down simultaneously, freeing my weeping cock.

My chest is rising and falling so fast that I can't seem to get enough oxygen into my lungs, and I'm afraid I may just pass out from the glorious anticipation. Two goddamn years of it.

Without skipping a beat, she leans forward to draw her pointed wet, pink tongue through the slit, closing her eyes while lapping up my precum like it's the most mouth-watering thing she's ever tasted.

"Mmmmm…"

Raising her eyes to mine, she encircles the head with her red painted, pillowy lips and grasping the base in one hand, she moves her warm, wet mouth down further and further, taking in as much of my length as she can before I hit the back of her throat, making her gag.

The sound makes my balls tingle when she retreats up to the swollen purple head of my cock before swirling her tongue around as she licks me like her favourite lollipop. The slurps and moans from her mouth make my balls draw up almost painfully with the need to fill her with myself.

Her free hand slides around to grab my ass, pulling me impossibly closer, her eyes and actions begging me to fuck her mouth into oblivion.

And being a man of action, that's what I do.

I withdraw my dick from her mouth, a trail of her saliva mixed with my precum keeping us joined as more saliva drips down her chin.

Running my thumb along her bottom lip, smearing that red lipstick she wears so beautifully, I force it inside her mouth before telling her, "Loosen your jaw."

My voice is low, hoarse with need.

"Good girl."

My words send a shiver through her as I lace my fingers through her blonde tresses, holding them above her head so tightly that she won't be able to move even if she wants to.

Using my other hand, I take hold of my dick and thrust it in her waiting mouth, driving it all the way back until her eyes water and her gag reflex kicks in.

"Relax your throat, Peaches. Relax."

For a minute, I don't think she's able to until I thrust forward, hitting the back of her throat, only to feel the muscles unfurl as she opens to take me to the root.

"Yes. That's it, baby. Take me."

And that opens the floodgates. I draw back and begin to

pummel her mouth with my cock, gripping her hair tighter and tighter, giving her all I've got because I can't hold back any longer.

This marking of her, claiming her in this moment, making her *mine.* The thought sends a tingling wave of pleasure down my spine, landing in my balls.

I'm seconds away from blowing my load down her slender throat as I choke out through gritted teeth, "Take it, baby, take it all."

She raises her eyes to mine, as much as I'll allow with how tightly I'm holding her hair. The sight of her taking my cock so willingly with tears and saliva streaming down her face is too much.

I still my pistoning hips to come in hot spurts down her throat, my dick pulsating in her warm, wet mouth, with a roar I know the entire floor had to have heard, though I don't give a rat's ass.

I hold my cock in her mouth as we stare at each other for several long minutes, not wanting to sever the connection, until I feel myself begin to soften. Then, pulling out and stepping back to give her space to move, she stops me as she bends forward to place a chaste kiss on the top of my depleted length before leaning back and running her tongue along her lips to taste the last of my essence.

I can feel my lipstick marked cock stir again at the picture she makes, so deliciously dishevelled with my cum and her spit all over her chin.

Tugging up my pants and haphazardly doing up the zip, I gently lift her from the floor, her eyes holding mine the entire time, still shining with innocence despite the deviant act we've just committed.

That combination of innocent sinner she pulls off so well is more intoxicating than any fine liquor, and I freely admit, I don't think I'll ever have my fill.

Picking her up, bridal style, I carry her to the couch in my office, where I lay her down as if she is the most precious thing in the world. Because she is.

As surely as I know my own name, I know now that after being near her, even just reading her replies to my emails, I can't go back to the world I lived in before she was a part of it.

She wipes her delicate fingers across her drenched chin as her other hand checks her tangled hair, her lips turning up in a self-deprecating smirk upon finding my handiwork.

I sigh deeply before forcibly ejecting the unwanted words.

"I have a meeting I can't miss across town, Peach."

Crouching down so that we are at eye level, I brush my thumb back and forth across her plump and deliciously swollen bottom lip, my eyes following the movement, completely entranced.

I've had more than my fair share of blowies, but my Peaches' mouth is out of this goddamn world; hot and sure, it wasn't the most skilled head of my life, but her enthusiasm was invigorating. The idea of her sucking another man's dick makes me want to smash someone's face with my fists. Mine may not be the first in her glorious mouth, but I'm going to make sure it's the fucking last.

"I can't miss it."

Stilling my thumb with her hand, she kisses it gently, the unfamiliar yet affectionate gesture making my chest tighten momentarily.

"Henry," she says my name like she's addressing an infant, "pull on your big boy pants and get back to work. I'll see you tomorrow."

She sits up, having taken it upon herself to decide playtime is over, and knowing just how stubborn this woman can be when she puts her mind to it, I hold out my hand to help her up before leading her to the private, oversized bathroom off of my office.

She stops dead on the threshold, taking in the sheer size and decadence of the room. I put in a lot of office hours, so no expense was spared when creating my sanctuary.

The entire room is white and chrome, with a rainwater shower that could fit six people easily, a free-standing claw-foot white tub sits off to one side, and glass doors lead to a modest enough steam room. There's a small selection of workout equipment to our left, including weights and a treadmill.

Shaking her head, she moves further into the room, and like the junkie I am for her, I follow at her heels.

She stands in front of the huge, gilded mirror above matching white Jack and Jill sinks, taking in her tousled hair and red smeared lipstick. I step forward to stand close behind her, placing my hands on either side of her waist.

"Take however long you need. I'll have a driver meet you downstairs to take you home when you're ready."

Accusation flashes across her eyes, mingled with pain as she spins to face me, shoving me backwards as she does.

"I get paid to be here till five, so why the fuck would I do that, hmm?" She all but hisses the words at me.

Feeling my brows knit together in confusion, I tilt my head, taking in my spitfire for a moment.

"I don't understand your anger, Peaches."

Covering the distance between us, she pushes her forefinger against my chest, stabbing me repeatedly with the offending digit.

"Don't. Don't you 'Peaches' me, Henry DeMarco. I refuse to be used as your little sex toy and only to get *rewarded* with the rest of the day off, you hear me? I won't…"

Gently but firmly, I place my fore and middle fingers over her lips, cutting off whatever she was about to say before meeting her eyes with mine in an intensely penetrating stare.

"Olivia, whatever you *think* I was insinuating is not the case. Firstly, this is not about sex. Secondly, it's not about work, or rewards for sexual favours at work, which, by the way, isn't how I roll."

I remove my fingers from her lips, confident now that she doesn't need to be silenced as the tension drains from her body and her eyes begin to soften.

"Third, I want this. Whatever *this* is. I want you, and that means no more Alex or anyone else scratching itches that I am more than ready, willing, and able to scratch. You get me? You are mine." My voice drops an octave. "And mine alone."

Her breathing hitches as she slowly nods once. Twice.

I allow myself a brief, smug smirk at her desire to please me.

Good girl.

"And lastly, Peach, I want you to go home and get ready because I'm taking you out tonight."

Her impossibly deep blue eyes light up as a broad smile spreads across her beautiful face.

"Like, on a date?"

The hopeful hesitance in her voice makes my heart swell as warmth fills my chest with a feeling I'm not entirely familiar with.

Dropping a kiss on her delectably flushed cheek, I inhale her scent in deep lungfuls. She smells like rainy days and wildflowers and something else, something entirely Olivia. And I'm addicted to it. Hook, line, and fucking sinker.

My lips move to her ear, my stubble rubbing along her cheekbone as I whisper, "Yes, Peach. *Exactly* like a date."

A shiver rocks through her body, reminding me that I need to get out of here before I spread her across my desk and feast upon her heavenly body.

"Now, Peaches, be a good girl and do as you're told." She swats at me playfully as I sidestep out of the bathroom.

I get as far as the office door, about to grab my briefcase and coat, when her soft words stop me.

"Miss you already."

My long strides eat up the floor as I reach her, unable to stay away following her gentle confession. Grasping both her hips and pulling her flush against my body, her soft curves mould to the hard planes of mine as though we had been made for each other.

I slide a hand up along her body from her hip, across the flatness of her stomach, into the flared rise of her heaving breast, unable to help myself from lightly squeezing her flesh.

Continuing upwards along her collarbone, I thrust my hand into the hair at the base of her neck, pulling her head forward to plunder her mouth with my own.

Tasting myself on the nectar of her tongue, I feel an impossible sense of ownership fill me to the brim. It's a feeling I'm entirely unfamiliar with, yet I don't ever want to go back to before experiencing its wonder.

Our kiss is a beautiful mess of tongues undulating and teeth clashing. It's unpracticed and raw and real in every way.

When the hand I've had on her hip slips around to grasp her flawless ass, she moans loudly into my mouth, and it's the most beautiful music my ears have ever heard. Then, in complete contradiction to the lustful sounds coming from her mouth, she pushes me away. Softly at first, but more insistent when I don't stop my onslaught.

I pull back, drunk on her, both of us drawing deep heavy breaths while our eyes find each other's and hold. Hers are the deepest blue I've ever seen, and I'd happily drown in their oceanic depths, but Olivia has other plans.

"Okay, enough for today. Get your ass out that door and to your meeting."

She takes a large step backwards, removing herself from my periphery before making a shoo-ing motion with her hands, effectively dismissing me from my own damn office.

Unable to help the edge of my lip tugging up in a half-smirk, I hold my hands up in defeat just as she swings the bathroom door after flashing her pearly whites.

Leaving the building, I begin the arduous and entirely unwanted trek across town while thoughts of my afternoon delight run rampant in my head. I don't see myself as that much of a reprehensible bastard that my brother won't come around over time, though the thoughts of Alex having her first is something I'll eventually have to move past. I've long suspected there was something more between them, and screw it if Peaches' admission earlier hadn't almost destroyed me.

But she is mine now. I'm giving Alex much more responsibility at the office and trying my utmost to rebuild bridges that had been razed to the earth years ago. But Peaches is a bridge too far at this point.

And one I won't—*no*—one I *can't* be without.

My phone ringing interrupts my musings, and I answer on autopilot.

"Henry, my motherfucking man! How are you, my friend?"

Without waiting for a response, in typical Caden fashion, he ploughs ahead. "Great, dude. Listen. Layla and I are tying the knot this weekend, and I need you and Nate there. You got me?"

My face breaks into a smile at his exuberance, and even if I'm not overly enamoured with his baby mama bride, Caden's happiness is contagious.

"Mail me the details, North. I'll ring my pilot ASAP. Wouldn't miss it for the world, Cade. Not for the fucking world."

Silence follows, then his signature boisterous laugh. "Thanks, man." And the call disconnects.

An email lands on my phone not thirty seconds later, and after skimming through it, I know precisely what my next move will be.

Ringing directly through to Alex's office, knowing damn well Peaches won't have left, she answers after three rings.

"DeMarco Holdings. You're through to the office of Alexander DeMarco. How may I help you?"

Shit. Cue the dick throbbing. Even her prudish secretary voice is sexy as all fucking hell, forcing my voice to drop to a husky growl.

"Peaches, baby."

Her surprised gasp has my dick jolting to attention in my pants. "Henry?"

Unable to stop the burst of laughter that escapes me, I ask, "Well, who else would be calling you baby after the indecency that we participated in less than a fucking hour past?"

I can almost see her turning that delicious shade of red that matches her lipstick from here.

"Umm… I… is everything okay?"

Gone is the cheeky sex kitten of earlier, and in her place, I'm gifted with that adorable rambling I want to memorise and replay when the desire hits. This woman is a walking contradiction, and I can't get e-fucking-nough.

"Everything is perfect, Peaches. But, I just had to let you know, you may need to pack a bag for our date."

"Henry…!" My name is a breathy admonishment on her lips, and I can't help the chuckle that escapes me.

"I have to fly to the U.S. later tonight, and I..." All of a sudden, I'm a little bit anxious.

What if she says no?

Having never grafted for a woman in my life, I'm facing a feeling of uncertainty that is entirely at odds with my usual cocksure self. Blowing out a breath, I do what she told me to do earlier and pull up those big boy pants.

"Peach, would you please come away with me for the weekend? My best friend is getting married on Saturday, and I can think of nothing I'd rather than for you to be by my side."

The silence is thick. I can't even hear her breathing over the sound of my racing heart.

When she eventually speaks, my stomach drops.

"When do we leave?"

Twenty-One

OLIVIA

As I clean myself in Henry's bathroom, I can't help the self-satisfied smile that stretches across my face. I had known exactly what I was doing, known that my words and attitude would incite a reaction. I'd wanted that reaction, craved it.

Hell, I'd *needed* it.

I just hadn't known how his demand that I suck him off would have excited me as much as it did. Upon hearing those sinful words, I realised how much I wanted to please him, to make him happy because it seems like he's had precious little happiness in his world of excess.

The complete and utter control I'd felt upon falling to *my* knees on the plush carpet of his office floor, combined with the knowledge that little old me had the ability to bring this powerful man to *his* knees, was a potent cocktail.

If I'd reached down and touched myself through my jumpsuit, I'd have gone off like a firecracker from the simplest brush of my fingertips on my needy clit, but I'd been too focused on making it good for him to give my own needs more than a fleeting thought.

I'd pushed all thoughts of inexperience to the back of my mind, let his body guide me, and when he'd spent himself at the back of my throat, roaring his pleasure as he peaked, I knew my pupils were blown and eyes glassy from how much I wanted him.

At twenty-two, it seems ludicrous to still be so carnally innocent. Sure, I've branched out and tried new, different, and fun things like karaoke, which I hated, and sushi, which I loved. But men and sexual exploration never appealed to me beyond that unforgettable night Henry and I had shared. No other kiss has ever made my body sing like being in Henry's mere presence does, and despite having distanced myself from the beliefs I'd been brought up with, I still believe that my virginity is a gift for whomever I choose.

And I am choosing Henry.

He is the only man to ever make me feel like I am who I'm meant to be when I'm in his arms. That I'm safe, protected and… home, wrapped in his embrace.

When he'd called me his, it'd been like something out of one of my favourite romance novels—utterly too fantastical to be real. But the zeal in his beautiful eyes had told me he meant every word.

So, I'm done fighting and second-guessing his motives. I'm ready now. I need to see what we could have—what we could become if given the chance.

Finishing my ablutions, I double-check myself in the enormous mirror, noting the main difference being my lack of lipstick, before making my way back down to the twenty-fifth floor. There's no way I'll be leaving before 5 pm. I have morals, and taking a day off after sucking my boss's cock is a little too close to sexual favours for my liking.

I've just resettled at my desk, having assured Freya and several other concerned PAs that I'm just fine after my run-in with Andrea, when I hear the shrill tone of my desk phone ringing.

Grabbing the handset, I turn my back to the girls who are still propped up on my desk, discussing what had happened.

"DeMarco Holdings. You're through to the office of Alexander DeMarco. How may I help you?"

"Peaches, baby." The smirk in his tone is evident, and I can't help my startled gasp, "Henry?"

His deep, unbelievably sexy laughter fills my ears, causing butterflies to flit from one side of my belly to the other.

"Well, who else would be calling you baby after the indecency that we participated in less than a fucking hour past!"

I can feel my cheeks blush heavily in memory of his reference, and I can barely string a question together.

"Umm… I… is everything okay?"

"Everything is perfect, Peaches. But I just had to let you know, you may need to pack a bag for our date."

"Henry…!" My mouth hangs open in shock at his gall. I'm overwhelmed by the urge to slap him!

"I have to fly to the U.S. later tonight, and I…"

My stomach does a somersault at where this conversation may be headed.

Deep breaths, Liv. Play it cool.

"Baby, would you please come away with me for the weekend? My best friend is getting married on Saturday, and I can think of nothing I'd rather than for you to be by my side."

Oh. My. God.

I take a minute, thinking about being cautious. Of being a good girl and doing what I'm supposed to do before I throw caution to the wind, allowing my heart to take the lead.

"When do we leave?"

Following a stunned silence, he relays all the info that I need, but refuses point blank to tell me where we are headed, insisting that it's a surprise.

Bidding me an unwilling farewell, I hang up the phone to turn around and see Freya has cleared the rest of the women from around my desk. But true to form, she stayed on and had a proper eavesdropping. Once I explain what I'm about to do, she can barely contain her delight, though I swear her to secrecy.

My fate has been sealed, and I can't stop the little thrill of delight that zaps through me. The ability to make decisions for myself will never be lost on me.

Hugging my friend goodbye, I race to the waiting town car, noting Samuel's absence when the driver, Colin, makes his introduction.

Since having made the move to my new place, the drive home takes even less time than on previous trips, but it feels interminable.

Upon reaching my apartment, I immediately begin packing for the coming days. I've never been so grateful to have Josie in my life as I am right now. She'd taken me on a mini shopping trip as a goodbye present when I'd moved out, so I know exactly what clothes to pack for this trip, Henry having told me to prepare for a warm climate.

After living with the girls for the previous two years, I'd become used to keeping my personal items in my bedroom, so having the entire apartment to myself has found me leaving things in the most random places. After eventually locating my body lotion on the sideboard of my itty-bitty kitchen, I realise it has taken slightly longer than anticipated to get my stuff together.

Having finished throwing together a smallish suitcase, opting to pack some fancy pants lingerie to sleep in instead of my go-to ratty t-shirt from the night I'd met Henry, I quickly shower. Afterwards, I scarf down some instant noodles, chuckling darkly to myself upon the realisation that the last thing I swallowed was Henry's salty climax.

Shaking my head at my depraved train of thought, I dispose of the remainder of my food before throwing a few last-minute items into my handbag. My mind is still utterly consumed by the difference a couple of hours can make when two people finally get their shit together.

It isn't long until the man on my mind arrives in a dark grey sports car that he later informs me is a Ferrari Roma and his "latest baby."

Gone is the business attire I've become used to and, in its place, he's wearing light wash, tight-fitting denims, which are ripped at both knees and moulded to his spectacular ass like a glove. He's paired them with spotless white trainers and a grey hoodie that's mostly covered by the sexiest black leather jacket known to man.

His dark hair looks freshly washed and holds none of the product it does when he's working, so it keeps landing in his eyes, causing him to brush it back in annoyance.

Just like when we first met.

And still as sexy as ever.

Upon reaching him, I see his green eyes glowing like precious emeralds as he takes me in from head to toe. I've opted for what I think is a chic yet casual look in an oversized cream jumper dress that lands just above mid-thigh, covered by a beige woollen pea coat and matching beige suede over the knee boots with a low block heel.

I think I've hit the nail on the head when he makes a fist, raises it to his mouth, biting it with a pained expression on his face.

"*Peaches*. What are you doing to me, baby?"

Launching my luggage at him, he catches it with an *oof* that makes me snigger softly. I step forward to open the passenger door.

"No way. Not happening."

Before my hand has even reached the handle, Henry has dumped my case on the pavement and has strode forward to spin me to face him so that I'm backed up against the door of the car.

He grins down at me, utterly boyish in his obvious delight, and I revel in this side of him that's so unknown to me.

"I need a proper hello, especially when my Peaches is looking positively succulent."

"My most sincere apologies." I slide my arms around his waist, tugging him impossibly closer. "Allow me to make it up to you."

Tilting my head back, his lips come down to brush gently across mine, his eyes still on mine, the green deepening with each pass his lips make over mine.

My eyes flutter shut when he runs the tip of his tongue across my slightly parted lips, seeking an entry I give only too willingly. Chills race up along my spine as he takes my mouth with his, as he deepens the kiss into something that makes time itself cease to exist.

It's as though in this moment, it's just he and I and this heart-pounding, soul-tasting, time-stopping kiss, and I want to live in it for always.

The blare of the horn from a passing car tugs the two of us unwillingly from our cocoon.

Henry's smile is impossibly wider as he looks down at me

with twinkling, laughing eyes.

"Hello, Peaches."

I snort. "I hope you don't say hello like that to just anyone."

A fleeting darkness crosses Henry's handsome face so quickly that I'm sure I imagined it as he steps back to pick up my bag from where he'd ditched it before.

"I can assure you, baby. *All* of my kisses are yours alone."

My heart is soaring when I slide into the swankiest car I've ever seen in real life, smiling happily at his words while he deposits my bag in the boot.

And it flies impossibly higher when he reaches across to grab my hand with his, proceeding to hold it tightly within his much larger one the entire time, a wholly intimate move that lights my senses on fire.

It's on the hour-long drive to the airstrip his private jet will be flying out of when he tells me what we'll be doing this weekend, thus blowing my mind.

"The wedding of your best friend, Caden? As in Caden North, lead singer of Misdirection, Caden?" He nods, a huge smile breaking across his face and lighting up his beautiful eyes as he laps up my rambling drivel.

"Oh. My. God. Oh my GOD!"

A bark of deep, rumbling laughter erupts from his chest, and I find myself momentarily distracted from yet another earth-shattering revelation that this man has *the* most intoxicating laugh. It touches me almost physically in places no one has ever touched me, lighting me up from the inside out and somehow balancing my skewed mind so that I can let him continue as the hits keep coming.

He informs me that Layla is several months pregnant, a fact that Caden and the record label have kept firmly under wraps up until now. I remember hearing several stories about stalkers and crazed fans taking things too far with exes of the band members. A pregnant girlfriend, or soon-to-be wife, would definitely bring out the crazies.

"And my other best friend, Nate, will be flying with us. I hope that's okay with you?"

I nod once, my eyes bulging out of my head. This is happening so fast, yet it feels like I've been waiting forever to get here. I'm only just beginning to face the fact that I like him a lot more than is wise despite myself.

To say I'm a little freaked out at how my weekend is shaping up would be the understatement of the year.

"So, only you and Nate and a handful of others are aware there's even a wedding, let alone *where* it's happening. Am I right in saying that?"

He nods, stealing a glance in my direction, his eyes softening when they meet mine before turning back to the road. "And I know, it's highly ironic considering I'm the CEO of one of the largest entertainment companies in the world when all Cade wants is to keep the media and all related to them out but, honestly? He knows the company means fuck all to me when it comes to the people I love, and there are precious few of those." Once I've calmed down, it takes only another few minutes before we arrive at the airfield. Henry introduces me to his pilot, Anders, and air hostess, Kyra.

Anders is a beast of a man, reminding me instantly of a WWE wrestler to look at, endearing himself to me immediately when I find him to be polite and friendly.

Kyra is, to put it mildly, a raging bitch. My sister always had a way with creative insults, and I think she would have said Kyra looked like a bulldog chewing on a wasp. Her expression is all twisted and sour upon discovering another woman will be on the flight.

And to make things worse, judging from how she made no secret of her longing glances at Henry with serious come-fuck-me eyes, I instinctively know they've slept together.

The thought sends a knife of tortured jealousy straight to my gut, and I can't help retreating into myself a little, unable to help feeling somehow less-than with her on our flight.

I'm stunned when I make my way onto the opulent jet, which has been fitted with oversized cream leather single seats on either side of an aisle, with accents of beige and gold throughout. The door into the cockpit, alongside a little galley and a seat for Kyra, are to the front. There are two other doors to the rear, which are both closed.

Nate arrives in a chauffeured car mere minutes after our own arrival. I instantly recognise him as the friend who'd spoken to Henry and me on the terrace at Velvet that night.

He is still as dark, as brooding, as serious, and as outrageously gorgeous as back then, but the smile that lights up his face upon our formal introduction turns him from a beautiful man to a living, breathing god amongst men. Jet black hair long enough to graze the collar of his white shirt, over eyes so dark a brown they are almost black, fringed by the longest eyelashes I have ever seen, make him impossibly magnetic.

His face is covered by a full, dark, immaculately trimmed beard, adding to the overall suave look he's got going on, though I can spot a single dimple on one cheek as he smiles broadly in my direction.

Henry rapidly throws his arm over my shoulder in a blatant caveman display of possession that has both myself and Nate laughing uproariously, despite my earlier peevishness.

For the early part of the flight, Nate takes great pains to get to know me, which ingratiates him to me even more than my first impression.

It turns out I have read and loved his three masterpiece works of fiction that he'd written throughout his teen and early adult years, eventually publishing them to worldwide acclaim at the age of twenty-one.

"You're Nathaniel Hawthorne? As in, Pulitzer Prize-winning Nathaniel Hawthorne?"

His eyes are jaded and sad behind his half-smile as he nods, indulging me.

"One and the same, unfortunately."

"I adored your last book, *Night For Days*. I think I've read it about ten times!"

Henry points out that Nate has suffered from writer's block for several years now, and despite knowing there must be more to the story, I don't push.

Two hours or so into our flight, Henry excuses himself to use the bathroom, which is behind one of the doors at the back of the plane, a bedroom behind the other.

Nate uses this time to confide that Henry has spoken about me to both himself and Caden on several occasions, surprising the crap out of me.

"Olivia, you have no idea how happy I am to meet you again. I wasn't sure Henry would ever just take the plunge. Especially considering he still feels a great responsibility to his father, even after two fucking years."

Sitting back in his seat, I file that tidbit about Henry's father away for later reflection as he continues. "In the end, we may be bound to our families by blood, but the bonds we've forged by friendship and love are what truly matter, above all else."

Slowly nodding, realising once again how close these three are, Nate confides in a hushed voice, "And it's not only the bonds of friendship for Henry. When that man lets someone in—and let me tell you, that's a fucking rarity, my friend—he's unwavering in his loyalty. I've only ever seen him lower his guard enough to let Caden and myself in before meeting his baby sister, Mila. But I can swear, hand on heart—if I had one of them, obviously—he's slowly letting you in. Just... be patient with him, okay? His emotions are... a little rusty."

Despite having *no* clue about the sister Nate mentions, our conversation really helps me see further into the man Henry is, rather than the one he has, for some reason, trained himself to be.

The fact that I am the only one to see that side of him makes me feel so privileged and, at that moment, I'm on cloud nine, excited as all hell at the possibilities for us.

And then that moment ends.

I smile up at Henry as he returns from his trip to the toilet, only for my lips to freeze in place when I see his grey hoodie covered in brown lipstick all around the neck, going along his skin up to the side of his mouth, as a smug, dishevelled Kyra slips by just behind him.

Twenty-Two

OLIVIA

My eyes fly to Nate's. My heart stops when I find his eyes as wide and shocked as mine. I push up to my feet, feigning tiredness and willing my face to remain impassive while unable to meet Henry's eyes.

Bidding both men goodnight, I slip past them, rapidly making my way to the back of the plane before I tug off my knee-highs, followed by my socks, and lie down with my back to the door, desperately begging my moronic heart to get it together.

It's not like we'd put a label on this, whatever this is, and obviously, my heart has been losing the damn run of itself, with my head thinking it's something it's obviously not.

Father T's voice flashes through my mind and I voice his words to the emptiness of the room.

"Fool me once, shame on you. Fool me twice, shame on me."

He's free to do what he wants with whomever he wants,

despite his earlier claiming.

"You're mine."

His words run through my head over and over on some kind of tortuous loop. I'm the biggest, most naïve idiot to walk the face of this earth.

My cheeks heat in embarrassment when I think of how easily I've fallen for his pretty declarations and delicious kisses.

Idiot. Idiot. Idiot.

It feels like it takes me hours to calm my racing, breaking heart, but in reality, it's probably only been a couple of minutes. I have just begun to relax, focusing on reading a book on my Kindle, when the bedroom door opens with a barely heard *click*.

"Peaches, everything okay?"

My eyes meet his concerned ones, and I shove my true feelings down, down as deeply as I can manage, hoping that I'm at least semi-convincing. I can't let him see what a fool he's played me for.

Again.

"I'm fine, Henry. Just tired."

"Give up talking shit, baby. You're pissed. So come on, just rip me a new one already!"

Refusing to take the bait, I reply with a popped brow and bland expression. "I have no idea what you're talking about, *baby*!"

I cringe internally at my inability to stop myself from throwing that last passive-aggressive tone in there for no reason other than the fact that I can't seem to prevent my emotions from bubbling over in the face of this man.

"Peaches."

His voice is a reprimand, his face anguished.

Coming closer and kneeling on the bed, Henry shucks off his trainers before pulling his hoodie over his head in that sexy, one-handed motion that I've never seen in real life, but all my book boyfriends have it down pat.

It's so much sexier in person. Fuck!

Frustrated with where my thoughts are headed, I sit up, depositing my Kindle on the nightstand beside the bed. Then, facing him head-on and closer than I'd realised, I let him have it.

"Fine. Let's just do this. You're a prick, Henry. It's as simple as that." I throw my hands up as words erupt from my lips, and then I keep going with the word vomit. I couldn't hold back now, even if I wanted to.

"I don't know why I thought things were finally changing between us. It's my own stupid fault for giving you the benefit of the doubt, despite *expressly* being told not to. I don't let people in, you great big twat, and fucking your air hostess while taking your current fling, or whatever the hell we are, away to a friend's wedding for the weekend has reminded me of why I shut myself off, so I guess I should be thanking you, really."

I extend my hand, waiting on him to shake it. "So, thank you, Henry—I mean, *Mr DeMarco*. I understand what this is now more than ever."

Taking a deep breath, I close my eyes, hold it for the count of ten, and then blow it out before looking at him again, hand still outstretched.

"Okay, Peaches. May I speak now?"

His sweet-talking tone sets me even further on edge, so my nod is a curt one, quick and unwilling, as I drop my hand from between us. I've said my piece, and there's very little he can say or do that will make me believe otherwise at this point.

"Okay, so firstly, I told my staffer to make sure an air host was on duty today. Not any of the hostesses. You may not like hearing it, but I want us to be honest with each other, so here it goes."

Pausing to suck in a deep breath, he ploughs on. "I've fucked Kyra and… several other air hostesses that work for the company."

My sharp inhale is the only sound that fills the room, and those noodles I'd had before Henry picked me up threaten to make a swift reappearance as he goes on.

"But surely, Peach, you understand the difference between fucking and what we have between us. I *know* you feel it too. I feel more connected with you than any other woman in my life, besides maybe my mother. That *right there* should tell you how much I am in this with you."

At the mention of his mum, my eyes burn with tears. Goddammit, I hate being such an empath. I hate being able to see where he's coming from, even as he hurts me.

"Secondly, Peaches, Kyra will continue on this flight, but only because it's not possible, or legal, to throw her into the middle of the Atlantic." My eyes shoot up to his, full of questions he is only too willing to answer.

"She let herself into the bathroom as I washed up, threw herself at me, and made sure to cover me with as much of that ugly fucking lipstick as possible. It was entirely uncalled for, unprofessional and, needless to say, she won't be working for me going forward."

Those damn tears just won't quit, my lower lids growing heavy with a barely contained torrent.

"And lastly, Peaches… you're not a fling, so get that out of your beautiful head. We're together now." His words are plain, his tone cursory, his eyes unrelenting on my own.

"I've waited two years to claim you, but I've waited my entire life to meet you. No one will come between us, you understand me? No one. I *promise you that.*"

Fat, salty tears flow down both cheeks at his final words, but the sincerity in his green depths tells me this is it; this is real.

A concoction of relief, fulfilment, and utter happiness overtakes me as I exhale a long breath, allowing the tears to just fall.

"I—I'm sorry, Henry. I—I jumped to conclusions. I—"

He moves up along the mattress to take me in his strong arms, wrapping me in tightly as though to shield me from all wrongs. It feels like belonging, a feeling I'm not altogether sure I have felt anywhere else.

"There's nothing to apologise for, baby. Not a damn thing."

We sit quietly wrapped up in each other, listening to each other's breaths and drinking deeply of each other's essence until I feel Henry's hard cock pressed against my leg.

The thought that merely holding my body in such a non-sexual manner could turn him on so obviously makes me clench my sex in longing.

"Is that a gun in your pocket...?"

The deep rumbling chuckle from within his chest where my head rests sets me off too, until I look up into his absurdly handsome face. We make eye contact, and all laughter stops abruptly.

His nostrils flare as his green eyes darken, the golden flecks disappearing entirely. Then suddenly, his mouth crashes to mine, taking it in an unforgiving, harsh kiss that is more a claiming than a kindness.

My arms reach up to wrap around his neck while my legs open shamelessly, allowing him to settle firmly between my thighs, forcing my dress to ride up and expose my white satin knickers. His jean-clad hardness grinds against the thin protection of my panties, hitting my quivering clit so delightfully I can't contain the moan of unbound lust that tumbles from my plundered mouth.

When he removes his exquisitely heavy mass from my

body, I cry out, reaching for him, desperate to keep him close. Momentarily fearful that he will leave me in this most agonisingly blissful state, I find he has slid down my body, pushing my dress higher to expose my almost concave stomach. He smirks smugly while unbuttoning his pants, allowing his mouth-wateringly rock-hard cock to spring free.

Laving kisses on my exposed belly, I writhe against his open-mouthed assault while silently begging him to descend lower.

I push down the anxious nerves that scream, I should be embarrassed to allow Henry to see me like this—so blatantly bared to his eyes. Like never before with another living soul.

And I can't help but send up a silent prayer of thanks to the girls for ensuring all of my parts are as McHottie-ready as they could possibly be.

My knees wobble slightly as nerves start to kick in, but they don't have time to take hold as Henry continues his world-altering assault.

His finger slips along my inner thigh as a flood of desire drenches my already soaked entrance before meeting the satiny placket of my panties. I inhale sharply as he gently tugs them to one side to run his finger along my slit, from my opening right up to my throbbing clit.

Circling my wetness several times, he stops his onslaught of kisses to my stomach to meet my eyes, his pupils blown so wide I can't see any colour at all.

"So fucking wet for me, Peaches. You're dripping down my fingers, and I've barely touched you. *Yet.*"

His final words are a growl, both a threat and a vow, as I feel my desire flow heedlessly from my core.

Slipping a finger inside, I hiss at his intrusion before jerking my hips forward, seeking more of this delectable brand of torture.

Sliding another finger inside to join the first, I feel myself stretching to accommodate him, sucking him further inside my greedy pussy as I throw my head back in utter abandon.

"So *tight*, Peach. Fuuuuuck! You're beyond my wildest dreams." His words are hoarse and filled with a need as great as my own.

This man.

Removing his fingers and earning him a desperate howl of disapproval from me, he shimmies my panties down my legs, tossing them to one side before moving down until his shoulders are between my thighs, his face right against my centre before looking at me, eyes on mine.

"I don't ever return the favour, Peach, but Jesus Christ, if I don't taste you now, I'll fucking die."

Without waiting for a response, his mouth covers my exposed pussy in an open-mouthed kiss, like the ones he's given my mouth, but oh-so-much more jaw-dropping.

I throw my head back, arching my body, as he eats me like a man who's been starved for years, and I'm his first meal.

He pushes my thighs farther apart with his palms until they are flush with the mattress, laying my glistening sex wide open to his ravenous mouth.

Flattening his tongue, he runs it from my opening to my pulsing clit before swirling it around and around in taunting circles, driving me higher and higher.

Pulling back to spread my lips apart, he gently blows a breath along my seam, causing me to jerk wildly. Desperately.

"Such a perfectly pink pussy, Peaches."

My hips move of their own abolition at his praise, seeking *more*, and Henry is more than willing.

Closing his mouth firmly over my clit while inserting two

fingers into my wetness, he sucks sharply, the waves of pleasure almost too much, causing me to jack-knife across the bed.

"Yes. Oh… fuck. Oh, *Henry*."

His name is a breathless cry that he's forcibly wrung from my mouth.

Bending my head forward, my eyes open wide as I take in his coup of my entire body. His stubble scratches against my tender flesh in the most pleasurably painful way, and I can feel my limbs begin to shake as I reach down and tightly fist his hair in my hand, holding him in place as I take over the momentum.

His eyes, which up till now have been closed as though in silent prayer, open, and our gazes clash. His are black pools of liquid desire as he continues to play my body like an instrument.

Our eyes hold each other's as I see and feel him grind his hardness against the mattress in an attempt to relieve himself. The idea that kissing me intimately like this turns him on so much makes me feel invincible. I'm almost there from the thought alone.

He pushes my dress impossibly higher with his free hand, shoving it underneath the wire on my bra to palm my breast. My nipples are hard as cut diamonds as he grasps one between his thumb and forefinger, rolling it, pinching it. Hard.

I gasp for breath as he thrusts his fingers inside my drenched pussy, sucking on my swollen clit before withdrawing his fingers and replacing them with his tongue.

His tongue fucks me fast and passionately, and I can feel my body reach for the stars just as he grasps my clit between two fingers and pinches before I detonate in his waiting mouth.

Voicing my pleasure for the world to hear, I come so hard I don't just reach the stars. They explode into a fiery mass all around me, and I don't think I'll ever come down.

Just as I begin to descend from my pinnacle, I see Henry has pulled back and is grasping his dick in his right hand, jerking himself off at a frantic speed.

Staring deeply into my hooded eyes with an intensity I can feel in my bones, he owns me as he proclaims gutturally, raggedly, "You. Are. *Mine*." Then he leans forward, making the sexiest sounds deep in his throat before coming all over my trembling stomach in thick white ropes.

The hot wetness that hits my belly button and the groans from his mouth send yet another flood of moisture through my core, despite having just come.

His face is contorted beautifully as he unleashes himself, as he coats me in his desire, and I find that all my earlier reticence is long gone in the face of his worship.

Reaching down, I run my fingers through his orgasm in lazy circles while Henry grips my thigh in a knee jerk response to my taunting movements. Then, needing to cite a blatant reaction, I go entirely on instinct.

I dip my cum-covered fingers lower, spreading it through my own wetness while watching, enthralled as I paint myself in Henry, utterly obsessed with *owning* this. With taking it as far as I possibly can.

With driving him to the point of insanity.

Our gazes are locked on my motions, hypnotised, until I gather our blended offerings on my thumb and bring it up to my parted lips before sucking our combined essences into my waiting mouth.

His jaw ticks, and his nostrils flare as he leans down over me, getting right in my face, our gazes rapt on each other.

"Whatever shall I do with you, Peaches."

Then he claims my mouth, alongside my heart, in a soul-destroying kiss.

We spend the remainder of the flight wrapped up in each other after Henry cleans us both up gently, so gently, like I'd shatter at any moment.

We land in Miami a little later in the evening, checking into the Fontainebleau, a stunning hotel right on the beach. The suite is just stunning, not that I'd expect anything less of Henry DeMarco and his proclivity for the finer things in life.

It all appears wonderful, but I'm not able to take any of it in. Instead, a potent mixture of sexual exhaustion and jet lag hits me with a bang, even as I try my best to take in my wholly alien surroundings. Contrary to where I'd assumed things were headed, Henry steers me towards the bedroom, where he helps me undress in the most tender and straightforward manner. It makes my heart swell with emotion, and before my head even hits the pillow, I am already fast asleep.

Waking the following morning, I find an almost naked Henry snuggled up against my back with his firm, corded forearm draped over my waist, holding my back tight to his front. I lie in the comfort and safety of his arms, listening to his even breathing for a long time, just soaking up the moment and committing it to memory until the need to relieve myself overpowers me, so I gently and unwillingly extricate myself from his hold.

When he eventually rouses thirty minutes later, I'm on the spacious balcony, dressed in a little white sundress I pulled from my still packed luggage while simultaneously tanning my naturally sallow skin and checking emails. After all, it is technically a workday, and as I've decided not to mention a word of this impromptu trip to Alex until I get back to the UK, it must appear as business as usual on my end.

He quickly nips that in the bud by kissing me so long and hard that it sets my head spinning, and as I'm busy recovering, he confiscates my phone.

Cheater.

But the kisses are so divine, I don't really mean it.

"No working whilst on holidays, Peaches. Them's the rules. For the next few days at the very least, you are wholly, completely, and thoroughly mine."

Huffing out an affirmative, I try and fail to keep the grin from my face as he leans in to drop another kiss on my always-willing mouth.

"A driver should be here shortly to bring us to the next leg of our trip."

My mouth drops open. "You mean, we're not at the wedding venue yet?"

"Nope." He pops the 'P' with a smug grin. "Just a seaplane away."

My mind is whirling with possibilities, but a seaplane from this location must surely mean…

"The Bahamas?"

He nods effusively, pulling me into his chest and hugging me to his beautifully moulded body. I could stay in his warm embrace forever. However, just as I feel all the tension begin to leave me, we're interrupted by a knock on the door.

"Let's get this utter shitshow on the road, folks!" Nate bellows from beyond before either of us has moved.

Giving my body one final squeeze, Henry opens the door to admit Nate and a bellhop, who proceeds to move our luggage onto a trolley alongside Nate's before moving on down the corridor toward an elevator.

Following both him and Nate out the door, Henry's hand

firmly holding mine, that's precisely what we do.

Twenty-Three

OLIVIA

Our secret destination turns out to be Isla De La Cruz, a private island not too far from Nassau that Caden bought as a wedding present for Layla.

On a scale of one to ten for best wedding gifts ever, it's a solid fifteen.

As the ceremony will take place on the beach tomorrow evening, Henry uses the afternoon as the opportunity to introduce me to his other best friend, the illustrious Caden North, alongside the other members of Misdirection, who all arrived last night.

Caden and Layla's villa is done in the Spanish style, with a large open courtyard in the centre, leading off to the various sections of the house. It's positively gigantic, almost like a castle minus the turrets, and as we journey across the courtyard, my stomach bubbles nervously.

Henry intuitively picks up on my anxiety and takes a moment

to pause in the centre of the open space, several formally dressed servers milling around us, to take my hands in his before bringing them between us. He gazes down upon me with such clarity in his eyes, such intent, that it momentarily steals my breath.

"They're going to love you, Peaches. Trust me."

Suddenly, his smile transfers to a grimace.

"Entirely too much, I reckon. Caden will love you, but the rest of the band will want to fuck you because they're complete horn-dogs who love nothing more than a banging body, gorgeous face, and tight as fuck pussy, so make sure you keep well clear."

Leaning up, I place a light peck on his soft mouth, so his scowl is replaced by my most favourite smile in the entire world.

"Let's go, McHottie."

Cocking a brow and tilting his head in the most adorable way that only he can pull off, his smile drops slightly as he questions me. "McHottie?"

I send a smug smile his way. "Yeah. Only fair I can give you a nickname since you insist on calling me Peaches. Which, FYI, I still don't understand? I don't even like peaches!"

"Well," he says, chuckling, "obviously, I'm referring to your peachy bottom, aren't I, baby!"

Waggling his eyebrows at me, he reaches around with both hands to palm the body part in question before using it to drag me closer. Then, turning my head to the side and, in doing so, exposing my neck, he takes it as an invitation to bite the sensitive area where my neck meets my shoulder, sending a shiver of desire straight to my core.

I suck in a breath sharply, then tell him, "It's what I called you in my head at Velvet, if you must know. The night we met. Henry McHottie. 'Cause you're… ugh, you *know* you're insanely hot."

Drawing back, he smirks an entirely too broad shit-eating grin.

"Don't you fucking know it."

"And modest too!" I snort.

We laugh as Henry throws his arm over my shoulder, and we round the corner at the end of the courtyard. My eyes widen in shock as he comes to a standstill, forcing me to stop alongside him.

Caden is front and centre on a lounger, naked as the day he was born, covered barely by an acoustic guitar that he's gently strumming. I don't recognise the melancholy tune he's softly singing, but it sends a jolt of sadness straight to my heart.

Tearing my eyes from him, I see the other four members of Misdirection are lying around the pool on loungers, buck naked. Two of them are taking turns being sucked off by a stunning Amazonian woman while two other women are writhing together on another lounger in a sixty-nine position, one obviously pregnant.

Holy motherfucker!

My eyes bulge from their sockets while my jaw hits the floor as Caden North's big baby blue laughter-filled eyes find mine. His mouth turns up in a ridiculously handsome smile as he takes in our arrival.

Henry moves before I do. Grabbing my hand, he spins us and turns back the way we'd come, shouting as he does.

"North, you prick, I'm going to fucking murder you."

Loud, boisterous laughter follows us as Henry leads me inside to an open living area that really needs a feminine touch. It's all dark browns and leather with the shades closed, and it smells of old books.

Just then, Nate walks through the door.

"Ah. So, you've found Cade, then."

Huffing out a sigh, Henry groans, "Yup. And some things

never fucking change."

Nate chuckles darkly. "They asked if I'd like to join, but you know me. Quiet as a church mouse."

Henry's answering laughter comes straight from his belly. It's so unrestrained and… happy. It's the most pleasant sound my ears have ever heard, and I greedily gather it up as I know it's a sound he doesn't make often enough by half.

"I see Layla is still fucking anything that moves."

The hinges on my jaw will need replacing with all the revelations I've been privy to lately.

"Yup, but Cade says that he's okay with it so long as it's not another dick. Whatever floats his boat. If you ask me, he just wants to make sure she doesn't do a runner with his fucking kid still inside of her. He says he loves her, so..."

He trails off, both men's eyes landing on me simultaneously.

My eyes are wide, lips clamped tight between my top and bottom teeth. The very picture of innocence, I'm sure.

"I can keep my mouth shut, okay. Pinkie promise!"

Taking in what I'm positively sure is my biggest *oh shit!* face, the two boys laugh uproariously at my blatant discomfort.

We spend two hours in the den, which I'm surprised to learn had belonged to Nate before he sold Isla De La Cruz to Caden for the low, low price of one pound.

One damn pound!

Nate's family had owned it since before he was born, but when his father had passed away a little over a year ago, the entire Hawthorne estate, which I'd come to realise is quite substantial, had been left to Nate.

Not that he wanted any of it, hence selling an actual *island* for a quid. But I learned his reasons were extremely justified.

"He was an angry old cunt anyway, right, Nate?"

"Yeah. Sadistic bastard. After coming home from that last book tour and finding him in bed with Zara, I never spoke to the prick again. I hope he died roaring." His words are vehemently spoken, almost spat from his mouth. It's so at odds with the man I've seen him to be up to this point. "Don't know why he fucking thought I'd want a goddamn penny off of him."

"Who's Zara?"

Nate huffs out a laugh, steepling his long, lean fingers under his chin as Henry answers, "She was Nate's fiancé, Peach."

Foot. Meet mouth.

"Don't forget her most recent title in my life was stepmother."

Oh, *fuck*!

Nate's sombre exterior and quiet demeanour make a lot of sense now. My heart hurts for this austere man with the beautiful soul he has purposefully shut away from the rest of the world.

Before I can utter an apology, Caden strides through the den door, fully dressed this time, thankfully.

"Sorry about that, man. The guys swung by, and Lay was so tense after the flight, we all just lost track of time."

His eyes land on me, tucked away in an oversized chair on the far side of Henry. His mouth creases into a smile that lights up his whole face, and I'm again reminded why he's been voted the world's sexiest man for the last two years running.

"Well, fuck me pink, Henry! You really did find her."

"Told you I did. She's *mine* too, so hands-off, yeah?"

A smile tugs at the corner of my lip at his possessive words, and I reach across the gap to thread our fingers together lightly, his jealous, proprietorial tone turning me on way more than it should.

Caden's eyes darken, and his nostrils flare slightly for a split second before he cackles so loud that I visibly jump in my seat.

"You know I gave my heart away a long time ago, Henry, my man. Otherwise, I'd give you a run for your money." He grins that million-dollar grin that has women dropping to his feet like flies the world over, then pops a light eyebrow before looking Henry right in the eye and deadpans, "Nothing I like so much as sinking my teeth into a ripe and juicy peach, though!"

Henry is up from his seat and out the door after a laughing Caden before I've even blinked.

"Are they always like this?"

"No, my friend. Unfortunately, they are usually a lot worse."

Nate sighs dramatically before rising and holding his hand out for me to take.

"Come on, Henry's Peachy one, let's get ourselves a nice strong drink." He raises a cynical brow. "I think we're going to need it."

Resting my fingers on his palm, I stand, allowing Nate to tuck my arm under his like a proper gentleman. He tuts and shakes his head, eliciting a giggle from my grinning mouth as he leads me away from the whooping and hollering of the two fully grown children chasing one another through the open courtyard.

We have an early dinner with Nate, Caden, Layla, and Beau, the drummer from Misdirection, who is covered head to toe in tattoos and, despite my first impression, is actually a great big sweetheart. It's rapidly becoming clear the more I'm around Henry's best friends, the more I can understand what makes him tick.

The way I've caught him watching me several times when he didn't think I was paying attention sends delightful shivers down my spine. His eyes hold the promise of so much more to come, and I'm like a kid at Christmas, letting the anticipation build to extreme heights, knowing the reward will be all the more delicious for the wait.

Once we're being served our dessert of the absolute best Tiramisu in the world, which Nate informs me is Caden's favourite dessert due to his lifelong love affair with coffee, Henry excuses himself to grab his gift for the happy couple.

He returns just as I'm taking my last bite, wishing I could ask for seconds without sounding like a complete piggy. He's carrying what looks to be a large, framed picture or perhaps a mirror, covered in brown paper and tied with an oversized red satin bow.

Gently depositing it on the floor, he reaches a hand up to rub the back of his neck, looking a trifle uncertain.

"I didn't know what to get the couple who has everything, so, umm... I went with this."

Slowly, he peels off the ribbon, letting it fall to the floor, before taking his time tugging the top two corners open and ripping the paper from the front to allow us to see what's underneath.

As we all absorb the painting on display, several gasps are heard around the table, mine among them.

Two blonde-haired boys, almost identical but for some slight differences, are holding hands with two vastly different girls. One is raven-haired and blue-eyed, with a small smile playing around her lips as she looks at one of the blonde boys.

The other girl has hair so blonde it's almost white, with big brown doe eyes that just look sad, and I can't stop the wave of sorrow that washes over me. The boy to her left is smiling broadly, in total contrast to her expression.

The foursome is set amongst the glorious colours of summer, and it is, hands down, one of the most detailed, enthralling pieces of art I've ever seen in my life.

Silence rings like a church bell throughout the room before Cade stands, all eyes drawn to him, watching him approach Henry.

"It's perfect, brother." The two men embrace for long minutes as Layla sniffles beside me.

Reaching for her hand, I give it a reassuring squeeze. "It's beautiful."

She hiccups, squeezing me back. "It's almost like being back there. With *them*—I don't know how he does it."

Nate, seated opposite, leans across upon seeing the obvious confusion on my face.

"Those two boys are Caden and his twin brother, Archer. And that's Layla in between Archer and Caden. We all grew up together, but Jesus, Henry has an eye for detail like no other."

Something finally clicks inside my head. "Henry *painted* that?"

The man of the hour sidles up behind my chair, dropping a kiss on the top of my stunned head as he chuckles deeply in his chest. "I'm a man of *many* talents, Peach."

Wiggling his eyebrows in a comically seductive manner, the whole table erupts into laughter, and though the rest of the evening is entertaining as all hell, I can't stop my mind, or my eyes, from wandering to the most beautiful artwork I've ever seen.

On the way back to our villa, I realise I never asked about the second girl.

Leaning my head against Henry's chest in the backseat of the chauffeured car, I plant a kiss on his stubbled jawline and find his eyes with mine. "Who was the second girl in the painting?"

He sighs deeply, dropping a kiss on my upturned mouth before taking a moment to respond.

"I'm glad you didn't ask at the meal, baby. I was unsure

whether to put her in there or not, but realistically, the four of them were joined at the hip for the majority of their childhood years, so it wouldn't have felt right to leave her out."

He inhales heavily. "That's Summer. She was like a sister to the boys, lived with the North family after her dad, who was a chauffeur for the family and her only living relative, died. She ran away when we were… maybe sixteen, I think. It wasn't too long after Archer's death, that much I do know."

"Did she ever come back?"

He shakes his head. "Nope. Tore Caden to shreds. Not so much Layla, despite what Cade thinks."

We sit in contemplation for the last few minutes of our trip and once we get back to the villa, I find that Henry has organised for me to have a full body massage and a mani/pedi. Henry and Nate made plans earlier to meet Caden for a bit of downtime before his big day tomorrow, and after the island staff arrive to pamper me, Henry lays a massive kiss on me before leaving for Caden and Layla's place.

By the time the staff has left, I'm completely blissed out, so decide to spend the remainder of the evening relaxing in our own private hot tub. It's there that Henry finds me when he returns from his time with the boys. Earlier than anticipated, but nonetheless more than welcome.

After the most epic massage of my life, I'm still a happy puddle of a human being, so I'm entirely unprepared for his mood change.

"Do you have something you'd like to tell me, Olivia?"

I lift my head from where I've been resting it against the back of the tub. I look up at him with my brows drawn together in confusion.

Olivia? What happened to Peaches?

I may pretend not to like it, but secretly I adore it.

He is looming right above me, closer than I had thought when I'd had my eyes closed. His jaw is tight, and his eyes are glistening emerald fire right at me.

He bends to a crouch and gets right down into my face when I don't answer before spitting his words at me through gritted teeth.

"I *said*, do you have something to fucking tell me?"

This man and his mood swings are going to give me whiplash.

I raise my body from the water and climb out in—what I hope appears to be a graceful way—before turning to face him while water drips from my bikini-ed body.

It pleases me to no end to find that even in his anger, he can't help but run his narrowed eyes up and down my wet curves before meeting my gaze with a feral look, but I refuse to be cowed.

"Henry. I have been *here*, minding my own business all evening. What could I *possibly* have done to set off this little tantrum?"

Making sure to effect as much condescension into my words as humanly possible, the newly found sadist in me, the one only this man can draw out, is overjoyed at his evident vexation as he steps closer so that we are toe to toe before bending at the knees to bring him right down to my face.

"Then why the *fuck* has my brother been blowing up your phone with missed calls and texts for the last several hours? Huh?"

My brows draw together as he rages on. "His texts tell me exactly what the fuck he's after, little Miss Fuck Buddy. 'I need you, sweet girl.' 'I need to see you, Liv.' What did I say about not having anyone else scratch those itches?"

Jesus, he's really the most insecure man I've ever met. But after my jealous episode on the jet, I can't really talk. So even though everything inside of me is screaming to give him hell for his assumptions, I opt for the gentle approach.

"This is easily remedied, Henry. May I have my phone please?"

If it had been possible for Henry's head to explode like a supernova, I'm altogether sure that this singular request would have done the job in record time.

Instead, he yanks my phone out of his pants pocket before dropping it onto the tiles and crushing it under his heel.

Twenty-Four

OLIVIA

When he raises his eyes to meet my stunned ones, his self-satisfied smirk sends me tumbling into a spiral of rage like never before.

Battle lines are clearly drawn. I suck in a deep breath before narrowing my eyes into slits, surprised steam hasn't begun pouring from my ears.

Game fucking on, asshole.

I knew it. I should have just gone mental to start with. Obviously. Hyde is gone, and I'm dealing with Jekyll once again.

Yeah, okay, so I can take partial blame here.

I may have allowed him to believe there was something between Alex and me before everything changed between us, but in all fairness, he's acting like a screaming toddler who can't be reasoned with.

Another Father Thomas adage flashes across my mind: cutting

off his nose to spite his face.

Hitting the nail squarely on the head once again, Father.

At this moment, this man is bringing out the very worst parts of me, and even though I know this, I *know* what I'm about to invite before I ever say a word, just as I'd known that day in his office when I goaded him, I can't seem to help myself.

I push back harder.

"Who the *fuck* do you think you are?"

I force the words out through gritted teeth while going up on my tiptoes, forcing him to pull back from my face. The slight accession makes me feel like I'm gaining advantage, despite our glaringly obvious size disparity, so I keep going.

"I will *not* be told whom I can, and cannot, see. What I can, and cannot, do."

Stepping forward, forcing him to step back, I continue, my voice rising to a shout.

"Never, *ever* again, you hear me? I will live *my* life how I want, where I want, *with* whomever I want, and you can go and—and... fuck a duck if you think you can force my hand, Henry DeMarco."

Spinning on my heel, I walk away feeling damn proud of myself, despite telling him to fuck a duck.

Seriously, Olivia.

Shaking my head at my absurd turn of phrase, I get all of two feet before being physically hoisted in the air, spun around, and thrown over Henry's broad shoulder in one smooth movement.

Beginning to kick and scream at his sheer audacity, he enrages me further with a sharp swat to my ass, the bikini brief giving zero protection from his hot palm.

"Put me down right this second, you fucking neanderthal! Who do you think you are?"

Pounding my fist against his rock-hard ass is getting me

nothing but a sore freaking hand, so I think of the long game and conserve my energy, going limp in his hold.

His feet step over the threshold, and as quickly as my world spun upside down, it returns to right again as he deposits me on my feet.

Hurriedly finding my bearings, I palm my long hair back from my face before hurling myself at him, fully intent on physical harm, though I've never hurt a fly in my life before now. That mishap with Andrea doesn't count because I never actually hurt her. Well, maybe her ego.

Ugh!

This goddamn man.

Before I can land my clenched fist on his chest, he catches both of my wrists firmly, walking me backwards to the nearest wall and pinning my trapped hands above my head with only one of his own, much stronger hands.

Despite the anger flowing through me, a zap of lust shoots down my spine, straight to my pussy, making me even angrier that my body could even think of sexual gratification at a time like this.

She's a dirty whore.

His eyes are stormy and unblinking, not a single golden fleck in sight as he glares down at me before speaking calmly and evenly.

"You will *not* be friends with someone you used to fuck. I won't have it. End of discussion."

Dropping my hands, he turns and walks away as though his word is law, but there's no way in hell I'm having that happen.

Over my dead body.

So, I coolly and confidently reply to his retreating back, knowing entirely too well the outcome my words will produce and still not having enough clarity of mind to give a rat's arse.

"I'll *fuck* whoever I want, and you *won't* stop me!"

He freezes, dead in his tracks, just as I'd known he would. And for a moment, spiteful delight surges through me at the knowledge that I've just gained the upper hand.

Until he leisurely turns to face me, his relaxed stance altogether at odds with the murderous look on his face.

Jaw clenched so tight it surely hurts, nostrils flaring with each deep inhalation he takes... and his eyes. Oh, his eyes are barely slitted and filled with unmitigated fury, sending a wave of panic right through me.

Realising I've gone too far, I murmur, "Oh shit," and try to run just as he closes the gap between our bodies. He grabs one of my hands before spinning me to face the wall, pinning me there with his chest pressed hard against my back and my hand trapped between us.

He leans in close, so close that I can feel his lips ghost across the back of my neck, making my entire body break out in goosebumps. His breath is hot on my flesh as he speaks the most sinfully divine words.

"I'm going to pound all memory of him right out of your sweet cunt until the only name you remember is mine—when you're screaming it at the top of your fucking lungs."

He runs the thumb of his free hand along my petulant bottom lip in a back-and-forth motion as I shudder openly against him.

Forcing his thumb between my lips inside my panting mouth, he presses down on my tongue before swirling the digit around once. Then twice, before removing it to rest on my quivering lips.

"This is *mine*."

Drawing his wet thumb down my chin to the curve of my breast, he splays his palm across my heaving chest before moving his hand down to tug my bikini top to one side roughly. He palms my exposed breast without mercy, my covered breast crying out for the same attention.

"And these are *mine*."

He pinches my nipple between his fingers, tweaking the erect bud almost harshly before moving down onto my bare stomach. Stopping his descent to swirl his finger inside my belly button, the gesture causes butterflies to come to life inside of me before he trails his hand around my hip to caress my ass almost reverently.

"And this is *mine*."

My body arches into his hand as he seizes one cheek in his large palm before moving back around to rest tantalisingly above my pubic bone, causing the butterflies in my stomach to take flight.

"And this…"

He dips his hand lower and lower until his fingers are resting ever so lightly at the edge of my bikini bottoms, achingly close to my fluttering, wet sex.

Teasing the briefs to one side with his pinkie finger, a flood of wetness drips out of my exposed core, coating my inner thighs, and he continues. "...Oh yes, this is *definitely* mine. Isn't that right, Peach?"

Barely able to draw a breath, let alone respond with how turned on I am, I nod mutely.

Goodbye feminism. It was nice knowing you.

Pulling his finger away, a cry of alarm is wrenched from my suddenly dry mouth. He lets go of the hand holding mine between us to catch the strings on either side of my bikini. Then he jerks them open in one swift, smooth move, allowing the material to fall to the floor before he uses his foot to kick my feet apart, giving him more access to the apex of my quivering thighs.

He skims his hand along my naked ass, taking his sweet time

caressing both cheeks before finally getting to my aching pussy.

Leisurely, as though he has all the time in the world, he dips a finger barely inside before drawing out even more wetness and covering my pulsing, engorged clit in teasing circles that make my toes curl in delicious anticipation.

I can barely remember how we got to this point; all I know is I don't want him to stop making me feel like this.

And he's right. I *am* his.

Entirely.

Completely.

Irrevocably *his*.

"Say it, Peaches. Say yes. Tell me you're mine."

"Henry, I… I… oh…."

Henry impales me with two fingers, stretching me so delightfully I can't speak. I can't think. I can only feel.

I only *want* to feel.

"Tell me, baby."

He withdraws his fingers to slap my pussy so hard it reverberates through my body, sending shocks of pleasurable pain from my core all the way to each extremity.

"Your body doesn't lie, Peach."

Another gush of pure desire leaves my heat, soaking his entire hand as he uses the juices that are surely covering his palm to grind it against my throbbing clit in the most sinfully decadent manner. I could come from the thought alone.

I'm a panting mess when he returns his long fingers to my aching sex, thrumming with a need only this man brings out in me.

Closing my eyes, I focus on the feeling of his fingers moving in, out, around and around, stretching me gloriously. Then, he begins planting hot, wet, open-mouthed kisses on the back of my neck, nipping at the joining where my neck meets my shoulder in the most sublime way.

"Say yes. Say it. Say the words. Invite me in."

He grinds his hard-on into my ass cheeks as his fingers plunge in and out of my dripping slit, faster and faster, the sound of my own wetness loud and utterly arousing as his fingers fuck me.

I can't hold back my moans of desperate pleasure as he drives me higher and higher.

"Yes, Peach. Come for me. Come all over my hand."

He curves his wrist so that his palm grinds against my clit with each forward thrust of his hand, giving me that exquisite friction I need, and my pussy convulses around his digits, my orgasm moments away from tearing through me as I scream.

"Yes, Henry. Yes, I'm yours. Only *ever* yours."

At my words, Henry turns his attention to my exposed throat, first flattening his tongue over the area before closing his lips and sucking hard while keeping up the delicious momentum of his hand.

And then I'm screaming his name over and over again until I'm hoarse as I come so hard, I almost black out.

I'm a sagging mess, jumbled inside and out, as I look up at him through barely hooded eyes, taking in his angry, beautiful face, knowing precisely what is happening here and needing it more than I need my next breath.

Twenty-Five

HENRY

Liv's impossibly tight channel contracts around my fingers as she erupts loudly, screaming my name just as I told her she would.

And I meant every fucking word.

I'm going to make her forget every other prick who's experienced her intoxicating responsiveness. Who's had her addictive cunt. The thought of another man touching her, touching what's mine, rips a low growl from my chest, vibrating through her shattered body.

She throws her head back against my shirt-clad chest, her eyes hooded, glazed and barely able to hold mine, her hair a tangled mess as she exposes her slender neck to me. Leaning forward, I lick and nibble along the sensitive area of her lower neck in that way I know she likes, making her moan loudly, her hungry cunt sucking my fingers in ever further. Her wetness dripping down my fucking arm makes me harder than I've ever been.

Feeling her legs go from underneath her while her body recedes from its crescendo, I pluck her from the floor, allowing her to snuggle against my broad chest as I carry her across the open living space to our bedroom.

Setting her gently on the bed, I unfold into a standing position, tugging the strings on her bikini top as I go so that my eyes can feast upon her spectacularly naked form. Only the light from the full moon reflected on the ocean lights up the room, and it's just about enough to appreciate the absolute perfection in human form that she is.

Her knees are pressed together and bent slightly, making her appear even shorter than her petite 5′3″. Her flat stomach flares out to meet generous hips that make her waist look impossibly small, in turn making her pert tits that are already a bountiful handful look even more full. Her nipples are pink, pebbled and standing proud in the barely lit room, and my mouth salivates at the thought of devouring her whole.

I shuck off my shoes and socks quickly, never losing eye contact as she nibbles seductively on her lower lip. The clink of my belt and the sound of my zipper are the only sounds that fill the darkened room as I strip down, my shirt following seconds later, leaving me in my tight, dark boxer shorts, my cock begging to be freed.

Lowering my body over hers, she opens her legs to grant me access until we are brow to brow, her bullet-like nipples slicing into my bare chest. The sensation of skin on skin is too heady to stem the moan of unfettered need that rips from my chest, which in turn makes her whimper my name softly.

"Henry." Her voice is a low whisper, an entreaty, as I taste her honeyed breath on my lips. "Kiss me. Please."

The desperation in her plea is too much. My mouth claims her in a plundering kiss, tongues dancing with unmatched hunger as we explore each other's mouths for long, luscious minutes, driving each other's needs higher and higher.

Grinding my hips and rubbing my hard-on against her soaked pussy in a delicious promise of what's to come, I pull my mouth back from duelling with hers as my eyes slowly peruse her flushed face.

"You never said *where* you wanted me to kiss you, baby."

One side of my mouth lifts in a smirk before I trail open-mouthed kisses the whole way down her body, from her jaw, along her neck, and onto that sweet spot that earns me a gasp of pleasure before I continue my assault.

Pressing butterfly kisses along her ribcage, onto her shivering stomach, before laving my tongue along the rim of her belly button, she arches against me, needing the friction only my body can provide as I continue descending lower and lower to my own personal paradise.

Her bare pussy is glistening in the moonlight as I slowly part her lips, exposing her plump, throbbing clit and take in the nectar dripping down, down to her puckered asshole and onto the white bedsheets. The sight alone makes my balls draw up, and I have to hold myself back from blowing my load like an unseasoned teen.

Bending forward, I trace the tip of my nose along her wet folds before nudging it against her trembling nub, sending a shudder straight through her while she draws in gulps of air frantically.

Seating myself firmly between her thighs, I press them further apart to display her to my eager gaze. I run my tongue the entire length of her shimmering sex, then flick her swollen bud with the pointed tip as her hips jerk against me, needing the touch of my waiting mouth. Finally, I move down to her entrance to ram my tongue into her wet core repeatedly, tongue fucking her without mercy. Her body writhes against my face, my scruff chafing the insides of the delicate flesh on her thighs as her slickness coats my tongue, my lips, my mouth.

Flattening my tongue, I glide it up from her gaping opening along her wet heat before engulfing her throbbing clit into the warmth of my mouth and sucking.

Hard.

She explodes without warning, grasping my hair roughly and holding my head in place. She rises to meet my plundering, drenching my mouth and chin with her essence as she cries out my name like a prayer.

Like a benediction.

"Oh, Henry, I'm coming. Don't stop. I'm coming."

Her screams are like music to my melody deprived ears.

I couldn't stop even if I wanted to. And I don't fucking want to.

I don't ever want to stop.

Savouring her sweet taste, I watch as she peaks, arching her neck and thrusting her breasts forward, nipples standing tall and prominent while grasping frantically at the sheets on either side of her body.

She's magnificent.

And she's mine.

It's in that fleeting moment, I realise—she's not just *mine,* I am *hers*. This goddess, this tiny being with a heart far too pure to exist—this extraordinary woman *owns* me. Body and soul, for all time. And she has since that night we met two long ass years ago.

Withdrawing my mouth, I'm still not satisfied I've done what I set out to do, so I run my hand along her quivering sex before pumping two fingers into her cum-soaked, still convulsing cunt and curve them to hit the sweet spot I know is *right* there.

Brushing the tips of my fingers along the throbbing bundle of nerves, I can feel more than see her stiffen, almost as much in surprise as in pleasure, as I wring yet another brutal orgasm from her enraptured body right on the heels of the last.

She arches her back off the bed, offering her luscious tits for my attention, which I freely give. I engulf one rock-hard nipple between my lips before moving on to her other one and sucking hard enough to mark her as she shudders to completion in the most beautiful surrender.

Watching as she descends from the heights I have driven her body to, I wrench down my boxers, allowing my hard, leaking cock to spring free almost violently. Finally moving up her writhing body, I push her thighs apart as her lash-veiled eyes lock on my own in the almost darkness of the room.

Kneeling between her open thighs, I palm my dick to line it up with her sweetness before looking down into her radiant face. Drawing myself along her slick folds, I wet my cock with her juices before pressing the barest tip just inside her dripping slit.

Her eyes fill with emotion as they rove along the moonlit contours of my jaw.

Breathing heavily, we both take a moment to revel in the other's body. To take in this moment that has been forever in the making.

Until there's only one thing left to say as I lean over her glistening, trembling torso.

"You're my every dream come to life, Peach."

She reaches her hands up to wrap them around the back of my neck, her eyes shimmering with a mixture of desire and longing as she brings my lips down to meet hers softly, so softly my chest tightens, almost in pain.

As I pull back, she runs her palm from my temple, down my cheek and along my jaw, holding it there as she smiles and nods once just before I sink into the warmth of her wet, tight pussy with nothing between us—the way we were meant to be.

But I freeze as my body meets resistance.

What?

Dropping her hand, she throws her arm over her face as her head falls away to one side, her body stiffening unnaturally whilst a low keen of pain meets my shocked ears.

"Peaches?"

Her nickname is a question and a sharp exhalation as I barely hold it together.

So tight. So warm. I've never experienced anything like it.

And the realisation hits.

I'm her first.

Shit. Shit. Shit.

Pulling back up onto my forearms, chest heaving with the effort, I move to withdraw from her tightness, but she stops me, wrapping her legs around my ass firmly and effectively seating my hardness a little further inside of her.

She drops her arm and turns her head to mine, meeting my crestfallen face head-on. Then, seeing the unspoken question in my troubled, turbulent gaze, a single tear forms in one eye, cresting her lashes before trailing slowly down her adoration filled face.

She reaches a hand up to brush it gently across my jaw as if I'm the one needing comfort, needing solace right now. The move is so quintessentially Olivia that it sends a surge of warmth through my trembling body.

"It was always meant to be you, Henry."

Her words hit me straight in the chest like a lightning bolt as

I feel something more intimate than lust, more unwavering than desire, begin to ignite the impenetrable walls I erected around my heart so long ago.

Our gazes are intent on each other, her pupils blown wide as she moves her hips upwards, searching almost experimentally.

The sensation of her untouched, tight sheath choking my cock makes me gasp for air. I have to be gentle with her.

No, I *need* to be gentle with her. Fuck knows she deserves better than this for her first time.

Christ, I'm a Grade-A idiot.

Swallowing hard as our gazes intensify, I choke out, "I don't want to hurt you, Peach."

Her other hand joins the one on my cheek as she places them oh-so-gently on either side of my face with a beguiling mix of tenderness and trust within her expression.

"You won't." She smiles, almost shyly. "You couldn't."

Her words fuel the fire in my chest as the walls encasing the unused organ held within begin to break and crumble, lighting an inferno that travels through me to places I'd assumed long dead.

Moving her hands around to the back of my neck, she pulls me down until my face is buried in her blonde tresses, her lips resting lightly on my ear as she softly whispers, "Now, fuck me like I know you need to."

Sucking in a breath, my nostrils flare as her heels dig into my ass in an attempt to pull me in deeper. I draw back enough so that our brows rest on each other, and then I drive my hips forward in one, quick thrust, breaking through her innocence.

Making her mine. For once and for all.

Her mouth opens in silent protest even as, in contrast, her thighs clench around mine to keep me embedded in her slick heat.

Closing the space between us, I capture her lips with my own, wishing with all my fiery heart that I could take her pain as easily. Instead, I plunder her mouth, dipping my tongue inside to spar with hers, to distract her mind and inflame her senses.

Soon she is panting as heavily as I am as she tears her mouth from mine to shout in desperation.

"Move, Henry. Oh, please. I need *more*."

Easing myself up onto my hands, I pull my hips back before I sink my cock into her tightness and rock my hips, circling them into hers, opening her up to me. I keep repeating this over and over, grinding against her clit with each delicious surge as I watch her undulate beneath me. Her long hair is fanned across the bed, and her tits sway lusciously with each slow thrust of my hips.

I've never seen a more beautiful sight than the one laid out in front of me right now, and the thought sends an exquisite shiver down my spine, settling heatedly in my balls.

When she reaches her tiny hands around to lay them palm down on my ass, I've almost reached my limit, and she knows it.

Biting her bottom lip before sinking her sharp nails into my flesh, she floors me when she widens her eyes innocently and pants, "More. Henry. I need more."

My reticence takes a hike while my need to fuck takes over as I hiss through my impossibly clenched jaw, "You asked for it, Peach."

Kneeling between her stretched thighs, I loom over her body, catching her wrists in my left hand and pinning them above her head. I lightly hold her neck with my right, keeping her in place before I fuck her the way we were made to fuck.

Her expressive eyes light up as I do what she's asked for, holding nothing back.

Pumping my hips at a ferocious pace, with my sweat-slicked

body sliding against her own, it's not long before I can feel her walls begin to vibrate, and I know that ecstasy is within her reach.

My hand leaves her throat, roughly moving along her breastbone to caress and pinch her hard nipples. I continue lower, never slowing my pounding hips, to reach between us and rub her clit in firm strokes with the pad of my thumb.

She cries out, then shatters into oblivion all over my cock, sending another flood of her warm wetness down my shaft when I press my thumb hard on her fully engorged clit.

Releasing her wrists, I kneel up, palming her thighs and holding them open for my onslaught. Fully sheathing my cock in her warmth, my balls draw up tight as I throw my head back with a roar to the heavens, filling her sweet cunt with hot torrents of my cum.

My dick is still pulsating, sending little tremors of pleasure through both of us when I look down on her naked, spent body, her hair spread across the sheets like strands of golden silk.

My heart, now beating freely, is no longer behind those impervious walls built over years of hatred and anger, now that this spectacular creature before me has somehow broken it down. The unused organ swells in my chest as I take in the glorious aftermath of our union, knowing without a doubt that both of our lives are now forever intertwined.

Twenty-Six

HENRY

Still seated within her warmth, I lean over to palm her cheek as she nuzzles her face to press a soft kiss to my palm. Then, stretching higher, I press a kiss of utter adoration to her flushed forehead before gently and reluctantly leaving her body's sanctuary.

She releases a hiss as she screws her eyes shut at the discomfort. "Ooh. That stings."

"I got you, baby."

Jumping up, I run to the ensuite, flicking on the light in there as I go. I glance at my dishevelled self in the oversized mirror as I let the hot water run for a moment. My eyes can't help straying down to my softening cock covered with our combined releases and Liv's virginal blood, and I am mildly disgusted at the entirely too fucking smug grin I can't wipe off my stupid face.

Quickly washing the evidence of our coming together before

dousing a small towel with warm water, I squeeze the excess and hurry back to find Liv turned onto her stomach, perfectly peachy ass on display, raptly watching my every move.

"Don't think I didn't see your self-satisfied smirk over there, McHottie, because I totally did."

Despite the sleepy tone in her voice, she raises a perfect eyebrow. Then, planting her tongue firmly in her flushed cheek, she giggles quietly at my grimace of apology before wincing in obvious pain.

Laying my hand on her hip, I urge her to flip over as I say, "Come on, baby. Let me take care of you."

Her dimpled smile sets my heart racing as she does what I've asked of her, allowing me access to her overwhelmed folds. The ensuite light shows me her red, swollen pussy, her slender thighs streaked with her innocence, as a wave of remorse washes over me.

Brow furrowed, nostrils flaring, and chest vibrating, I feel like the piece of shit that I so obviously fucking am.

"Don't you dare do that."

"What?" Our eyes meet, mine pained, but hers are blissfully happy, marred with an edge of annoyance at my apparent discomfort.

"Don't you dare take this away from me. I wanted this. I wanted it just like this. Just me and you and nothing between us. No other people. No doubts. No expectations. No condoms. Just *us*."

"I'm clean, I swear. I'm—"

"I know," she cuts me off. "You wouldn't have touched me without protection if you even suspected otherwise. And I know that because I know *you*, Henry. The real you—the one you showed to me the night we met."

My eyebrows draw together at the realisation that she's right. Whatever it is between us, I've known from the start that I could be who I *want* to be with her—not who I'm supposed to be.

She smiles as she sees my thoughts play out across my face. "I felt it then. I've felt it every day since… and I feel it now."

She rests her hand on mine, pulling herself into a seated position before she says, "It was so perfect. *You* were perfect, Henry."

The purity shining from her deep blue eyes almost cleanses me of my selfish actions while sending a muted thrill of unbridled elation through me. Her words validate all my years of oppressed feelings, allowing me to unleash everything from my freshly unrestrained heart.

"Peach. I… I…" My voice falls away hoarsely.

Words fail me.

Words never fail me.

Placing a soft kiss on my jaw before looking up at me with eyes that sparkle, I find myself entirely at the mercy of this small, celestial being as she moves to take the rapidly cooling towel from between my hands.

As if her movement rouses me from my stupor, I stop her and place a hand lightly between her breasts to push her onto her back delicately, exposing her flooded core to my eyes.

"Please, baby, let me soothe you."

Letting her knees fall to the mattress, giving me unrestricted access to her razed body, I bring the towel up and softly wipe it through her tender folds, taking special care of her red, puffy clit.

The sight of my cum mixed with her own pleasure dripping out of her freshly fucked pussy while I cleanse her of our coupling has my cock twitching against my thigh. But before she can catch sight of my arousal, I throw the towel to the floor, and in one fluid move, lie down on the bed, gathering her close with her back to my front.

We stay there for several long minutes, just breathing each other in. Inhaling the other's very existence.

I don't recall ever feeling so present. Ever *being* so present with another human being, other than my mother, which was so long ago now, the memories don't even feel real.

Nuzzling my nose into the nape of her neck, I breathe deeply. Her floral scent mixing with the sweet smell of our exertions causes my dick to swell against her ass, earning me a groan.

"I can't again. Henry!" A deep chuckle vibrates through my chest into her back and all along her divine nakedness.

"Oh, baby. I may be a bad bastard, but I'm not that much of a shit. At least not to you."

I drop a kiss on that sweet spot before drawing her even closer against my chest.

"Never to you, Peach. Never ever."

And we lie like that, wrapped up in each other's souls, each other's essences, as her slow and even breathing eventually lulls me into a deep and peaceful slumber unlike any I've had in as long as I can remember.

I wake the following morning to an empty bed, the sound of the waves outside our villa a whisper against the shore.

I soon realise there's another sound. That of the shower, meaning one thing.

A wet, naked Peach.

Throwing the covers from my bare body, I all but sprint to the ensuite, throwing the door open to find her under the showerhead. Naked and soaped.

In other words… perfection.

And I have plans to make peace with her pussy before the nuptials later today.

Sensing my presence, she looks over her shoulder right at me while putting her perfect ass on display for my viewing fucking pleasure. I just stand and take in her unequivocal flawlessness for a long moment before I close the distance to the shower, my eyes never leaving hers.

I rip open the door and allow my eyes to drift slowly down along her body, finally landing on her sweet, bare pussy before falling to my knees at her feet.

Our eyes meet and hold as she draws in several frenzied breaths when she sees the intense resolution in my eyes.

The showerhead sprays water down her shoulders and back, dripping from each delicious curve while I kneel in reverence at her feet, like the divinity she so clearly is, before palming her taut stomach to guide her back until she meets the tiled wall.

Grasping her ankle, I run my hand upwards until I meet her knee, bending it before hooking her leg over my shoulder, exposing her core to my eager gaze.

I run my open hands up the inside of both soft thighs until they land on either side of her centre, gently parting her pink lips, allowing me to glimpse her already swelling nub. The desire to please this woman, *my* woman, goes through me like a lightning bolt when I see her pussy begin to glisten with her own moisture, now mixing with the water from the shower.

"I need to apologise for last night, Peach."

Placing her hand atop my head and holding me at arm's length, she says, "There's nothing to be sorry for, Henry. I told you that."

Furrowing my brow, my lips lift into the biggest shit-eating grin.

"I never said I had to apologise to *you*, baby."

Her brows lift quizzically.

Innocently.

I fucking love it. "I have to apologise to *her.*"

Pushing my head against her restraining hand until my tongue meets her clit and all her reticence drains away, I lay siege to her pussy, fully intent on kissing her better until she forgives my jealous ignorance.

Being the most sexually responsive woman I've ever known, Liv takes no more than thirty seconds before she drenches my starving tongue with her honey.

"Yes, baby. Give me that sweetness." Her hips buck against my face, urging me closer.

Taking her ass cheeks in both hands and using the wall as leverage, I push her upwards, settling her other leg over my shoulder so that I have full access to her weeping folds.

And I lap it up voraciously. Every single drop of arousal she leaks into my greedy mouth, I want it all.

"Fuck my mouth, Peach. Use me. Come for me."

My words send her into a frenzy as she grips my hair tightly in her fists, using my face to get herself off. Flattening my tongue, she moves up and down against my drenched mouth, her body tremoring exquisitely.

Sensing she's almost there, I move one hand from her perfect ass where I've been holding her up to slide two long fingers into her leaking core, causing her to throw her head back forcibly, hitting it off the tiled wall as she voices her pleasure.

"Oh fuck, I'm coming, I'm coming."

Rolling my tongue along her convulsing cunt, I lap up every single drop of her pleasure as she shudders to completion all over my mouth.

First, setting one leg on the floor, followed by the other, I wait until she's a little steadier before I lean forward to rest my head against her stomach while wrapping my arms around her waist to pull her close as she recedes from her orgasm.

She begins to play with my wet hair in the most soothing way as I feel any and all tension just drain away from me.

Sighing contentedly, I whisper, "Thank you, Peaches."

Snorting softly, she says. "I think that's meant to be my line."

I turn my face to place a chaste kiss on her stomach before raising my eyes to meet hers, resting my chin on her.

"I mean it, Peach. I feel lighter, freer... less shackled by the past than I've been in the longest time. *You've* given that to me. *You* make me feel at peace. *You* make me feel like I could become a man who's *worthy* of you."

Rising to my feet, I catch her face between my palms, gently running my thumbs across the light pink blush staining her cheekbones as I stare intensely into her wide, deep blue eyes.

"So, thank you."

I drop a kiss onto her upturned mouth before wrapping my arms around her wet nakedness, gathering her against my chest as we stand holding each other. The water sluices down our bodies for an age until her gentle voice breaks the silence.

"You already *are* worthy, Henry. I know you are. You just have to believe it too."

This woman. I don't know what I have done to deserve her, but I know now, in this moment, that I'll spend the rest of my life trying to become the person she believes me to be.

I press a kiss atop her head. "Come on, Peach. Let's have a quick swim before lunch."

Looking up at me, her brows furrow adorably. "Lunch?"

Popping a devilish brow, I smirk as I shrug a shoulder. "Well, since I've already eaten the most delicious breakfast. *Oof!*"

She cuts me off, swatting my chest, and I'm unable to stop the peel of laughter that rings out as I take in the furious blush on her cheeks.

My good girl is out in full force now that I've licked the temptress into submission. That contrast of personalities will never get old for me.

We somehow manage to fall out of the shower laughing, and just as I stand behind her, placing a white satin robe over her shoulders, unable to stop myself from placing a kiss on the exposed skin of her neck, I hear the shrill tone of my mobile phone ringing from the bedroom.

Not bothering with a robe for myself, I stand in the doorway of the ensuite, towelling my hair as she crosses the room to get the phone, tying the robe as she goes.

After glancing at the screen, she spins to face me, all levity gone from her features, brows furrowed as her eyes peer intensely into mine.

My stomach sinks before she says the words.

"It's Alex. Shit! He can't know I'm here with you. I need to talk to him face to face—we left things unresolved…"

Crossing the distance between us, I close my hands gently over her upper arms, peering down into her concerned face. Nibbling on her bottom lip as she tends to do when she's feeling overwhelmed, her blue eyes are impossibly dark as she weighs up what to do next.

"Let me deal with my brother. Come on." I steer her in the direction of the pool, shrugging off her concerned words and half-hearted attempts to push me away. "I've got this. Okay?"

Giving up, she sits on a lounger, tugging her robe tighter around her body to outline each delectable curve as I walk back to the villa to grab a towel and her Kindle. Handing both items over, I run my knuckles along her face, from temple to chin, gripping it gently as I drop a kiss on her soft mouth. I take a long moment to thrust my tongue inside once, then twice, and upon feeling her relax with the third thrust, I break our lips apart to stride back to the bedroom.

Reaching the bed, I grab my phone, quickly finding Alex's number and hitting the *Call* button.

He answers on the second ring, no greeting in sight.

"About time. Look, I've fucked up with Liv, and, as much as it kills me… I need to clear the air with you so that I can make things right."

Scrunching up my face in utter shock, it takes everything in me to form a sentence. "What—" I cough, clearing my suddenly dry throat before trying again.

"What can I do?"

Clearing his own throat, I can hear him swallow deeply before he launches into an explanation at top speed.

"I lied to you." There's a pause, followed by a deep breath before he goes on.

"Not initially when I said Liv was just a friend. I lied at the DeMarco Holdings Gala—when I claimed she was something *more*. There's nothing more than friendship between Liv and me. There never has been, and there never will be. It's taken me this time in Dubai, and a poorly timed revelation from the woman herself, to realise I was wrong to manipulate the situation to suit my skewed view of you. Maybe everything you touch *doesn't* turn to shit these days."

Jeez, thanks for the vote of confidence.

Instead of rising to the bait, I keep quiet to allow him to continue.

"Since we've reconnected, you've been nothing but good to me. Fuck knows why you've bothered, really. I've been a proper wanker of the highest order, but I can't–"

My stomach clenches when I realise *exactly* where this conversation is headed, but still, I remain mute.

Silence permeates our connection before he's ready to finish what he obviously needs to say. "But Jesus, don't make me say it, Rico."

Inhaling sharply through my nostrils, I repeat the overused phrase through gritted teeth. "It's Henry."

Huffing in irritation, my half-brother goes on. "Henry. Okay, so look, I thought my actions were justified in protecting my friend, considering, well, you know."

"I can assure you, brother, your actions were entirely *unjustified*."

He sniggers darkly. "Excuse me if I'll have to disagree with you there, brother. I would do anything for that girl. *Anything*. Which is why I'm even making this stupid fucking call."

"Then don't insinuate things you know nothing about, *brother*."

"Henry—please, don't patronise me. This isn't how I wanted this call to go. We've never spoken about it, but… surely, you know that I remember what happened. I know *everything*."

My stomach bottoms out when I feel all the blood draining from my face, but he continues.

"I was there that night."

Rapidly sitting on the bed, in case I keel over, my recently unchained heart palpitates in my chest as memories start to rush back in, no matter what I do to keep them at bay. My stomach roils nauseously and my whole body breaks out in a panicked sweat that has nothing to do with the heat of the day.

When I speak again, my voice is barely a rasp as I choke out,

"You. Know. Fuck. All."

Hanging up the phone, I throw it across the room, uncaring if I smash it to pieces.

My head is a fucking mess as I stalk past Olivia, who is quietly and blissfully oblivious, reading on her sun lounger. Her robe is opened to bare her naked, perfect tits to the sun's early rays, but I'm not in the mindset to appreciate any goodness today. Not right now, at least.

And so, I launch myself headfirst into the coolness of the seawater swimming pool as I allow years of repression to rush to the forefront of my consciousness, entirely unprepared for what's to come, yet knowing it's long past time.

Twenty-Seven

OLIVIA

Seated by the pool, I'm not too far removed from the entrance to our bedroom, where I can hear Henry's side of his conversation with my best friend. And judging by his tone, it's not going at all well, despite his earlier confidence.

My perception is proved correct when he stalks past me on almost silent feet, naked as the day he was born, only to propel himself into the deep end. After surfacing, he does lap after lap as I watch his gloriously defined shoulders slice through the water with ease and precision.

I can almost feel the tension emanating off his body from where I'm perched. And though I want nothing more than to discover what happened to bring on such a change of mood, I'm insightful enough to know when I need to stay back and allow him to work through whatever is going on inside that beautifully broken soul of his.

After what feels like a very long time, he surfaces, resting his forearms flat against the tiled pool area while remaining in the water as he stares at me, and though his eyes may be fixed on me, I know innately that his thoughts are a million miles away.

Eventually, I push into a standing position, allowing my robe to fall away, boldly bearing my nakedness to his veiled gaze before slowly padding closer. His eyes remain steadily on my own until I reach the edge and dive in alongside him, surfacing only a couple of feet away.

Treading the water, I greedily soak in his profile, taking in every curve and feature of this man I'm coming to care for more than I'd readily admit.

"Henry?" My voice is low and hoarse from lack of use, but he turns to push himself off the wall at my tentative tone. He reaches me in a nanosecond before taking me in his arms. I immediately wind my legs around his waist, locking them lightly behind his back, and he simply holds me against his smooth, primal nakedness. We remain unmoving for the longest time until my overwhelming need to comfort him in this time of distress becomes too great.

"I want to be in this bubble we've created, Henry DeMarco. For as long as we can. Just me and you."

His arms encircle me even tighter as I go on. "But if there's something that you need to talk to me about, not just now but *ever*—I'm here... in whatever capacity you need me."

I feel the stress slowly ebb from his body at my words, and I'm filled with sheer joy at my ability to ease his mind. I think my heart may just burst out of my chest at any minute.

"Peaches." My moniker is a quiet sigh on his lips.

"There are things you need to know to understand the dynamic of my relationship with Alex."

Taking a deep breath, he then spits out, "His mum was my nanny first."

I don't give away the fact I'd already learned this from Martha, not wanting to betray her trust, and instead allow him to speak.

"She was hired to take care of me when my mum got sick, though I don't remember her doing much of anything except mooning after my father. Then, a day or two after my mum's funeral, she found him almost passed out drunk in his study. So, she dressed in my mum's clothes, doused herself in Mum's perfume and—"

My sharp inhalation cuts him off, eyes wide in disbelief. I nod for him to continue, even as my stomach bottoms out, instinctively knowing the next words to leave his lips.

"And she took advantage of a very drunk and grief-stricken man. The result of their questionable... *union*, being my brother. Bear in mind, I didn't know *any* of this until my father told me right before he died. I just assumed the selfish bastard had fed me to the wolves while he'd fucked off having a grand old time." He snorts a dark laugh, shrugging his shoulders. "I never understood why he hated her so much..."

He trails off in quiet contemplation, the pool around us motionless as his eyes remain fixed on the still waters. Until his loud declaration makes me jump in his arms and the water goes sloshing over the sides of the pool onto the deck beyond.

"Well, eventually, I understood *every*-fucking-thing."

Turning and tugging me toward the pool's edge, he pins me against the wall with his body, my legs now wrapped firmly around his waist and my core snug against his well-defined abs.

"Anyway, when she told him, he couldn't even remember sleeping with her. He demanded a DNA test. Obviously. When it was confirmed that the baby she was carrying was indeed his, he tried to pay her off."

He pauses at my grimace. "Yeah, Peach. Not his finest hour, I know. In all fairness, he just wanted her gone, but the devious bitch knew she had him by the short and fucking curlies. She threatened to sell her story to the paps, knowing a sex scandal on the heels of his wife's death would destroy his life's work, his father's legacy, my birth right, and so… he gave her what she wanted. The status of being the wife of one of the richest men in the UK, with her own private bank balance to prove it. But he couldn't bear the sight of her, devoting more and more time to the company, and eventually buying a separate apartment in the city, effectively living an entirely unrelated life that didn't include me. Or Alex."

He drifts off, his eyes still fixed intently on mine, but his conscious mind is somewhere else. Somewhere far off in the past, reliving years of horror, neglect, and pain that I can only barely begin to touch upon.

I feel my brows draw together in concern and can't stop myself from bending forward to lay a kiss on his own puckered brow, bringing him back to the here and now.

"For the most part, we lived in barely concealed hate, Peach. Dad rarely showed his face at the house, and when he did, the fights between them were explosive until he told her he was done with their sham marriage and stopped coming not long after I turned 17. It was then things became intolerable at home… I left around then."

Pain flashes through his eyes as his brows furrow further, his childhood memories washing over him like a wave. Overwhelming him entirely.

I wrap my arms around his waist and lay my head on his chest.

Father Thomas once again whispers in my subconscious. "I

won't push you, but please know I'm here for you. A good friend once told me, 'A problem shared is a problem halved.'"

His whole body stiffens as his breathing stops.

"I *want* to be your safe place because I don't think you have many of those. If any..."

He leans closer, enveloping me in a full-body hug, which I return with my whole self, holding nothing back. I know now that whatever happened in his past still lives within him, eating away at his beautiful soul like a disease that keeps him from fully healing.

And at that moment, I vow to do whatever it takes to make him whole again.

I vow to *be* whatever he needs because all I know is that this man... he completes me.

"Ladies and gentlemen. I give you Mr and Mrs Caden North."

Everyone rises to their feet, clapping loudly and shouting even louder, as the bride and groom turn to face us, Caden smiling that super-sized pearly white smile I know has definitely made *many* panties grow legs and run away.

The cheers, catcalls, and whistles get astronomically louder as Caden pulls Layla into his chest, both smiling broadly before he dips her back, taking care of her small bump to capture her mouth in a soft kiss.

They are the very picture of perfection. Layla's long, poker-straight black hair is streaming down her back, settling at the base of her spine, adorned with a crown of white flowers. Her ankle-length white dress is simple and elegant, flowing down her fragile body, made to look even more slight by her barely protruding bump. According to Henry, she's got to be around five months pregnant, but it seems as though she's had a fairly big dinner instead.

Caden is wearing a black tuxedo, and oh my—does he wear it well. He's left the black dickie bow untied to hang around his neck and has gone barefoot, as has Layla.

I'm finding it hard to reconcile this bride in front of me with the woman engaging in oral sex with a groupie at that Misdirection orgy yesterday, but it's most assuredly her. I'm puzzled by Caden's acceptance of her sexual proclivities, especially as Henry confided earlier that while Layla has been less than discreet about her dalliances, Caden hasn't been with anyone else sexually in at least two years.

And when news of this wedding breaks, the media will have a field day while women and men the world over will mourn his newlywed status, never knowing he's given his loyalty to a woman who clearly takes it for granted.

My eyes meet Henry's across the heads of the guests as his lips lift in a smile meant just for me, causing the ever-present previously dormant butterflies in my stomach to take flight.

He, like Caden, is dressed in a black tux minus the dickie bow, instead opting to leave his shirt open several buttons, giving all and sundry a glimpse of his tanned, broad, sexy-as-fuck chest.

Having snapped several photos of us together before leaving the villa, I was delighted to see we look really well side by side. I've chosen to wear a flowy full-length dress with a generous cut at the chest, but the best part is the colour.

I'd baulked when Jo told me to get it, all things considered, but Henry's face was a picture as he'd taken in the peach-coloured gown draped along my curves.

Smiling to myself at his reaction, I watch the wedding party, consisting of the newlyweds, Henry, Nate, and Layla's two younger sisters, whom I believe are called Sienna and Giana. They lead the way to the celebrations, which are taking place in a massive specially built pavilion just off the beach, where the ceremony had taken place at sunset.

It was beautiful and wholly un-rock and roll. Beau, who'd sat on one side of me, told me that Caden had insisted on the whole traditional vibe even though Layla just wanted to elope to Vegas.

Walking silently behind the members of Misdirection, whom Beau had introduced to me before the ceremony began, I can't help my mind straying to the events of the past twenty-four hours.

My body is aching in delight at the memory of the delicious acts Henry and I performed while also aching. Period.

When he'd realised I was a virgin, his face was a beautiful contradiction of pain, pleasure, and unbridled delight at the knowledge that he was my first.

My only.

When he'd apologised this morning in the shower, he'd looked at me like I'd hung the moon. Like I was the only light in his darkness, and I want nothing more than to be that for him.

This whole thing just beggars belief. Things like this don't happen in real life to girls like me.

I daydream of fixing those broken parts of himself that he's unveiling to me bit by bit, piece by piece, if only he'll let me.

I could see it had really taken a lot for him to tell me as much as he did in the pool earlier this morning, and though I was obviously hurting for him, I couldn't help my joy in having him open up to me even more than he already had.

Realising that I've stopped at the edge of the dancefloor, I raise my head to see the most gorgeous man in the entire world on the opposite side. His hands are hanging on either side of his body, his jacket gone, and his rolled-up shirt-sleeves display his muscular forearms, lightly dusted with dark hair on his olive skin. A large silver watch glints on his wrist in the millions of tiny, twinkling fairy lights surrounding the pavilion.

His impassioned eyes find mine, his face serious, and I am just blown away at the height of the emotions this man brings to life within me.

As if on winged feet, I cross the space, with him meeting me halfway. He takes me into the safe haven of his arms in a move that looks completely rehearsed, but I know deep, deep down, it's because our souls were made to mirror the other.

We sway around the dancefloor for several long minutes, my head tucked under his chin, his heart a soft, steady thump beneath my ear, fitting just perfectly in his embrace. Neither of us uttering a single word, just soaking up the feelings we elicit in the other.

I can see Caden and Nate joking at the side of the dancefloor. Both men's faces are filled with such delight it brings a contented smile to my lips.

"Having fun, Peaches?"

His voice is a husky intonation, sending a jolt of awakening to my centre. Will I ever get enough of him?

Incorrigible hussy.

Giggling softly, I nibble on my bottom lip while looking up at him through my lashes, his nostrils flaring, sending a jolt of electricity through me at the knowledge I can affect this powerful man so easily.

"It's been wonderful, Henry. Thank you for having me as your guest."

He raises his eyebrow while one side of his lips quirks up in a smile.

"You've been an exceptional plus-one."

"Oh, is that right, McHottie?"

"Don't make this harder than it needs to be, Peach. I'm serious. I'm not good with the words."

Choosing that moment to move closer so that my stomach is flush against his body, his eyes darken before I taunt provocatively. "I'm not making *anything* hard."

Arching a brow at him, I can't help the smirk that appears on my face. I love riling him up and sparring with him. I'm so utterly unlike my usual self. Yet somehow it fits the me that I am when we're together.

The me that I want to be.

He narrows his eyes imperceptibly. "I don't do girlfriends. I've never had a one, or a partner, or a lover, or any other label you want to put on a significant other." He stops, his intense eyes levelling me with their sincerity. "I fuck, Peaches."

My stomach roils at the bare, naked honesty in his voice, and I remain silent, allowing him to continue, though I have no desire to hear his words.

"I've only ever fucked. Nothing more, nothing less. And I've fucked probably more than my fair share, to be frank."

I want his candour, but hearing it doesn't make the thought of him being with other women any less shit.

Is this the cliché part where he pushes me away after starting to open up to me?

I pucker my brow in thought as my mind kicks into overdrive.

No way, not now. Not now that I know how this feels. Not now I know how intimacy tastes. How he makes me come alive in ways I could never have dreamed of.

I'm not fucking having it.

Placing my hands on his broad chest, I look him right in the eye, not wanting him to finish what he has to say because screw this, I'm not letting him ruin what we have started to build here.

"Henry. I want you. I want what we have together. I told you last night. I just want *us*."

I grit my teeth and narrow my eyes as I seethe, "And you can get *fucked* if you think you can push me away after what we've already shared. I'm stronger than I look, so just know that when you push me, I'll push *back*. Ten times harder."

He tilts his head to the side questioningly before his face mirrors my own, brows furrowed, eyes spitting fire.

"Why do you do that? It drives me *insane*, woman!"

Glancing over his shoulder before turning to me with a face like thunder, he grabs my shoulder and swiftly marches us both off the dancefloor and out of the pavilion, Caden's hoot of "Get it!" ringing loudly behind us.

I barely have a second to take a breath before we land on the dark beach at the far side of the wedding party. Stomping across the sand, I rip my arm from his grip before I lean down to take my heels off, toss them over my shoulder, and continue down the beach alone.

I can hear him jog to catch up to me just as I spin to face him, my emotions at a fever pitch right now.

"What is with this hot and cold you've got going on? Because I can't deal with you being Dr Jekyll one minute and Mr Hyde the next, okay? You tell me about your childhood, open up to me, let me *in*, and Lord help me because I *want* that. I want to inhabit your every living, breathing, waking moment. I want in. But then you ruin it—you ruin *me* when you call me an 'exceptional plus-one' before launching into, what I'm sure is, your usual speech to get rid of stage five cling-ons. But I'm not having it. We're *more* than that. I know it. *You* know it. So, no! I'm *not* having it."

Dropping my discarded heels to the sand, I throw my hands to the sky in exasperation, laying my cards on the table and letting the chips fall where they may.

"As fucking *pitiful* as it makes me sound, as it makes me *feel*, I have no pride when it comes to you, so I'm here. Putting myself on the line, being vulnerable for *us*. The us we can be if you just *let me in*."

He invades my space without saying a word and grabs hold of my chin, forcing me to look into his eyes as he says the words that blow my mind and make my spirit soar.

"What I was *trying* to say is that I want you. No, that's not enough. I don't just want you. I fucking *need* you, Peaches."

His pupils are blown and glassy as he continues. "I have only had you in my life for a couple of weeks, barely even two months, but my mum always said when you know, you know. And fuck this, but even I know that what we have isn't something you come across in every lifetime."

His eyes flick back and forth between my own as his stare penetrates me down to the fibres of my being. A surrealistic feeling saturates our moment as my dreams and reality distinctly collide and intertwine like paint on a canvas.

His words are a whisper, coiling innocuously around my frantically beating heart, tightening with each layer he peels back to display his own vulnerability alongside mine.

"I've known it since that very first night."

My breath hitches in my throat, and fleetingly the thought of what I must look like flashes through my mind as I hope my mouth hasn't dropped open too wide because I was not expecting this.

I wasn't expecting him to want what I want. To be ready to fight for it. To be as in this as I so surely am. Chills race along my spine, despite the heat of the evening.

My head feels light, as though I may faint, until I realise I've been holding my breath in anticipation of his next words.

"The night I experienced my first real kiss. I gave it to *you* because I knew then, as surely as I know now."

His first real kiss?

"I was drawn to you then, like a moth to a flame and even since, when I knew I could get burnt, I couldn't keep myself away. Not when your light had the power to chase away the darkness."

My head is racing. My brain can't process his words quickly enough at the intensity shining from his beautiful eyes, giving me the very air I need to breathe.

"Peaches." He rasps out the word as though his lungs have been deprived of all oxygen.

"What I was trying to say in the pavilion is I've only ever wanted women for one thing. To fuck them. End of story. But you. It's been you since the moment I first laid eyes on you. I want you in every way. I want to see you. Be with you. I want to know you. To touch you. To kiss and hold you. To *make love* to you. To share my joy—and even my fears. All of it."

My heart is about to leap right out of my chest, and I feel my eyes glisten with unshed tears. My senses are utterly overwhelmed by everything Henry and I can't get enough—I'll never get enough.

"I want you to be *mine,* but Olivia Marie Parker—I *need* to be yours."

Twenty-Eight

OLIVIA

The faint sounds of the ongoing wedding celebrations and the gentle lapping of waves upon the shore fill the night, as the sound of my galloping heart fills my ears.

Henry's face is angled towards mine. His eyes are as earnest as his words, forcing my pounding heart to skip a beat in my chest.

Without conscious thought, my arms slide up his chest to entwine around his neck, pulling his mouth to mine in a desperate kiss.

The need to show this man how his honesty has just ruined me takes control as my lips press against his, softly at first, but once he groans deeply—and oh so sexily, in his chest while pressing his hips forward in search of friction—it's game over for me.

I take control of the kiss, running my tongue along the seam of his lips. Teasing him, tasting him, taunting him, until he opens his mouth and touches my tongue with his, tangling them together as we delicately savour each other.

Electricity sparks through every nerve ending in my body as I feel my whole self come alive. Moving my hands from around his neck, I place them on either side of his face, cradling him gently. Carefully, like he needs in this moment of absolute vulnerability.

He shudders against me, tugging me closer and taking control of our kiss from my grasp. No longer soft and gentle, his tongue spears my mouth mercilessly, reminding me of the delicious tempo of his cock plundering my innocence last night. The exquisite memory sends a flood of warmth straight to my panties as his wet tongue continues to ravage my mouth.

Pulling back to meet my eyes, he pins me with a look that makes time stand still as his eyes look back and forth between mine.

"You take my breath away, Peach."

His mouth is on mine once more before I can say a single word, not that I could speak around the ball of emotion lodged in my throat.

He wastes no time picking me up with each of his hands firmly grasping my ass, encouraging me to wrap my legs around his waist before I can feel him move further down the beach, away from the revellers.

Pulling back from our kiss, he sits on the sand. His eyes never leave mine as he motions for me to sit on his lap. Dropping to the sand, I straddle him with my legs on either side of his hips, my core snug against his hardness.

Gently drawing the thin straps of my dress down to expose my breasts to the night and his hungry gaze, he ravishes first one nipple for several long delicious moments until moving to the other one, almost drawing the whole globe into his warm, wet mouth.

It's not long before I'm a desperate mess, driving me to reach eagerly for his belt between our writhing bodies.

"Please. Please. I need to feel you inside me."

My panties are a sopping mess with my need for this man.

Placing his hands on my cheeks, he looks at me intensely. "Liv. I don't want to hurt you again." His eyes are filled with a mixture of heady desire and intense regret.

"But I want you, Henry." I ghost my lips across his, my breath mingling with his. "Fuck me *now*."

Flicking my tongue out, I lick his top lip and continue unfastening his belt.

"Fill me up with your cum. I *need* it."

And as I'd known they would, my words break his restraint. His mouth claims mine in a deep, hungry kiss, our tongues undulating against one another in the same rhythm as our bodies, which are far too clothed for my liking.

Wrenching open his belt, button and zipper, I tug his underwear forward, allowing his big, beautiful cock to spring free into my waiting hand. We continue kissing each other senselessly as I slowly but firmly grasp his satin encased hardness under the bulbous head. Henry wraps his own hand over mine, moving my hand in rhythm with his increasingly desperate kisses before he roughly stops, pulling back.

"Enough."

The single word is a hoarse bark. "I need inside before I blow in your tiny little hand, Peach."

Sitting back onto the sand, I raise the hem of my dress until it meets my knees before popping a brow and lifting my chin in challenge.

"Well, come on in, then."

Before I know what's happened, he's spun me over as though

I weigh nothing so that I'm kneeling on the sand facing the ocean. Henry gently raises my dress from behind until my ass is exposed to his ravenous eyes.

He palms first one cheek, then the other, before squeezing hard, pulling a low groan of pleasure from my throat. Leaning over my back until his mouth is pressed to my ear, he says, "I'm going to take you like this now because, firstly, I don't think you'd enjoy the feeling of sand in your pussy for the remainder of the evening."

We chuckle together softly as he plants a kiss on my exposed shoulder blade while running his hand around to grip my swaying breasts firmly. He twists and plays with my nipples, sending another pool of arousal straight to my already soaked underwear.

"And secondly, because I want to see your gorgeous ass bouncing on my dick as I fuck you from behind."

He moves back, removing his heavy warmth from my spine when I suddenly hear a ripping sound before feeling him tear my panties from my body. I look over my shoulder just in time to see him pocket my ruined knickers in his tux pocket, shooting me a wide smirk in the process.

Leaning forward, he places an open-mouthed kiss on one cheek, followed by the other, as he runs a single finger from slit to clit, drawing my wetness the entire length of my throbbing wet core. Nipping my ass cheek with his teeth, he makes me yelp, and I can feel the vibrations from his laughter roll through my body just as he moves back further, pressing my ass cheeks apart, encouraging me to arch my back, exposing my wetness to him fully.

Just when I think he's going to fuck me, he leans his face forward, closes his mouth firmly over my clit, and licks me into a frenzy. His groans of pleasure and the sound of his mouth on me make my desire laden veins feel as though my entire body is on fire.

"Your pussy tastes sweeter than your name, Peach. Come on my tongue, baby. Feed me that delicious honey. I'm starving for you."

I feel so open, so exposed, and his dirty words send me that much closer to the edge. I'm *this* fucking close to coming all over his face. I'm sure he can feel it from the jerky movements of my hips as I push back into his open-mouthed assault.

Adding first one finger, then two to my stretching sex, he pumps them in and out faster and faster while flicking his pointed tongue back and forth across my engorged nub. When he adds a third finger, the painful pleasure sends me spiralling over the abyss as I chant his name over and over.

"Yes, that's it, baby. Come all over my fingers." His words are a growl as he bends over my back to lick the entire length of my exposed spine before seating himself firmly behind my quivering thighs.

He presses his dick between my ass cheeks, slowly pumping between them. Looking back over my shoulder, I can see his eyes have darkened, glued to the sight in front of him in absolute thrall.

"One day, Peach. One day *real soon*, this hole will be mine too." His eyes lift to meet mine, the promise behind his words shining brightly from his eyes, and I feel a shiver of premonition run from the top of my head right to the tips of my toes.

He grasps his rigid length in his right palm, pumping it once, twice, three times as a bead of precum appears on the slit. My eyes light up and I chew on my bottom lip while my mouth waters in yearning, a look he doesn't miss as his eyes promise more to come.

He dips two fingers into my still pulsating centre, drawing out my release and covering his cock with my essence, running his fingers up and down, making it slick. The sight makes me whimper in need from deep within my throat.

"You want this cock, Peach?"

He slides it along my wetness, the tip nudging my clit as I moan loudly. Impossibly turned on, I feel another gush of arousal flow from my pussy to drench his already slippery hardness.

He groans. "Fuck yes, you do. You want to come all over my cock, my greedy girl."

As I try to push back in an effort to guide him closer to my waiting, needy slit, he holds me in place. His hardness poised teasingly at my centre. "Henry." My voice is a throaty whisper. "Please."

He pulls back his hips ever so slightly before placing a hand on either side of my waist, holding me in place before thrusting forward sharply into my waiting heat. The force of his possession tears a sudden scream from my hoarse throat as he holds himself buried deep inside of me.

"So… fucking… tight…" he hisses from between clenched teeth before drawing back and pumping in and out, in and out, deliciously slowly for several minutes while clenching my ass cheeks in his large palms.

"Your pussy looks so fucking beautiful taking my cock, Peaches. She stretches perfectly for me like the good girl she is."

His praise soaks my centre with even more of my slick arousal, and he notices, judging from the low groan of pleasure that rumbles from his chest.

"I'm going to fuck you now, baby. Hard…" Both of us are panting loudly, bodies strained and on the edge. "And fast."

And with those words, he picks up the pace, driving himself

into my wetness, over and over, until I can feel another orgasm begin to build quickly in the pit of my stomach.

Henry leans over my back to wrap his arms around my chest, pulling me up, so we are kneeling, his front pressed to my back, the new angle making the sensations even more jaw-dropping as he hits parts of me I've never dreamt of.

"Oh fuck, Henry. I'm going to come… I'm going to come."

My words are the impetus to drive him impossibly deeper, his already impressive member growing harder, if that were even possible. I'm on the edge of the cliff, just about to fall, as he frantically gathers the front of my dress to allow him access to my clit. Placing a finger on either side of my sensitive nub, he scissors them up and down, matching the tempo of his thrusting length.

It's a teasing, gentle touch, just enough to make my body light up, wanting, begging for more, but before I even have to ask, Henry knows exactly what I need.

Squeezing his fingers to pinch my clit sends me flying headfirst off that precipice, and Henry follows seconds later as I feel my pulsating core milk every last drop of his seed.

We remain kneeling, motionless, for a while. Time passes as we both come back to reality, as our bodies come down from the heights we've taken them to, and the entire time, he keeps his arms wrapped around me, his stubble-covered jaw resting on my bare shoulder.

If I could bottle this moment, I'd keep it forever.

"Get a room, fuckers!"

Another voice draws us from our cocoon as Caden comes into view along the strand, propelling Henry into action. Sliding from my body, he grabs his tux jacket, which he'd tossed on the sand earlier, draping it over my exposed shoulders and wrapping it tightly around me to cover my naked breasts.

"Too late, you two. I was taking a leak down the ways and couldn't help having a sneaky peek when I heard obligatory wedding sex. I see why he calls you Peaches."

His eyes flare in amusement as he raises his eyebrows in a way he definitely knows will annoy Henry, who is currently tucking himself away and trying to not look so freshly fucked.

I can't imagine what I must look like. Still, Caden's laidback nonchalance is so refreshing compared to the stuffiness in my upbringing, and I can't help choking on the chuckle I try to withhold as Henry scowls at both of us before standing, holding a hand out to help me up.

Once we are set to rights again, Caden having had the wherewithal to turn his back lest Henry do him physical harm, our trio makes the shorter than I remembered trip back to the pavilion.

Nate is the first person to cross our paths. He takes one look at me and, in a move entirely uncharacteristic of him, at least at this point in our friendship, he bursts out laughing.

Proper, deep belly laughter that lights up his almost black eyes like polished onyx.

"Oh Jesus, DeMarco. Couldn't you have waited till afterwards at least? Come on, Peachy, I'll show you the facilities. You might want to… fix… fix…" Nate trails off, obviously not wanting to hurt my feelings, but Mr North has no such qualms.

"You can use the main house, Peachy, because, Jesus Christ, you look like you've been fucked six ways from Sunday!"

Flushing bright red at the realisation he's spot on with his description, I look around to find the correct exit to bring me to Caden and Layla's house, but Nate presents his arm with a flourish. "Allow me."

Levelling him with a serious face, trying my hardest to keep the threatening smirk at bay. "So long as you quit with the nickname."

Nate quirks an eyebrow, nodding slightly before stepping forward to take my arm, until Henry slides his arms around my waist and rests his chin on my shoulder. I can feel his smirk against my neck, and I can't stop myself from grinning idiotically.

"Not so fast. Where's my kiss, Peach?"

Tilting my head to the side, I look up into green eyes hazy with adoration. Eyes that I could happily drown myself in before Henry closes the gap and covers my lips with his in a soft, far too fleeting touching of our mouths.

As he pulls back, I spin in his hold to place a quick peck on the rumpled shirt covering his chest. "Be right back, McHottie."

I step back to find Nate watching us closely, a joyous expression taking over his face.

Once again, holding out his forearm for me, he smirks. "If the lady is *quite* finished."

I narrow my eyes playfully before accepting his arm to allow him to walk me through the party, which is in full swing and out the far side of the enclosure. The house is perched on the clifftop just above the celebrations, and he leads me along the beach, reminding me that I've lost my shoes somewhere in the sand as I'm still barefoot and up steps set into the cliffside. The entire walk is lit by suspended lanterns, and it's one of the most beautiful places I've ever seen in my life.

I say as much to Nate, to which he grimaces, though pained. "Yeah. The old man was all about image, you know? Pained him to no end when I didn't go into the family business and became a 'starving artist' instead. Aesthetics, of course. Not because the old bastard actually gave a shit about mum or me. Pawns, that's what we were. And when a measly pawn dared to go up against the King, he didn't take it too well."

He's talking as though in a trance, like he's forgotten about my presence entirely.

"When I found him with Zara… fuck. I thought my life was over. He'd planned it." He chuckles darkly. "Obviously. But somehow, she managed to get him to marry her, not that riding his wrinkled old dick got her anywhere. He left her with barely the clothes on her back when he finally kicked the bucket."

We've reached the top of the cliff, the house about thirty metres away when he stops in his tracks. "I fucking hate this place. I wrote my three novels here, holed up from the world with only Zara for company. For inspiration. This place is toxic as fuck. It reminds me of everything I'm not supposed to want…"

Awareness comes back into his body with a visible shudder, and he shakes his head to dispel the memories of another lifetime.

"Anyway. Needless to say, I hope this place brings better luck for Caden and Layla."

Squeezing his arm in solidarity, we continue to the house, finding the large wooden doors thrown wide open, the sheer white curtains blowing softly in the light breeze coming in from the ocean.

"Right. Oh, Captain, my Captain. Where are the ladies' facilities in this monstrosity?"

A smile splits his handsome face, revealing that single dimple in his left cheek, winking at me in delight underneath his impeccably groomed, dark beard.

"Whitman. Nice."

I preen under his praise; poetry having been one of my father's favourite pastimes, so I'm more than familiar with the greats.

"This way. Come on. We'd better get you back quick sharp." His tone is light-hearted now as a smirk tugs at the edges of his lips, his eyebrows wiggling. "Before Henry loses his shit and storms up here thinking I'm having my wicked way with his woman."

Twenty-Nine

HENRY

"I'm telling you, Henry. Lock. That. Shit. *Down*."

I can't deny the roguish cat-who-got-the-cream grin that appears on my face at North's proclamation.

"I'm fucking serious, DeMarco. She's a proper worldie if I've ever seen one. And fuck me, I've seen them all." We both burst out laughing, Cade's inimitable guffaw ringing loud and sincere through the whole pavilion. His merriment, his unbridled happiness encouraging me to laugh even harder, feeling lighter than I have in years, and that's not thanks in small part to one tiny, little Peach.

He sobers, leaning forward to place his elbows on his knees, his hands hanging between his thighs. "In all seriousness, I've never seen you as happy, man. Peachy looks good on you! I mean, Henry, I've not seen you as chilled since, well… since ever. You usually look slightly constipated."

He chuckles easily when I flip him the bird, but even his usual antics can't bring me down from this high.

I don't remember ever feeling as light, though the burden from the shit Alex dredged up earlier still lingers like a bad smell, and I can't help the thought from racing across my mind. Maybe what Liv said earlier is true.

A problem shared is a problem halved.

Sounds like something my mother would have said.

"Besides, I can see why you'd be happy. Those tits are the stuff of legend, man. Perfectly pink and puckered *juuuuust* right—*ouch!*"

He's not expecting it when I kick my leg out at the annoying little prick. He almost falls forward off his seat, but he does it with that shit-eating grin plastered to his face, knowing full well he's succeeding in his never-ending mission to irritate the ever-loving shit out of me.

Can't say he's not wrong, though. Peaches' tits *are* spectacular. Full, firm, and just enough that my palms barely contain their plumpness.

Jesus, despite having come—and come fucking hard at that—less than half an hour earlier, I can feel my cock stiffening in my already restrictive pants. I'm forced to adjust myself, a move the wanker beside me doesn't miss, ripping another loud guffaw from his throat, his face telling me he knows precisely where my mind has wandered.

Layla's little sister, Sienna, who I'd been paired with earlier for the ceremony, is just finishing a song she'd written especially for the occasion. The applause of appreciation from the crowd surrounding me brings me back to the present.

Shaking his head with a shrug, he shifts his gaze from Sienna as she softly thanks the crowd, then back to me, suddenly deadly serious.

"When you've found your other half, you just *know*, right?"

At the severity of his usually unfettered features, I want to ask him what he means. But when I open my mouth to voice my thoughts, I catch sight of Peaches returning, and I'm once more floored that this woman could possibly want *me*. She enters the pavilion with Nate on her heels, both smiling and laughing together as though they've known each other their whole lives. It's been a long ass time since Nate's been so relaxed with anyone other than Cade or me.

I realise then that while I've been openly gawking at the hottest girl in the room, Caden has walked over to the stage and grabbed the mic.

"Okay, fuckers. Before this decadent shindig turns to rack and ruin, courtesy of my Misdirection comrades, among several other unmentionables—" His eyes swing around laughingly to find mine and Nate's before he winks broadly. "I want to take the opportunity to thank a few people."

Cade goes on to thank everyone and their mother; no one could claim the man isn't thorough.

"And my thanks wouldn't be complete without thanking my brothers, Nate and Henry. The best fucking girlfriends anyone could ever want. Cheers dickheads."

Nate rolls his eyes, but his full black beard can't hide his smirk, identical to my own.

"Finally, I'd like to thank my *wife,* Layla. Where are you, babe?"

Tucked away in the far corner, almost hidden out of sight, Layla is standing beside Noah, Misdirection's manager.

Making a demure walk toward the stage, she approaches Caden, who's smiling his signature Cheshire Cat wide grin, all white teeth and tanned skin.

Dropping a kiss onto her lips, Caden settles the mic into its stand before gesturing for Layla to sit on the stool beside the one he takes and then picks up his guitar to rest it on his legs gently.

"Lay, babe. We've had our ups and downs, but we're here now. Living the dream. With a kid on the way, for Christ's sake!"

He holds up his free hand to stall the cheers his words have wrung from the crowd.

"I wanted to play a little something you and Duffy—"

"Caden North!" She slaps his arm, cutting him off sharply. "You can't keep calling the baby Duffy!"

He just grins that motherfucking shit-eating grin he can't help doing when he's in the throes of annoying someone. "But, babe, I have to. It stuck when you told me you were 'up the duff'!"

Chuckles and sniggers run through the room as his winning sarcastic sense of humour takes centre stage, even drawing a small smile from the bride with his signature outrageousness.

"So, I know this hasn't been the easiest pregnancy for you, babe, and I want you to know how grateful I am for how much you're sacrificing to bring a symbol of our love into the world." The guests' cries of adoration almost drown him out as he finishes. "So here we go."

Caden strums a soft, lilting melody, so soothing it's almost hypnotic.

"I love you, Layla."

Then his low, gritty voice begins to sing softly. The song lyrics are so familiar, but I can't pinpoint them, despite knowing they mean something to the newlyweds, though you'd not know it to look at Layla's furrowed brow.

My entire body is alive with pins and needles at the palpable love and devotion in his voice, and the crowd stands enraptured by the scene playing in front of us.

Liv leans up on her tiptoes. "It's so romantic. I've never heard this song without the bells and whistles before." Nodding, I draw her into the circle of my arms as we sway gently to the tune.

He's barely starting the second verse, when Layla cries out, her eyes wide, skin as white as snow and her brow covered in glistening drops of perspiration. She glances frantically around the watching crowd as though searching for something before her body folds in on itself. She crumbles like a house of cards from her perch on the stool as Caden drops the acoustic with a *clang* reverberating throughout the hushed space before he grabs her mere centimetres from the floor.

Our trio is pushing through the shocked, gasping gathering and have reached his side almost immediately as the whole room erupts into screams and hysterics.

Nate, ever the cool-headed one, is already leaping into action, sending Layla's other sister, Giana, to get the medical staff Caden had made sure were standing by, refusing to take any chances with his new wife and unborn child's lives.

There's a buzzing in my ears as I grip Liv's hand even tighter while we take in the devastation. Turning horror-filled eyes to mine, I'm overwhelmed with the need to pull her close, to make sure she's okay in every way. She hides her face against the width of my chest while her body trembles, and I can't help tightening my hold around her in response as my eyes once more stray back towards my best friend and his whole world imploding.

Caden has pulled his unconscious wife of mere hours onto his lap, cradling her head in his hands while rubbing absentmindedly at her long black hair. She's motionless but for the slightest rise and fall of her chest.

Giana is quick to return, medics in tow, and it registers that the buzzing in my ears is, in fact, the low hum of a helicopter in the distance. Relief fills my chest cavity, realising that help is close at hand.

One of the medical personnel pulls Cade to the side, allowing the rest access to Layla. They check her vitals, and with several quiet, seemingly brisk words between them, they mount her onto a waiting gurney and carry her from the still crowded pavilion onto the beach and down aways to what looks like a cleared area I hadn't seen before, but it's perfectly shaped into a makeshift helipad.

Cade is led out after her, his face in his hands, blonde locks falling forward, hiding him from the onlookers, with Noah close behind. Nate, Liv, and I are hot on their heels, my arm loosely draped over her shoulder just tightly enough to keep her to my side.

A helicopter begins the process of landing, whipping up a storm of sand and ocean, spraying both over the onlookers, despite the distance between us and the pad. Nate and I turn our backs momentarily to shield Peaches and Layla's sister, Giana, who's close behind us.

By the time the sand has settled, Layla is being rapidly boarded with two medics climbing on alongside what looks to be another onboard. Cade and Noah draw up the rear.

At the last second, Cade looks back, meeting first my eyes, then Nate's, before tipping his head and indicating, using his hands, that he'll call us. Then, climbing into the medivac helicopter behind Noah, they are in the air and moving closer to safety within less than a minute.

The staff have already begun to wind everything down, ensuring that all the guests have somewhere to sleep or a way to return to their own living spaces. In addition to the main house, several smaller villas like ours are dotted across the island for visiting guests.

Nate, who's staying at the main residence, walks us to a waiting car without so much as a word, but after embracing first Liv and then myself, he says, "I think it's time to call it quits on this shithole. If today taught me anything, it's that this place is as fucking cursed as I'd thought."

Shaking his head, he scrubs his hand from his forehead to his chin, rubbing the dark beard in contemplation for a moment. "Can you have the jet ready for us in Miami tomorrow afternoon?" I nod once, slapping a hand on his shoulder in solidarity, knowing just how hard this will have hit him, considering where this shit has gone down.

"Thanks, Henry. I'll confirm a seaplane for the three of us if you can handle your end."

Our return trip is sombre as Peach nuzzles against my chest, quietly dotting my shirt with her steady stream of silent tears.

Once we arrive at the villa, I shoot off a text to my pilot, alerting him to have the jet ready for tomorrow. We then go about the business of defrocking our finery—an elegant reminder of a disastrous evening.

"Such pain…"

Peach is bent over the bed, placing the last of her luggage in her case as she murmurs so quietly that I strain to hear her. Suddenly, she turns to look at me. The tear tracks marring her cheeks only serve to make her even more heartbreakingly stunning as she tries and fails to stifle a low sob in the back of her throat.

"On their happiest day, Henry. Such *pain*."

Closing the gap between us, I envelop her in my arms, wanting so badly to take this pain away—to bear it for her. If there's one thing I know about my Peaches, it's that she feels others' pain. Deeply. Profoundly.

And having witnessed something as traumatic as what had happened on that beach, well, we both need to just take a moment and find gratitude in each other's embrace.

After a time, she pulls back, her eyes bright and puffy, but a small smile graces her lips where there'd been none before. I feel elated at having brought her even a semblance of the peace she so easily brings to my soul.

"I promise, baby. It'll all be okay in the end."

Her smile brightens. "As Father Thomas says, 'if it's not okay, then it's not the end.'"

I chuckle quietly as we both go back to packing up.

Despite having packed her own nightwear, Peaches looks good enough to devour in an oversized grey t-shirt she pinched from my drawer. She's in the process of putting some white cream all over her face when I step up behind her, pulling a surprised shriek from her when I spin her to face me.

Internally chuckling at her reaction, I wrap my arms around her, soaking up the comfort her mere presence brings me. When I'm with her, I can just about believe that there *is* good in this world. Good in the female species as a whole. Up to this point in my life, women seem to leave me worse than when they found me. Peaches makes me think that, maybe, not every woman will hurt you, that they aren't out for what they can gain, whether it's cash or cock, because it's always been one or the other.

Maybe, just *maybe,* people don't always leave.

"My heart speeds up when I'm near you. It's like…" I circle my hand around the back of her neck, lacing my fingers through her thick locks. "It's like until I met you, it was only half beating. Just enough to live, but not really be *alive*. When I met you, it came to life for the first time… recognising the missing beat was within you. As though, only when we came together, our hearts could be whole and beat as one."

There's silence for several long moments as we stand there just absorbing each other. Her breath gently plays across my lips and her big deep blue eyes widen impossibly further.

"Henry, I—"

"Shhh, baby." Placing my finger over her soft lips, I go on, unsure if it's feelings that have been simmering underneath the surface all along, or if the events of the evening frightened the fucking shit out of me.

Or maybe I need to get the words out now, while I still have the balls to say them because fuck knows, she's waited on my confession for a long ass time now.

Maybe it's a combination.

"I didn't comprehend how… dead I was inside until I met you. I was breathing, not living. Not really. And you slipped through my fingers back then. I'm *so* sorry I never fought for you, Peaches. I've punished us both by staying away, but having had you now, I can't go back to the human husk I was before you filled me with life. To hell with everything and everyone else."

I pull her into my chest in a bear hug as I feel her shoulders relax under my touch. "Henry." Her voice is muffled against my bare chest, but I don't ease my hold. "In case you missed the memo, I've always been yours. *Only* yours."

Her lips find the space over my heart, her nose nuzzling back and forth over the rapidly increasing beat before she plants a firm kiss on my skin as goosebumps break out underneath her soft touch. She tilts her head back, her eyes finding mine when she speaks once more.

"Meant for *only* you. Alex will be fine; he's my best friend. Leave him to me." Then, taking a deep breath, she quietly continues. "And if you're asking for my forgiveness, you surely must know you already have it."

My breath freezes in my lungs as my mind registers the truth of her words.

"I forgive you for all of it. Everything. For whatever you think you need absolution from. Truly, there's nothing to forgive."

Before she can continue, I've hoisted her into my arms with my large palms under her perfect ass. Her legs wrap firmly around my waist, her arms winding around my neck when I crush my lips to hers, immediately opening my mouth to invade hers with my tongue.

She's mine. I'm hers. And the knowledge is intoxicating.

I walk to the bed, still carrying her in my arms, before depositing her on the white sheets, the picture of seductive innocence.

I climb in behind her, pressing my almost naked body against her softness while drawing a sheet loosely over us.

Placing my mouth just by her ear, I whisper, "I'm ready to half that problem now, Peach."

Her body tenses in my embrace before she visibly relaxes and slowly turns to face me. She places her hands on either side of my face, gently tugging me forward to drop a soft kiss on my brow.

"You're shaking, Henry." Her eyebrows draw together in concern as I realise she's right. I am indeed shaking, yet I also realise that for us to move forward and be *in this*, then I need to tell her everything. No matter what she'll think of me afterwards.

I swallow roughly before blowing out a heavy breath as she clasps my hands in her much smaller ones, squeezing reassuringly. "I'm ready, Peach."

She smiles softly. Encouragingly. "If you're sure. I'll be that safe place for you."

Taking a deep breath and hoping beyond hope that this won't change things for us, I start at the beginning.

Thirty

HENRY
AGED SEVENTEEN

"Thanks for the lift, Mr North. Bye, Cade."

"You're such a fucking suck-up, DeMarco."

Slamming the door of their Range Rover while smiling broadly at my best friend's insult, I run toward my front door, kicking up a shit ton of brown and beige stones from the huge-ass driveway before turning to wave my farewell at their receding car.

Pulling the door open, I spot a briefcase just by the door, and my mouth immediately lifts into a massive grin.

Dad's home.

Flying up the stairs, two at a time, I hear raised voices just as I reach the landing. I follow the sound on silent feet, stopping outside Lauren's bedroom.

The door is cracked open about an inch, but still enough that I can hear what's being said.

"I'm done, Lauren. *Ho finito con te*. You hear me?"

I hear several drawers slamming and a zip closing, before the quiet sobbing of my stepmum meets my ears.

"And none of those bullshit tears either. I've given you everything you demanded. I refuse to do it any longer. You're a poisonous psychopath, and I won't stand for it anymore. It's bad enough you've turned my sons against me—"

"You've done that without any help from me, Rico." All signs of upset have disappeared as she hisses the words. "So just go. LEAVE! I don't fucking want you anyway."

Ducking into the bathroom opposite, as I hear footsteps approach, I barely make it inside, when my dad throws the door of the master bedroom open. I can see him through the slit between the door and the jamb; his face is scarlet, his green eyes identical to mine like thunder. He's carrying a small case, which he heaves under one arm as he turns one last time.

"I gave you the last two years to try to mend fences with my sons, to form *some* kind of bond with them, but that's been a fucking waste of my time. I can't do this anymore."

He's leaving us, leaving *me*, leaving *Alex*!

Not that I should expect anything else after years of his form of absentee parenting, but hearing it stings.

It stings so badly that I immediately shoot off a text to the boys, telling them I'm on board for the party Cade's older sister Cassidy is having later.

Having never touched a drink before, being too fearful of my stepmother's wrath, tonight is different.

I know she'll be too busy burying herself in plans of revenge to hit him where it hurts—my best bet being the company. He cares for nothing else anymore.

Not to mention her little gin habit that she thinks I don't know about. She'll be off her tits by teatime, so all I have to do is steer clear of her, and I'll be home and dry.

Realising the coast is clear, Lauren having retreated to the confines of her room, and my father very obviously disappeared, not even bothering with a goodbye, I leave the bathroom and make my way to Alex's room. I'll need to get him settled for the night before I can go anywhere; otherwise, he'll want to sleep in my room and then I can kiss goodbye to sneaking out.

"Hey, Al, you in here?"

His bed is impeccably dressed, not a single item out of place, and no sign of my little brother until I hear a noise from underneath the bed. Bending down to look underneath, I see his light brown head face down on the hardwood floor, his shoulders shaking as he sobs his heart out.

"Hey, buddy. Got room in there for one more?"

His head shoots up, his unusual amber eyes that he got from his mum focusing on me as tears fall silently down his cheeks. Whereas Lauren's eyes are cold and full of hate, my baby brother's are always brimming with his absolute devotion to me.

"I'm coming… out… Ri." His words are choppy as his voice quavers, but he doesn't waste time climbing out and into my waiting arms. I bury my nose in his neck, inhaling his comforting scent and allowing him to do the same with me.

"I don't like when they shout, Ri. It hurts my ears."

Frowning in frustration at his useless parents, glad that I'd had at least six years of decent parenting compared to his zero years, I rub soothing circles on his upper back as I begin to hum some Johnny Cash. It's our thing, always has been, and within a couple of minutes, he's calm and has stopped crying.

"Can we do some art before bed? Please?"

Swallowing a sigh because now I know I'll be late to that party, I nod my head anyway, knowing I can't deny my brother a damn thing.

And so, we spend the next hour painting and sketching, and what he lacks in talent, he more than makes up for in enthusiasm. Finally, we wind down laughing and splashing paint on each other, resulting in both of us needing to wash up before I settle him down into his bed.

"Please sing me the empire of dirt song, please?" Then, seeing that I'm about to shake my head, he ploughs on. "Please, pretty please, I'll love you forever!"

Rolling my eyes, I launch into the latest Cash song that we've been singing together, *Hurt,* the words spilling easily and with conviction from my lips and before I've reached the second chorus, he's out like a light.

Tiptoeing from the room, I quickly and quietly descend the staircase, noting the place is in pitch-black darkness, which I find strange. Lauren is always overly concerned with how things are perceived by the outside world and our mansion in darkness on a school night won't look well to the neighbours.

Despite that, I'm in a rush, so I don't ponder and instead leave via the French doors at the back, ensuring it's latched before grabbing my bike and hot-footing it to the North's house two miles away.

When I arrive, the party is in full swing, and it doesn't take me long to find Nate with his flavour of the month stuck to his lap.

I love my boys, but they are fucking manwhores of the highest order. Cade was the first to pop his cherry, having fucked Mrs D'Onofrio on her desk the day we finished Year 10, and I don't think he's ever fucked the same girl twice since then.

Nate wasn't long after that, though he'd kept the details quiet.

I'll get them out of him one day.

With Alex as my sole responsibility, it doesn't leave a lot of time for a relationship, and call me old-fashioned, but I kind of want my first time to mean something, so I'm the odd man out.

If they ever found out I've never even kissed a girl, they'd never let me live it down. Not from lack of opportunity. Mind you, I was only really interested in one girl, and she was out of bounds.

"Hailey, grab Henry and me a drink, yeah?"

The willowy blonde on his lap smiles prettily before dropping a kiss on his cheek and wandering off through the throng to, no doubt, do as she's been told. Nate may be the quiet one, but he's got this ability to just get people to do what he says without ever needing to raise his voice.

Lucky fucker.

"This is it, DeMarco. The night you pop that motherfucking cherry."

And now it seems he's trying to use that ability on me because I find my head nodding enthusiastically. "But how do I make it happen with Cassidy, 'cause she's the only one I'm interested in, yeah?"

He rolls his eyes. "Man, if you touch Cass then you can expect Caden to fuck. You. Up. You know his sisters are off-limits." Then, chuckling darkly as he leans closer, a devilish smile forms on his face. "Which is exactly why it'll be so much more fun."

We spend the next hour knocking back plenty of liquid courage in the form of tequila shooters and some expensive ass Irish whiskey that Nate whipped from his old man, until I'm slurring my words and can barely stand up.

Nate's not that much better off, and then his skinny as fuck latest squeeze—*Hannah? Harper?*—whatever her name is, carts him upstairs to one of the guest bedrooms. Moments later, I catch sight of Cassidy grabbing a beer from the kitchen, so I throw caution to the wind, deciding to shoot my shot.

Weaving through the mass of bodies, I eventually get to the kitchen, where she's just popping the cap off a bottle of lager.

"If Carlsberg did sisters…"

What the fuck am I saying? She's going to think I'm calling her my sister. Giving myself a mental slap, I note her eyebrows are raised questioningly as she comes closer.

Pull it together, idiot.

"Where are your sidekicks, Batman? You look a little worse for wear. How about you call it a night?"

I'm about to defend my inebriated state, when nausea swirls in my stomach, and before I can stop it, I bend over, turn my head to the side and empty the contents of my stomach pretty much right on Cassidy's bare feet.

I'm too many sheets to the wind to care about being embarrassed right now, and that's my final thought as the floor rises up to meet me.

The next thing I know, I'm being tucked into my super king bed, Cassidy looming in and out of focus just above me.

"Ah, there you are, Batman."

Her gentle smile reaches her eyes as her long curly brown hair falls forward, brushing across my arm.

"You were out cold on the way over here. I hope it's okay; I've had to strip you down to your jocks. Umm, your clothes were kind of gross after all that mess..."

She tucks my sweat-soaked hair off my forehead in such a motherly gesture I'd shed a tear if it didn't take so much effort.

"I've left a glass of water and some painkillers here on your bedside locker, and there are towels on either side of the bed in case you need to throw up, okay?"

Her tone sounds like she's speaking to a toddler, and my eyes start to close again as she rises to leave, but I summon the energy to reach for her hand, my fingers grazing her knuckles, stopping her in her tracks.

"I like it when you call me Batman." She smiles softly, tucking a wayward strand of her mass of brown hair behind her ears. "Stay. Please."

My words are a hoarse whisper, and whatever she sees in my face makes her smile grow before settling herself back on the bed beside me.

"I'll stay until I'm sure you'll be okay. Sleep now, Batman."

But I'm asleep again before she's even finished her sentence.

I rouse again to find Cassidy's lips on mine as she kisses me awake, her tongue moving passionately against my own, her wild curly brown hair covering both our faces to shield us in our own bubble in the already dark room.

I begin to kiss her back, pulling her against me and devouring her mouth with my own. Before I even know what's happening, she breaks our kiss and moves down my body, kissing my pecs and my abs before tugging my boxers down, allowing my hardness to spring free.

She kisses the head softly before swirling her tongue around and around, lapping up the precum that is undoubtedly seeping from me.

My head is thrown back as I can't help my hips from rolling upwards, shoving my cock deeper inside her hot, wet mouth until she pops her mouth off and in a move I've only seen in those pornos that Cade always sticks on during our study sessions, she turns and spins so that her pussy is right on my face.

Taking my dick back into her mouth, she goes to town, and I

respond in kind as I lick at her like a man possessed. I have no idea what I'm doing, but she doesn't seem to mind as she grinds into my face, coming loudly within no more than thirty seconds.

My cock pulses in her mouth, my delight and male pride at making her climax so easily, giving me the confidence to do what I do next.

I grab her narrow hips, urging her to move onto the bed on her knees before kneeling behind her and lining my cock up with her wet centre.

"Do it, Rico."

Her voice sounds strange to my still very inebriated ears, deeper and huskier, and it's weird that she didn't call me Batman, as that's always been our thing. Still, my drunk, horny side doesn't care about that right now, so I thrust my hips forward, breaching her wet cunt as a long, low moan of exquisite pleasure leaves my lips.

It only takes a handful of pumps before I'm thundering towards coming hard in her tight sheath. When she screams her own pleasure, her pussy clenches around my dick, forcibly pulling my cum from my body as I groan my own release before falling forward onto her wet, sweaty back.

It takes several minutes to come down, my body still enveloped in her tight heat. It's when I eventually lean back and am just about to withdraw, I see a tattoo on her lower back.

My heart beats so fast and loud that I can hear my blood pumping in my ears. The sound is deafening, forcing me to screw up my eyes in pain.

I know that tattoo.

Jerking back from her as though I've been hit by a thousand volts of electricity, I can see my release leaving her body, dripping down onto my bedsheets, and it's the catalyst for my reaction.

I turn to the side of the bed and begin to throw up violently. So violently that I don't stop until there are dark splats, which I fundamentally know are blood, on the towels that Cassidy had spread on my floor.

Once I've purged my stomach of everything, I know I can't delay the inevitable.

Turning to confirm my suspicions were correct, my horrified eyes meet the amber gaze of my stepmum as she sprawls unashamedly naked across my bed, a sadistic smile on her face.

"I'd like to see that cheating prick have a relationship with you now that you've fucked his wife."

Thirty-One

OLIVIA

"I grabbed some clothes off the mess on my floor, yanking my pants up while hopping toward Alex's room." Then, for the first time since he relived the most horrifying day of his life, Henry's voice breaks as he says his brother's name.

I drop a kiss on his knuckles, then lace his fingers through mine as I try to send the strength to continue from my body to his.

As though it's worked, he inhales a deep, steadying breath before continuing.

"Alex wasn't in his room, so I started to shout for him. I didn't have to shout for long before I heard his quiet cries from within my room." He swallows audibly as though he must force the following words past his lips.

"I found out later from Cassidy that he'd come to my room in the middle of the night, as he liked to do most nights. Cass had settled him back to sleep on the daybed. Since we've never spoken of it, I'm assuming he heard and saw most, if not all, of what happened, and the fact that I'd slept with his mum, *my* fucking stepmum… Jesus, Peach. Who could blame him for hating me?"

"You didn't." My voice quietly intrudes on his revelation.

His body stiffens behind me. "What?"

My heart breaks for this man who is so cool, calm, and confident, but who, underneath it all, is so utterly clueless that he blames himself for something that he had no control over.

"Henry, you didn't sleep with her." I keep my voice steady, but my tone is soft, not wanting to spook him. "She coerced you. She *forced* you."

I can feel his head shaking behind mine, his arms holding me tighter. "No, baby. I *fucked* her. I did. There's no escaping it. Trust me. I've bloody tried."

"Would you have done it if you'd known it wasn't Cassidy? If you hadn't been too drunk to realise? If she hadn't insinuated herself into your bed and taken advantage of you, her *stepson*, for crying out loud, in some crazy attempt to ruin your father's life? To ruin his relationship with his sons?"

Confusion runs riot in his green gaze, and I know immediately that this thought has never occurred to him. Not once.

I know now, as surely as I know the sky is blue, that Henry DeMarco has seen himself as the villain in his own story for the last twelve years of his life and something inside me snaps, knowing I will go to the ends of the earth to fix what's broken.

"Henry, you understand what I'm saying, right? You are *not* to blame. You are the victim here, okay? Not the villain."

"Not the villain?" He sounds utterly incredulous at the idea.

He places his hands on either side of my head, pulling me closer to rest our brows on each other. I set my hands on his warm pectoral muscles, feeling his heartbeat slowly recede to a normal level until his deep, even breathing tells me he's succumbed to the exhaustion of both the day and reliving his nightmare.

Sleep doesn't find me as I replay everything he's told me on a continuous loop in my mind, desperately searching for ways to mend these brothers' bond that had been so irreparably broken by someone who was supposed to care for them.

And hating Lauren DeMarco with every fibre of my being for what she's taken from these two exceptional men.

The flight home is a quiet affair. Neither man has heard a word from Caden about how Layla is faring, and having not gotten any the night before, I sleep the entire way. Finally, about an hour outside London, Henry climbs into bed behind me, tugging me close before his deep, even breathing tells me he has nodded off.

Disembarking from the jet, we find two black town cars waiting for us, and while our luggage is being transferred to the appropriate vehicle, we say our goodbyes. Nate wraps me in his embrace. "Don't be a stranger, Peachy." He pulls back with a wry grin on his handsome face as I playfully narrow my eyes at his ongoing play on Henry's name for me. Waving goodbye, he disappears into the back seat of his waiting car before the driver whisks him away to his countryside retreat. The enormous estate is yet another bequeathment from his late father, though this one of sentimental value as it had been his mother's childhood home.

Sensing his unwillingness to be apart and perhaps my own need to be close to him, I grasp Henry's hand in mine in the backseat of the town car, gently squeezing. "Will you stay with me tonight?"

I strive for confidence instead of neediness, unsure how our relationship will progress now that we've broken our bubble to return home. I'm sure I've blown it upon hearing the waver in my tone, that hesitant optimism ringing loud and clear even to my own ears, but Henry doesn't seem to care when his face lights up with a beaming smile that makes the golden flecks in his eyes sparkle as he nods.

Henry has someone magically swing by with clothes and a new phone for me before we've even reached my apartment door. His face is the very picture of sheepish regret, putting a self-satisfied smirk on my face at the memory of my old phone and what had happened following its untimely demise.

"You're an idiot."

I shove his bicep playfully before depositing my luggage on the small kitchen table. Before I've turned to see his reaction, he's gathered me into his embrace to nuzzle his nose against my neck.

"And you fucking love it, Peaches."

His lips move against my neck as he says the words, causing his scruff to chafe my sensitive skin in the best way before I nod softly in acknowledgement. I do love it. This soft side of Henry that no one else sees. I love it, and I can't get enough of it.

Sidestepping out of his embrace, I reach for his hand to tug him to the bedroom. Once we've crossed the threshold, I turn to take in his reaction.

My room is small but brimming with personality.

Inside the entryway, there's a chest of drawers that I've painted a matte dusty pink with odds and ends strewn across it. Sunglasses, several tubes of lip balm, a bunch of spare keys, including one to Nola and Jo's place and a large photo of me and my sister, Holly, taken a couple of weeks before her accident.

Henry moves around me, evidently having spotted the photo, and stares at the two girls in the frame for the longest time. Then he turns to me, his eyes suspiciously sparkly, and his words make my heart hurt even more than before. But this time, not only for this beautiful man but also for myself and what I've lost.

"She'd be so proud of the beautiful woman you've become, Peaches. Because despite it *all*, you're the most amazing person I've ever known. Inside and out."

His lips quirk on one side ever so slightly. "You've overcome so much and rather than hiding away from the world and ceasing to live like *some* of us..." His self-deprecating sneer makes me giggle as he continues.

"You've grown and adapted and embraced every single part of what makes you *you*. I can't say it any more plainly, Peach. I'm in awe of you."

Swallowing heavily, I step forward to plant a kiss on his mouth before resting my hands on his cheeks.

"I'm in awe of *you*, Henry DeMarco. Despite every single obstacle, every single thing that happened to you and around you and yet you've grown into a man your mother would be *so* proud of."

I'm gathered against the warmth of his broad chest before I've even finished the sentence, my ear resting over his heart, listening to the now-familiar galloping cadence and allowing its melody to soothe my weary body.

As though Henry has read my thoughts, he pulls back gently to look down into my upturned face.

"You've had *quite* the hectic few days, Peaches. Let's get ready to turn in."

Placing his hands on my shoulders, he spins me in the direction of the small ensuite bathroom, excusing himself to get a glass of water from the kitchen. I make short work of my regular night routine and, throwing on one of the satin pyjamas Jo insisted I buy, I return to my bedroom to find Henry holding my ratty, yet irreplaceable, night t-shirt in his fist as though the mere sight offends him.

His horrified eyes rise to meet my entertained ones while I try to keep my impending laughter under wraps.

"What the *fuck* is this, baby?" I can't help the snort that escapes at the tone of utter incredulity in his question.

"Things are worse than I fucking thought. Is *this* what you sleep in?"

Widening my eyes, the very picture of innocence, I clamp my lips between my teeth and nod slowly. He runs his free hand through his hair in disbelief, allowing it to fall forward boyishly over his forehead. The urge to brush it back almost overwhelms me until his eyebrows very nearly hit his hairline, and I can't hold my sniggering in any longer. Folding at the waist, I double over as laughter flows through my body, escaping from my upturned lips.

Walking forward, I pluck the offending garment from his outstretched hand, tossing it on the chest of drawers to my left.

"Oh, Henry." I shake my head. "This t-shirt holds a lot of sentimental value for me." Obviously, he couldn't know this was the t-shirt I slept in the night I met him; the night I lost almost all my belongings in the fire that killed my parents, but it holds such a special place in my heart that I'll never part with it. No matter how tattered it gets.

He looks sceptical for a long beat. Then, shrugging his shoulders, he crosses his arms across his chest and arches a brow devilishly. "I prefer you naked anyway, baby."

Unable to help myself when it comes to taking him down a peg or two, the retort has left my mouth before my brain has even registered the thought.

Mirroring his stance with my arms crossed and brow popped, one side of my mouth lifts in a taunting smirk. "Well, I hope you took a picture because you won't—"

Moving forward with the speed of a rattlesnake, he grabs my biceps to pull me to him, tucking his face into the crook of my neck to nip the sensitive skin gently before soothing the area with his flattened tongue. His words are a whispered promise that sends tingles of anticipation through my instantly attuned body.

"You'll pay for that."

But instead of following through, he moves his hands to my face and pecks my lips chastely. "I've got one last thing to attend to with Martha. I've just received an email alerting me to a disgruntled ex-employee wanting to cause a stir..."

My eyes widen when I realise what he's saying.

Andrea. Oops!

Nodding understandingly, I move around him and pull the satin shorts down along my legs, allowing them to puddle at my feet before flicking them to one side. Then, turning my back to him, I bend over, allowing him to glimpse my naked rear end as I crawl across the mattress on all fours. Spinning around to sit, I tug the sheets over my bare legs and meet his darkened, lust-filled gaze.

"I'll be here. Waiting." Barely suppressing my laughter, I snuggle under the covers, drawing them underneath my chin. He bites his lip as his nostrils flare. "You're *killing* me over here, Peach." Then, without another word, he marches out of the room to the sound of my chuckling.

I try my hardest to stay awake but evidently, I fail, as the next thing I remember is waking to the smell of sausages cooking. The morning sun shines through a crack in my dark curtains, and there's not a single sign of Henry other than the Henry shaped indent in the mattress behind me.

Grabbing my satin pyjama shorts from where I'd kicked them last night, I tug them up quickly. Then, after a quick trip to the ensuite to relieve myself and brush my fuzzy teeth, I tiptoe out of my room into my kitchen to find the most unusual sight.

Naked from the waist up, Henry is tugging off a frilly novelty apron that Freya bought me as a housewarming gift. He's dressed in the hottest grey tracksuit pants that show me *exactly* how lucky I am and nothing else.

He catches sight of me, and his face lights up as though he's not laid eyes on me in months, not just mere hours. His eyes are more gold than green, something I've noticed when he's happy, and my stomach fills with butterflies at the thought of being the reason for his joy.

He insists on plating me up a huge breakfast, though I've no idea where any of this food has come from. Without voicing my question, his reply is as Henry-esque as ever. "I have my ways, Peach. And, just a heads up, I've told HR you're taking some personal days, so until the world comes a-knocking, I'm all yours.

Two gloriously normal days follow where we play house, mapping each other's hearts, and make love for hours, memorizing each other's bodies.

On the afternoon of day one, we get the call we've been waiting for. Caden video calls Henry and Nate in their group chat to let them know that Layla and bump are both perfectly fine. Though she has been placed on strict bed rest for the remainder of her pregnancy—something to do with her blood pressure, though Henry did say that Caden was quite vague.

"There's some concern that news has leaked to the media

about the wedding and the baby. Noah has organised a full feature spread for some big magazine in the hopes it will brush Layla's hospitalisation firmly under the rug."

My brows pinch together in confusion. "But why would he want to cover up her accident?"

Henry rolls his eyes skyward. "I've known Noah fucking Spellman my whole entire life. If anything that affects him smells like a scandal and can be painted by the media to look like a scandal, then he's on it quicker than a dog on a bitch in heat!"

I can't help the unladylike snort of laughter from erupting as he smiles indulgently at me from his perch on the sofa, where he's been rubbing my bare feet like the domesticated, diligent lover he so clearly is.

"But why would it be a scandal? I don't understand."

"With Spellman, he'd never take any chances. Could be to keep news of Layla's rehab from hitting the tabloids. She was on her second week at the Priory when she found out she was pregnant. Could be any number of things really, baby. Spellman knows way more than he'd ever let on. Suppose that's how he got to the top of his game!"

"Are you sure? He was so lovely to me."

He pauses massaging the ball of my foot to meet my eyes with a deadpan look. "Takes a shark to know a shark, Peach."

"He seemed so nice at the—"

Obviously finished with my little twenty questions, Henry takes matters into his own hands and tickles my feet relentlessly until I'm a weak, laughed out mess on the sofa.

"Fancy a cuppa, then?"

His eyes twinkle with withheld laughter when I narrow mine playfully in response before nodding profusely.

"Yes please. Two—"

"Sugars. More milk than tea, you dirty animal." He pinches my big toe gently as he pulls a face at my tea preference. "I know your taste in tea at this stage, my Peaches!"

Eventually, after a day of light and laughter, lounging and love-making, Henry takes it upon himself to draw me a bath, which I find weird as all get-out.

"You don't have to do this. I am plenty capable of running my own bath, McHottie."

After dumping almost half a bottle of my favourite bubble bath under the running water, he turns to me, a grin plastered to his face and bubbles covering his cheeks.

I can't stop the bark of laughter, and soon I'm doubled over as he looks at me, askance, the bubbles dripping from his chin down his plain white t-shirt. "What, baby? What's so amusing?" His deep voice is droll, though barely containing his own mirth.

He tugs me against him, and too late, I realise his intent because before I can stop him, he's smushed his face against mine, rubbing lavender-scented bubble bath all over my laughing face. He pulls back after dowsing me sufficiently, all laughter draining from him. The suds dotted along his jawline would look hilarious if it weren't for the intensity in his eyes.

"Let me look after you, Peach. Isn't that what you're supposed to do for the people you care about?"

A lump the size of the Grand Canyon forms in my throat so that all I can do is nod as he gently rubs my suds-soaked cheeks before turning back to finish drawing the bath.

While I'm marinating underneath the bubbles and Henry is dealing with some transatlantic calls that require his attention, I come to the realisation that my feelings run deep, deeper than anything I've ever felt for another living soul before. I'm hesitant to call it love, but I *think* it could be something I've read about in my books.

It feels the way I've always imagined love to feel—the intimate love I've long dreamed of experiencing.

Whatever it is, I'm grabbing it with both hands and holding on tight because I never want this feeling to end. What we have is so much more than on a physical level, though he's the most gorgeous man I've ever seen in my life and the mere sight of him makes me weak at the knees, but that's a moot point.

We connect emotionally, and spiritually too. Body, mind, and soul. And mine are all his, because never having had that trifecta with another living soul, this feeling is an addictive combination.

Thirty-Two

OLIVIA

The following afternoon, after one particularly robust session, Henry gathers me close in his arms as our sweaty bodies stick together in the most delicious way. A ball of desire forms in the pit of my stomach, despite the four orgasms Henry has just wrung from my body with his fingers, mouth, and glorious cock.

"Peach, I don't want you to freak out, but… we've never had the conversation about being safe." I look up into his handsome face with a frown playing across my brow.

"Safe?" I'm not following.

"In the sexual sense. I just want you to know, I've been bare with one other person in my life and… well, you know who I'm talking about. I know I'm clean, so that's not an issue."

"Well, I'm obviously clean if you need me to reconfirm." However, once the words have left my mouth, I realise he's not asking me if I'm clean. Instead, he wants to know if I'm on birth control.

"Oh, sorry. You mean, am I on the pill or something, right?" His nod is slow, hesitant.

"Nope. I'm not taking the pill, Henry." His face falls, and that sadistic side he brings out in me rubs her hands in glee at this shock I've just given him.

"No, the pill doesn't agree with me. Can't take it. Is that an issue?"

His voice comes out high and pitchy, and I fight really, *really* hard to maintain my composure, wanting to wring as much out of this moment as possible.

"No. No—*ahem,* I mean, no. That's not a problem at all." His hard swallow, as though to contain a spew of word vomit, or perhaps actual vomit, is the cherry on top, and I can't hold back any longer.

Extricating myself from his embrace, I climb astride him and lean all the way over until my face is no more than an inch from his, my long hair shielding us from the outside world.

Unable to contain my giggles at his reaction, I release them into our little space as I tell him, "I get the Depo shot every three months, you great big idiot. Really, for a smart man, you can be quite obtuse at times."

As I finish my sentence, my giggles turn to a shriek of surprise as Henry grabs my hips and, in one smooth move, he flips me so that I'm underneath him. His hips grind into the soft flesh of my thighs in painful pleasure while his cock, having sprung to life at the speed of light, pushes into my still soaking wet core.

His movements are delightfully slow and measured, his long, thick hardness pressing against the swollen nerve centre inside me with every delicious thrust.

"You think you're funny, do you?"

I'm so focused on the tingling that's spreading throughout my extremities, I don't answer him. I can't.

"Answer me, Peach."

I try to nod, but I'm a slave to sensation, the slow rhythm so at odds with how we usually come together. He reaches between us, rubbing my engorged clit, spreading my juice across my lips and nub in divine circles, driving me higher and higher while keeping up the slow, deep fucking hitting that sweet spot inside of me—over and over again.

Until he withdraws, looking down to where the head of his cock is sitting on my wet centre, covered and glistening with my slickness. He grasps himself to tap his dick repeatedly on my clit, drawing a low moan of pleasure from deep within my chest.

"Do." *Tap.*

"You." *Tap.*

"Think." *Tap.*

"You're." *Tap.*

"Funny?" And upon gritting out the final word, he pulls me up onto his lap, sinking his cock deep inside, the new angle in the aftermath of the taps from his wet cock to my throbbing nub almost too sublime, but I, somehow, choke out an affirmative, because hello?

Yes, I'm *very* fucking funny.

My answer seems to set him in motion as he seizes my hips in both hands and moves me up and down on his cock, setting a punishing pace while using me to get both of us off.

All the while, his green eyes hold mine, looking deep down inside me as his hips piston up and down, in and out; the intensity in his gaze, the searing heat, the longing—it's too much.

"Henry, yes, yes, fuck me harder. I'm almost there. Harder."

He pulls me against him, burying his face in the nape of my neck, his pants of exertion hot on my skin as I feel his hand move from my hip, around my ass to my pussy, drawing a finger through the wetness, gathering my juices as he feels where we're joined. Extracting a surprised yelp as he moves his slick finger back to my untouched puckered hole, he inserts the barest tip while maintaining the ferocious speed he's built up as he fucks my pussy.

He simultaneously bites the sensitive spot on my neck, driving me wild with wanton abandon.

It's all too much. And instantly, I'm hurtling off the edge, shouting Henry's name at the top of my lungs as I come harder than ever before.

Henry follows with a long bellow, and I feel hot jets of his essence fill me as his cock pulses in my overwrought pussy, sending shivers of prolonged pleasure through my core, propelling them throughout my entire body.

As we both come down, he pulls back to place a gentle kiss on my forehead before meeting my eyes. Our intermingled breaths are short pants while we both descend from a height, with Henry reaching solid ground before I do.

"I'm not afraid of being all in this with you, Peach. And if that were to mean kids sooner than later, sign me the fuck up. I can't say it any more clearly than this."

His eyes are so intense on my own that I feel like I would happily drown in a sea of green and gold.

"I want you. I want us. I want nothing between us ever again. Secrets, lies, miscommunication, even a goddamn condom—nothing will separate us ever again. I want *everything*, Olivia Parker. I want everything with *you*."

We're brought back to earth with a bang later that evening

when he gets a call that he's needed back in New York to settle the ruffled feathers of one irate board member, though he manages to put off flying out until the following day.

We spend the night, once more, wrapped up in each other until the sun shines through the cracks in my apartment blinds before we drift off to sleep, wrapped in the safety of each other's embrace.

I wake several hours later to an empty bed with a note tied to a single blue rose, putting an unwilling smile on my lips, even though I'm heartsick he's left without saying goodbye.

Please forgive me.

You look too peaceful to rouse, Peach.

And honestly, if I wake you, I doubt I'll ever leave.

I hope to be back over the weekend, but I'll call and email while I'm gone.

I miss you already.

Yours,

H

My heart races at the promise in his words, even as I miss him with my whole self.

A sharp rap on the door draws me from my musings. So I slip on a light robe and cross the short distance from my bedroom, through my living area, to my front door.

I smile as familiar raised voices hit my ears. I throw the door open wide to find Nola and Jo standing side by side, tugging a package back and forth between them as they bicker loudly. Such typical behaviour from two of my favourite people, alongside the fact I've not seen them in what feels like forever, has me slamming into them. I throw my arms around both their bodies as they immediately stop their dispute to gather me up in their joint embrace.

"About time, girl! I'm sick of knocking and getting no answer. *Where* have you been?"

At Jo's words, I realise that I've been so deep in my Henry bubble I've neglected to touch base with anyone—my destroyed phone meaning I've been unreachable.

Drawing them into my apartment, I launch into an entirely unbelievable story, obviously leaving out Henry's secret. By the time I've reached the end, both women are staring at me wide-eyed, jaws dropped, resulting in a fit of uncontrollable giggles from yours truly.

"I think I need a stiff fucking drink, Liv. What a wild ride!"

Wagging my eyebrows at Nola earns me a chuckle at my response. "It surely was!"

"Come on, little nympho." She pauses to look at Jo. "Who the fuck knew she had it in her?"

"Well, she's definitely had *it* in her now!" Jo's response makes the three of us collapse into gales of laughter before Nola composes herself.

Flourishing a wooden spoon from a drawer, she pretends it's a magic wand as she gently taps the crown of my head. "I officially decree today *Girls' Day*. So, as the inimitable Pink said, let's get this party started!"

In true Josie style, she doesn't do things by halves. Leaving my building quickly, we discover Samuel waiting outside.

Jo rounds on me with a wink as we approach the sleek black car. "Courtesy of the cock and balls himself, no doubt."

It takes no time at all before Jo has demanded he bring us to her salon post-haste, which he does as stoically as ever.

Our trio are preened and pampered to within an inch of our lives over the following three hours, and I send more than one teasing photo to Henry, letting him know exactly what he's missing while he's away. I've lost track of the number of treatments, trims, and tweaks I've had by the time we're set to leave, with Josie warning me that *she* will be styling me from her own wardrobe.

"It's bound to be short and slutty, so—*ouch!*"

I burst out laughing at Nola's words, which earn her a solid smack on the ass from her girlfriend, just as I hear my phone chime in my bag.

Without checking the caller ID, I slide the button across to answer.

"Hello?"

"Liv! At last," a hyped-up Alex calls down the line. "Martha forwarded me your new number this morning. I was so worried when your phone was turned off and I couldn't get in touch with you."

I wasn't planning on having this conversation right now, but no time like the present, right?

"Alex, I'm sorry I needed time to figure out what I wanted without any outside influences; you know? And before you say anything… I *know* I should have told you your brother was the guy from Velvet as soon as I realised, but I wasn't sure I… I didn't think you'd…"

My words stumble to a halt, fearful of destroying the friendship that has meant the world to me for so many years, until Alex speaks again, allaying all my doubts.

"Liv, sweet girl. No matter your choices, I just want to be here for you. No matter what, I will *always* be your biggest supporter."

His words bring tears to my eyes, and it's hard to get past the ball of emotion lodged in my throat. Swallowing hard, I manage to choke out a meek *thank you* without allowing any tears to ruin my makeup, lest Jo pitch a shit fit.

"Alex, underneath all that bluster, your brother has one of the most beautiful souls I've ever encountered. I know you don't see it, but if you gave him a chance, you'd know what you're missing by not having him in your life."

"I'll have to take your word that he's changed because the man I knew was soulless… and I'll never understand how he could just leave so callously that night, without a word."

His flat tone and harsh words cause my stomach to drop, and my response is a low murmur, not wanting to remind him of things I know he'd rather forget.

"Alex, that was the night your father…"

He huffs an affirmative, sounding more like his brother than he knows. The thought brings a half-smile to my lips, despite the serious topic.

"Ah, yes. The night my sperm donor took his turn. I'd almost forgotten about that."

My heart breaks once more for my friend, whose relationships with both his father and brother were stolen from him by his conniving mother.

"Henry's not who you think he is. *Talk to him,* fix whatever is broken between you. It's not too late."

I want nothing more than to tell him that I know about what happened back then—the night Henry left—but I would never betray Henry's trust, so instead I must settle with nudging these brothers in the right direction.

"Fix *this*? Oh, Liv. Your optimism is one of the things I love most about you."

His words are nonchalant, but there's an inflection in his voice that sounds sad, troubled—regretful even. Sensing this is as far as I can hope to push things today and just grateful in general to still have my best friend, I choose to ignore his last remark.

"When will you be back in London?"

His answer surprises me. "I've been back since Sunday, Liv. Boss's orders."

My heart falls even further at the realisation that he's brought my best friend back from Dubai, knowing that I need to clear the air between us.

That man.

Jo chooses this exact moment to grab my phone clean out of my hand. "Loverboy, you need to give your girl a break. All that sex on the beach in the Bahamas not enough for you?"

Her eyes widen as she discerns it's not "loverboy," but Alex on the line. It would be comical if it wasn't so horrifying. Mutely handing the phone back, she turns to point at the door as she clamps her lips between her teeth.

"Well, a little TMI, but… um, that'd be our Jo all over!"

I'm met with silence for several moments before he exhales deeply. "A vacation together, Liv? It's serious, then?"

I don't miss a beat, answering with a firm. "Very."

"Well… okay, then. For you, I can do this. Just… Liv, I swear—if he hurts you, I will kill him. I'm not joking, okay?"

Snorting a sob mixed with a giggle that makes me sound like some demented version of Peppa Pig, we end the call with laughter on our lips and a smile in my heart.

After thanking all the employees in the salon, I follow the girls onto the curb to where Samuel is parked and waiting for us. Bless him, that man must have the patience of a saint.

I slide into the backseat, looking askance at Jo, whose eyes are still wide, face the very picture of sheepish regret, and I can't stop the bark of laughter from escaping my grinning lips.

"Oh, Josephine O'Malley. You and that damn mouth!"

Thirty-Three

OLIVIA

The trip to my old apartment is quick, and upon depositing us safely, Samuel gently tips my arm as I step out of the backseat of the car.

"Ms Olivia, I need to make a quick trip, but I'll be back to collect you girls when you need me. Would that be alright?"

His light blue eyes are fixed on mine earnestly as I reply, "Honestly, Samuel, there's no need to keep looking after me like this. The DeMarco boys will have you run ragged." His lip quirks up in an almost smile on his always so impassive face. "We can just get an Uber."

My words land on deaf ears, and as it begins to rain, he whisks me along the footpath and into the foyer of my old building, promising that he'll be back within the hour.

Jo meant business when she said she was styling me. So, after devouring a quick dinner of lasagne and two large glasses of my new favourite Sauvignon Blanc, I spend the following two hours as Jo's personal mannequin. Most of that time is spent trying on countless outfits, each one skimpier than the last. Eventually, I walk out of the bathroom after squishing my ass into a short black satin ruched dress with sparkly sequins scattered throughout and one long, sheer sleeve.

Nola squeals when she catches sight of me, and once Jo pulls her head out of her mobile phone with a guilty shrug, her face also lights up with glee.

"I know *exactly* what you need, girl."

Jo spins and reaches for her jewellery case to pluck a simple pair of sparkly silver earrings from within. She gently drops them into my outstretched palm before grabbing a pair of plain black, barely-there sandals from her shoe rack.

Once I've popped in the earrings and fastened the straps of the heels around my ankles, I stand up straight, awaiting their judgement.

My hair is sleek, split down the middle and flowing straight down my back without its usual bounce, but it perfectly fits this dress.

"That's the one. Cha-cha-ching! You look *amazing*, girl." Jo's enthusiasm is infectious as she jumps on the spot in unfettered glee while Nola laughs at her lover's signature zest for life. As we leave the apartment only moments later, our trio is smiling from ear to ear.

Walking out onto the street, we find Samuel standing in front of a black stretch Hummer, a self-satisfied grin lighting up his usually stiff features.

"Boss's orders."

After thanking him profusely, our trio climbs in to find all our favourite drinks and almost enough room to stand. The sheer decadence of the interior is on another level, and I make a mental note to thank Henry profusely upon his return.

The boy done good!

It doesn't take Jo long to get the music pumping and the drinks flowing as Samuel drives us through the city. Charli XCX's *Out Out* is blaring over the Hummer's speakers on repeat.

"This is it, girl! Our song for the night—it's been *far* too long since we've been out-out." A louder than usual Jo sets to getting the drinks in right off the bat while Nola settles beside me, eyes filled with dreams. She's always been the romantic one out of the couple.

"Please tell me again about the wedding, Liv. I'm swooning after the little tidbits you fed us earlier!"

Grateful that Henry had told me about the announcement coming through the media, I know I'm safe to touch on some wedding details with the girls so long as I leave out Layla's hospitalisation.

"I think the full ten-page spread *Hello!* magazine did today kind of hit all the valid points. They are very much in love, and really, they're both very normal and down to earth."

If you could call an open marriage, for all intents and purposes, normal!

"But honestly, girls, as bad as it sounds, especially for a massive Misdirection fan like me, I was far too focused on my own dramatics to see much outside of my own bubble!"

Crossing my fingers that deflection is the best tactic, lest I let something spill whilst I'm drinking, my redirect pays off when both girls swoon dramatically—and wholly over the top.

"Liv, you are entitled to your own life. I *know* that we may have had issues and you were caught in the middle..." Nola trails off, glancing sideways at Jo, who jumps right in.

"Basically, you've kept us together, Liv. If it weren't for you mediating some of our… disagreements—" Nola stifles a laugh while Jo rolls her eyes, continuing. "Okay, but you know what I mean. You've been the glue so many times for us."

I snap my head around to meet her eyes, but she leans forward before I can utter a word.

"Don't do yourself a disservice, baby girl. Karma *owes* you at this stage!"

She grasps me into her loose embrace, tugging a tearful Nola in with her left arm as she shouts, "Next on the playlist, Sammy boy!"

"Roses Imanbek Remix" blares through the car's speakers, and I pull my head back to level her with a droll face.

"Really?"

"You hardly thought we didn't see you mooning over those blue roses every day, did you?"

I shrug sheepishly. "Well, I—"

"Olivia Parker, *you* are the most transparent person I've ever known. It was as obvious as the nose on your face that that man had you by your girly balls from the jump!"

She throws her head back, laughing boisterously before loudly instructing Samuel to bring us to Vivaldi, a brand-new bar with several floors, live music, and the most amazing cocktails, or so she claims.

"Wow!" The word leaves my lips unbidden as we walk into the latest London hot spot, Vivaldi.

From the entry area on the ground floor, I can see floor-to-ceiling glass windows on four different levels, each with a different theme that's obvious even from this vantage point.

The four seasons, no doubt inspired by the composer and name of the bar Vivaldi, are represented in each area, which Nola tells me indicates the different styles of music on those levels.

I barely glimpse the various hued tiers, each with their own individual styling looking like something out of a magazine, before I'm ushered into an elevator. It reads *VIP ONLY*, prompting me to send a questioning look to both girls who are standing side by side, an aura of unmistakable guilt emanating from them.

Putting on my most austere mum's voice and frowning at both girls, I ask, "What did you two do?"

Nola shakes her head in silence, unable to meet my gaze while Josie stands there with her arms crossed, openly sneering with a brazenly arched brow.

The elevator *dings* as we reach our destination, which turns out to be a roof terrace, not unlike the one I'd sat on with Henry into the early hours of the night we'd met. The main difference here is that the entire place is absolutely glowing with lights, and there's music coming softly over prominent speakers that dot the area.

Stepping out of the elevator, I take it all in before I turn to ask my friends what the hell is going on, only to find the doors have closed, and I'm standing here alone.

I'd like to think it's my new adventurous side that encourages me to move further into the space, but in reality, it's probably the slightly too strong margarita I'd had in the Hummer buzzing through my veins, giving me newfound confidence.

Moving forward, I can make out the song playing much more clearly.

It takes a moment to realise it's the lyrics from *These Arms of Mine*, the song from *12 Monkeys*, the same song Henry and I danced to the night of the DeMarco Holdings Gala.

My heart quickens as my mind races.

Turning a corner, I'm suddenly speechless as a lump forms in my throat, so large it almost cuts off my oxygen supply.

"Henry!"

Standing front and centre with his broad back facing me, hands resting in his pockets and looking the epitome of sex god almighty in a tight, dark grey shirt, and black slacks, which are perfectly moulded to his pert rear, my barely breathed exclamation sees him pivoting to face me head-on. His mouth turns up in his smug, handsome smile that I've come to adore so much.

Before he's even fully turned to me, I'm racing as fast as my sandals will allow before propelling myself into his open arms. I wrap my legs instinctively around his waist before giving him a full-body hug with my whole heart.

"Oh, Henry. I've *missed* you! How have you only been gone less than twenty-four hours? How are you back already? What—what happened?"

Pulling back to look into his mischief-laden green orbs, a laugh breaks from his chest as he takes in my bewilderment.

"I couldn't leave, Peach. I didn't go to New York. I was able to resolve everything over a conference video call, that's not long after finishing up. I've been kept from you for so long, I won't be forced away from you anymore, not when I can appoint someone else to oversee international operations going forward."

My breath hitches in my throat as he goes on. "I'm going to offer the position to Alex. Not only is it his birth right, but I think, with some guidance, he could be really great. And plus…"

He trails off when I place my palm on his face, forcing his eyes to mine, overjoyed at what I know he's going to say. "And plus, you know it is a big step toward fixing things with him. Oh, Henry—I'm so proud of you."

His eyes blaze with intensity as he nods sharply before slamming his lips to mine, almost assaulting my mouth with his warm tongue until he's eating each and every deep-seated groan that he tears from my mouth as though they are an aphrodisiac of the highest merit.

Stepping backwards, he sits so that I'm straddling him, my dress around my hips, never once breaking our kiss. Deliciously, his hands move around to clench my ass, hard, making me whimper into his hot mouth before he draws his thumbs up along my hip bone slowly, teasingly, to find the tiny string of my barely-there thong, and rips both sides.

Unable to contain my yelp of surprise any more than I'm able to stop the flood of moisture to my now bared pussy, Henry tugs my bottom lip between his teeth, biting lightly before growling, "Let me in, Peach."

At his words, my movements become erratic as each touch of his lips, each brush of his fingers across my bared skin, sends me to dizzying heights long before he's so much as glimpsed my slick folds.

Reaching between us, I undo his belt and zipper in seconds, freeing his cock before lowering myself onto his hard length with a desperation I didn't know was possible.

"That's it, baby, ride me."

I grind down onto his lap, his hardness angled to hit deep, while I pepper his face with butterfly kisses.

"Use me, Peach."

Circling my hips, I open myself up more, needing this man more than life itself.

"Take all of me."

And I do. Pulling myself up until only the head remains inside, I push back down faster and faster with each downward thrust.

Reaching his hand behind me, he grasps my long hair, wrapping it around his hands once, then twice before tugging it back, forcing me to arch against him, displaying my neck to his ravenous gaze.

Pressing open-mouthed kisses all along my bare skin, he drives me wild with need as I grind my pussy against his groin with every thrust. My low moans give way to much louder, less inhibited cries of pleasure, each sound from my hoarse throat encouraging Henry to push up into me harder. Faster. Deeper. Until he begins hitting that sweet spot inside that's almost too painful to be pleasurable.

Almost, but not quite.

"Shatter for me, Peach. Come all over me. Soak me, baby. *Drown me* in your sweetness."

It's as though his words are the impetus for my climax. My eyes roll back in my head, loudly proclaiming my pleasure, uncaring of anyone or anything but this moment, here and now.

"Yes! Yes! Harder, more, yes!" My words set off something inside of him as he begins to hammer upwards, driving into me, drawing my orgasm out further until I feel I may just pass out from the force of it.

From the force of his full body worship.

His cock pulses inside my tight channel, unloading stream after stream of his seed into my greedy pussy. The feeling of taking what he gives me sends another smaller orgasm rippling through me as we both shudder to delicious completion.

Coming back to earth, Henry lets go of my hair still clenched in his fist, allowing me to roll my neck before dropping his hand to my bare ass, drawing lazy circles along one exposed globe.

"Let's stay just like this forever." His quiet words, barely a murmur, reach my ears, making my heart skip a beat at the honest sincerity in his voice.

"*Please*, Peaches."

I can feel his hardness still pulsing oh-so-sexily deep inside me as we stay connected in the most intimate of ways before I reluctantly move, only for Henry's arms to tighten around me.

Turning his head so that his green orbs penetrate deep down into my soul, I feel a rush of air leave his body as his voice breaks the sweet silence surrounding us.

"Move in with me."

Thirty-Four

HENRY

Having received snaps from Peaches earlier in the day and knowing she was having the time of her life, I'd sourced the number for her friend's salon. Both girls had been only too happy to go along with my idea.

At Josie's suggestion, I'd booked the roof terrace of the swankiest new bar in the city and had arranged to have what I've now come to think of as our song piped over the speakers. The initial plan had been to ask her to move in—a little quick if you reasoned that we'd only just started this thing between us officially, but not quick at all when I put the extent of my obsession for the last two fucking years into context.

If only she knew.

But instead, we'd succumbed to our base desires, proceeding to fuck like animals, heedless of everything outside of our bubble.

This woman consumes me, and I'll gladly allow her to if it

means she will keep me.

Stay with me.

Be mine.

Coming down from the heights our bodies have been driven to, I cradle the love of my life in my arms, my eyes blowing wide as I realise that's exactly what she is.

The love of my life.

I love her.

A feeling more potent than anything I've felt before flows through my veins, igniting my body and setting my soul on fire, knowing I'd give anything, that I'd give *everything* I own for her to love me back. Knowing that if I could just have one taste of her brand of loving, I'd be filled to capacity for the rest of my days.

And so, cock still buried deep in her hot, wet core, I blurt out the words in my heart as my gaze meets her navy blue one, taking in everything about this moment.

"Move in with me."

Her breathing falters, and her expressive eyes open impossibly wider. Time ceases to exist as her dimples appear, and her face breaks into the most captivating smile, eliciting a mirroring one on my own face.

"Yes." One word with so much meaning, so much emotion, I can't stop myself from skimming my hands up along her sinful body before settling them on her delicate neck to close the distance between our mouths.

I kiss her with all the years of emotion stored up inside me, with all the words I'm desperate to voice, willing her to take what she needs from me because everything that I am, everything that she makes me wish I could be, it's all hers.

This woman owns me.

Body.

Soul.

Dare I say—heart?

Although I've only just come so hard, I swear that I saw stars; I can feel my dick start to twitch and harden, still seated within her heat as she presses her heaving breasts against the hardness of my chest, like a cat wishing to be stroked.

"No!" she moans, trying to stop me as I grudgingly pull my hardening length from her body. I can't help but chuckle at the sexual fiend I've created.

Forcing myself to ignore her displeasure, I stand, setting her on the ground in front of me as I fix first her dishevelled state and then my own.

Reaching out my forefinger, I rub it under her swollen bottom lip, wiping away the remnants of that red lipstick she loves so much until only her naturally pink lips are visible.

"That's better, Peach."

She smirks before running her thumb all around my mouth. "Might want to fix that."

I playfully nip the offered digit, and a melody of her unique laughter chimes across the empty terrace at the sight of my irreverent grin as I clasp her hand in mine, pulling her gently towards the elevator.

"Come on. The night isn't over yet."

Her eyes narrow in suspicion, and I pull her closer, having pressed the call button on the lift.

"Let's get to know these girlfriends of yours. Only fair, since you put up with my two idiots."

Finding Nola and Josie holding court on the second floor, in the Autumn inspired section brimming with yellow, orange, and brown hues with Coldplay's *Yellow* playing under the din of raised voices in the crowded bar, I'm caught off guard to find my brother seated with them. I push the sharp pinch of envy down as deep as I can when Peach shouts his name, drawing the attention of everyone within a ten-mile radius.

Wincing, she squeezes my hand in that reassuring way she has about her before flying into his waiting arms.

"Hi! I'm Nola." A pretty redhead with a spray of freckles across her petite features holds her hand out as she tosses an easy smile my way, alleviating some of the tension in my chest.

I take her hand, pumping it up and down several times as she points with her free hand. "And *that* over there is my girlfriend, Josie."

The woman in question is dancing with much more gusto than the song requires, her antics putting a smile on the lips of everyone nearby.

Catching my eye, she tosses a saucy wink my way before starting to dry hump her stool, her short black curls bouncing as she laughs heartily.

"We call her Jo, but I'm fairly sure by the way she's grinding against that bar stool we should rename her 'Ho.'"

Unable to help it, I throw my head back and laugh loudly. I definitely like these two.

As my laughter fades, I meet Peaches' eyes to find her big dimples on display while she watches me get to know her friends. The unrestrained happiness on her face is worth everything and more as she and Alex continue to speak quietly between themselves.

We settle into the booth with the most important woman in both our lives placed surreptitiously as the buffer between my brother and me. About an hour passes quickly and easily. The drinks have flown freely, and the banter even more so when the ladies excuse themselves.

"The little girls' room calls. We'll be right back." Peaches moves to sashay away, only to fall back onto my lap when I grasp her hand.

"That's *not* how we say goodbye." Slamming my mouth over hers in a brutal claiming, my tongue forces its way past her teeth in my sudden desperation to taste her again. She melts against my chest and moans into my mouth, her own tongue duelling with mine.

I pull back to find her pupils blown wide and her chest heaving, tits thrust hard against my own breathless chest before I slip my hand into the hair at the back of her neck to draw her closer, raising my head higher to drop a soft kiss on her forehead.

"Aww!" The girls can't hold back their simpering as Peach ducks off my lap, tossing me a promising wink before taking her leave.

"Looks serious, Ri."

Raising my head, my eyes meet his remarkably unusual ones questioningly.

He has a half-smile aimed at me playing across his lips, something I've waited forever and a day to see again, but never thought I would.

"I didn't use your nickname in error, if that's what you're thinking. I've been gravitating toward a reconciliation for quite some time. Since before I even started at the company, if I'm being candid, having discovered for myself that my mother is… well, she is who she is."

He casts his eyes downward as though unable to meet mine.

"Look." He wrings his hands anxiously in his lap. "I… I don't know why I fought it for so long or why I interfered between the two of you. All I can say, I suppose, is that old habits die hard and, for that, I'm truly sorry."

He lifts his head, meeting my eyes. "Once she told me how important you were to her—that you were the *one*—"

He cuts himself short upon spying my puckered forehead and grins ever so slightly. "Ah, I see. Did she tell you she called you McHottie when she didn't know who you were?"

I nod, realisation dawning. "She spoke of me after that night?"

"Spoke of you? No. Not if she could help it. Mooned over you… well, as her best friend, I have no comment."

We exchange small smiles as my heart feels both lighter and fuller than it has in longer than I can remember.

"I can see it in your eyes, you know. How much you care for her. It makes me happy—for you both, Ri."

Straightening up in my seat, I hold my free hand out in a gesture I've thought about so often over the years but have been too afraid to complete for fear of his absolute refusal.

For fear of what I'd see in his eyes, but right now, I can almost hear Liv and her adorable euphemisms egging me on.

It's now or never.

Without missing a beat, my brother reaches his hand out to grip mine tightly, pumping it up and down twice, a lopsided grin on his features that used to make me want to move the earth and lasso the moon for him when he was a kid.

Before all that had been stolen from us.

"I don't know if I'll ever fully move past… you know—what I saw, but—"

My grip tightens around his hand. The move is wholly subconscious as my body tenses in an almost fight-or-flight mode, unwilling to go into this right now.

"No."

His eyes narrow in confusion as he tugs his hand from mine.

"Pardon me?"

"I won't get into this today with you, Alex. Maybe never. If you truly want to put the past where it belongs, *now* is the time."

His face is reminiscent of a confused child, all big eyes and furrowed brows.

"Jesus Christ, Henry. I'm confused as all fuck about the whole thing—I can't move past it without getting answers. Without knowing what happened. I need to *understand*!"

His tone brings me back to his fifth birthday when he couldn't fathom why his mum wasn't home for cake, and it was just the staff and I who sang him "Happy Birthday" as he blew out his candles.

My reply is my stony silence.

"Have you told Liv?"

Holding his eyes, I rasp out a single, impassioned word.

"Everything."

Sitting there in the tense atmosphere, I'm willing the girls to return so we can make our excuses and get the fuck out of here, but the world obviously has it out for me today because there's no trace of them in the crowd.

"Henry." His voice breaks on the second syllable. "Someday we need to iron this out. I get that right *now* is not the time, but I just need to know we'll clear the air. Someday. *Please*."

I'm still mute long minutes later until I see his shoulders droop, and my stubbornness wanes in the face of his defeat.

"Someday, okay?"

That same old grin reappears, forcing an unwilling upward tug on one side of my mouth in response, just as the girls crash back to the table with yet another round of shots.

"This one's for my McHottie." Liv, blatantly flying high on her mix of margaritas, tequila shots and, dare I say orgasms, provided by yours truly, holds out a shot of tequila to me. The lime is balanced on the side of the glass, and her other hand is held out, offering me a salt cellar.

Standing, I walk around behind her, pinching the cellar from between her fingers as I go, watching her body begin to hum under my intense gaze. Standing behind her, I pull her long hair to one side, displaying her slim neck, before drawing my tongue from her sweet spot right to just below her ear.

Her body visibly trembles, and I swear I can smell her arousal in the air, causing my dick to thicken in the suddenly tight confines of my pants.

I slowly and deliberately sprinkle the salt along the glistening trail of my saliva on her neck before pinching the lime from the side of the glass that's still held between her thumb and forefinger.

I place it between her teeth, and plucking the glass from her fingers, I quickly lick the salt, making sure to flatten my tongue all the way up before I tug her earlobe between my teeth, biting softly.

Her unchecked whimper does nothing to ease the heaviness in my balls as I knock back the shot, then fuse my lips to hers, sucking the lime while offsetting its bitterness with her luscious sweetness.

The second I break away, Peaches' eyes find mine as her words ghost across my mouth. "You remember that night at Velvet, you told me to call you get-your-coat-love-you've-pulled?"

"And that's all she wrote, folks." Alex and the girls move forward to bid us both farewell as Peach gathers her coat and bag and begins tugging me toward the exit to copious catcalls from both girls.

Having left the bar unexpectedly, and unwilling to hold on for a couple of minutes while I call my driver, Liv hails the first black cab she sees. As we slide into the back seat, she chants off her address, but placing a hand on her leg to squeeze gently, I cut her off to give him the address of my penthouse.

"I'd like to go home, Peach."

"But, Henry, my place is closer."

Sliding my hand along her bare leg until I reach the hem of her short dress, I run my pinkie finger underneath, climbing higher and higher as a shocked gasp leaves her mouth.

"*Our* home, baby. I want to go to our place." Finding her clit already wet and swollen, I barely dust my pinkie across her throbbing flesh, gathering her juices before withdrawing my hand to find my finger shimmering in her honey.

"To *our* bed."

Her eyes are hooded with barely concealed desire. She watches, enthralled when I slip my coated finger past my lips, sucking her essence into my mouth, swirling it around on my tongue like the finest vintage cabernet before releasing the cleaned digit with a loud *pop*!

Moments later, we pull up outside my building with unconcealed sexual tension crackling between us. I toss the driver two one-hundred-pound notes before we rush along the path and into the lobby, both of us uncaring of passers-by in our desperation to have one another again.

Keying in the code for the penthouse, the elevator ride is a moaning mess of undulating tongues, teeth clashing, and hips grinding, as though we are trying to inhabit one body instead of two.

Once the car arrives at our floor, we stumble into our space, lips not once breaking apart.

Reaching around her back, I frantically yank down the zipper of her dress as she tries to unbutton my shirt with trembling fingers.

Too slow.

Stepping back, I grip either side and pull, sending buttons flying everywhere as Liv's sweet giggles reverberate through the ample space. Then, advancing on her with a heated intensity in my eyes, she sobers before retreating several steps until her back is against the full glass windows of our home.

Reaching her, I peel the dress from her body, letting it fall to the floor. She steps out of it, kicking it to one side, then leans forward to unbuckle my belt.

She toes off her heels while unbuttoning my pants, her hard nipples jutting into my chest when I tug her long, straight hair back to force her eyes up to meet mine.

"Leave them on."

At my command, she stops her efforts to remove her shoes, but juts her chin out insolently before snaking her hand into my underwear, freeing my hardness into her waiting palm.

I hiss sharply when she squeezes the head of my cock, both of us fixated on my length in her petite hand as she moves in rhythmic tugs.

Planting butterfly kisses all down my chest, she falls to her knees at my feet, her wide ocean blue eyes on mine—the very picture of innocence as she licks me from my balls all the way up my shaft to my oozing slit, where she laps up my precum covetously.

Slamming my palm against the window, I throw my head back, releasing a low moan of approval when she opens her mouth and takes me deep into her throat until I hit the back, making her gag around my rigidness.

Instead of forcing me back out of her mouth, I feel her swallow around the tip of my cock, drawing me in further until a slight pop that I can feel more than hear allows me to bury myself balls deep in her divine mouth.

A shiver runs the length of my spine, settling with a glowing heat in my balls, making them draw up, sending a shot of precum down her slim neck.

Removing one hand from the glass, I softly place my palm around her throat, feeling her hum deep inside her chest.

"I can feel my cock right here, Peach. *Fuuuuuuck*! You're absolutely spectacular, baby."

Her wide-eyed, trusting gaze finds mine as I pick up the pace, my hand feeling the movements deep in her throat only adding to my pleasure.

Several slow thrusts later, and I'm in danger of finishing this way too quickly.

Pulling myself from her mouth, I swipe my thumb across her chin, cleaning the excess saliva before pulling her to standing with her chin firmly gripped between my forefinger and my thumb.

I pillage her mouth with a passion bordering on violence until she is sobbing into my mouth.

"Please, Henry, oh please. I need you."

I spin her body around, pinning her nakedness to the glass with my bare chest pressed to her back. Then I nip roughly at the tender spot on her neck, my hardness between her peachy derriere, making her squirm against me deliciously.

The city is laid out right at our feet, a combination of dark and light as far as our eyes can see.

"Everything you see before you, Peaches. Everything, baby. Every. Single. Fucking. Thing. It could wither and perish into oblivion and still, my heart would beat because of *you*."

Her whole being convulses at my words, even as I know words don't compare with how I feel for this beautiful woman who fills me with her vivacity, her awe-inspiring light in the face of all obstacles.

"For you."

Gently nudging her feet apart so that I can run my engorged head through her silky folds, her moans of anticipation exhilarate me.

Leaning closer to her ear, my breath runs across the shell, causing goosebumps to rise in its wake.

"Always for you."

Thrusting forward on my final word, I seat myself fully within her warmth as my growl of possession mingles with her gasp of pleasure.

"And now, I'm going to take what's mine. What will only ever be mine."

Thirty-Five

OLIVIA

All oxygen is pushed from my lungs when Henry draws back and penetrates my wet heat with a force I didn't know was possible.

And I fucking love it.

My hot centre clasps tightly around his hardness as he moves inside of me at speed, hitting parts of myself I had read about but had never dreamt were real outside of my romance novels.

It takes no more than thirty seconds, thirty-five at a push, before I'm coming and coming hard all over his cock.

Wrapping his arms around my waist, encouraging me to arch my back even further, Henry pulls my ass back, seating himself impossibly deeper inside me. And my greedy pussy swallows his onslaught, begging for more.

Harder.

Deeper.

Our bodies are in perfect alignment, and nothing in this world has ever felt more right. More destined.

"You love that, don't you, Peach? You love when I use your body—when I fuck this juicy cunt."

Henry's hand reaches up from my hip to tweak my nipple. It hurts oh-so-good. Sending a flood of moisture to my centre, drenching his shaft in my arousal before moving his other hand to my clit. Slapping my pussy with the flat of his fingers, I whimper against the glass before he circles them several times, gathering my juices and then moving his hand to where our bodies meet. He gently runs along my outer lips once, then twice, before slowly inserting his middle finger alongside his ravaging cock. The added friction of his thumb pressed firmly against my clit while his finger stretches me even further, has me pushing back against him with utter abandon.

He groans blissfully, his mouth on my shoulder, his breath coming in heavy pants as he hits deeper with every emphasised word, "So… fucking… *wet*."

Biting into my shoulder blade, not at all softly, I can feel my pussy begin to clench. That pained pleasure once again brings me closer to completion as I press harder against the cool glass.

"Don't stop, don't stop, don't stop." My chant only encourages him as his hips pump faster and faster, and without warning, I erupt around him, howling his name as a mind-blowing, earth-shattering orgasm rips through me, milking his cock. He groans loudly, holding himself far within my centre—so deep that I can feel his savage warmth jettison deep inside as each thick rope sends undulating waves of pleasure through my ravaged body.

My forehead is pressed against the cool glass. Chin down, desperately gasping for air as though all the oxygen had been sucked from the room. I begin to recede from our coming together when he presses a soft kiss on each shoulder blade before tenderly pulling his still rock-hard cock from my aching folds.

Taking breath after deep breath, Henry meets my eyes before smiling that devastating smile of his, the delicious one that turns my insides outside before he scoops me up into his arms, hugging me close to his broad, sweat-slicked chest.

"That was quite the welcome. I hope you don't treat all your house guests like that."

My lips quirk while his chest rumbles with deep laughter.

Having crossed the living space, Henry carries me down a very unlived-in hallway before entering the master bedroom and crossing to the adjoining ensuite. There he cleans me silently and gently of our dual releases, planting adoration filled kisses on the most random of body parts—my right knee, my left eyelid, over my heart, the tip of my nose.

Shucking his ruined shirt, he places it over my shoulders, tugging it closed over my exposed breasts before taking my hand in his, a small smile playing on his lips.

"Firstly, you're *not* a house guest, Peach. Tomorrow, we'll move you in properly, and we'll make this place our home. Okay?"

I can't quell the surge of delight that flows through me at his words as I smile broadly in reply.

"And secondly, come with me." He softly pulls my hand, encouraging me to follow him. "I need to show you something."

Walking back out of the bedroom and further down the hall, he opens a door right at the end. I enter just behind him to see all the odds and ends that make up a very much lived-in artist's studio—in total contrast to the rest of the penthouse.

"Is this where you painted your gift for Caden and Layla?"

He nods. "This is the only place I use when I'm here. I've lost count of the number of nights I've fallen asleep on that goddamn futon."

Shrugging his shoulders with a self-deprecating half-smile firmly in place, he lets go of my hand to stand at my back. Then, placing his hands on either bicep, he slowly turns me to face the door we've just come through, and the sight before me drives all breath from my body.

Directly above the door, there's an exceptionally detailed painting of a beautiful blonde woman dressed in black, tight-fitting clothes, her arms raised above her head as though in motion. Eyes closed with a slight smile on her upturned face, she looks… utterly happy. There are various hues of greens, reds, and yellows dotted throughout, giving the image an almost lifelike presence. It's stunning.

Once I manage to tear my eyes away, I look at the paintings and sketches tacked haphazardly to the wall on either side to find dozens of blue eyes staring back at me in darker hues.

"It took forever to get the colour *just* right."

My stomach drops before filling to bursting with a myriad of butterflies, ready to take flight at a moment's notice.

"Is that—" I swallow roughly and try again. "Is that *me*?" My voice raises in incredulity on the final word, earning me a deep chuckle from the man pressed close to my back.

"Peaches, I kept my distance out of respect for my father's wishes. I've spent two years telling myself that. I forced myself to swallow that you were with my brother when I had *no* reason to believe it. Not after the undeniable connection we'd shared that night."

Stepping in front of me, he puts a finger underneath my chin and gently meets my awed gaze.

"It wasn't until after the night at the O2 that I realised the truth and made a vow to fight for you. I had stayed away because you deserve so much more than the half-man I have spent my entire adult life being. But in choosing to fight for you, I also choose to fight to be the man you deserve."

I can't stop my eyes from filling with unshed tears, my heart picking up speed at his sincere, impassioned words.

"I'm going to spend the rest of my life fighting for you, fighting to be deserving of you because… I love you, Peach. I love you so fucking much, and I'm tired of not being honest with you. Of not being honest with myself."

He pauses, his eyes peering even more intensely into my own as he cradles my face between his palms. My body thrums under the heady concoction of his words and his touch, while my mind races to catch up in the silence that envelops us.

"Having you in my life, being a part of your world—it's like I've spent my entire life existing in the grey matter, the in-between. Not alive, all but dead inside, but meeting you, knowing you—*loving* you, it's like you've painted my heart with all the light within your beautiful soul, chasing away the darkness of before."

As the magnitude of his confession settles around me like a longed-for comfort blanket, a single tear falls down my cheek so that he bends forward, gently kissing it away before pulling me in against his broad chest.

"Please don't say anything tonight. Sleep on it, baby." Henry gestures around the room, including himself. "Let all of *this* settle first. Okay?"

Despite wanting nothing more than to tell him how I feel—how I'm sure I've felt for a while now—I nod almost shyly before he scoops me up, earning him a yelp of surprise.

His long strides eat up the hallway until we're once again in his room.

No, *our* room.

Depositing me on one of the most enormous beds I've ever seen, he pulls his ruined shirt off my shoulders, tossing it on a chair before stepping out of the rest of his clothes and climbing under the covers.

Pulling me against his side, I slide my leg over his and cuddle close, already feeling sleep tugging at my eyelids. The last thing that registers before I'm pulled under is his soft whisper into my hair, his words landing on my ears and travelling straight to my soul, to be cherished forever.

"I can't wait to make a life with you, Peaches."

I wake a couple of hours later, firmly entrenched in Henry's muscular arms, the lights of the still sleeping city illuminating the room around us.

Disentangling myself as quickly and quietly as possible, I make the short trip to the loo to relieve myself, my bladder fit to bursting after the amount of alcohol consumed in the previous twenty-four hours.

Once I've washed up, I walk back into the bedroom and grab a t-shirt from Henry's drawers. He's still sleeping so soundly, handsome as ever, with a relaxed brow giving him a peaceful, contented look that I need to see on his face more often.

Deciding I want to do something nice for the man that loves me, I tiptoe quietly from the room in search of sustenance, only to find Henry's cabinets are bare, apart from a half-full bag of sugar and some coffee beans for a machine that wouldn't look out of place at MI5.

His fridge is mildly better. There's a little milk, some eggs, and a block of hard cheese. But it's way stinkier than what I'm used to. Maybe it's rich people's cheese; perhaps it's gone sour. How would I know?

I wonder if he's got something like a pantry, so I move around the open-plan kitchen slash living area, the epitome of a woman on a mission, opening and closing doors to find precisely nothing.

He wasn't kidding last night when he said he just uses his studio. The memory of the words spoken in his private, sacred space last night sets my senses aflame as I decide today is the day. Today, I'm going to show him how much I love him before saying the words I so desperately wanted to say last night.

Right, enough is enough. The day is beginning to break over the city, and there's got to be a corner shop down the street, so I grab a pair of clean grey jog pants and a matching sweater from the laundry room, winding the waistband up several times before leaving a note.

We need to get groceries sorted, McHottie.
Your love cannot live on sex alone, no matter how flutter inducing!
Gone to find sustenance.
Back in five, ten at a push!

Since Henry's feet are *way* bigger than mine, I've got no choice but to slip on my heels from the night before. Ready to go, I hit the call button for the elevator, which arrives in moments, and I can't help grinning like an absolute idiot as I take in my ensemble in the elevator mirrors.

Shaking my head at the absolute state of myself, the elevator has hit the ground floor by the time I'm able to wipe the entirely too pleased grin from my face. Except for a lone door attendant, the foyer is empty. I hold back a grin as he bids me good morning while trying to withhold his look of judgment.

"Good morning. I'm just wondering if there's a corner shop

somewhere nearby?"

"There sure is, Miss. Out the door, take a left and McKellan's is a stone's throw."

Nodding my thanks, I step out into the cool morning air before turning left in search of food.

McKellan's is indeed precisely where the door attendant said I'd find it. But, alas, it's still closed. My brow puckers before I turn and begin to walk back to Henry's building, when a car pulls up alongside me.

"Ms Olivia?"

Relief fills my body at the sight of Samuel dressed casually, light blonde hair slicked back over his forehead, in the driver's seat of a silver Range Rover.

"Oh, Samuel, you frightened me for a minute!"

He grins easily, but something about it feels off. I can't put my finger on it. Perhaps I'm unused to seeing expressions on his usually stoic face.

"Do you need a lift home or anything? I'm just on my way back from my girlfriend's place." His sheepish grimace immediately makes me feel like an idiot for my paranoia, and I step closer to the vehicle as a sharp breeze hits me, making me shiver.

"Come on, climb in. I'll drop you off before I head home."

"Do you know if there's a place I can get some groceries nearby? I've been at Henry's and his fridge…" I roll my eyes exaggeratedly. "Well, let's just say, it leaves a lot to be desired."

"There's a small shop that never closes about a three-minute drive that way." He points straight down the street. "Can't miss it. But honestly, I don't mind dropping you."

"It's okay! Thank you so much, Samuel. I could use the walk." The words have barely left my mouth, when the heavens open, covering me in a big fat wet downpour as I quickly realise that

I've got no bra on, and this situation could get uncomfortable fast.

"Actually, I'll just run back to Henry's. Perhaps his building has a service for grocery delivery. I'm sure I'll see you later once you're on duty. Thanks!" I move away, shouting my words over my shoulder in my haste to get inside, out of the drizzle. Glancing skyward, I can see it's rapidly turning into a deluge.

I'm so caught up in teetering as fast as I can in my heels, attempting to get out of the sudden shower, that I don't hear the pounding footsteps on the path behind me.

In fact, I barely feel the sudden knock on the back of my head before I fall forward, the world spinning on its head.

Thirty-Six

OLIVIA

The first thing I register is the barely-there breathing of another person in the room with me. After that, my heart kicks up a notch.

Slowly opening my eyes, I blink several times, allowing the world to come into focus. Above me, I see a canopy on what looks to be a very luxurious, exceedingly large bed.

I remember leaving the apartment in search of breakfast for Henry.

Something is missing there, and though I know it's important, my pounding head won't let me remember.

Pushing up into a sitting position, the room spins, and my head beats like a drummer has taken up residence inside. Blinking my eyes several more times, I attempt to collect my bearings and then slowly take in my surroundings.

It's a private dwelling, I think. Looks to be somewhere in the countryside, owing to the view of open fields and copious trees through the dark-framed window. There is about an inch of dust on the bedside locker, and the room itself smells unused. As though no one has been inside for many years.

Reaching out, I pick up a photo frame from the locker, which is also covered in so much dust I can't see the image within until I slide a finger across the dirt, slowly unveiling the picture underneath.

What?

Two boys aged several years apart are cheek to cheek, smiling broadly for the camera as they hug each other close. My brows pull down, and my heart pumps quicker at the realisation that I recognise both of those gorgeous faces.

Henry and Alex!

The door is thrown wide open, making me drop the frame to the ground with a loud clatter. Every muscle in my body goes rigid when I jerk upright, shock playing openly across my face.

"Good to see you're awake, dearest Olivia."

I blink twice, unwilling to believe the sight before me. Blinking hard a further three more times before rubbing my eyes, I clear my throat and then croak out a single worded question. "Samuel?"

"Would you like a drink? Some breakfast, perhaps?"

My mind is racing faster than my heart, which is really saying something as he looks at me, the very picture of innocent hospitality.

"Samuel." I speak slowly, so far beyond terrified I can't find a word for the emotion. "Where am I? How did I get here?"

He continues to busy himself with something over by a daybed in the corner of the room before turning to me with a broad smile on his face.

This smile of his sends prickles of fear and wild desperation down my spine, settling there and chilling me to my bone marrow.

And, just like that, the memory hits me as I remember how I've ended up here.

I feel utterly helpless just as I hear a low moan from behind his back.

It gets louder, as though the owner is trying to shout, but something is stopping them. Drawing gingerly onto my knees, the world still a bit topsy-turvy, I look beyond him to spy another person. They're obviously female from both the sounds they are making, and the long, dark brown poker-straight hair splayed across the pillow behind them.

Momentarily forgetting Samuel and my own fear, I crawl forward, wholly focused on this other person, clinging to the realisation that I'm not alone. "Are you okay?"

The only response is more mumbling.

Trailing my eyes up and down along her back, I can see her hands are tied at the base of her spine, and I suddenly realise she must be gagged, hence the incoherency.

"Samuel, may I have some water, please?"

"Of course, dearest." His voice is entirely at odds with the deranged look in his wide, pale blue eyes.

He moves to the door, walking into the hallway beyond, and I count to five before I slide off the side of the bed, almost falling to the ground, weaker than I'd anticipated.

Stumbling as quietly as I can, I reach the girl's side within seconds, yet it feels like so much longer.

"Here, let me help you." Unfortunately, her eyes are also covered, so I tug that off first.

She's young, can't be more than fifteen, sixteen at a push. She's stunningly beautiful, with sallow skin and petite features.

And then she opens her eyes.

"Mila?"

Her golden flecked green eyes widen as she nods her head frantically.

Henry's sister! Their eyes could be mirror images of each other.

"I'm Liv, your brother's girlfriend—or well, you know? Umm, I'm also Alex's best friend. Of course, he's your other brother, but I guess you already knew that!"

I shake my head rapidly, trying to stop my penchant for rambling.

Not the time, Liv!

I tug the gag, barely loosening it. It's been tied much too tightly. I pull again, but Mila's eyes widen as she jack-knives across the bed, and I realise, she's trying to warn me of danger behind me.

I see, almost more than feel, a glancing blow to the side of my already aching skull, saved from its brunt by Mila's quick thinking. Rolling forward, I pretend I've been more hurt than I am, knowing it could work to our advantage, only to draw to an utter standstill as I take in the person before me.

Dressed head to toe in white, her long dark, normally curly hair pulled back in a high, sleek ponytail, that arrogant look I have come to associate so well with her plastered to her face and Samuel drawing up the rear. I cannot silence the audible gasp of shock that passes through my lips.

"Mrs DeMarco?"

Her perfectly manicured hand rears back before connecting with my cheek in a stinging slap that leaves me breathless.

"Who the fuck did you think it would be, you home-wrecking whore!"

My ears ring with the force behind her assault, taking in the entire picture while simultaneously reeling at this latest development.

"Samuel," she barks, all signs of her usual high-class accent gone, "get this bitch tied up alongside her bastard spawn."

Striding forward with a menacing frown on his usually pleasantly passive face, Samuel grabs me by the shoulders, hoisting me to my feet before depositing me into a desk chair. He tugs my arms behind my back and, looping a cable tie around my hands, pulls tightly, so tight that it cuts into my skin, freeing an unwilling hiss of pain from my clenched jaw.

He proceeds to bind my feet, too, all under the watchful gaze of my best friend's mother.

Drawing back slightly, a familiar scent of soap and citrus emanates from his body. He runs his finger softly across my lower lip, his eyes intent on the movement, and I barely suppress a shiver, unwilling to risk angering him.

"Remember our deal, Laur. This one's mine. Mine to fuck. Mine to hurt. Hands off her."

My eyes meet Mila's green orbs, so like her brothers, as nausea swirls in my stomach at his words, because the look in his light eyes sends a ripple of cold fear straight to my heart. His fervour is shocking and bordering on scarcely constrained violence.

"Fine. You can have the daughter momentarily as a warm-up if you wish. I need the mother to witness the child's pain."

And with those words, she produces a knife before stalking towards me slowly. Desperate to slow her even more, I grab onto something she's said that makes no sense.

"You know I don't have any children, Mrs DeMarco."

Something passes over her face as her eyes darken, and her brow draws in as much as her overly botoxed face will allow.

"What I *do* know is that you tempted Enrico away from me. I know you've dug your vicious claws into my son, too, as if stealing my husband wasn't enough, you slut. And I know that *today*, you and your spawn here will pay. For everything."

Mutely, I shake my head, confused, but that only seems to draw her wrath even more.

"Samuel!"

He winks at me, stepping forward with a savage smile slashing his face, before twisting to face Lauren. "Yes."

"Take her for some playtime. And make it *hurt*."

Her eyes meet mine and I can feel every inch of her hatred when she speaks again.

"I want her mother to feel her pain."

"Of course, Laur."

His manic grin and wide eyes are the last I see of him before he slinks out the door as Lauren DeMarco, once again, takes centre stage.

"Please, Lauren." I try reverting to her given name in an effort to stop this madness. "I am begging you here. You don't want to do this."

At my words, she grabs my chin, forcing my head back before spitting in my face.

"You couldn't possibly know what I want, Charlotte. And you definitely don't care. Not after you stole my husband and the love that was *owed* to me. The love that should have been *mine*."

Realising I'm not getting anywhere, I go along with what she's saying, playing the part of this Charlotte, or whomever she believes me to be.

"Why do you think I stole your husband? Or his love! The way I hear it, he never loved you."

Staring down her nose at me, the only physical sign that my words have affected her shows on her flushed cheeks.

"He never gave himself a chance to love me before you seduced him, Charlotte. And you sank your claws in so fucking deep, he'll never be free of you. Or your bastard spawn."

She leans closer until our noses are almost touching, her breath brushing my cheek when she whisper-shouts, "But he'll be free when you're both dead and buried."

And with that parting shot, she pushes my horrified face away with force, then strides from the room without a backward glance, twisting the lock on the outside before her footfalls can be heard in the hallway beyond.

"Mila?" My voice is a whisper. Lauren's crazed ramblings were scary but worse still, the deranged look in her eyes. She fully intends to carry out her threat and definitely has no idea that I'm not who she thinks I am.

Alex has often mentioned she has the tendency to flip a switch, but I'd no idea just how bad he had meant.

Even in our dire situation, my heart can't help but break for both my lover and my friend at how life must have been under her category of care.

"How did you realise who I am?"

Having loosened it sufficiently before Lauren's attack, Mila has managed to push the gag from her mouth, surprising me in my musings.

I can't help the small, wistful smile that graces my lips. "You share the same eyes."

"We do. Dad had the same ones. Mum's are whiskey coloured, and she always tried to claim the golden flecks in mine were her contribution."

She laughs softly, but her words have begun turning cogs in my brain as I try frantically to connect the dots. "Mila, is your mother called Charlotte?"

Her laughter cuts off abruptly as she swings her shocked gaze to meet my own. "Yes, though she goes by Lottie. Dad used to call her that."

Shit. If Lauren DeMarco thinks I'm the one who took her husband away, I don't see any way out of this. And by default, Mila is facing the firing squad.

Our eyes widen in sync when heavy footsteps come down the corridor, both of us visibly jumping when Samuel throws the door open with such force that it bounces off the dresser beside it.

"I'm back."

He moves around behind me, running his hand down the front of my hoodie, plastering his palm to my breasts and groaning upon finding them braless.

"You came prepared, dearest Olivia. I knew you could feel it too. You don't have to hide your feelings anymore. We can be together now."

Despite the ice-cold fear that snakes down my spine, I take a defiant stance. Having never been touched intimately by anyone but Henry, his proprietary words and actions give rise to repulsed anger.

How dare he!

I jut my chin out, narrow my eyes into slits, and allow pure hatred to fill my body as my jaw ticks so tightly it hurts.

"You. Are. Fucking. Crazy."

Resting his hands lightly on either shoulder, he squeezes softly.

"About you? Yes, dearest. I am." His words are softly spoken, almost caressingly, as his next statement makes the fine hairs on the back of my neck stand to attention.

"I've watched you for a long time, Olivia. From when we first met at St. Fintan's, although I look a lot better these days. Homelessness and drug addiction are hard to come back from, you know."

He winds a finger around my long blonde hair, tugging firmly until I meet his gaze, rapt upon my face with the adoration of a would-be lover, yet sending a ripple of icy cold fear through my veins like nothing I've ever felt before.

If I've given away any physical display of my fear, he's either not noticed or he doesn't care as he runs his free hand from my temple to my mouth. While absentmindedly rubbing his forefinger over and back across my trembling bottom lip, Samuel continues as though bewitched by his own revelations.

"Still, with the help of my golden goose sponsor from the shelter, the drug and drink addled Lauren DeMarco, I was able to get clean and move in here with her. All while bleeding her dry of every last penny, feeding her delusions, encouraging her paranoia, biding my time until me and you could *finally* be together. I've been patient, taking care of you from the side-lines. Setting that fire to free you from your parents—"

I cut him off with a sharp gasp before he moves in front of me and continues with an immoral smile on his lips. "I had no choice, my dearest one. They were stifling you. Dulling your sparkle, that light in your soul that makes you so unusual, so intoxicating. That sets you alone, apart from all others. Taking their lives demonstrated my endless love for you, don't you see?"

Regardless of the nausea swirling in the depths of my stomach, I nod, knowing that if I try to speak right now, I will, without a doubt, throw up.

"Driving you to work, collecting you, being there when you needed me—not to mention, supplying the apartment."

Wrinkling my forehead, the cogs begin to twist in my mind, and the reason it had never made sense hits me like a bolt from the blue.

"You own my apartment?"

He shrugs his shoulders. "Well, *technically*, Lauren owns it, as the paperwork all leads back to her. You were so much easier to get to when you moved away from your friends, not that I didn't spend time with you at any given opportunity." He sighs as he obviously remembers something, and his following words have my stomach bottoming out, threatening to eject what little contents within.

"I've lost count of the nights I've watched you sleep."

Closing my eyes, I swallow hard, pushing the tears that threaten behind my lids back down. Forcing myself to not break.

"Of the night I embraced you while you slept so fitfully."

The scent of soap and citrus assaults my nostrils as my sense of smell brings me back to the night I know he's referring to. My stomach roils dangerously, and I frantically try to think of what I can say or do to make this stop.

To make *him* stop.

"You wanted me."

Father T's comforting old phrases yet again come into my mind. That man really does have a saying for everything.

You catch more flies with honey than with vinegar, Liv.

I shove my disdain, my hurt, my anger, my frustration, my skin-crawling repulsion—everything I'm feeling, deep down, and opt for the honeyed approach, injecting as much pleading kindness into my voice as I can.

"Why are you doing this, Samuel? You don't have to do this. I can *help* you, my friend. You don't need to go along with whatever she's making you do."

And in a flash, his personality flips as he gets right up in my face, his eyes burning fanatically.

"Because you *fucked* him." He snarls the words at me as spittle flies from his mouth, landing on my face and making me retch as he draws up to his full, formidable height.

"He took something that was meant to be mine, so I've taken you from him in return."

Tilting his head to one side while looking at me with such intensity, I can't help but squirm under the scrutiny. When he speaks again, his tone is soft once more, almost indulgent.

"Besides, dearest Olivia, little Mila here and even the almighty Lauren DeMarco herself are surplus to my plans. Now that I have set things in motion, we can be together just like I'd always planned. She made me wait—kept me on a leash for the *perfect* moment."

His face contorts when he grits out, "Until *him*. And as a result of her delay, he stole the innocence that belonged to me and for that"—he raises his shoulder indifferently—"she'll be the first to go."

With those words, he brandishes a gun from the waistband of his pants while grinning maniacally, our conversation at an apparent end.

"Time to play."

Thirty-Seven

HENRY

Opening my eyes, I find sunlight streaming into the room and no Olivia in sight.

This most assuredly will not do.

Rolling out of bed, I check the bathroom first, followed by the rest of the apartment, and finally land on a handwritten note on the table by the elevator doors.

I dial her number, only to have the call go straight to voicemail.

My brow furrows deeply, and a chill of unease creeps up my spine when I see it's not long past 9 am, but this note could have been written an age since. Grabbing the phone, I ring down to the lobby and Garry, a long-standing employee, answers.

"Morning, Garry."

"Good morning, Mr DeMarco. How may I help you?"

I chuckle quietly, suddenly feeling like an overactive bunny boiler, but ask my question, nonetheless. "I'm wondering if you'd perhaps seen a blonde woman leaving the premises this morning?"

"I'm afraid I have not, sir. I've been here since before 8 am and not one person has come or gone since I've been on duty."

Thanking him, I hang up, feeling justified in what I'm about to do.

Grabbing some clothes, I quickly dress, intent on going in search of her. Unfortunately, the elevator ride is interminably longer than usual, even though I know that's impossible.

Stepping into the foyer, I almost collide with someone walking onto the lift.

"Nate?"

I've never been as pleased to see this wanker's depressed face.

"The fuck, Henry. Watch it."

Gripping his elbow, I steer him out and onto the street.

"You fancy telling me why you're acting even stiffer than usual?"

Scrubbing my hand down my face, I can feel my brow knitting together in a fusion of concern and frustration.

"Peaches went out to grab breakfast this morning and hasn't returned. I don't know why, but I can't help feeling that something's off. It's strange, but I just can't shake it, brother."

Instantly, Nate's entire demeanour changes and his take-charge persona comes to the forefront. There's no better man to be around in a crisis. I take solace in that fact, knowing he's got my back.

"Right, first things first. What's the closest shop?"

We make our way to McKellan's, a small tobacconist and sweet shop a couple of doors down. The woman behind the counter tells us that they opened at 6 am, and upon showing her a snap of Liv at Caden's wedding in the Bahamas, she confirms she hasn't seen her this morning.

"I *know* something has happened to her, Nate. I can feel it."

He narrows his eyes in thought. "Your building must have CCTV, no?"

The words haven't even cleared his lips before I spin on my heel and race back the way we'd come.

Garry is just getting off a call when I slam into his desk, my nuisance hair flopping forward, blinding me momentarily. I impatiently push it from my face. "I need to see your CCTV footage. Now." Raking my hands through my hair, I realise I must look crazed, so I try to rein it back, softening my tone slightly before speaking again.

"Please, Garry. I need to see the street outside the building in the early hours before your shift had begun."

Sensing that I'm hanging by a thread, Garry shuffles off to do my bidding, and at that moment, Nate arrives with my brother not far behind.

What the fuck?

Marching straight up to me, face like thunder, Alex pulls no punches as he drops three disposable coffees and a bag from Mucho Muffins, Liv's favourite breakfast spot, on the reception desk. "What's going on, Ri? I was dropping off breakfast, but Nate says Liv's *gone*? Gone fucking where, may I ask?"

My brother's closeness with Olivia would have bothered me before, but knowing now how much they care for each other in a strictly platonic way, it only soothes me to know someone on this earth cares for her as much as I do.

Clapping my hand on his shoulder and squeezing gently, I can feel some of the tension leave his body. And my own.

Muscle memory.

Our bodies remember the ability to ease each other as we did in childhood.

"Mr DeMarco?" Garry gesticulates that we should follow him before turning back into a small rear office full of monitors from floor to ceiling.

We take up the small space behind him as he sits at a desk, the monitor in front of him clearly displaying the street outside.

"It was easy to find her. The only person who entered or left since you both flew through the lobby last night."

His side-eye would discomfit me if I could give a shit about anything other than Peaches right now.

"Here she is. Walked out of the building shortly before 6 am and turned left. Here's the footage of the next couple of minutes. You might need to take a seat. Or call the authorities. Or maybe both. It isn't pretty, sir."

His words turn my stomach, but my eyes remain rooted on the small screen in front of us. So, we watch as a quite dishevelled Liv walks down the street, almost disappearing from view before she stops and throws her hands in the air, openly exasperated.

Such a Liv thing to do. Alex and I share a small smile as the thought surely hits both of us simultaneously.

She returns along the path and is almost within reach of home when a silver Range Rover, top-end I note, pulls up alongside her. It looks like the driver calls to her, and after a moment's hesitation, she steps closer, and I *think* she's smiling, which says that *maybe* she knows the occupant.

Suddenly the heavens open, and she turns to run toward our building, towards safety, and although my subconscious knows what's about to happen, I can't help willing her to run faster. It's like watching a horror movie, and I can't look away.

She's within a hair's breadth of the doorway, when a large man exits the vehicle and sprints after her with a speed that belies his sheer size.

He doesn't look to be much older than me, if at all, though the resolution of the footage is less than clear. He has short, cropped blonde hair, but other than that and his size, there's nothing to distinguish him from any other Joe Soap.

Reaching Liv, he jerks her back before clocking her over the back of the head in a practised move. Then, in contrast with his actions, he picks her up gently, pushing her hair away from her face slowly.

He stands there looking at her for several beats, then places a soft kiss on her forehead before returning to the Rover, depositing her tenderly in the back seat and driving on his way.

My breathing has quickened, my pulse pounding at a ferocious pace, and I feel the urge to hit someone, to hit that fucker who's taken my girl.

"Garry, can you see if you can find a licence plate on any of the footage from this camera or the ones further up the building, perhaps?"

Nodding his understanding, Garry moves swiftly to do my bidding—or at least as swiftly as his old frame will allow him to.

Stepping away, I level Nate with a look. "I'm sure you know someone who can help us discreetly, right?"

His face is as pale as a ghost, but he nods succinctly, already fishing his phone from his pocket as he walks out into the lobby.

Turning to Alex, my face falls. He's still fixated on the screen, not having moved a damn muscle.

"What?"

No response.

"Alex? What the hell?"

He turns his head as though in slow motion, meeting my rising ire, which rapidly turns into full-blown horror at his next statement.

"I know him."

"What?" The single word is a growl reverberating from deep within my chest.

"Henry." He looks as though he might throw up as he chokes the following words from his throat. "He's a driver for us—I mean, for DeMarco Holdings. His name is Samuel Hastings. He's always been quiet and steady. He's driven both of us on occasion—"

"Christ almighty. Get to the point!"

Alex swallows hard, like he's unable to get the words past his lips. "He mostly works for…"

He trails off, his head dropping into his hands as he shakes it back and forth, repeatedly as though to dislodge whatever thoughts or memories are playing inside. I grip his shoulders, shaking him back to reality. Now is not the time to fall apart. If I'm not allowed, he certainly doesn't get the fucking luxury either.

"For who, Alex? Who the hell does he work for?"

His nostrils flare while his jaw clenches and unclenches several times before he swallows. Hard.

"My mother. He mostly works for my mother. She hired him, and I… well, I've asked him to drive Liv. On *many* occasions."

I blink rapidly as my mind processes this information while swallowing back the threatening vomit. If the mention of one of the vilest human beings ever to walk this earth wasn't bad enough, the fact this Samuel prick is clearly ob-fucking-sessed with my Peaches makes my stomach bottom out while my mind spirals.

"Nate!"

His name is a loud bark, and in no way respectful, but I'm so far gone that I don't give a shit. My oldest friend knows it.

Striding back into the room, the very picture of calm under pressure, Nate takes in the image my brother and I present before he raises a sardonic brow.

"What did he do now?"

Ignoring him, I let go of Alex's shoulders and exhale deeply, preparing myself for what's sure to come.

"Alex recognised the fellow who took her. Says he works for his mother."

Neither he nor Cade knows for sure what happened the night I left home, but I'm sure they have an apparent understanding, considering what came in the period afterwards.

I lived with the North family until I came into my inheritance at eighteen. Nate practically lived there, too, for almost our entire teen years. Both of us were openly envious of the beautiful family from which our best friend came.

Having had too many nightmares to number, Caden had gone to his father. Being an incredibly perceptive man, though more often than not playing dumb just for the hell of it, Sutton North had sought a sex therapist.

Ergo, I'm sure they are all aware, but we've never openly voiced the words.

"What do you need?" My pragmatic friend is at my shoulder, concern dripping from his features.

Just then, my phone rings. I almost don't answer it until I see Lottie's name on the screen. She *never* calls, though my little sister never stops.

Swiping the button across, she launches into a tirade that chills me to my marrow.

"Henry, Mila's been taken. She went to study at school yesterday evening, but she never made it there. I've checked with everyone and had the school run through their CCTV footage."

This is all sounding far too familiar.

"They said a man in a silver SUV pulled up beside her after her driver dropped her at the school entrance. They exchanged some words, and she shouted at him before giving him the middle finger."

In the face of it all, I can't help but smirk. My sister is a force to be reckoned with, even at the tender age of sixteen.

"The stranger got out of his car, hit her across the back of her head and—" She breaks off in hysterics before eventually choking out, "My baby girl. Henry, what am I going to do!"

"Lottie, calm down." Her sobs get even louder, so I cut the bullshit. "Charlotte." My voice is stern, reminiscent of my father's, as I attempt to get her under control. "I've got this, okay. I've *got* this. Calm down, hang tough. I'll keep you in the loop. I already know exactly where she is."

Okay, so maybe not exactly, but I've got a hunch.

Her response is barely intelligible in her distraught state, but somehow, she chokes out an "Okay."

Promptly facing Alex, I grasp his arm, putting pressure on his bicep, until he meets my eyes. "Did she bring them home?"

"Th-them?"

"Liv and Mila. They're both missing. Taken by that wanker, from the sounds of it."

Nate stiffens beside me, his lowly muttered profanity drawing my gaze. I know he's had a soft spot for Mila since meeting her last year, bonding over their mutual love of the old English Classics.

"I've called a friend of mine who handles issues of a sensitive nature for the right price. No police. We can get this sorted and both girls back with minimal intrusion and still keep the media hounds out of it."

He meets my eyes. "You know if it leaks, this shit will be front-page news for weeks, months, even. Neither woman wants that, especially if…"

He doesn't finish. He doesn't need to. And I know if either Liv or my baby sister have been touched, I will kill this fucker with my bare hands.

It takes several hours, which is way more time than I wanted to wait before making a move. But eventually, Nate's contact, Jesse Ramirez, an American ex-special forces sniper who runs his own private sector retrieval team, Elite Forces, or just Elite, as he's insisted, has given the all-clear.

His team consists of two men called Bull and Joel, and a woman, Billie, all suited, booted, and kitted with cutting-edge technology, the likes of which I couldn't have imagined.

Jesse has done his homework, having located floor plans of the mansion I grew up in. Even going as far as having infrared eyes in the sky, confirming the girls are indeed being held within those walls.

The Elite foursome has agreed to allow me, Alex, and Nate to accompany them to the outskirts of the building. It's a hard-won agreement, but I need to get to the only important women in my life as soon as possible. My own safety doesn't even come into it in my need to be reunited with them.

Nate is quick to remind Jesse that he's an excellent shot—a product of his stellar upbringing.

Jesse huffs out a laugh. "How could I forget? You can out-shoot me on a really good day. I've seen it."

Nate nods darkly, momentarily thrown into some unwanted reminisce or other, but he quickly pulls himself together as, on the way to my childhood home, Jesse lays it all out for us.

"Okay, so what my guy has been able to dig up is this... Hastings is currently twenty-eight years old. He went off the grid in his late teens into his early twenties and in those years, he popped up here and there for some petty crimes. Breaking and entering. Carjacking. You know, small shit that kept him in the wild, but fed a very blatant drug addiction."

Glancing at Alex, I can see he's gone as pale as a sheet, but upon catching my gaze, he stiffens his shoulders and nods briskly before returning his full attention to Jesse.

"He eventually began staying at St Fintan's, a homeless shelter for which Miss Parker was a volunteer, before being sponsored by one Lauren DeMarco."

One phone call to Martha confirmed that Hastings is indeed a paid staff member on the books for my company, and his home address was given as my childhood home. He must have been living here with Lauren for the last couple of years while also being her driver.

We've reached the outskirts of the property and have been suited up like the team with bulletproof vests over our casual wear, when Jesse's number two, Billie, steps forward.

"Okay, guys, when we get the nod, we move as one. Elite will take up the front with your three sticking firmly on our six. If anyone decides to be a damn hero and break out of formation, I *will* shoot you myself."

Jesse nods proudly as she returns to his side before being momentarily distracted by his earpiece.

"That's the go-ahead. Let's move."

Our party of seven slowly closes the distance as a unit until a woman's scream rips through the stillness of the countryside, followed by a gunshot.

Before anyone can say or do anything, I've taken off across

the wide-open gravel driveway and thrown open the front door, Jesse and Billie right on my heels.

The sight before us is of complete and utter carnage. Dressed head to toe in white, which only makes the blood staining the marble floor underneath her body more shocking, the bane of my existence is staring lifelessly at the vaulted ceiling, a single gunshot wound right in the middle of her forehead.

Without coherent thought, I whirl around to intercept my brother, loathe to have this visual be the last image he has of his mother, regardless of my personal feelings towards her, but I'm too late.

Moving as though in slow motion, his face falls like a house of cards when he registers the sight before him. The other two members of Elite pull Nate and Alex backward as I follow willingly while Jesse and Billie scout the house for signs of Lauren's killer, presumably Hastings.

"Alex, I—"

He holds his hand up, palm facing me, and instantly I stop speaking. His face is harsher than I've ever seen it, and it's as though I can see his walls, identical to the ones I spent years erecting, have been thrown up at speed.

"Ri, let's just get everyone home safe and sound, okay? This can wait."

Putting up a wall in the face of devastation is something I'm somewhat of a professional at, and knowing that this is what he needs, I give it to him, dropping it.

For now, at least.

Billie appears on the steps leading to the front door on silent feet, gesturing for the remaining members of Elite to join herself and Jesse inside, having cleared the downstairs.

"Jesse said one of you three knows how to shoot a handgun?"

Bulls' question in his deep Texan accent has Nate stepping forward. "Here, the safety is on, but let's hope you won't need to turn it off."

Then he disappears inside after the rest of his team.

Nate and I remain by the entryway, watching as the foursome ascend the massive staircase onto the landing, splitting into two teams of two, with Jesse and Billie turning right, and Bull and Joel going left.

Alex has taken to pacing along the side of the mansion, hands buried in his pockets and his brows firmly drawn together. The tension within our trio is almost intolerable.

We are on the verge of throwing caution to the wind and following them up the stairs when several minutes of radio silence have passed, but two things happen in perfect synchronicity, thrusting us into motion.

Jesse appears at the top of the staircase, holding my little sister, her arms wrapped loosely around his neck. Her face is much paler than her normal olive complexion, standing out even more so with the mass of long dark hair clouding her petite features and a steady stream of bright red blood from a gash across her forehead.

I'm about to move toward them, assuming Billie has my girl, when a strangled scream from somewhere to the rear of the mansion pierces the air.

And my heart.

Thirty-Eight

OLIVIA

Mila and I take each other in as Samuel brandishes a small, shiny handgun from the waistband of his trousers. Assuming the worst—that he is about to kill one or both of us—I brace myself, only to stare in silent disbelief as he walks to the door and pleasantly calls, "Laur!" down the hallway, in contrast to the manic gleam in his eyes.

Turning back to us, he looks… gleeful. Giddy almost.

"Not exactly how I'd planned things to go, but"—he raises his hands unconcernedly—"she's played her part, and I'm sick of simpering to her inane whims."

At that moment, Lauren re-enters the room. "Get a move on, Samuel. Stop faffing about and do as you've been told."

She tuts, but the twisted grin on her face belies her sharp tone as she strides further into the room until she's directly in front of Mila. Reaching down, she fists Mila's long locks in her manicured hand and jerks her upright with enough force that Mila whimpers in pain.

Shouting my outrage, hoping to draw her wrath, I find she's entirely focused on the girl who's little more than a child. Her eyes don't seem so glazed, so foggy anymore, and she looks to be wholly together as she unleashes years of pent-up anger on an entirely innocent soul while I thrash around uselessly.

"The *bastard* daughter of the great Enrico DeMarco brought low—you're not so high and fucking mighty now!" Her words are spat with such vitriol, such evil, that I'm momentarily silenced.

"I've changed my mind; I think I'll play with you instead."

And at that, she rakes her nails down one side of Mila's beautiful face, deep gouges opening up directly as blood streams from the wounds.

When another person would surely cry or scream, Mila stares straight into Lauren's face, unmoving as she regards her aggressor.

"No wonder Dad fucking despised you."

The words are spoken easily, factually, and with the newfound knowledge that Mila, unlike her father, won't bow to her threats, Lauren flies into a rage, using her hold on Mila's hair to press her firmly face down into the daybed mattress, the younger girl bound and powerless to stop her.

I hear someone shouting for her to stop. Pleading with Lauren to please stop and it takes a long moment to realise that the voice is mine, though Lauren is too far gone to cease this madness.

"Samuel? Please, stop her."

He stands unmoving, turning his lips down detachedly, lifting a shoulder. "None of my concern. One less for me to kill, innit?"

As I watch Mila thrash harder, my lungs feel deprived of oxygen and I desperately pray she's hanging in there, so I do the only thing I can think of.

Flies with honey.

"Samuel?" I purposely inject a sensual tone into my voice, surprised to hear my words are steadier than I'd have thought they would be, even to my own ears.

"If you save her, I'll come willingly. I'll never leave you. We can be together. Forever. Just like you've wanted."

Shock crosses his face before he jumps into action, ripping Lauren from Mila and roughly removing her from the room despite her cries of displeasure.

Returning to me, he produces a small knife from a strap on his ankle underneath his trousers, which he uses to cut my cable ties before softly massaging my aching wrists in his gargantuan hands. Then, surprisingly, he presses the knife into my palm, obviously trusting me to keep my word.

"Cut her free, and then we'll leave, dearest Olivia. I've syphoned more than enough funds from Laur over the last five years that I'll be able to keep you in the lifestyle you deserve."

Placing a kiss on my forehead, as I compel myself to not shudder at his touch, he straightens up, pulling me to a stand beside him.

Clucking me under the chin, he sneers, "I have one last thing I have to do here, and then we'll be on our merry way."

Knowing exactly what he means, I must try to stop him from murdering anyone else. "Please, Samuel, let's just go. *Now*. I don't care about these people. I can't wait to have you to myself."

He groans deeply, running his hand the length of my body while I will myself to stay strong enough to see this charade through.

Leaning forward suddenly, he grazes his lips against mine while I suppress a shudder.

"I promise, my dearest love. This won't take a moment. I'll be right back."

He marches from the room, leaving the door ajar before I can even think of what to say next.

Knowing there's no time to waste, I jump into action, rushing to Mila's side to cut off the cable ties binding her hands and feet before gingerly turning her onto her back.

Her chest is rising and falling, but it looks as though she's passed out, whether from shock, blood loss, or both. I'm not sure.

Grabbing one of the many pillows on the daybed, I rip the pillowcase from it before reaching up to staunch the blood flow. It's hard to believe nails could do so much damage as I take in the gouges running from Mila's hairline right to her cheekbone.

Her eyelids flutter open, her beautiful eyes glazed with pain, more green than gold.

"Go!" Her voice is a bare croak before she clears her throat, repeating herself.

"Go, Liv, run. You're the one who he wants; he won't care about me, and if I know my brother at all, he's not far away even as we speak. Just—"

Her words are cut off by a scream, followed by a gunshot.

Mila's eyes open wide and urgent, all signs of pain and shock gone. "Run. Now. Please, Olivia, *go*!"

She rolls off the side of the daybed, showing me that she plans on hiding underneath, before giving me a small smile. "Do it for Henry, if not for me."

Then she disappears into her hiding place, all but invisible, before I slide the small knife along the floor, knowing I'll feel better if she has at least some way of defending herself when push comes to shove.

Her mention of Henry makes me spring to my feet, desperate to get back to him. Then, checking the hallway for signs of life, I turn right, hoping beyond hope that I've chosen correctly.

Reaching the end of the hallway, I come to a dead-end. Several doors surround me, leaving me with no option but to check inside. Finally, on the fourth door, I find a small staircase. Glad to be barefoot, I make it down to the floor below, which I'm assuming is the ground floor, in no time at all. Glancing around, I realise that I'm in a massive kitchen opening up onto a raised patio at the back of the house. I sprint across the kitchen and out of the French doors onto the patio beyond without another thought.

Pressing my body up against the side of the house, I take a minute to assess my best chance of escape. There are green fields and forest all around, though I don't see a road or hear any cars, and I can't help my heart sinking a little at the thought that this is all for nothing.

Abruptly, I hear a crash in the kitchen behind me. Chancing a peek inside through the nearest window, I can see Samuel enter through the same door I did, the front of his shirt covered in red spatter, and I'm horrified to realise it must be Lauren's blood.

Please, oh please, don't be Mila's.

Edging my way along the side of the house, scarcely daring to breathe, I reach the corner and peer around, surprised, to put it mildly, to find Alex pacing intently.

My mouth breaks into the biggest smile, realising that help is *just* within reach. However, before I can push off from the wall, an arm like a steel band wraps around my waist, lifting me off the ground while a hand clamps down over my mouth unforgivingly before I can make so much as a whimper.

Drawing me up so that my back is to his front, I suck oxygen in through my nostrils as tears flow freely from my eyes.

"Running just makes me want you more, dearest Olivia."

He taunts me as he grinds his pelvis into my rear, tearing a muffled cry of frustrated hopelessness from me when he moves off the way we'd come.

"Nothing will ever come between us again. You'll forget all about *him*, and we'll be happy together. I promise we'll be happy forever, just you and me."

I've been teetering on the edge of despair this whole time, but his words send me flying into the abyss, and I no longer care about the consequences. I'd rather die than be forced to go with him, especially when help is within arm's reach.

I bring my bare heel backwards against his shinbone, just hard enough that he loosens his grip on my mouth, allowing me to fill the silence around us with a shrill cry before he rapidly regains control.

Snapping me back against him, he snarls into my ear, "Why couldn't you just come easy?"

He takes off around the other side of the house, where I see an oversized garage standing separately just to the side of a huge gravel driveway leading to massive iron gates and a road beyond. And houses. There are a lot of houses, meaning people. Meaning *help*!

Out of the blue, there's a noise behind us, and Samuel spins around to find Henry barrelling toward us, a man possessed. The anguish and outright vengefulness on his handsome face raze me to the ground as Samuel all but tosses me to one side, preparing to tackle the man I love.

Both men collide with the strength of a nuclear explosion as Henry throws the first punch, but Samuel is faster than I'd have thought, considering his larger size. He moves at the last minute so that Henry's fist barely skims along his jaw.

Samuel gets a solid body shot in, forcing Henry backward as I stifle a cry. Henry rapidly lands one of his own and Samuel stumbles back, holding his gut in apparent pain. Both men go for several minutes, and they're evenly matched until Samuel decides he's had enough.

Reaching into his waistband, he produces the gun from before, levelling it right at Henry, and I can't stop the cry that flies from my lips as I push off the ground to go to him.

"It's okay, Peach. Stay there, baby. Everything's going to be okay."

Henry, *my Henry,* is in the line of fire. He's in this position because of me and still trying to soothe my fears. It's too much.

"You couldn't just leave well enough alone, could you?" Samuel moves closer to Henry, the gun still firmly trained on his chest. "Oh well, she'll get over this. Eventually."

He squeezes the trigger as Henry's gaze meets mine, unapologetically fearless in this moment of pure terror. Our life together, the one we never got to have, flashes before my eyes as I hear a single solitary gunshot ring out.

"What the—" Samuel sways on his feet, teetering like a house of cards. He looks down to see a hole in his t-shirt right over his heart. Moving forward toward Henry menacingly, his legs buckle and fold underneath him as he falls to the driveway with a heavy thud.

Pulling myself to my feet, I race to an astounded Henry, who's still checking himself for a bullet wound. He gathers me in his arms, kissing every inch of my face as tears stream unchecked down my cheeks.

Catching my face between his palms, he pulls back a little to capture my teary eyes with matching ones of his own. His eyes rake over every contour of my face, checking for signs of injury while my own just soak in the sight of him before me—the feel of his warm body against mine. Everything I feared I'd never have again from the moment I'd woken up in this place.

A single, fat tear falls from one green eye, making a track through the dust on his handsome face from the gravel of the driveway. "I thought I'd lost you, Peach. For good this time. I don't think I could… I don't—"

Reaching up, I wipe the tear from his jawline before bringing my hand up to swipe his messy hair back from across his forehead. "I'm here. I'm okay. We're okay."

His eyes hold mine for a long beat before he nods, blowing out a heavy breath as we turn together to find Nate standing a little way behind us, his jaw unhinged.

Mila is slightly in front of him. In her small hand is a gun, pointed in the direction of Samuel, and there's no doubt in my mind that she's the one who pulled the trigger to save her brother's life. Her outstretched hand is shaking in complete contradiction to the next words that leave her bloodied lips.

"Fucker had it coming."

She drops the gun, turning into the safety of Nate's arms as he rambles incredulously, "She grabbed it. She grabbed the fucking gun."

Three exceedingly large, burly men and a powerfully built woman stride purposefully towards us, taking in the scene. Finally, the most prominent man shakes his head. "Fuck, Hawthorne. You owe me. *Big*!"

With two dead bodies on the ground, the retrieval team—or Hulk team, as I've begun referring them to in my head—Nate hired to get Mila and me out safely have no choice but to go through the proper channels. But unfortunately, as recovery is their primary job description, murder, even self-defence, is a whole different ball game.

Having rallied themselves faster than the rest of us, both Nate and Henry take control of discreetly filling in all the blanks as to how we got here and how Lauren came to such a violent end.

Sitting beside a cleaned and bandaged Mila, our arms linked as we huddle close for comfort, we can hear the detectives grilling both men, calmly but firmly.

The woman, an elderly lady with a mass of curly red hair bound at the nape of her neck, curls springing wildly around her face, puts her hand on Henry's arm in a reassuring manner, her kindly face twisted in understanding.

Her companion, a tall, thin man with minimal hair on his head but the most ridiculous overgrown moustache I've ever seen, looks less than impressed with how neat a bow the boys have managed to tie on their tale.

"Almost done, gentlemen, if you don't mind one last thing." At their nods, he continues. "Just give me the rundown of Mr Hastings' final moments. I'm confused as to how he was so fatally injured."

Henry's nostrils flare as he hits on all the key moments, all of us undoubtedly wondering how on earth he's going to explain that his sixteen-year-old sister shot that psychopath to save his life.

An investigation is not what she needs, especially after the trauma of the last twenty-four hours.

"Mr Hastings pulled the gun from behind his back and held it on me. I… I saw him begin to squeeze the trigger and then heard a shot."

"Leading me to the real question: who shot Mr Hastings?"

Jesse Ramirez, the largest member of the Hulk team, walks up behind Henry, opening his mouth to take the heat in Mila's place.

"It was me. I shot Mr Hastings. I killed him." Nate's voice rings out coolly over the group. "I was entrusted by one of the Elite Forces with a loaded gun for our protection. When I saw Henry's life was in danger, I made a decision. I stick by my actions, no matter the cost."

From across the driveway to the grass Mila and I are sitting on, I can see both of them hold each other's eyes at his final words. Mila tries to stand, but I grip her arm tightly as Nate shakes his head almost imperceptibly.

She huffs in anger beside me, but doesn't struggle. "Idiot. I'm a minor." The words muttered under her breath would be comical if not for the severity of the situation.

Thankfully, the detectives advise Nate, and the surrounding men, that there will be an investigation, but at this point, it's basically a formality.

And at Henry's firm reminder, they confirm that things will be handled quickly and diplomatically before telling us that they will be in touch.

Rather than ringing for a driver from DeMarco Holdings to come all the way out from the city, Alex, who has circumspectly been taking everything in from a distance, suggests we take a car from his mother's garage.

"I'll drop Mila. She's on my way."

I catch Mila's eye at Nate's announcement, my wide eyes mirroring her own before she insolently rolls hers to the heavens.

Shooting Nate a look that would have a lesser man quaking in their boots—and entirely reminiscent of her oldest brother—Mila hugs Henry and me before awkwardly patting Alex's shoulder in farewell. I guess it's a start.

Before she can leave though, Henry reaches for her again, pulling her roughly against his chest. His voice crackles ever so slightly, the only indication of his barely held emotion as he whispers.

"I love you, Mouse."

My throat closes up when I hear his nickname for her. This man of mine, who's spent years perfecting his ability to reject the world before the world can reject him, and his penchant for nicknaming the women he loves.

"One time. That's all you get." Her words are muffled against his chest before she pulls back and looks up into his face. "I love you, too."

They smile softly at one another for a moment before Mila shoves Henry away.

"Enough with this soppy crap. You'd swear we'd just escaped from a life-or-death sitch!"

Moving toward the garage as she cackles at her own joke, Mila shouts back in our direction, "I'm driving."

Nate rolls his eyes before raising his hand in farewell, about to take his leave when Henry's words stop him. "Why did you take the blame, Nate?"

A half-smile playing at the edge of his lips, Nate shrugs. "My gun, my responsibility, brother." The two men embrace for a long moment before Nate slaps Henry's back, pulling back with a chuckle.

"Besides, she's just a kid, for Christ's sake."

Both men nod in understanding as Nate follows in Mila's footsteps. I catch hold of Alex's hand when Henry throws his arm over my shoulder, pulling me close so that he can clap his palm down on his brother's shoulder too. The three of us draw strength from each other as we cross toward the garage.

As we reach the massive entry, Nate peels out of the garage with Mila in the passenger's seat of a white sports car that has both men whistling.

"Lamborghini Aventador. Sweet choice!" Alex's exclamation makes Henry smile broadly while our trio walk toward the garage to follow Nate's lead.

The love of expensive sports cars obviously runs in the DeMarco family.

I'm barely through the massive door when, despite the horrors of today, a huge smile breaks across my face as I hear the brothers begin to bicker about the finer points of Porsche versus Maserati. Although their words are gibberish to my ears, I can't help but draw solace from their brotherly antics.

Everything is going to be okay.

Thirty-Nine

OLIVIA

We've almost reached the city, when we get the call from Nate that he'd dropped Mila home safely to her exuberant mother, Charlotte, who had proceeded to bestow hugs and kisses galore on her daughter's knight in shining armour, as she had called him, to the point of discomfort.

"You owe me, dickhead."

Henry's mouth draws up at one side as he answers with unmistakable sincerity in his words. "Anytime, Nate."

Henry is about to disconnect the call, when Nate's voice comes through the speaker again. "And *try* to keep our girl safe from gun-wielding psychopaths while I'm not around. I can't guarantee I'll be able to swoop in and save the day the next time."

"She's *my* girl, you wanker."

Nate's laughter rings through the car as the call ends, with

Henry shaking his head and mumbling, "That prick needs to find his own ass and stop looking at mine."

Biting my lip to quell the rising laughter, I look out the window at the city lights until I get myself under control.

Instead of dropping Alex at his own place, Henry drives straight to the underground car park by his building, instructing his brother that he'll be spending the night with us.

Alex nods mutely and just continues to hold my hand in the back seat as he has done the entire drive back.

Still being barefoot, Henry insists on giving me a piggyback ride, both of us chuckling softly, appreciatively, when we catch sight of my blackened feet in the lift mirrors.

Putting me down onto the heated marble flooring of the penthouse, Henry drops a kiss on my forehead, then walks to the island in the centre of his open-plan kitchen before opening a drawer and flourishing a whole host of delivery menus from within.

"What do you two fancy for dinner?"

Alex and I side-eye each other, knowing there's only one food we reach for when we need comfort, a slight smirk tugging on both our mouths despite the day's events as we answer in sync. "Italian!"

"Give me *all* the carbs, please!" And I rattle off some of the favourites that we always share when we go to our favourite place. "Make sure you order arancini. Maybe even two orders because *someone* doesn't like to share."

Raising his hands in defeat, Alex smiles that lopsided grin I haven't seen in an age, and I'm just so happy to be seeing him now after the events of today that I can't stop my own face from copying his.

Snorting at our display, Henry throws the menus back in the

drawer, and once he's placed the order for enough food to feed a small army, he shows Alex to the guest bedroom. "There's a shower and full bath in the ensuite if you want to get washed up before dinner, Al. I'll lay out some of my clothes for you on the bed; you've filled out a lot since you last wore my shit."

The brothers share a smirk at some long-ago memory before Henry leaves to get the clothes from his closet.

Once Henry has departed, Alex's face crumples like a piece of paper, his amber eyes filling with tears. "I'm sorry all of this happened, Liv. I don't think I'll ever forgive myself."

Marching across the room, I wrap my arms around his waist and settle my head against his chest. "Alex. This was *not* your fault. How could you even think that?"

Huffing out a tense breath, he rests his chin on the top of my head, silent for several long moments.

"If I'd not had him drive you. Get close to you; maybe this wouldn't have happened."

His voice rises, his words spoken at top speed, almost frantically. "If I'd paid closer attention to her instead of being involved in my own life. If I'd gotten her more help or given her more money... maybe this wouldn't have happened. Maybe she—"

His breath catches as a sob breaks from his throat. He takes a deep breath, followed by another. "Liv, maybe she would still be alive."

"Oh, Alex." My words are a faint murmur as I gather him as close as possible, willing my body to send him the strength to get through this. To realise it's *not* his fault.

"It's not your fault, Al." Henry's deep baritone echoes my own thoughts from his stance by the door's threshold. "If it was anyone's fault, it was Samuel Hastings and his deranged infatuation with Olivia."

Alex's chest trembles underneath my ear as I feel him inhale deeply into his lungs, his brother's words a salve to his anguish.

"Your mother was in no way blameless having played her part too, but you, brother, are entirely innocent here."

At Henry's absolution, I can feel some of the tension drain out of him before he plants a kiss on the top of my head and pulls back, focusing on me.

"I'm so grateful you're safe, sweet girl. Now, no offence, but you *reek*." Stepping out of his hold, my mouth dropping almost to my chest, the two men throw their heads back as loud, hearty laughter rings through the apartment. After the day from hell, I soak in their mirth with a contented heart as I fake flounce from the room, if only to encourage more of their camaraderie.

Reaching Henry's room—no, correction, *our* room—I grab my phone to see a barrage of missed calls and several messages in my group chat with Nola and Jo.

NOLA

Thanks for saying goodbye, horn-dog!

JOSIE

Leave the kid alone, woman. She's gotta go get some. It's been a long time coming! Geddit?! *devil emoji*

I know you were probs busy last night, but you should have cancelled lunch. I waited for hours, and you were a no-show.

NOLA

She sits on a throne of lies, Liv. We ordered after like 5 minutes. If even. Enjoy your day, whatever, or should that be whoever you're doing *wink emoji*

JOSIE

You know we're just joking, yeah?

Come on. Your vajayjay will be raw if you keep this up. You must learn to pace yourself, my young padawan *eggplant emoji*

Seriously, Liv. Where are you? Answer your bloody phone.

If I knew where loverboy lived, I'd be rocking up to the door. Seriously girl, I'm worried. Call me back!

It feels like a decade has passed since the events at Vivaldi when I last saw my friends. I hit Josie's name by accessing my favourite numbers, and she answers after half a ring, practically screeching down the line.

"The dead arose and appeared to fucking many! Jesus, Liv. You scared me. You scared *both* of us!"

In a spur of the moment decision, I decide to withhold the events of the last twenty-four hours from my best friends. Having barely accepted what happened and not yet having processed what *could* have happened, I'm not in a fit state to go there right now.

Not even with my best friends.

"Oh, you know. We were doing exactly what you'd imagine we were doing!"

Her squeal on the other line, alongside her next question, means all is forgiven and forgotten.

"Did your fanny fall off yet, then?"

We spend the next ten minutes laughing and bantering in the way Jo and I always have before I ask her to give my apologies to Nola, who's away on a work trip overnight, and hang up, heading straight for a hot shower.

Upon finding no clean towels in the ensuite, I slip quietly back to the hallway, intent on grabbing some fresh ones from the laundry room. On my travels, I hear Henry and Alex's quiet voices coming from the guest room, and I immediately stop, intent on their words despite knowing I shouldn't be eavesdropping.

"Ri, I—I had no idea. I knew Mum was ill; we *both* knew it, but Jesus Christ. She tricked our father into sleeping with her, for Christ's sake. She was obviously barmy before I even came into the picture."

"I didn't know about that until Dad told me before he died. He never told a solitary person, so how could we have known her actions were anything out of the normal. My mum died when I was so young… the memories I have are only fleeting. Lauren became my primary caregiver at the age of four, so her… unique brand of parenting was really all I knew. All either of us knew, for fuck's sake."

"Well, either way, she damn well coerced you into sleeping with her and ruined any chance you had at a normal relationship with your dad—"

"*Our* dad, Al. She ruined any chance of him having a relationship with *either* of us."

"And you just never came back. You left me with *her*. Alone."

I can hear the reproach in my friend's voice, the agony. It's like a wound that won't heal, and both men feel its never-ending pain.

"After I moved out or ran away—whatever you want to call it—I couldn't go back, Al. I just *couldn't*. The idea that you hated me after witnessing my greatest mistake…"

Henry stops abruptly to clear his throat.

"Initially, it wasn't even about you, if I'm honest. I couldn't face her. The sight of her, hell, the idea of breathing the same air as her was enough to turn my damn stomach. Eventually, with a *lot* of help, I began to move through my issues. But, Al, so much time had passed between us..."

Trailing off, Henry heaves a world-weary sigh.

"I just couldn't see how you'd ever forgive me. I didn't know how we could ever get back to being *us*. The 'us against the world' version, you know? For so long, Al, you were my whole entire world. Helping the staff to raise you… that was the only thing that got me through those dark years after my mum died and our dad all but checked out. The years where your mum used me as her whipping boy…"

My heart stops while anger churns in my chest at this new revelation. Jesus, if I didn't hate her before now, I'd be damning Lauren to the seven circles of hell for all eternity.

I'd long suspected they couldn't have had an easy time with her as their mother or pseudo mother, but hearing the words from Henry's mouth physically hurts me.

"...I was glad to spare you. Both from her ire, but also from seeing what she was capable of."

Silence permeates the room, and I slowly edge further down the hallway, not wanting to be caught snooping until Alex's low murmur stops me.

"She never treated me like that."

"And that's something I will be forever grateful for. The one good thing your mother managed to do was to ignore your existence for the most part, which is ultimately a blessing. Even though it may not have felt like one back then."

Alex huffs out a bitter laugh. "Yeah, that's true. Eventually, once I came into my inheritance, I became an ATM to her. The years after you left were identical to the ones that had come before. She continued to live her life as she wanted, without a care for anyone outside of herself. Our father called once—around the time of my sixteenth birthday, I believe, to tell Mum that if she continued to use our surname and deny him the divorce he'd been after for so long, she had to do some philanthropic work. So that's how we started volunteering. How I met Liv. How Samuel came into our lives—and our home."

"And everything worked out how it was supposed to. We're here. Safe. Together. Starting afresh?"

I can hear the unmistakable hope in Henry's voice. Then, there's some rustling, followed by an odd pounding sound, and I can't help myself edging closer to take a peek inside the room through the slightly ajar door.

The sight that greets my eyes makes my heart fill to bursting. The brothers are standing, arms thrown around each other, alternately slapping each other on the back, in that utterly masculine and wholly useless manner the male species use to communicate happiness.

Moving backwards and down the hall, I quietly grab some fresh towels out of the dryer before making my way past the guest bedroom on silent feet. Then, finally, I can hear one of them moving, and unwilling to be caught in the act, I rush to the master bathroom.

I quickly turn on the shower and strip out of Henry's soiled tracksuit, tossing it into the laundry hamper before moving under the warm spray and closing my eyes, allowing the heat to cascade along my whole body, removing the grime, filth, and unwanted memories of this day.

When my body is thoroughly drenched, I open my eyes to find Henry's gaze on me, a strange look on his chiselled features.

Tilting my head to the side, my forehead puckers as he just continues to look at me—his chest rising and falling slowly at first, but getting faster and faster the longer he stares.

I shake my head and throw my hands up. "Okay, what is it now? Give it to me straight."

After the day I've had, I'm just glad to be back here, but if there's something that needs airing, now's the time to let it out. Henry steps closer, his fists clenching and unclenching repeatedly until I realise, he's not meeting my eyes. I follow his line of vision to land on my arms, my torso, my thighs—all of which are covered in deep bruising that up until now I've not even felt, let alone noticed.

"I want to drag that bastard back from the bowels of hell just to kill him all over again." His vehement words are a deep growl brimming with frustrated anger, and despite the sudden throbbing ache throughout my body, I reach for him, grasping his t-shirt in my fist to tug him closer.

Running my hand across his temple, I push his hair back from his forehead over and over until I can feel some of the hatred ebb from his body.

"I'm *fine,* Henry. I'm here. You found me. You got to me in time—it's a couple of bruises. Nothing I can't handle."

Pained eyes meet mine. "I can't lose you. I don't think I could survive it. I—I think I know now. How he felt when she died… not that I can excuse his actions, but… I can appreciate how his world ended the day she left. I couldn't—"

His voice catches and his head drops, unable to get the words out, but I know instinctively what will help him—what will help *both* of us.

"Will you wash it away? Everything? I need to just erase the past twenty-four hours, okay?"

Turning to the side, I reach for Henry's body wash, but his hand shoots into the open shower, stilling my movement.

"Please, Peach. Allow me."

Ducking down to the cabinet underneath the matching his and her sinks, he returns to his full height, flashing a bottle of shower gel.

My brand of shower gel.

"Lavender and waterlilies. I could never pinpoint it until those days we spent at your place."

My eyes meet his, the question in mine apparent. Kicking off his shoes, he steps fully clothed into the shower, squirts some gel into his hands before rubbing them together to make a lather, and proceeds to paint delicious bubbles across my chest and abdomen.

"I made a note when I stayed over and had Jas organise to have all of your home comforts delivered here."

"Who's Jas when she's at home?"

He chuckles at my presumption before correcting me. "*He* is my PA. Jasper Knowles, though he's been working from home these past couple of months following the adoption of his little girl."

"Then why would Martha—ooh, yes, right there!"

My train of thought is utterly disrupted when Henry finds a knot at the base of my spine—a knot he's exceptionally good at working out. He grins down at me, continuing to knead my back until I'm almost boneless.

"You're *much* too good at that."

He narrows his eyes. "Trust me on this—I've never massaged a living soul in my life. I just know your body, Peach. Considering it was made to fit mine. Besides, I believe I've already expressed my opinion on how we take care of those we care for..."

Excuse me while I swoon—if I had the energy after that massage, I mean.

"I still can't believe you bought my shower gel. How did you know I'd agree to move in?" I quirk an eyebrow playfully.

"I told you before… I have my ways!" He smiles into my eyes for a long moment, absentmindedly rinsing the bubbles from my biceps, until he sobers, raw emotion manifesting rapidly in his handsome features. "Either way, *this* is your home now." His voice is low, eyes boring into mine with an intensity that knocks my breath from my lungs.

"For as long as you'll have me and all that comes with me, everything I have, everything I am, everything I want to be… it's *all* yours, Peach."

At that moment, I don't just feel his love for me. No, his love breathes new life into my soul, filling parts of me I didn't even know existed. And there's just one thing I need to do. That I've wanted to do for the longest time now. Possibly from the night we first laid eyes on each other, as insane as that sounds.

"Meeting you lit a fire inside me, Henry. I tried to extinguish it in the years after, but it refused to die away."

He lifts his suds-soaked hands up to place them on either side of my face as his eyes hold mine deeply, his brows drawn as he listens to my words intently. "When you showed up in my life all those months ago, your presence stoked the fire within me. It fed that fire until my heart became a blazing inferno of unadulterated *love* for you."

His nostrils flare as his hands on my face stiffen with anticipation.

"I love you, Henry DeMarco. I love you; I love you; I love you to the depths of my soul and back again. And I always will."

Crushing his drenched t-shirt and jeans covered body up against my equally as wet naked one, I wrap my arms around his waist, pulling him impossibly closer as he rests his brow against mine, eyes closed as we both soak up this moment.

"I love you, Olivia Parker. And I'm going to keep falling in love with each little piece of you. Each and every day for the rest of my days. I want your happiness and your sadness, your weakness and your strength. And everything in between."

Then his mouth comes down on mine. Just a meeting of mouths, gently at first, before he's nudging my lips open with the tip of his tongue, teasingly caressing mine with his.

He groans deep within my mouth when he moves to deepen the kiss, gripping my ass with his strong hands while grinding his jean-clad hardness against my stomach, and I can't stop the whimper that escapes from my throat.

The sound of knocking permeates the bubble Henry had placed around us as I register Alex's voice. "Food's here. And there's only one order of arancini… I can't promise they'll last long, Liv!"

Henry ducks his head to rest it on my shoulder, huffing out a mixed laugh of frustration and humour. "To be continued, hmm?" He nips at that sweet spot, eliciting a squeal as I jump from the shower, grabbing one of my towels to wrap around my chest.

"For sure, McHottie. But for now, priorities, please! Get dressed and come on. He's insatiable when it comes to arancini."

Forty

HENRY
SIX WEEKS LATER

Walking into our apartment, I inhale deeply—like a junkie taking a hit of the inimitable scent I've been missing these last four days while in New York, getting my brother fully invested in his new title.

Chief Operations Officer has a nice ring to it. Though I'll have the final word in all business-related matters, domestic and international, he's already excelling far beyond my expectations. He's taken to the role like he was born for it.

My brother had been through a rough couple of weeks. The loss of his mum. The revelations that came alongside that. We both felt that he'd needed the change of scenery that the New York office would provide just as surely as I needed the space to be with my heart's desire.

Following on from a thorough investigation mainly handled

by Jesse Ramirez and his crew, we'd discovered that Samuel Hastings's obsession had been more deep-seated than we'd ever imagined.

They had discovered spy cameras in every room of Liv's apartment, with coinciding footage in Samuel's quarters of my childhood home. Also, hidden apps on her phone to alert him to her location, allowing him to track her emails, her messages—her entire goddamn life.

He'd watched her closely for years. Having been sponsored initially by a delusional Lauren, he'd eventually found ways to insert himself into her life.

Alex and I had both agreed that Liv had been through enough, our bond strengthening even further over our mutual desire to keep her safe. To allow her to live freely and without fear—or as much as she could, considering the current circumstances.

And so, we'd opted to keep it between just the two of us, seeing little to gain by sharing our findings with the woman we both adored.

Her inner strength is second to none, and she continues to astonish me each and every day.

"Yes, Al. I'm just in the goddamn door. Give me a chance, for fuck's sake."

It's safe to say the idiot misses me now that I've left him on his lonesome on the other side of the pond, although I'll still be flying over once a month just to keep him on his toes if for no other reason.

"Christ, Ri. I was only asking. Tell my girl I miss her, and we'll video chat tomorrow."

Glancing around the apartment, my eyes land on the woman in question. Her back is facing me, the black fitted skirt she's wearing displaying her faultless ass in all its magnificence as my palms itch with the demand to hold her close. Her white shirt is half tucked in, half out, and she's got those hideous socks that I despise pulled all the way up to her knees.

She turns, her face breaking into a bright smile that only broadens when she catches sight of the single blue rose in my hand. Her dimples perfectly pop while I see her chest start to rise and fall faster, as though my mere presence is enough to set her heart to racing.

And, if her heart is anything like mine, then that's certainly the case, as I feel my own speed up in response.

Kicking off my shoes and leaving them by my briefcase at the elevator doors, I fall onto the couch, my eyes trained on the most beautiful and wholly irreplaceable part of my life.

"One, darling brother, Peach is most definitely *not* your girl. And two, she's on the phone, so you'll just have to wait. I'll get her to text and confirm the time."

We both hesitate. I know he's worried about how he will manage to fly solo after having me as a crutch this past week. However, I remember the sheer terror I felt at taking the helm when our father passed, so I genuinely can put myself in his shoes right now.

Lowering my voice, I drop my head onto the cushion behind me and close my eyes.

"Alex. Brother. You are going to kick ass and take fucking names, yeah? And if you need me, I'm only a couple of hours away. So look—how about I talk to Liv and see if we can make our U.S. trips fortnightly for the next few months while you get settled? Might that help?"

I can almost feel the tension leave his body at my words, and he concurs wholeheartedly with my plan before saying goodbye.

"That's great, Martha. I look forward to going through those proposals with you."

I can hear chatter coming from my head of Human Resources on the other end of the line before Liv giggles melodically. "No! Of course, I haven't forgotten dinner with you, Ted, and Father Thomas on Friday. Neither of us has."

Popping a brow in my direction, I know that she knows I had absolutely put all thought of dinner with Martha, her husband Ted, and the legendary Father T out of my head within moments of hearing said plans.

"Mm-hm, wouldn't miss it! We'll see you then. Bye!"

Ending the call, Liv plops down on the opposite end of the couch before gently placing her fluffy stockinged feet on my lap. My Peaches loves her comfort items, like these ugly-ass pink socks and an ugly-as-fuck yellow ratty old t-shirt that she likes to sleep in whenever I haven't successfully managed to orgasm her to sleep.

It's got a hole under one of her tits, showing just a hint of curvature. And all the stitching is gone from the hem. I even think it was white in a previous life, but still, she insists on keeping it.

And what Liv wants, she gets. From me anyway. I'd give her anything she asked for, but in true Olivia Parker style, she doesn't ask for much, and she expects even less.

Having known almost from the start of her employment of Liv's ability to manage an office and her infectious enthusiasm for a job well done, I'd asked her a little over a fortnight ago if she'd like to run a new division of DeMarco Holdings for me. Something my mother had always spoken about but never gotten around to. Martha had confirmed my vague memories when I had gone to her for advice.

She'd jumped at the chance, delighting me with her passion.

And so, the non-profit *Katherine's House* was born. Liv had, of course, insisted on calling it after my mother, and honestly, I didn't put up a fight. It's the perfect way to remember the woman who *gave* me life while handing it over to the woman who *gives* me life.

Martha is also balls deep in the planning aspect, as is Ted, a retired attorney, and only too willing to pitch in at any and all opportunities.

Of course, Liv's first port of call had been to the man who I'd heard so much about.

Father Thomas Vasquez of St Fintan's parish was absolutely *nothing* like I'd imagined him to be—just an inch or two shorter than my own considerable height, bald with a neatly kept light brown moustache and bright hazel eyes twinkling with such irreverence I couldn't help liking him on sight.

His first words to Liv and me, alongside his slow, mischievous wink, had cinched the deal.

"A pretty face gets old; a nice body will change, but a good woman will *always* be a good woman."

They had spoken tirelessly about a great many things, not only the development of a worthwhile non-profit, in those first weeks, but most importantly I believe it was due in no small part to Father T's help and encouragement that Peach was able to accept that her parents deaths were in no way her fault.

That was something I don't think I could have convinced her of singlehandedly—Alex either and, for that reason, if no other, we'll always be grateful to the man she views as more of a father figure than her biological one.

There had been many contenders for this first non-profit. And, although I haven't yet told her she can start as many as she damn well pleases, there was only one that held my Peaches' heart. When she'd suggested a homeless intermediary service where inhabitants of St. Fintan's and surrounding shelters in London could go to get back on their feet, I don't think I've ever been as proud. And once registered on the service, the team at Katherine's House would work on re-homing and rehabilitating their lives.

Her face shone with light, love, and a vivacity that I wanted to see from her each and every day as she ran with the project of her heart.

Plucking the flower from my grasp, she holds it under her nose, breathing in the delicate scent before raising her smiling eyes to mine.

"Martha said she's found a building not too far from St. Fintan's. Father T put her in touch with the developers. Isn't he the best? Because then, we'd be within the same area the lodgers are used to being around. We'll view it next week, but I think I'd almost take it now, sight unseen, just from the specs and proximity alone."

"I think it's a great idea if that's what you want, Peach."

Pulling the socks from her feet and tossing them to the floor, I massage the arch of her foot as she straightens her leg, a groan of pleasure escaping from between her teeth and sending a spark of desire straight to my already hard dick.

It's been like a rock since the second I walked off the lift and drank in her delicious essence.

I rub harder before skimming one hand up along the back of her calf, drawing lazy circles as I slowly climb higher. Her skin pebbles with goosebumps I've put there with my touch as I continue my ascent, our eyes locked, gazes unyielding.

Skimming my fingertips across the soft placket of her underwear, I tut as a devilishly filthy smile graces my features.

"Soaked through, Peach. Whatever shall I do with you, my naughty girl."

Raising her delicate chin in an act of defiance, making me work for her in a way that I adore, she pulls no punches. She nibbles on that plump lower lip and gives me the biggest come-fuck-me eyes I've ever seen before tossing the rose onto the low coffee table beside us.

"*Whatever* you desire."

Fuck, I adore this woman.

Grabbing her underneath the ass, I lift her as though she weighs nothing until she's straddling my lap, her tight skirt now up around her waist and her delicate pink lace, obviously dampened panties on display for my hungry eyes.

My hunger for this beautiful creature in my arms is no longer a want; it's a need. And I can't quite believe she's all mine.

As I rise to a standing position, she wraps her legs around my waist, nestling her hot core right over my aching cock while I march in the direction of the bedroom at breakneck speed, my heedless scramble ripping a wild laugh from both of us.

Tossing her on the bed, she bounces twice before slowly peeling her panties down along her slender legs, balling them up and tossing them at me. I catch them easily, grinning wolfishly when I inhale her musky scent before sliding them into my pants pocket.

Eyes never leaving the others, we slowly divest ourselves of our layers until she's naked before me. Liv drops her legs wide open, allowing me to glimpse her glistening folds in an act entirely at odds with her outwardly demure persona. She runs two fingers through them before circling her clit roughly and holding her soaked fingers out to me in an invitation I can't refuse.

Kneeling between her legs, I grab her offered digits before wrapping my lips around them and sucking them clean. Her flavour explodes on my tongue, but it's not enough. I need more.

"You should know that a taste is never enough for an addict, Peach."

Dropping to my elbows, I throw her legs over my shoulders, unapologetically burying my face in her pussy. Flattening my tongue, I run it from slit to clit before proceeding to lap at her delicious arousal voraciously. She arches her body off the bed, head tossed back as that tell-tale pink flush of a building climax blooms across her chest.

Squirming wildly against my ravishment, her hands reach down, fingers entwining in my hair as she holds me in place, moving her hips, using my mouth and face to get herself off.

"Yes, yes, yes. Right there. Oh, oh, *yes,* Henry." I can tell she's almost there, not only from how her rhythm begins to falter, but by the taste of her juices thickening and sweetening even further on my tongue.

Hugging her legs with my arms, I reach around to hold her firmly on my tongue while pressing my flattened palms over her lower abdomen before latching onto her pulsing nub and sucking hard.

Liv's legs clamp tighter around my head, and her arousal explodes in my mouth as she screams through her orgasm, my name falling from her lips like an invocation until her quivering body comes back down to earth.

As I raise my head from my place of worship, her head bends forward to lock gazes with mine. Then, grinning broadly in self-satisfaction, I run my tongue around my lips, savouring the flavour that is uniquely hers, before scrubbing my hand down my face, divesting it of her offering.

Standing up, I stroll around the foot of our bed to my bedside table and open the drawer, pulling out a small bottle of lube as Liv's orgasm heavy eyes open wide, her sharp inhalation like a shock straight to my hard shaft standing tall right at her eye level.

I lift one brow, my smile becoming more devilish with each passing second as her chest rises and falls rapidly in anticipation of what she *knows* is coming next.

Tossing the bottle onto the bed, I reach across to grasp her ankle and roughly tug her around so that her feet are hanging off the side of the bed on either side of my hips.

Running my hands up along either side of her body, I skim along her hips, past her slender waist and palm her tits, squeezing, tugging, pinching her erect nipples as she twists and writhe deliciously under me. Then, leaning over her body so that my face is right above hers and the tip of my cock is resting on her wet clit, I slide one hand higher to grip her neck, feeling her pulse pounding at pace beneath my fingertips.

"I'm going to fuck you so hard, my sweet Peaches; you'll still feel my cock inside of you this time next week."

Slamming my lips down on hers, I devour the groan she lets loose at the sound of my words, taking it into my mouth and feeding her with an answering growl of my own.

If I could merge our beings into one and live inside her forever, I'd do it in a heartbeat. This woman is my favourite place to be. Her body is my sanctuary, her heart my home.

Breaking our lips apart, she cries out at the loss of contact as I rub my hardness through her folds, lining myself up with her heat and plunging inside mercilessly.

I pump my hips several times before circling them to grind the short hairs at the base of my cock against her hooded pearl with each pass as the feeling of being *exactly* where I belong washes over me.

Standing to my full height, I hold Liv's legs together, forcing her tight walls to clamp down even harder on my cock.

"So wet. So tight. Fuck, your greedy pussy is sucking me in, Peach."

I can feel the new angle hitting that distended bundle of nerves within her core with each rapid thrust of my hips just as her pussy convulses around me. Her orgasm flows through her body faster than a lightning strike, ecstasy exploding across her face and inside her heat so suddenly that my balls draw up as that tell-tale tingle begins at the base of my spine.

She's still shuddering in completion, with my cock impaled deep within her warm cunt, her skin dewy with perspiration, when I grip her hips and, in one fluid movement, flip her onto her stomach. She bends her knees so that her delectable, peachy cheeks are laid out before me in all their glory.

Seizing the bottle of lube from its resting place on the bed, I pop the lid and slowly drip a few drops onto her pert ass. The sensation of the cool fluid trickling down along her puckered hole causes Liv to gasp as I run my thumb along the trail the liquid has left behind before settling right on her little rosebud. Circling my thumb, nudging gently at first, then harder when I see a shiver ripple along her spine as she arches her back, pressing herself closer to my searching hand.

I reach around her hip with my other hand, softly skimming the pad of my thumb across her clitoris. Her whole body jerks from that slightest friction as I lean over her back, taking her earlobe between my teeth, before I whisper, "I'm going to take you here now. Just like this."

Probing my thumb deeper, I can almost hear the small *pop* as it breaches her tight ring of untouched muscle while, in tandem, I increase the pressure of my other thumb on her engorged nub, sending a flood of moisture pooling between her thighs.

I press open-mouthed kisses all along her neck, shoulder and onto her back, drinking in her cries of pleasure as I pump my thumb deeper and faster into her ass.

"Oh please, please fuck me. Fuck my ass."

Jesus Christ, she's never talked dirty to me, but hell, if those words don't have me almost coming all over her perfect cheeks.

Her cry of displeasure when I remove my thumb quickly turns into a loud moan of encouragement as I line up my cock and squirt some more lube onto both of us, rubbing it in quickly.

Gripping her hip with my free hand, I press forward, her lubricated asshole initially rejecting this considerably larger, new intrusion.

"Relax, Peach. Let your body go, and I'll take it to heights you've never even dreamt of."

Surging forward, I feel her body accept mine as I sink slowly, oh-so-slowly inside. Then, picking back up where I'd left off, I resume strumming her clit until she's pushing back against me, seeking more, and it's then I sink deeper, burying my length inside her virgin hole.

"Oh fuck. Oh fuck. Oh my GOD!"

Stilling my movement, I allow her to take all of me—to become accustomed to my body's invasion into hers. My whole being is trembling with the effort of giving her the time she needs to adjust, my brow dripping heavy beads of sweat onto her lower back as I take in the view before me, my cock seated as deep as it can go in her perfect ass.

All the while, I'm continuing my assault on her clit, giving her more and more friction until she pushes back against me, encouraging me to move.

"Henry. Move. *Please* move. I need… I need—"

"What do you need? Tell me what you need, Peaches."

Dropping her head onto the mattress, she lifts her ass impossibly higher as I clench my jaw at the wondrous sight before me.

"I need—" Her words are barely a whisper as she struggles to catch her breath. "I need *you*. I need *everything* you have, Henry!"

Her declaration travels through my ears, along my entire body and settles heavily in my cock, willing me to take, take, take.

"Your wish, baby...."

Our bodies move in perfect synchronicity as I pump in and out several times, not stopping my movements on her swollen bud while holding her firmly by the hip, but it's too good. It's too much.

The visual feast spread before my eyes. Her moans of pleasure tantalising my ears. The feel of our naked skin on skin. The scent of our combined arousal mixed with our joint perspiration.

I'm going to come, but not before her.

"Come for me, Peach. Come *now*."

"Henry, I'm so close." She reaches her own hand down, pressing my thumb against her clit harder, before sinking her own finger inside her pussy while I continue to fuck her deep in her ass.

"Jesus, Peach, I'm going to come. I can't stop it."

I can't hold back. Leaning over her body, I bite that sensitive spot on her neck, and that's all it takes to send us both spiralling over the edge as I almost black out with the force of my orgasm.

Falling forward over her perspiration-soaked back, I'm careful to protect her from most of my weight as we both come back down from the crest of our passion.

I'm careful to ease myself out of her body. The sight of my load flowing freely from her ass is almost enough to get my cock throbbing again, if such a thing were possible after how hard I've just come.

"I'll just grab a towel and get us cleaned up, baby."

Her response is a bare murmur, face down on the mattress.

Making my way to our ensuite on jelly legs, I wet a hand towel and clean myself, then toss it in the hamper before soaking a second one for Liv.

The sound of her heavy breathing is apparent the minute I re-enter our room, and a satisfied smile spreads across my face.

Mission a-fucking-ccomplished!

Forty-One

OLIVIA

Within two weeks of signing the deed to the building for Katherine's, we are almost ready to open our doors to all those who need us. I can scarcely believe how quickly things can get done when the right amount of cash is involved, but Henry had insisted we move swiftly. I don't think I have the heart to deny him anything, especially when his main goal is just to make me happy.

And I am. I'm happier than I've ever been or ever dreamed I could be. Even with the knowledge that my parents deaths are on my hands; I'm slowly making progress. With the help of Father Thomas, I'm in the process of forgiving myself, letting go of the ingrained guilt and finding peace.

After the events with Lauren DeMarco and Samuel Hastings, the police investigation had been quick and painless, though both Mila and I, as well as Alex, had struggled in the coming weeks.

I've been exceptionally fortunate with the bond I have with Father T. He's like a friend, teacher, father figure, and therapist, all rolled into one.

Together, we'd thrown ourselves into the project of setting up the non-profit, Katherine's House, and Alex had done the same with his new title at the DeMarco offices in New York. We'd both made a pact to always be there for each other as we had always been over the years, and as much as it pained me to see my best friend move so far away, I knew it was what he needed to allow himself to heal.

I'm not utterly obtuse. I know there are things both of my men are keeping from me… however, I also know, these men would take a bullet for me—one already tried to—so I'm willing to allow them to keep their secrets, knowing that whatever they've retained is to keep me safe.

Mila—possibly the least affected, on the outside, at any rate—is seeing a counsellor that Henry and the boys had known from his college days, a Dr Taylor Jameson, twice weekly, and he seems to really be helping her. In addition, she has become a regular overnight visitor at our apartment, where we've bonded over a great many similar interests and our mutual adoration of her older brothers.

And I'm entirely sure she uses me to get out and see some boyfriend called Simon she's yet to tell Henry about—but after what Mila and I shared, we deserve to have something we keep between us.

Her relationship with Alex took flight once they eventually talked, and despite being polar opposites, their newfound closeness is apparent for all to see.

I'm in the process of sorting through RSVPs for the launch event for Katherine's seven short days from now, when Henry strides from his studio at the far end of our apartment—shirt-sleeves rolled up to display his hair-dusted forearms, hands liberally coated in blue and white paint and a smile as wide as London Bridge gracing his absurdly handsome face.

Glancing up from the tedious work that I'd insisted upon doing myself, despite having a whole team at my disposal, I can't help my lips lifting into an answering smile.

"I just got off a call with Cade." I jump to my feet, my stomach bottoming out while simultaneously filling with butterflies. "Layla delivered their little girl last night. Both of them are just perfect, even if her arrival is slightly earlier than anticipated."

Thrilled by this, I launch myself into his waiting arms as he spins me around in delight, ecstatic to hear Caden's unbelievably good news.

"Bella Blue North. 5lbs 8oz. Can you believe North has a kid!"

"Do you think we could visit them in two weeks when we fly out to see Alex? Would that be okay, do you think?"

Having just returned from the first of his bi-monthly visits to his brother, I know he'll be due to fly out again in two short weeks.

"Of course, baby. Cade has already asked us to come. He's desperate to show her off. Do you think you can organise someone to stand in for you for the couple of days we'll be away?"

What he really means is, can I bear to hand the reins over to someone else while I take a step back for a hot minute, something I haven't done in weeks now—but he's smarter than that. Good for him!

Having precisely zero experience in the administrative side of running a non-profit, I am heavily reliant on Martha, who is one of those people who inherently knows what needs to be done, and so I trust her judgement implicitly.

On her advice, and Father T's encouragement, I'd decided to

throw a charity dinner to entice donors to give generously to such a worthy cause, so I know immediately Martha will take the helm while I am away.

I nod, making a mental note to email her to double-check.

Martha has become infinitely more like family than a friend. Her reaction to the news that Henry and I were a couple was highly enthused, to say the *very* least. If I hear her talk about shopping for a hat for "the big day" one more time, I'll kindly throttle her.

She'd also come clean on my "promotion" just the other day, telling me that Henry had never asked her to promote me to his PA, which is hilarious considering Jasper had been his long-standing PA from before he'd even taken the helm. She'd done it under her own steam in an attempt to push us together, having seen the sparks between us at the DeMarco Gala.

And so now, Henry and I have decided to nickname her Meddling Martha—not that she cares, having claimed her work was done.

Plonking my ass back down on the couch, I'm surprised to find Henry settling himself beside me, only to pick up a handful of RSVPs and begin sorting them.

"You don't have to do that, you know."

Raising a sardonic eyebrow, he retorts, "Neither do you, Peaches."

Flattening my lips against my teeth, I deadpan him with slitted eyes.

Touché!

He grins easily, something that would have been a hard-won emotion to see on his face only months ago, and my chest tightens in gratitude.

"In the words of *you*, many hands make light work, right? So, the quicker *you* can finish *this*, the quicker *I* can finish *you*."

His grin turns heated as his intention becomes more than evident. Shaking my head at his insatiable appetite, I try to suppress my own grin and fail miserably.

"Well, get to it then, soldier. Chop, chop."

Saturday rolls around much quicker than I'd like, but somehow, we manage to get everything organised, and by *we*, I mean Martha. Because holy shitballs, that woman is a machine!

Jo had taken it upon herself to give me the works once again, insisting on a soft curled up style sitting on the nape of my neck and that smoky eye effect she is so fond of, which, she tells me, makes my eyes shine.

I'm feeling entirely like a princess in my blue full-length ball gown. The draped sleeves sit below my bare shoulders, and the tightly fitted bodice hugs my body to my hips before flaring out into a tulle skirt that floats around my legs as I walk. My sandals are the exact same shade of blue as the dress, and the only jewellery I've chosen is some low hanging diamond earrings that sparkle with each movement.

Standing in the entryway to the marquee we've hired for the event just half an hour outside of the city, I take in the stunning display before us.

Ten black Chiavari chairs surround each circular table, which are covered in bright white linens. Black candelabras tower above the guests with various white flowers climbing from the base to nestle among the tall white luminescent candles. The full lights within have been dimmed so that only warm white fairy lights glow around the space, giving the room a magical effect.

The dance floor is front and centre, black and white squares alternating and the area where the band will set up after the meal is shrouded in darkness, though I know from the event manager that there's purple up-lighting in place to set the musicians apart.

I've gotten to the venue with Martha and Father T around thirty minutes before we should be seeing others arrive, just to do some final checks, finishing up as the first guests make their way inside.

The first half of the evening is a blur of faces I don't recognise. Still, Martha smooths the way with Ted taking up the mantle of my protector of sorts, standing close beside me and whispering the names of each potential donor discreetly in my ear moments before I greet them while Father T makes sure the rest of the venue is running smoothly.

It turns out to be a perfect strategy, and we've smashed our pledge target within the first hour and long before the meal has even started, though there's still no sign of Henry.

Pushing down my nerves at his absence, Father T, Martha, Ted, and I take our seats with the tenth setting at our table, Henry's, remaining empty for the entirety of the meal. Martha clucks over me like a mother hen.

"Liv, sweetheart. He will be here in no time. But, really, I didn't think he'd take this long—"

She trails off, turning to her husband on her other side and Father T beside Ted as I try to quell my nervousness.

Mila, who is seated on the other side of Henry's empty one, keeps sending me anxious looks, both of us fearing something has happened as that's where our minds go now after the events of two months ago. Graciously, our worries are unfounded as, just when the band sets up, Henry appears looking slightly more dishevelled than I've come to expect, but even more heart-stoppingly sexy as a result.

Dropping a kiss to my lips, he sits beside me before grabbing Mila's hand to squeeze it reassuringly, having noted the apparent distress on her face.

"Where were you? You missed dinner."

Holding my chin, he looks deeply into my eyes, smiling broadly. "You'll see."

The servers have just finished clearing the tables, when Martha, seated to my right, gently taps my shoulder, her eyes lit up suspiciously, to let me know she's going to get the speeches started.

Forgetting about that glint in her eyes, for now, I try steeling myself, not at all looking forward to this part. I inhale a deep breath, knowing she's about to announce my name to make a thank you speech that I've struggled to write for days now, if not weeks.

"Ladies and gentlemen, thank you so much for such a wonderful turnout as we launch Katherine's House, an intermediary home for those who don't currently have a residence to call their own. We are taken aback by the support you have given us before we've even opened our doors, and here, to thank you in a unique way all of their own, I give you Henry DeMarco."

Unhearing the final words that come from her lips, I'm already pushing myself into a standing position, when the realisation strikes. Henry gently eases me back into my seat, gifting me with an exceedingly smug grin before all but skipping toward the podium where Martha awaits.

The crowd applauds loud and lingeringly when I realise another body has filled Henry's seat.

"Nate?"

The man in question just smirks beneath his impeccably groomed dark beard, handsome as ever, before placing his forefinger over his upturned lips in a shushing gesture and turning to watch as Henry addresses all and sundry.

"Thank you, Mrs Goode. You've been a wonder, as always."

Martha's face flushes a deep crimson as her smile encompasses the entire space before eventually landing on mine to send me her signature kind smile.

"I'm late to the party, unfortunately." Henry continues. "However, judging from Martha's words, it seems you have all developed an affinity for Olivia and her passionate work with those less fortunate than we.

"I'd like to take this opportunity to pay homage to the most amazing female influence in my life. My mother was a firm believer in kindness, in doing right by others, in living your life without regret but with compassion and in loving with your whole heart."

I plead with myself to not allow the tear that threatens to fall at his entirely out-of-character declaration.

"She told me once that when I knew I'd found my love, my *forever,* that I'd fall hard and I'd fall fast, and Jesus if that didn't happen years ago when I saw Olivia Parker dancing in a crowded room as though no one was watching."

His eyes meet mine across the space—meet and hold and fill me to bursting with love and wonderment.

"I fell in love with you then. I have fallen in love with you more each and every day since then. And I'll continue to fall in love with you each and every day between this day and my last day. Even then, I'll continue to love you all the way into eternity."

He steps from the podium as my heart beats with a pace to rival the speed of light when Nate nudges me and gestures that I should stand up.

I glance around past Martha's empty seat to Ted, who shoos

me forward, smiling broadly as though everyone is in on the joke and I'm the last to know.

I stand hesitantly, looking around the space, but everyone's eyes are trained on Henry in wonderment. Finally, I turn back to face him, his eyes capturing me and holding me prisoner so that I begin to close the distance between us, helpless to fight that gravitational pull.

My gown swishes around my feet, the tulle moving freely around my legs until I'm within touching distance.

"Liv." His voice drops to a harsh rasp. "Peaches. May I have this dance?"

I can't help drawing my brows together as I glance around, my consciousness held so tightly in Henry's thrall that I am wholly oblivious to all present. "There's no music."

I've barely finished my sentence, when an acoustic guitar strums tunelessly from the darkened area set up for the band. Light slowly fills the space until I see Caden sitting on a chair with his guitar resting on his lap, a mic in front of his lips.

As though they'd rehearsed it, Caden winks once, face breaking into his signature shit-eating grin, before breaking into the opening of *These Arms of Mine*.

My stomach fills with anticipation as Henry pulls me into his embrace, slowly moving me around the dancefloor, our eyes holding for an age before he speaks. His words don't carry over the music and are intended solely for my ears.

His gaze becomes even more intense, if that were even possible.

"When I kept us apart… when I was trying to do the right thing and making us both so fucking miserable as a result, I'd often listen to this song. I'd have it on repeat, purely to torture myself with thoughts of having you in my arms just once more. I fed myself a whole load of bollocks, a stomach full of lies, a billion and one painted truths to keep you at arm's length, and I can promise you, Liv, I'll never lie to you or to myself. Ever again."

I bite my inner lip to keep my emotions over his confession at bay, though I'm sure I can feel tears tickling my bottom lashes, threatening to fall at any moment.

"You're my beginning, and you're my end. You're my yesterday, my today, and all my tomorrows, Peach."

He steps away slightly, no longer filling my vision as I unintentionally realise that the dancefloor is full of other couples. Then, out of nowhere, Alex is beside Henry, handing him something before slapping him on the shoulder. He turns to me with his lopsided grin, pulling an answering one from my own mouth. Bending close, he drops a peck on my cheek before giving us a one hand salute and disappearing just as quickly and silently as he'd appeared.

"What was that? How did he—"

My question cuts off abruptly as Henry drops to one knee before me, my heart threatening to leap from my chest.

"Jesus, I didn't think I'd be as nervous, but shit—"

The man kneeling at my feet raises his shoulders in a self-deprecating shrug as those around us begin to notice what's going on and move backwards, watching intently. Henry's grip on my hand, held within his, strengthens, and I draw stability from his action even as my whole being threatens to take flight.

He holds his hand up, a small navy box held within his palm, and I'm trying to keep it together as he pops the lid allowing it to fall to either side, displaying the most beautiful square diamond ring nestled on a pillow of navy satin.

Raising my eyes, I meet his deep green gaze, his intensity and his passion holding me as a willing prisoner.

"Marry me, Peaches. Let me love you now and through

forever."

His face takes on an anxious look, his jaw tensing as he waits for my response.

My throat closes as I try to swallow the ball of emotion that threatens to choke me, so the only thing I can do is nod.

I nod, again and again, tears filling my eyes and flowing freely as he leaps forward, catching me around the waist and spinning me around to the sound of several catcalls, the loudest being Caden, of course, even without a mic as an amplifier.

Setting me down onto quivering legs, Henry plants a hard kiss on my lips before licking the seam of my lips and drawing my tongue into his own mouth, swallowing my gasp of delight. He pulls back, bestowing me with his perfect grin before leaning forward to drop his brow to mine, his hand finding its familiar home at the nape of my neck.

My eyes close automatically at the comforting gesture as I feel his breath whisper across my smiling lips.

"I love you so fucking much, baby."

Epilogue One

HENRY
TWO YEARS LATER

"We're in here."

Liv's sweet voice carries to my ears through the hall where I've just entered. "Where's *here,* Peach?"

Her giggle is as melodic as always and I hear several voices murmuring, followed by her reply. "The kitchen."

Having just moved into our new home a short six weeks earlier, I'm still getting the hang of living in such a large space.

Liv had tried to warn me when I'd gone through the plans with the architect that it was too much for just the two of us, but I'd insisted. Our double front doors open into a vast entrance hall with several corridors leading off of it in various directions. To my left lies our joint home office, something I'd never thought to have until meeting my wife, but the appeal of being near her as often as I can means this was a must-have.

We both have our own space, separate but together, so that I can continue to run the more successful than ever version of DeMarco Holdings while she manages the admin side of running three non-profits.

Yes, three. Katherine's House alone wasn't enough, oh no. My Peaches has branched out, opening two further intermediary services within London, with another in the works up north in Manchester.

Beyond our office is the hallway leading to a substantial open-plan kitchen and living area. Further, there's a formal dining room, formal living room, library, home gym, two bathrooms, a laundry room, and a mudroom.

Upstairs, there are eight bedrooms and nine baths, probably a bit on the excessive side. Okay, so definitely extreme—but Mila has her own room for when she stays, just like she always had at the penthouse, and Alex also stays with us when he's home visiting from the States, so there are at least a couple of rooms always in use.

Drawing closer to the kitchen, more giggling meets my ears, and I wonder who else is in the house. I don't have to wonder long as I enter the rustic living space to find Mila, Josie, and Nola holed up around the oversized island, poring over something on the counter beneath them, laughing sporadically while speaking quietly amongst themselves.

They haven't seen me yet, so I take a second to admire my wife. Having spent the last few days in New York with my brother, I've missed appreciating her beauty in the flesh. Her body is displayed perfectly in casual dark blue jeans and a light blue fitted sweater. She's barefoot and smiling, which only broadens when she spots me over my sister's shoulder.

Crossing the space between us, she throws herself at me, wrapping her legs around my waist, holding me close to pepper my face with kiss after kiss.

She eventually pulls back, hands on either side of my face. "I missed you, husband."

The titles are still relatively new, having finally tied that knot good and tight a little under four months previously. "I missed you more, wife."

I press a kiss to the tip of her button nose, her laughter ringing out through the large open space as I walk toward the island and our guests, Liv hugging tightly to my body like a baby koala.

Setting her ass down onto the marble top, I peer over her shoulder to look at what's so interesting that my own sister hasn't even glanced in my direction.

"Isn't it wonderful? Mila is thinking about going to university after all."

Liv's words are a shock to me because just last week before I left, Mila was dead set on taking an entry-level position at DeMarco, just like I had.

"And," Josie jumps in, "she's bought her first apartment too!"

I send a questioning glance at my sister, who just so happens to be staring at the counter rather than meeting my curiosity filled gaze. She can easily pull the wool over everyone else's eyes, but we're too alike for me to not realise when something's off in her demeanour, and I plan on getting to the bottom of it once we're alone.

For now, I'll play along. "That's *great*, sissy." Her eyes find mine and narrow into thin slits as she huffs out, "Thanks, *bro*! Keeping my options open," knowing full well I'm onto her and not letting it go.

"We were just about to head out," Nola interjects. "Did you

want to come with, Mila?"

My sister squints her eyes in thought, blatantly weighing the pros and cons of sticking around under her big brother's scrutiny. Self-preservation seems to be the clear winner when she grins straight at me.

"That would be *wonderful*. Thank you, girls! I just have to grab a couple of things. I'll meet you outside in two."

Shooting a mischievous smile at yours truly, she bounces from the room in that way nineteen year olds girls can't help when excited. Or, more likely, happy to be getting away from the inevitable grilling brother dearest is set on.

Bidding farewell to Liv's best friends, I turn to my wife, only to find her with a popped brow and an accusatory look in her eyes.

"What?"

She deadpans, remaining mute.

"What? What's with the look?!"

Huffing a sigh, she closes her eyes and shakes her head almost wearily. "You need to let her live her life, Henry. She's an adult now. She can make her own life choices, and we should support her."

I'm on the verge of raising a sardonic eyebrow at my empathic wife when she tightens her legs around my waist from her perch on the island, pulling my always-ready cock close until I can feel her heat even through her denims. A groan falls from my mouth at the delicious friction the move creates.

"You were saying?" Then, arching a perfectly shaped brow, she lifts her chin in that way that drives me wild. I catch her by the waist, tossing her over one shoulder as she yelps loudly before I march directly to the hall and up the stairs, passing an eye-rolling Mila as I take them two at a time.

Her passing words are my sister to a T. "Be safe, kids."

Smartass.

After giving Liv more orgasms than I can count, we doze for a couple of hours before I get up, intent on drawing her a bath.

She rolls over to her stomach, reaching to grab me as I move off the bed. "But I don't need a bath."

"I beg to differ, stinky." Throwing a smirk over my shoulder, I can see her narrowed eyes from her comfortable position on our super king bed, eliciting a bark of laughter from my chest.

Turning on the taps on the oversized free-standing bathtub, I reach for some lavender essence in Liv's drawers, and after adding a couple of drops to the running water, I grab some towels from the rack, leaving them within easy reach.

I hear Liv's soft footsteps as she sits on the edge of the tub, watching me intently before she grabs her hair and scoops it up messily, tacking it to the top of her head. My eyes are drawn to her movements like a moth to a flame. She is the most beautiful woman in the world with an even more beautiful heart, and she doesn't even realise it.

"Come on, Peach. Let's get you all clean."

Her mouth lifts on one side as her eyes twinkle mischievously. "Why? So, you can dirty me up all over again?"

Growling playfully, I grab her hand and yank her to my chest, our unclothed bodies rubbing against each other, making my dick thicken once more.

"Don't you fucking know it, baby."

She shudders against me when I drop my mouth to her neck, biting lightly before pushing back from her, knowing where this is headed but needing to pamper her first.

I help her, then climb in myself, settling her between my thighs, her back pressed against my chest. Sighing contentedly, she drops her head back so that she's resting against my shoulder as I begin the process of lathering her up.

She arches against me like a cat as I rub lazy circles along her arms and shoulders, slowly edging my way toward her perky tits and drawing her nipples between my thumb and forefinger; I can't help giving them a tiny pinch.

"How was your trip?"

Continuing to lather her body while she preens under the attention, I ignore my blatantly hard cock and focus on answering her question.

"It was good. He's good. Missing home a bit now and then, but settled quite well in New York. The Big Apple suits him. He's even been on some real, genuine dates."

The smile on her face is bright and genuine as her eyes meet mine. "I know. We talk every day. Twice a day, most days. His date last week was with a girl called Krista. I think he liked her. He said they had a fun time!"

I snort internally, knowing precisely who Krista is and why my brother would like her. She's a daughter of one of the board members renowned for her blowjobs—so much so that her nickname is Dyson.

"When you're speaking to him tomorrow, you should ask him about Krista's nickname, yeah? It's a good story!"

Liv nods against my chest, shoving her breasts further into my waiting palms.

"Jesus, Peach. Your tits have gotten bigger since last week, I swear. Look at that. They're spilling over the side of my palms!"

She grins up into my face, delight playing behind her ocean blues as though I've walked into a carefully laid trap.

"That's something that happens to women sometimes."

I furrow my brow in confusion. "That's news to me, Peach. It's never happened before, has it?"

She narrows her eyes slightly. "I *meant;* it happens to women like me sometimes."

My eyebrows pull together as I send her a questioning look.

"I mean, women in my condition..."

"In your condition? Is something wrong, baby?" My heart speeds up, fearful of her answer.

Liv takes hold of the hand still sitting on her chest and moves it further south until it's resting on her flat stomach.

The realisation of what she's saying hits me like a bolt out of the blue.

"Peaches, are you...?" My eyes are blown wide, mouth surely hanging open, as she laughs, fucking *laughs* at me before nodding enthusiastically.

"You know what they say—new house, new baby!"

Epilogue Two

NATE

"Thank you so much, Professor Hawthorne. If there's *anything* I can do for you—"

Pushing down my ire, I force a semblance of a smile onto my lips, cutting her off before she can say or do anything to make this exchange even more inappropriate than she already has.

"That won't be necessary, Sabrina. You may turn in your project within the next seven days. No penalties." I move from behind my desk to open the door of my office for Miss Turner, the seventh student today, to blatantly attempt propositioning the current guest lecturer at Walden-Forbes University.

"Now, if you'll excuse me. My office hours were finished more than forty-five minutes ago. I'll see you on Monday."

She slowly stands from her seat, brows drawing together in confusion. This is obviously *not* how she saw this evening going.

What these co-eds don't know is I have zero interest in fucking anyone barely out of nappies, without a decent thought between their ears and the conversational skills of a blow-up doll.

Liar. You want her though, don't you?

I push the disgusting thought out of my head as quickly as it flashes through, instead focusing on nodding at Sabrina as she slips past me into the hallway beyond.

Shutting the heavy oak door of my office behind her, I rest my head against the cool wood and close my eyes in silent thanks that this day is *finally* over. Slightly rotating my head, I spy my decanter of Rémy Martin on the sideboard, an empty tumbler alongside it, just whispering my name.

Straightening up, I make short work of sloshing a hefty measure into the glass, then seat myself back behind my desk with a heavy plonk.

My stomach is twisting and churning with the need to tamp down on the thoughts that threaten to run riot in my twisted brain, and even downing the fucking snifter in one gulp does nothing to tame my racing heart or clear my galloping mind.

Maybe if I just ask where she is, or how she's doing, then I'll at least know she's okay.

Fuck, I can't unsee the look in her eyes. It haunts me every damn day. Even when I dream, which is a damn rarity, I can't escape the pain there either.

I can't stop myself as my head tips back onto the headrest of the oversized office chair, letting the memory of Henry and Liv's wedding assail me.

"Now," Caden's voice booms over the mic, "let's get the wedding party out on the dancefloor with Peachy and the Grump." He flashes a

self-satisfied wink alongside his shit-eating grin at a droll Henry. "Come on then, folks, move your asses!"

Mila rises from her seat beside me, grabbing my hand and pulling insistently.

"Come on, before I'm left to partner up with Caden. He'll do something like pinch my bum just to get a rise out of my brother!"

Chuckling low in my chest, I shrug while nodding easily. She's not wrong there.

Still holding her tiny hand, I follow Mila out onto the dancefloor set amongst the surrounding forest in Devon where the new Mr and Mrs DeMarco had tied the knot in utterly excessive fashion—not that I'd expect less from a DeMarco, in fairness.

I tug my dance partner's hand gently, spinning her around and into my waiting arms to pull her close as Misdirection begins to play. Beau Maxwell, their burly drummer, is singing in Cade's place, his deep chocolatey voice breaking into an acoustic version of Rewrite The Stars.

Mila's golden eyes, so reminiscent of her brother's, find mine as they widen impossibly.

"Shit, I didn't think he'd actually do it!"

I can't hold back my laughter. This girl is one of the very few people who can easily bring my true emotion to the forefront—another reason we've spent basically every weekend together over the last two years, since the incident that changed the course of so many lives.

She's a safe place to be me. A true friend—and fuck knows, I don't have many of them. Not truly.

Still slowly rotating across the dancefloor, I can see several other couples have joined in. "You didn't think he'd do what exactly, Mila?"

She worries her pink lip between her teeth, narrowing her eyes in contemplation before deciding to disclose whatever it is she's referring to.

"Well… I was joking with Beau earlier and he said Caden had laid

very specific rules; for the setlist, you know?" Her wide eyes meet mine, seeking acknowledgement, so I nod encouragingly.

"So… I dared him. To play whatever his heart desired."

I can't help snorting. "And his heart desired a cover of this?" I glance over Mila's shoulder to find Cade, who's dancing with a hysterically laughing Josie, shooting daggers at his drummer.

My laughing eyes turn to find hers, only to see her brows drawn in deep thought.

"I—I need some air."

Jerking herself from my hold, she spins on her heel and takes off at the speed of light across the dancefloor and into the darkened forest beyond. Before my brain can draw a conscious thought, I'm moving after her.

My eyes take several long moments to adjust to the mostly darkened state surrounding me—the lights of the ongoing wedding party at my back with pitch-black stretching out before me. Yet, I move forward, needing to make sure the kid is alright.

"Mila? Where did you go?"

A whispered "Shit!" meets my ears somewhere to my left, but I still can't make out her form in the darkness. "Come on, Mila. I can't go back until I know you're okay. Where did you go?"

As I ask the question, the moon breaks free of the night sky's hold on her, shining between the darkened clouds to light up my quarry. Her blush pink dress shimmering in the light like a beacon.

"There you are."

She throws her hands up in exasperation. "Even the fucking moon is out to get me tonight. I can't even have a drink without brother dearest monitoring me like an overbearing father. He knows he's barely turned fucking thirty-one, right?"

I step forward, slinging my arm over her tiny shoulder. Mila is well over a foot shorter than my 6'5", so it doesn't take a massive effort in fairness.

"Let's get back to the party, Mouse."

She stiffens before pulling out of my hold. "Don't call me that, Nathaniel."

Widening my eyes at her severely hostile tone, a wholly new sound to my ears, I can't help crinkling my brow as I stare at her in confusion.

"Henry calls me Mouse. It's a pet name for a little girl. And in case you haven't noticed it—I'm far from being little anymore."

It's hard to miss her thrusting her considerable chest forward and I curse myself for taking note.

Sick fuck.

She steps closer, her head tilting questioningly as her eyes narrow in what I'm guessing is astute speculation.

"Have you noticed, Nate?"

She closes the distance with another bold step, then another, while I step backwards, my eyes never leaving her face.

She quirks a perfectly shaped brow, one side of her mouth drawing up in a smug, knowing smirk. I need to steer this conversation to safer waters sharp-ish!

I clear my throat, shrugging. "Henry has you all wrong, littlest DeMarco. You're no Mouse." I can't stop my mouth from twitching with a threatening grin.

Her smirk blooms into a fully loaded smile, her eyes twinkling mischievously. "That so, Nathaniel?"

"It sure is. He can keep calling you Mouse, but we both know you're not the prey."

The words lay unspoken between us. Fierce, funny, tough, strong-as-fuck Mila DeMarco takes no nonsense from anyone, and woe betide if you hurt with someone she loves when there's a loaded gun at hand.

"You're the predator, Mila. A real Hellcat."

A name I've kept to myself for years now, but I can't help the small relief I feel at just speaking the word aloud.

Stepping forward, I link her arm with mine to escort her back to the festivities, optimistic that whatever sent her flying heedlessly into the darkened woods has passed, but she remains rooted to the spot. Unmoving.

"I slept with Simon."

She turns her head to find my eyes blown wide, and a sick feeling settling in the pit of my stomach. I don't know if I want to vomit or kill this fucking Simon—either way, I don't like it.

Her eyes glisten with tears. "I just did it because everyone else—all my friends, I mean, had already had sex, you know? And the person I truly want… never mind. Anyway, it was absolutely awful, and the worst part was when he… finished—" I openly grimace, closing my eyes as though to block out this conversation I want no part of, before I nod for her to continue, knowing she needs to tell someone.

And a twisted part of me is rejoicing at being the person she goes to when she needs to talk.

"Well, he got up and… disposed of the… condom, but then he said, 'We need to break up.'"

My jaw clenches so tightly that I think my teeth might just chip until the next words leave her mouth.

"He said he's been sleeping with his best friend Erick and he'd only fucked me to make sure he wasn't into girls."

"Oh, Hellcat." I gather her against my chest as she soaks my dress shirt with tears, her small frame shaking underneath my hold. I feel utterly incompetent, and it's a feeling I'm not at all too keen on.

"Do you want me to kick his dumb ass, littlest DeMarco?"

She nods in my hold, still quivering. "Your wish," I whisper our special words against the top of her head, and her body loosens slightly.

"Am I ugly, Nate?" Her words are muffled against my chest. "Am I such a turnoff to the opposite sex that I can make a man gay just by sleeping with him?"

Instinctively, I place my hands on either side of her head, tilting it back until my eyes meet hers.

"Hellcat, any man would be crazy not to want you."

Her eyes drop to my lips and I'm unable to stop my tongue from darting out to wet them, her gaze fixed on the movement as her nostrils flare. Then, before I know what's happening, she's thrown her hands around my neck to pull me closer, planting her soft mouth firmly on mine.

My mind tells me to push her away immediately, to shut this the fuck down, but her mouth—it's like nothing I've felt before. And I don't want to damage her self-confidence any further than this fucking Simon already has, or at least that's my excuse for what I do next.

Pulling Mila firmly against my chest, I tease her lips with my tongue, gently running the tip across her closed lips, probing, needing her to invite me inside. When I move my hand from her face down her body, along each lush curve to land on her tiny waist, she gasps and I'm ready and waiting.

Thrusting my tongue inside, I'm simultaneously stunned and assaulted by the taste of vanilla milkshakes as she purrs deeply inside her throat, her tongue tangling delightfully with mine.

My senses are alight, and I can't help the thrill of sheer happiness that fills me from head to toe as a feeling more powerful than I've ever known permeates my entirety.

Her little whimpers are music to my ears, and I'm so in tune with her that at first, I don't hear his voice until he is almost right upon us.

"Hawthorne? Where the fuck did you go, man?"

I jerk away at the sound of Cade's voice, Mila's eyes still closed in apparent bliss as I roughly shove her behind the nearest tree, following and clamping a hand over her mouth, lest she disclose our location.

Shit, what the fuck are you doing, Hawthorne?

As Cade searches nearby, I have several long moments to plan my attack, and as his voice moves further and further away, I turn Mila towards me.

Her eyes meet mine in the half-moonlight and my resolve almost wavers. But not quite. I'm a heartless cunt, truth be known.

"Kiss me again, Nathaniel. Please."

Her words tie my insides up in knots even as I step back from her. "Sorry, Hellcat. I'm not into fucking little girls. Best sticking with someone your own age, yeah?"

Her face falls, almost undoing my resolve, and I want nothing more than to give in to the sickness inside of me—this illness I have for my best friend's baby sister that I've striven desperately to get a motherfucking handle on.

"Now run along, Hellcat. It's past your bedtime."

Her pained eyes meet mine and I almost give in—I almost tell her what she wants to hear. What she needs to hear.

That she's the light in the motherfucking dark. That she's the calm in the chaos. That she's the right to my wrong. The Heaven to my Hell.

But I can't. Instead, I allow her to rip herself from my embrace, anger and frustration taking pride of place on her beautiful face.

"You'll regret that, Nathaniel Hawthorne. Mark my fucking words, you'll live to regret this fucking moment."

In a flash, she's ducked under my arm and taken off through the trees. And out of my life.

I'd taken the lecturing job at Walden-Forbes that following week, despite turning down a multitude of better offers. I had just needed to distance myself from the temptation that was Mila De-fucking-Marco.

Which had landed me *here*. In a gig that saw every Sarah, Mary, and Winifred Sanderson attempting to bewitch me with their supposedly skilled attempts at seduction.

I huff a breath deeply, just wanting this to be over so I can go home and back to the life I had ten months and five days prior. Before Hellcat unleashed her truth and blew all my denials right out of the water.

My phone rings on my desk, jolting me forward from my reverie, and when I glance at the screen, I can't help the thought that I've manifested her from my thoughts into reality.

Without conscious thought, I answer. "Mila?"

Hysterical sobs, utterly unlike Mila, greet my ears, as I feel my stomach bottom out. "Mila. What's wrong?"

I can hear her gather her breaths, taking long moments to find enough air to say the words she's so desperately trying to get out.

"Deep breaths, littlest DeMarco. I'm here." I run my free hand through my hair as a feeling of deep foreboding cloaks my body, chills running up and down my spine like iced water through my veins.

"I can't Nathaniel. I can't *breathe* right now. I—I need you."

The End

Mila DeMarco and Nathaniel Hawthorne's forbidden love story, *Unwritten Rules*, is available now!

Also by Pamela O'Rourke

THE BROTHERHOOD SERIES

1. *Painted Truths*
2. *Unwritten Rules*
3. *Broken Strings* (COMING 2023)

Acknowledgments

When I was seven years old, I told my Nan that one day I was going to write a book.

Look, Nan! I did it, I fucking did it!! And you were with me each and every step of the way—whispering in my ear when the late nights got lonely, or the early mornings got tough. When the self-doubt crept into my soul, threatening to steal my joy away. I couldn't see you, but I could feel you. Beside me, encouraging me—the same way you did in life. I miss you.

My first readers – Danielle, Jenny and Selena. When I had the crazy notion of writing this book, you three were in there like swimwear. Shouting loud and proud, ready and willing to read anything and everything I threw at you. Thank you, from the bottom of my heart, for the support and encouragement. I love you, girls!

To my Beta readers, Joan, Amy, Anna, Vicki, Robin, Fiona and Katie. Your help and feedback were utterly invaluable. I grew as a writer from every single comment, good and bad. Thank you for taking the time out of your lives to help me out—you are angels!

For my powerhouse PA, Jasmine Kasper. Girl, if you didn't keep me on the straight and narrow, I don't know who would. Thank you so much for doing all that behind-the-scenes stuff that I am literally allergic to. You are a Queen!

Mackenzie at NiceGirlNaughtyEdits, editor extraordinaire!

Thank you, thank you, thank you for that sample edit back in January. Your feedback on, possibly, the worst words I've ever written, was a game-changer for me. Your critique and honesty influenced my whole process, and, for that, I'll be forever grateful. Thank you for loving these characters as much as I do.

This story flew from my fingertips between December 2021 to February 2022. It consumed my every waking (and oftentimes sleeping) thought. Writing it was the easy part—little did I know the amount of behind-the-scenes work that goes into bringing a dream to life.

T.L Swan, J.C Hawke, Lilian Harris and V.H Nicholson are four amazing ladies who helped guide me along this process, building me up and encouraging me. Four absolutely beautiful souls and I'm so lucky to have you all in my corner. Thank you for all the time and knowledge you have bestowed upon me; I shall be forever in your debt.

To THE best writing group in the world. Tee's Cygnets! I love you all. Thank you for the wealth of knowledge and overflowing positivity. Thank you for allowing me to be a part of the best little village.

I've always been a dreamer—away with the fairies is what Mam says. Thank you to my parents and my sister Michelle, for putting up with my incessant daydreaming. For all the times I left you hanging when I was "nearly finished" my latest book addiction. I'm sorry to say, writing is ten times more addictive. You'll have to suffer on!

For what it's worth, I love you beyond measure.

Last year, I met a girl on Instagram. We got chatting about our love of books and our mutual desire to write our own stories someday. Together we encouraged and supported each other, a friendship blossoming bigger and brighter every day. Had I not met Katie Lamdin, I can, hand on my heart, promise you that these characters would never have seen the light of day. She's buoyed me when I've been adrift. She's kept me on the straight and narrow, given me a talking to when I needed one—to say we overshare would be putting it mildly. I'm so grateful for the day we met because I know that, in you, I've found a friend for life.

A ride-or-die.

Katie, this one is for you, my *good* girl!

For my long-suffering husband, James. For all those years you tried to 'reverse psychology' me into writing this book—or any bloody book! I hope you see now that I react *much* better to positive encouragement, and at times, outright bullying! For being my unpaid PA, looking up all the boring-ass things I really didn't want to know about. For picking up the slack with the kids when I was trying to hit a deadline. For believing in me when I didn't. James – WE did it! We made a book baby.

To my five living, breathing, walking, talking miracles—Will, Jamie, Ben, Zachary and Isabel. You guys mean the absolute world to me, never forget that. Thank you for everything you've sacrificed to make this a reality for me. I promise I won't let the next one dominate my every waking moment. I love you bigger than the sky xoxoxo

For every single blogger, bookstagrammer and booktoker who has read and reviewed my debut book baby—thank you for taking a chance on this indie introvert with a filthy mind. The support I've received from the bookish community has been mind-blowing. It's truly a wonderful community to be a part of.

And lastly, to *you*. My reader.

Thank you for reading my words. Thank you for taking a leap of faith with me. Thank you for being a part of my dream come true.

Pamela O'Rourke lives in Ireland with her husband, James and their five young children. Life is hectic, but she wouldn't change a single second of it. She loves sunny days, strong coffee and daydreaming about her next book boyfriend.

Her debut novel in the Brotherhood series, *Painted Truths,* is currently available on Amazon alongside *Unwritten Rules*.

Watch out for Caden and Summer's heart-wrenching love story, *Broken Strings,* coming in early 2023.

In the meanwhile, come and join my Facebook reader group, O'Rourke's Raunchy Readers, for a first look at sneak peeks and teasers. Please note that this is a private group, so only other members can see posts and comments.

Follow on social media!

Facebook: www.facebook.com/authorpamelaorourke
Instagram/TikTok: @pamelaorourkeauthor
Amazon: https://tinyurl.com/PORourkeAmazon
Goodreads: www.goodreads.com/pamelaorourke
BookBub: www.bookbub.com/profile/pamela-o-rourke

Printed in Great Britain
by Amazon